My Sister Jodie

MY SISTER JODIE
A DOUBLEDAY BOOK 978 0 385 61012 4

Published in Great Britain by Doubleday,
an imprint of Random House Children's Books
A Random House Group Company

This edition published 2008

1 3 5 7 9 10 8 6 4 2

The Random House Group Limited supports The Forest Stewardship Council (FSC),
the leading international forest certification organisation. All our titles that are
printed on Greenpeace-approved FSC-certified paper carry the FSC logo. Our paper
procurement policy can be found at www.rbooks.co.uk/environment

Mixed Sources
Product group from well-managed
forests and other controlled sources
www.fsc.org Cert no. TT-COC-2139
FSC © 1996 Forest Stewardship Council

RANDOM HOUSE CHILDREN'S BOOKS,
61–63 Uxbridge Road, London W5 5SA

www.**kids**at**randomhouse**.co.uk
www.**rbooks**.co.uk

Addresses for companies within The Random House Group Limited can be
found at: www.randomhouse.co.uk/offices.htm

THE RANDOM HOUSE GROUP Limited Reg. No. 954009

A CIP catalogue record for this book is available from the British Library.

Printed and bound in Great Britain by William Clowes Ltd,
Beccles, Suffolk

JACQUELINE WILSON

MY SISTER JODIE

Illustrated by Nick Sharratt

DOUBLEDAY
London • New York • Toronto • Sydney • Auckland

For Trish

*With special thanks to Natasha West and
Annelies Hofland*

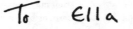

To Ella

lov

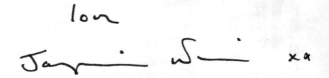 xa

'I told you so!' said Mum triumphantly.

1

Jodie. It was the first word I ever said. Most babies lisp *Mumma* or *Dadda* or *Drinkie* or *Teddy*. Maybe everyone names the thing they love best. I said *Jodie*, my sister. OK, I said *Dodie* because I couldn't say my Js properly, but I knew what I meant.

I said her name first every morning.

'Jodie? Jodie! Wake up. *Please* wake up!'

She was hopeless in the mornings. I always woke up early – six o'clock, sometimes even earlier. When I was little, I'd delve around my bed to find my three night-time teddies, and then take them for a dawn trek up and down my duvet. I put my knees up and they'd clamber up the mountain and then slide down. Then they'd burrow back to base camp and tuck into their pretend porridge for breakfast.

I wasn't allowed to eat anything so early. I wasn't even allowed to get up. I was fine once I could read. Sometimes I got through a whole book before the alarm went off. Then I'd lie staring at the ceiling, making up my own stories. I'd wait as long as I could, and then I'd climb into Jodie's bed and whisper her name, give her a little shake and start telling her the new story. They were always about two sisters. They went through an old wardrobe into a magic land, or they went to stage school and became famous actresses, or they went to a ball in beautiful long dresses and danced in glass slippers.

It was always hard to get Jodie to wake up properly. It was as if she'd fallen down a long dark tunnel in the night. It took her ages to crawl back to the surface. But eventually she'd open one eye and her arm went round me automatically. I'd cuddle up and carry on telling her the story. I had to keep nudging her and saying, 'You *are* still awake, aren't you, Jodie?'

'I'm wide awake,' she mumbled, but I had to give her little prods to make sure.

When she *was* awake, she'd sometimes take over the story. She'd tell me how the two sisters ruled over the magic land as twin queens, and they acted in their own daily television soap, and they danced with each other all evening at the ball until way past midnight.

Jodie's stories were always much better than mine. I begged her to write them down but she couldn't be bothered.

'*You* write them down for me,' she said. 'You're the one that wants to be the writer.'

I wanted to write my own stories and illustrate them too.

'I can help you with the ideas,' said Jodie. 'You can do all the drawings and I'll do the colouring in.'

'So long as you do it carefully in the right

colours,' I said, because Jodie nearly always went over the lines, and sometimes she coloured faces green and hair blue just for the fun of it.

'OK, Miss Picky,' said Jodie. 'I'll help you out but that won't be my *real* job. I'm going to be an actress. That's what I really want to do. Imagine, standing there, all lit up, with everyone listening, hanging on your every word!'

'Maybe one of my stories could be turned into a play and then you could have the star part.'

'Yeah, I'll be an overnight success and be offered mega millions to make movies and we'll live together in a huge great mansion,' said Jodie.

'What does a mansion look like?' I said. 'Can it have towers? Can our room be right at the top of a tower?'

'*All* the rooms are our rooms, but we'll share a very special room right at the top of a tower, only I'm not going to let you grow your hair any longer.' She pulled one of my plaits. 'I don't want you tossing it out of the window and letting any wicked old witches climb up it.' Jodie nudged me. She had started to have a lot of arguments with our mother. She often called her a witch – or worse – but only under her breath.

'Don't worry, I'll keep my plaits safely tied up. No access for wicked witches,' I said, giggling, though I felt a bit mean to Mum.

'What about handsome princes?'

'*Definitely* not,' I said. 'It'll be just you and me in Mansion Towers, living happily ever after.'

It was just our silly early-morning game, though I took it more seriously than Jodie. I drew our imaginary mansion, often slicing it open like a doll's house so I could illustrate every room. I gave us a huge black velvet sofa with two big black toy pumas lolling at either end. We had two real black cats for luck lapping from little bowls in the kitchen, two poodles curled up together in their dog basket, while twin black ponies grazed in a paddock beside our rose garden. I coloured each rose carefully and separately, deep red, salmon, peach, very pale pink, apricot and yellow. I even tried to do every blade of grass individually but had to see sense after dabbing delicately for half an hour, my hand aching.

I gave us a four-poster bed with red velvet curtains and a ruby chandelier, and one wall was a vast television screen. We had a turquoise swimming pool in the basement (with our twin pet dolphins) and a roof garden between the towers where skylarks and bluebirds skimmed the blossom trees.

I printed the title of each of our books in the library in weeny writing and drew every item of food on our kitchen shelves. I gave us a playroom with a trampoline and a trapeze and a jukebox, and one of those machines you get at the seaside where you have to manoeuvre a crane to pick up little furry teddies. I drew tiny teddies every colour of the rainbow, and I had a shelf of big teddies in our bedroom, and a shelf of old-fashioned dolls with real hair and glass eyes, and a splendid rocking horse big enough for both of us to ride on.

I talked about it to Jodie as if we'd really live there one day. Sometimes I imagined it so vividly it seemed like a real place. I just had to work out which road to take out of town and then I'd round a corner and spot the towers. I'd run fast, through the elaborate wrought-iron gates, up to the front door with the big lion's-head knocker. I'd know how to press the lion's snout with my finger and the door would spring open and I'd step inside and Jodie would be there waiting for me.

I wasn't stupid, I knew it wasn't really real, but it felt as if it might be all the same.

Then one morning at breakfast everything changed. I was sitting at the kitchen table nibbling at a honey sandwich. I liked opening the sandwich up and licking the honey, letting it ooze over my tongue, but I did it quickly and furtively when Mum wasn't looking. She was very strict about table manners. She was forever nagging Jodie about sitting up straight and spooning her corn-flakes up quietly without clanking the spoon against the bowl. Jodie slumped further into an S shape and clanked until she nearly cracked the china. Mum took hold of her by the shoulders and gave her a good shaking.

'Stop winding me up, you contrary little whatsit,' she said, going *shake shake shake*.

Jodie's head rocked backwards and forwards on her stiff shoulders.

'You're hurting her!' said Dad, putting down his *Daily Express* and looking anxious.

'She's not hurting me,' Jodie gasped, waggling her head herself, and then she started da-da-da-ing part of that weird old 'Bohemian Rhapsody' song when everyone bangs their heads to the music.

'Stop that silly row! I suppose you think you're funny,' said Mum.

But Dad was laughing and shaking his own

11

head. 'You're a right head-case, our Jodie,' he said.

'Trust you to encourage her, Joe,' said Mum. 'Why do you always have to take Jodie's side?'

'Because I'm my daddy's girl,' said Jodie, batting her eyelashes at Dad.

She was too. She was always in trouble now, bunking off school and staying out late. Mum could shake her head until it snapped right off her shoulders but she couldn't control her. But Dad could still sometimes make her hang her head and cry because she'd worried them so.

He'd never say a bad word against Jodie.

'It's not her fault. OK, she's always been a bit headstrong, but she's basically been a good little kid. She's just got in with the wrong crowd now, that's all. She's no worse than any of her mates at school,' he said.

'Quite!' said Mum. 'Moorcroft's a rubbish school. The kids aren't taught properly at all. They just run wild. Half of them are in trouble with the police. It was the biggest mistake in the world letting our Jodie go there. She's heading for trouble in a big way. Just *look* at her!'

I thought Jodie looked wonderful. She used to have pale mousy hair in meek little plaits but now she'd dyed her hair a dark orangy-red with streaky gold bits. She wore it in a funny spiky ponytail with a fringe she'd cut herself. Dad said she looked like a pot of marmalade – he'd spread her on toast if she didn't watch out. Mum said Jodie had ruined her hair and now she looked tough and tarty. Jodie was thrilled. She *wanted* to look tough and tarty.

Then there were her ears. Jodie had been begging Mum to let her have her ears pierced. Mum always said no, so last year Jodie went off and got her ears pierced herself. She kept going back, so there are five extra little rings up one ear.

'You've got more perforations than a blooming colander,' said Dad.

Mum was outraged at each and every new piercing.

'Hey, hey, they're only pretty little earrings,' said Dad. 'It's not as if she's got a nose-stud or a tattoo.'

'Yet!' Jodie whispered to me.

She'd tried going to a tattoo parlour but they said she was too young. She inked butterflies and blue-birds and daisy chains up and down her arms and legs with my felt pens instead. She looked incred-ible in her underwear with her red-gold hair and her earrings and her fake tattoos – but her clothes were mostly as dull and little-girly as mine. Jodie didn't have enough money to buy much herself. Mum was in charge when it came to clothes-buying. Dad didn't dare slip Jodie some money any more. She'd told him this story about her clunky school shoes rubbing her toes sore, so he gave her forty pounds for some new ones. She bought her first pair of proper high heels, fantastic flashy sparkly red shoes, and clacked happily round the house in them, deaf to Mum's fury. She let me try them out. They were so high I immediately fell over, twisting my ankle, but I didn't care. I felt like Dorothy wearing her ruby slippers in *The Wizard of Oz*.

Jodie was wearing the clunky school shoes this morning, and the grey Moorcroft uniform. She'd done her best to customize it, hitching up the skirt as high as she could, and she'd pinned funny

13

badges on her blazer. She'd inked little cartoon characters all over her school tie. Mum started on a new nag about the tie, but she interrupted herself when she heard the letterbox bang.

'Post, Pearl. Go and get it, pet.'

I'm Pearl. When I was born, Mum called me her precious little pearl and the name stuck. I was born prematurely and had to stay tucked up in an incubator for more than a month. I only weighed a kilo and was still so little when they were allowed to bring me home that Dad could cradle me in one of his hands. They were very worried about Jodie's reaction to me. She was a harem-scarem little girl who always twisted off her dolls' heads and kicked her teddies – but she was incredibly careful with me. She held me very gently and kissed my little wrinkled forehead and stroked my fluffy hair and said I was the best little sister in the whole world.

I picked up the post. A catalogue for Mum (she wrote off for them all – clothes, furniture, commemorative plates, reproduction china dolls – anything she thought would add a touch of class to our household) and a letter addressed to Mr and Mrs Wells – Mum and Dad. A proper letter in a big white envelope, not a bill.

I wondered who would be writing to them. I hoped it wasn't a letter from the head of Moorcroft complaining about Jodie. I knew she and her friends had been caught smoking once or twice, and sometimes they sneaked out of school at lunch time to go and get chips and didn't always bother to go back again. Jodie didn't *like* smoking, she told me privately; it made her feel sick and dizzy, and she also said the school chips were much better than the pale greasy ones in polystyrene pouches from the chippy, but she was trying to keep in with Marie and Siobhan and Shanice. They were the three toughest girls in Jodie's class. If you kept them on your side, you were laughing.

'Pearl?' Mum called.

I fingered the letter in my hand, wondering if I should stick it up under my school sweater until we could steam it open in private. But then Mum came out into the hall and saw the letter before I could whip it out of sight. She barely glanced at the catalogue, even though it was the one for little enamel pill boxes, one of her favourites. She took hold of the letter and ran her finger under the seal.

'It's for Dad too,' I said quickly. He'd be softer on Jodie; he always was.

'Mr *and* Mrs,' said Mum, opening it.

There was a letter inside and some sort of brochure. I peered at it as best I could. I saw the words *boarding school*. My heart started beating fast. *Boarding school, boarding school, boarding school!* Oh God, they were going to send Jodie to boarding school. I wouldn't be able to bear it.

'No, Mum!' I said, my voice a little squeak.

Mum was reading the letter intently, her head moving from side to side. 'No what?' she murmured, still reading.

'Don't send Jodie away!' I said.

Mum blinked at me. 'Don't be silly,' she said, walking back into the living room. She flapped the letter in front of Dad's face.

'Look, Joe, look!' she said. 'Here it is in black and white!'

'Well I'll be damned!' said Dad.

'I told you so!' said Mum triumphantly.

Jodie pushed her cornflakes bowl away and got up from the table, taking no notice.

'Sit down, Jodie,' said Mum.

'But I'll be late for school,' said Jodie.

'It won't matter just this once,' said Mum. 'Sit *down*! You too, Pearl. Your dad and I have got something to tell you.'

'What?' said Jodie, sitting back on the very edge of her chair. 'You're getting a divorce?'

'Don't be ridiculous!'

'You're going to have another baby?'

'Stop it now! Just button that lip of yours for two seconds.'

Jodie mimed buttoning her lips. I copied her, zipping mine.

Mum glared. 'Now, don't start copying your sister, miss! Shame on you, Jodie, you're a bad example. It's just as well you'll be making a move. I can't believe how badly you behave nowadays.'

'You *are* sending her off to this boarding school!' I wailed.

'*What* boarding school?' said Jodie, looking startled. 'You mean you're getting rid of me?'

'No, no, of course we're not,' said Dad. 'We're *all* going. I've got a new job. We both have, your mum and me.'

We stared at them. New jobs? At a *school*? Dad worked as a carpenter for a small building firm and Mum was a waitress at Jenny's Teashop opposite the town hall.

'Are you going to be teachers?' I said doubtfully.

Dad burst out laughing. 'Heaven help any pupils

16

if I had to teach them their reading and writing! No, no, sweetheart, I'm going to be the school caretaker and your mum's going to be the school cook. We saw this advert for a married couple and it seemed like we might fit the bill.'

'It's time for a move,' said Mum. 'We need to get you girls away to a decent environment where you can grow up into little ladies.'

Jodie made a very unladylike noise. 'We like it here, don't we, Pearl? We don't want to go to some awful jolly-hockey-sticks boarding school.'

I picked up the school brochure. I shivered when I saw the coloured photograph of the huge grey Victorian building. My fingers traced the gables and turrets and the tower. It was called Melchester College, but it was just like my dream-world Mansion Towers.

'Look!' I said, pointing. 'Look, Jodie!'

Jodie looked too. She bit her lip, fiddling with the little row of earrings running down her left ear. 'We'd live *there*?' she said.

'There's a special caretaker's flat,' said Dad.

'It's got all the mod cons even though it all looks so old fashioned,' said Mum.

'So you've both been to see it? When?' said Jodie. 'Why didn't you tell us? Did you fix it all up behind our backs?'

'Hey, hey, none of it's been fixed up,' said Dad. 'We haven't even been to see the college ourselves. We went to this interview at a hotel in London while you two were at school. We didn't say anything because we didn't want to get your hopes up. To tell the truth I never thought in a million years they'd take me on. I mean, I'm fine with wood

17

but I'm a bit of a botcher when it comes to plumbing or painting.'

'Don't be silly, Joe, you're a skilled carpenter and a fine odd-job man. What else could they possibly want?' said Mum.

'No, no, I think we got the job because of your cooking and management skills,' said Dad, reaching out and patting her hand. 'You were dead impressive at the interview, Sharon – the way you had that list of sample meals all sorted out, that was fantastic.'

'Where *is* this Melchester College? Why can't I still go to Moorcroft? I don't mind a long bus ride,' said Jodie.

'It would have to be a *very* long bus ride – it's a good hundred miles away, right out in the country,' said Mum. 'No, you'll be moving, thank heaven.'

'No I'm not,' said Jodie. 'I'm staying with all my mates at Moorcroft.'

'I hate that word. It's *friends*,' said Mum. 'And that's the whole point of us moving away. I'm sick to death of you hanging around with that deadbeat crowd, acquiring bad habits. We're moving in the nick of time, before you start seriously studying for your GCSEs and before Pearl starts secondary school. You girls need to make something of your-selves – and now we're giving you a golden opportunity.' Mum stroked the shiny brochure. 'Melchester College,' she said slowly and reverently, as if it was a magic word like *Abracadabra*.

'Melchester College!' Jodie mocked. She glanced at the brochure. 'It looks dead posh. It says it's for four- to thirteen-year-olds. Who could send a little kid of *four* to boarding school?'

'It's a day school too; not everyone boards. It's very select, naturally. It prides itself on the teacher/pupil ratio and the outstanding pastoral care,' said Mum, quoting.

'So what does that mean?' said Jodie.

'It means it's a very good school,' Mum snapped. 'It costs a great deal of money to send a child there. It's a wonderful opportunity for you two.'

'You mean we're supposed to have lessons there?' said Jodie.

'That's the whole point!' said Mum. 'You've learned nothing this last year at Moorcroft. We're going to have you repeating Year Eight, getting properly taught.'

'I'm not repeating a year with a lot of posh kids all *younger* than me!' said Jodie.

'But given the right coaching, you could pass this Common Entrance exam and win a scholarship to one of the public schools,' said Mum.

'*What?* Are you crazy, Mum? I'm not going. Ab-so-lute-ly no way!' Jodie was shouting.

'Hey, hey, Jodie, listen to me,' said Dad. 'We'll be there all through the summer holidays so you'll have lots of time to settle in. I know you're going to love it when you get there.'

'I won't, I'll hate it. I'm not going. You can't make me.'

'Of course we can. You'll do as we say. You're our daughter.'

'I wish I wasn't! Maybe I'm not. Maybe you adopted me and that's why I'm so different and never feel like I fit in,' Jodie yelled.

'Don't start, Jodie, you're doing my head in,' said Dad. 'Don't spoil it all. Like your mum says, it's a wonderful opportunity. We thought you girls would be thrilled to bits.'

'Well, we're not, are we, Pearl?' said Jodie. She looked at me.

I looked back at her helplessly.

'Do you really want to go there?' she asked, astonished.

I struggled. I nearly always copied Jodie, even if it got me into trouble. But we didn't always have the same ideas, although we were such close sisters. Jodie had hated it at Moorcroft at first. She'd been horribly teased about her girly plaits and neat uniform and nice manners. She had cut off her hair and changed her clothes and learned to talk tough so now she was fine, one of the gang. Some of the kids were even scared of her. I'd be scared of her myself if she wasn't my sister.

I knew *I* wouldn't be able to manage Moorcroft. I had nightmares about going there in September. I got horribly teased *now*, in Year Six in the Juniors. I was still very small for my age and looked very babyish; I worked hard and came top in class; I was useless at sport; I always had my head in a book; I blushed whenever a teacher talked to me in class; I never knew what to *say* to all the others. It was as if I had an arrow up above me: *Tease this kid!*

Melchester College looked like the sort of place where *everyone* wore proper uniform and worked hard and tried to come top. And even if the lessons were awful, Jodie and I would still be living in a real-life version of Mansion Towers. Maybe we'd even be able to share a tower room!

'You *can't* want to go there, Pearl,' said Jodie.

'I think I do,' I mumbled.

20

'Well, I *don't*,' said Jodie. She folded her arms. 'You go, Pearl. Fine. But no one's going to make *me* go there.'

'I can't go without you!' I said, starting to cry.

'There now, you've reduced your sister to tears. I hope you're proud of yourself,' said Mum. 'Why do you always have to spoil things for everyone? Poor little Pearl. Say sorry to her, Jodie, she's sobbing her heart out.'

'I think you should all say sorry to *me*, trying to force me off to this stupid snobby school. I'm not going. I'm not changing my mind, not in a million years,' Jodie shouted, and she slammed out of the door.

But that night when I started crying again in bed, she sighed and slid under the duvet beside me.

'Stop all that blubbing, silly. Do you really really really want to go to Melchester College, Pearl?'

'Yes. But not without you,' I sobbed.

'You're going to have to stand on your own two feet *some* time,' said Jodie. 'But all right – I'll come too. Just so as I can look after you. OK?'

'You'll really come to Melchester College?' I said, putting my arms round her neck and hugging her tight.

'Yes. I'll hate it. But I'll come, just for you,' said Jodie. 'Now quit strangling me and snuggle up and go to sleep.'

'Drunk!' Mum exploded, and she slapped Jodie's face.

2

I wonder how many times we said the words *Melchester College* over the next few weeks. Mum tried out special traditional school-dinner recipes every day: shepherd's pie, toad-in-the-hole, meat loaf. They were all pretty horrible but she did real puddings too, jam roly-poly and treacle pudding and sherry trifle, and they were absolutely wonderful. Dad kissed his fingertips and said each dish was truly scrumptious. He even sang the 'Truly Scrumptious' song from *Chitty Chitty Bang Bang* to Mum, and she giggled and did a little dance, swishing her skirts and twirling around. They were fooling about like teenagers all of a sudden, not acting like Mum and Dad at all.

Mum didn't nag Jodie so much, although she got really really mad when Jodie went out with Marie, Siobhan and Shanice on Thursday night, supposedly to a church youth club. Jodie promised she'd be in around half ten. She didn't get home until way past midnight, wobbling in her high red heels.

'Drunk!' Mum exploded, and she slapped Jodie's face.

I was sitting at the top of the stairs, shivering in my nightie, anxiously gnawing at a hangnail on my thumb. The slap was such a shock I ripped the hangnail halfway down my thumb, making it bleed. It was so sore that tears sprang to my eyes. Jodie didn't cry, though when she came up to our bedroom, one side of her face was still bright scarlet from the slap.

'Oh, Jodie! Are you *really* drunk?' I asked, wondering whether she was going to start reeling round and falling over like comic drunks on the telly.

'Not really *really* drunk,' said Jodie, peering at herself in the mirror. 'I did feel a bit weird when we came out of the club, but then I puked into the gutter and I felt better.'

'Did they have real drinks at Shanice's youth club then?' I said.

'As if!' said Jodie. 'We weren't *at* her youth club. We went proper clubbing – the under-eighteens night at the Rendezvous.'

'You never!'

'You *didn't*, dear – you've got to remember to speak nicely now you're going to Melchester College,' said Jodie, imitating Mum's voice.

'Ssh, Mum will hear!' I said, giggling. 'So what was it *like*, clubbing? Was it scary? Did you dance with any boys?'

'I danced with heaps of boys,' said Jodie. 'More than Shanice and them, and they got a bit narked and went off without me. Marie said I was a slag because I let this boy snog my face off.'

'You *never*! Didn't. Whatever. *Which* boy?'

'I don't know. He told me his name but I couldn't hear it properly because it was so noisy. Marty or Barty. Maybe it was Farty?'

'Jodie!'

'He wouldn't leave me alone and I let him slobber all over me just to annoy Marie because she'd said she fancied him. She was welcome to him actually To all of them. Just as well I couldn't hear them talk. It was just rubbish anyway. I don't like the way boys just want to dance and snog and touch you up. They don't want to be *mates*.'

'I don't like boys either,' I said. 'Some of the girls in my class have got boyfriends. They say I'm a baby.'

'Well, I'm a baby too, because *I* haven't got a boyfriend, and I don't want one either,' said Jodie, rubbing her lips fiercely with the back of her hand.

She flopped down on her bed and pulled the duvet up to her chin even though she was fully dressed, with her high heels still on.

'Night-night, Pearly Girly,' she said, closing her eyes.

'Hey, you've still got your shoes on!'

I knelt on her bed and wiggled her shoes off her feet. She had a hole in her tights, her big toe sticking through comically. I waggled it and Jodie giggled sleepily.

'Give over. Come to bed, Pearl,' she said, reaching out and pulling me in beside her. 'You're freezing, like a little snowman!' she said, cuddling me close.

'We don't ever have to have boyfriends, do we,

Jodie? We can still have our own place together, can't we?'

'Mansion Towers,' Jodie mumbled.

'I can't believe we're going to live in Melchester College,' I said.

I closed my eyes, nestling against Jodie in her warm bed. I saw us wandering the grounds of the college together, having picnics on the lawn, paddling in the lake, picking raspberries and strawberries in the kitchen garden . . .

We didn't have any kind of garden at home, because Dad's workshop took up all of our back yard. He pottered out there most evenings, but I don't think he ever did much *work*. He watched his little portable telly, brewed himself a cup of tea and enjoyed a bit of peace and quiet. Mum was forever on to him to make her new kitchen units but he never seemed to get round to it, just managing the odd cupboard or shelf.

I'd begged him to make me a doll's house. I'd hoped for a miniature Mansion Towers, but he made me a small square four-roomed house with a wobbly chimney stuck on top. He'd tried so hard, sticking special red-checked paper on the outside to look like bricks. I gave him a big hug and kiss, but privately I thought the house was hideous. I furnished it with a plastic bed and chair and tables and tried to play games with a family of pink plastic people, but it wouldn't become real. I had much more fun playing house in a cardboard shoebox with a paper family.

Jodie had never wanted a doll's house. When she was little, she'd asked Dad to make her a rocket, which was a challenge for him. He struggled hard,

26

because he could never say no to Jodie. He handed over his rocket proudly. It was hollow, with a little hinged door, pointy at one end, touched up with shiny grey paint. It looked like a big wooden fish. Jodie held it in her hand, looking puzzled.

'What *is* it, Dad?'

'It's your rocket, sweetheart,' said Dad.

Jodie wasn't good at hiding her feelings. Her face crumpled up. 'But it's much too small. I can't get in it!' she wailed. 'I want to go up to the moon!'

'Daddy can't make you a real rocket, you noodle!' said Mum.

Jodie howled. Mum laughed at her. Even Dad found it funny, I wasn't there – I wasn't even born yet – but the story had become family history, passed down like a folk tale.

We found the rocket at the bottom of Jodie's wardrobe when we were sorting through all our things for the big move.

'My rocket!' said Jodie, dusting it with an old sock. She made it swoop in and out of her clothes, and then she stood back and chucked it into the air so that its pointy wooden nose hit the ceiling with a satisfying *thuck*. It made a little dent in the ceiling plaster and then hurtled back to earth. Jodie caught it one-handed.

'We have lift-off, brief landing on ceiling and perfect re-entry,' she said.

'What was that noise?' said Mum, bursting into the room, a pile of our old clothes in her arms.

'Nothing, Mum,' we chorused.

'Well come on, girls, get a move on. Get all those old toys sorted into cardboard boxes, then Dad will take them to the hospice shop in the car.'

Mum glanced up at the ceiling. 'Where did that mark come from?' she said, frowning.

'What mark?' we said in unison.

'You two!' said Mum, but she was in too cheery a mood to get really angry. We heard her humming 'Truly Scrumptious' as she went back into her own room.

'I don't know what to keep and what to chuck,' I said, stirring all my toys. 'I never play with my Barbies now, or my cut-out paper dolls, or my giant set of wax crayons – they're just for babies, but I don't really want to throw them *out*.'

It was easier for Jodie. Most of her old toys were broken. Her old Barbies had skinhead haircuts and tattoos and assorted amputations; her teddy had led such an adventurous life that his head was hanging off his shoulders by a thread. Her crayons were stumps and her paints a sludgy mess.

'Junk, junk, junketty junk,' she chanted as she threw them rhythmically into a black plastic rubbish bag.

She grew wilder, throwing in her cream clutch bag and cream pumps, her pink crocheted poncho, her white fluffy towelling dressing gown, her floral toothmug and flannel and washbag, her pink alarm clock in the shape of a heart.

'Jodie! You'll hurt Mum's feelings,' I said.

'She never minds hurting mine,' said Jodie.

'They were presents from her.'

'Yeah, but they're all stuff *she* likes, not me.'

'I quite like them too,' I said. 'Can I have your dressing gown if you don't want it?'

'Sure,' said Jodie, wrapping it round me. She

laughed. 'You look like a polar bear. Here, bear, want a fishy?'

She pretended to feed me the wooden rocket, and then chucked it carelessly into the black plastic bag – but that night I heard her scrabbling in the bag, searching for something. I kept quiet. The next morning I saw she'd wedged the rocket beside her red shoes in her small suitcase of treasured possessions.

We lived with cases and cardboard boxes all around us for days, never quite sure where anything was, suddenly needing something that was packed right away. Dad was out all day and half the night, trying to complete all the bookshelves and bathroom cabinets on his order book. He had a farewell do with his mates at work and came home all tearful, saying they were a cracking bunch of lads, like brothers to him.

We had a farewell Sunday lunch with Dad's real brother, Uncle Jack, and Aunty Pauline and our two little cousins, Ashleigh and Aimee, and Dad's mum came too. They all wished us the best, and Gran kept saying how much she'd miss us, though whenever we went round to her house she was always telling us off, especially Jodie.

Mum didn't say goodbye to any of her family. She didn't keep in touch. She always sniffed when she spoke about them. Jodie and I would have loved to meet this other gran who always 'went down the boozer', and the granddad who'd been on benefit all his life, and we especially wanted to meet the uncle who'd been 'in and out of the nick', but Mum had left home at seventeen and never gone back. She did her last shift at Jenny's Teashop, coming home with a carved wooden spoon and a new apron with

SUPERCOOK embroidered in white across the chest – gifts from her regular customers.

Jodie missed school altogether for the last couple of weeks. Marie and Siobhan and Shanice had turned against her and it was simpler and safer to keep out of their way. Jodie said she mooched around the town in the mornings, ate the packed lunch Mum made for her down by the river, and then mostly hung around the park until it was time to come home. She liked the children's playground. She always loved little kids. She'd had plenty of practice looking after me. They all ran at her as soon as they spotted her, hanging on her arms, begging her to pick them up, to whirl them about, to give them a push on the swings or help them up and down the little slide. The mums made a fuss of her too because they could sit on the bench and chat amongst themselves while Jodie leaped about like Mary Poppins on skates.

'Maybe I'll be a nursery nurse when I'm older,' Jodie said happily. 'I seem to have the knack for it. Or I could be a nanny. Or maybe I'll just have heaps of kids of my own.'

'I thought you said you didn't want to get married,' I said.

'I don't! You don't have to have a husband to have lots of children,' said Jodie, winking at me.

'Mum would go spare if she heard you saying that,' I said.

'Mum goes spare at *everything* I say,' said Jodie.

'What if she finds out you're bunking off from school?'

'She won't. I'm leaving anyway, so what does it matter?' Jodie said carelessly.

She didn't bother to go back to say goodbye to anyone. I didn't actually say goodbye to many people at my school either. I didn't really have any proper friends. I did say a proper goodbye to my teacher, Mrs Lambert, because she was always kind to me.

'I'm so happy for you that you're going to this boarding school, Pearl. It's a wonderful opportunity. You're a very bright girl. I know you'll make the most of it.' She straightened up, shaking her head now. 'What about that big sister of yours? How does she feel about going?'

I shrugged awkwardly.

'I was very fond of Jodie, though she was always a handful,' she said, smiling. 'Still, maybe she'll turn into a lovely young lady at boarding school.'

She'd guessed my wish, word for word.

3

We got up at six sharp on moving day, even Jodie. Mum had been practising big breakfast fry-ups – egg and bacon and sausage, sometimes black pudding and hash browns and bubble-and-squeak as well – but this morning we had a marmalade sandwich and a mug of tea as we worked, doing all the last-minute packing up. Dad was useless, fretting about his work tools, taking them out of their boxes and unwinding all the bubble wrap.

'I'm just checking, just checking,' he kept muttering when Mum screamed at him.

I tried to help Mum pack up in the kitchen but I was trying to be too quick, too eager, because I knew she wanted everything out of the way before she gave the floor one last scrub. The milk jug slipped right out of my hands and crashed on the floor, shattering into blue and white shards and splashing all over my socks.

'For pity's sake, Jodie!' Mum snapped. It came out automatically – she was so used to telling Jodie off and not me. 'Pearl, I mean, you silly careless girl.'

Jodie herself was clearing up the bathroom, packing all the washing things into one last box and then cleaning the basin, the bath, the toilet, the floor.

'I'll give it a going-over after you. You'll leave it all smeary,' said Mum, but when Jodie called for her inspection, she had to shake her head.

'Well, you've made a really good job of it, Jodie. Look at that shine! There, it just shows what you can do when you put your mind to it.' Mum sounded almost put out, as if Jodie was playing a trick on her.

As soon as the two removal men came, Mum got them clearing the living room first while she vacuumed busily behind them. We followed when they went on to the big bedroom, trying to help with the small stuff while they tackled the heavy furniture and the carpets. Jodie rolled me right up in a rug, calling me her Pearl Swiss Roll, while Big Alf and Young Bernie roared with laughter. Big Alf seemed the same size as Bernie and they looked about the same age too, but these were their official names for each other.

'I'm Big Jodie then and you're Young Pearl,' said Jodie.

They laughed again and started chatting away to her as they collapsed the bed and swathed the mirrors in bubble wrap. Jodie tore off a strip herself and started popping it, sitting on the edge of the dressing table. She kept giggling at their jokes. I giggled too, though I didn't understand half of them.

Mum peered round the door and looked cross. 'Jodie, how dare you! Get *off* that dressing table, you'll make marks on the wood. And Pearl, why is your dress all creased? Whatever have you been up to?' She glared at Big Alf and Young Bernie too. When she was gone, they waggled their eyebrows and pulled faces. Jodie pulled faces too and they pretended to tut at her.

'You're a saucy baggage,' said Big Alf. 'You're going to be a handful in a couple of years.'

'I reckon she's a handful right now,' said Young Bernie. He pursed his mouth up like a goldfish and made slurpy kissing noises at Jodie.

I suddenly stopped liking him, but Jodie laughed and made kissing noises back at him. I tried to tug her away, telling her I needed her to help me bubble-wrap my doll's house.

'That's it, you go and pack up all your dollies – but we need Big Jodie to give us a hand here,' said Young Bernie.

Jodie jumped down from the dressing table, doing a little tap dance in her red shoes and finishing with a flourish, so that Big Alf and Young Bernie clapped. But then she smiled at me. 'Come on, Pearl.'

She marched us out of the room, neatly avoiding Young Bernie's patting hand with a twitch of her hips.

'You don't *like* him, do you?' I whispered on the landing.

'Of course not,' said Jodie.

'Then why were you mucking around flirting with him?'

35

'Because it's fun,' said Jodie. 'Take that look off your face, you look like *Mum*. Now, let's get your doll's house done.'

She wrapped it up expertly, stopping for a few last pops of the bubbles. 'There! All done.'

'I don't really play with it any more,' I said, running my fingers over the chimney and sighing. 'And it'll make our new bedroom look ever so babyish. But I can't chuck it out. Dad would be so hurt.'

'Maybe we'll be able to shove it in a cupboard,' said Jodie. 'So, we're having a grown-up glamorous bedroom, are we? No fluffy teddies, no fairy lamps, no posters of cute little puppies?'

I hesitated. Jodie laughed. She knew I was devoted to Edgar, Allan and Poe, the little triplet black bears who lurked in a cave under my pillow all day and came out to play with me at night. She knew I was frightened in the dark, even cuddled up close with her in her bed. I needed my fairy night-light to shine softly so I could see if there was anything creeping up on me. She knew how much I wanted a puppy, though Mum thought all animals were nasty messy nuisances and wouldn't even let us have a hamster. I had one lovely poster of white poodle puppies that I pinned above my bed. I gave all four puppies names: Ice Cream, Sugar, Salt and Mashed Potato.

'*Mashed Potato?*' said Jodie, snorting.

'Well, I wanted white food things and it was all I could think of,' I said huffily. 'I think it's a *lovely* name for the big puppy. He *looks* like fluffy mashed potato.'

I pretended he was the naughtiest, forever

fighting with his brother Salt and pushing his dainty little sisters out of the way. I even used to pretend to take them for walks, whistling to them and slapping my knees, but I'd grown out of that now.

I supposed I'd grown out of my poster and the lamp and the three teddies, but I couldn't bear the thought of chucking them in a black plastic rubbish bag.

'Don't look so worried, Pearl,' said Jodie. 'Of *course* you're keeping them. You can have your lamp by your bed, and the puppy poster above your bed and the teddies *in* your bed, same as always.'

'But it won't be very glamorous then,' I said.

'Yes it will! It'll have *us* in it,' said Jodie, striking a sexy-lady pose, her chest stuck out and her hand on her hip. 'Come on, look glam too!'

She grabbed two rolled balls of socks out of my suitcase and stuck them up under my T-shirt. 'There you are, Pearl, instant boob job. Show them off, then!'

I stuck out my socks and waggled my bottom, pursing my mouth up to do fishy kisses like Young Bernie. Jodie shrieked with laughter, clutching me so that we both over-balanced, falling onto my suitcase.

'For pity's sake!' said Mum, poking her head round the door. 'What are you two up to? We haven't got time to mess about. We've got to be packed and out of here by lunch time.'

'We've packed ourselves, Mum!' said Jodie, tucking her legs right into the suitcase.

'She's a card, that girl of yours,' said Young Bernie, putting his head round the door too.

Mum glared at him. 'She's a very silly little girl,' she said. 'Now, I think we'd all better get on.'

Young Bernie bobbed back to the bedroom to help Big Alf with the wardrobe.

'What are you *playing* at, showing off like that!' Mum hissed at Jodie. 'I won't have you making eyes at that man!'

'He's the one making eyes at *me*,' said Jodie, climbing out of the case.

'You go out to the shed and help your father,' said Mum. 'Pearl, tidy this mess and then come and give me a hand. What's that stuck up your T-shirt? Oh, for goodness' sake!'

We were all exhausted by the time we'd emptied the house. Big Alf and Young Bernie went off for an early lunch break while Jodie and I wandered around the house hand in hand, saying goodbye to each room. It looked so strange now it was empty, almost as if we hadn't really lived there. It was a comfort seeing the pencilled marks on the kitchen door where Dad measured our height each birthday, Jodie on the left, me on the right.

'It's not fair, I won't ever be able to catch you up now,' I said.

'Quite right too, little Titchy Face,' said Jodie, squeezing my hand.

When we looked round, there were marks made by Jodie everywhere: biro scribbles and paint spills, scuffs where she'd kicked the doors, crumbling plaster where she'd once whirled her school bag and it had banged the wall, a cracked window pane where she'd thrown a tennis ball, a splintered floorboard where she'd stamped hard. I'd been scared she'd stamp her way right through the floor like Rumpelstiltskin in the fairy tale.

We walked this Jodie devastation trail, telling each other the story of every mark and crack and splinter, both of us giggling.

'It's not a laughing matter!' said Mum. 'You're a total disgrace, Jodie. The landlord will think we've been keeping a wild animal in the house. I don't think we stand a chance of getting our five hundred pounds deposit back.'

'Every house has to put up with a little wear and tear,' said Dad. His voice was hoarse, his eyes overly bright as if he was about to cry.

'I'm sorry, Dad,' said Jodie, sobering up. 'Look, I'll save up and pay the deposit out of my pocket money.'

'Well, we'll all be in our graves by the time you've paid it off.' Mum sniffed.

Jodie glared at her. 'I'll get a Saturday job when I'm old enough, you'll see. And I can do babysitting now, easy-peasy. *Please* don't look so upset, Dad.'

'No, no, it's not the deposit, pet. I'm just – well, it sounds so soppy, but I'm sad to be leaving. We've been so happy here, the four of us.'

We stared at him.

'My three girls,' said Dad, holding out his arms.

'You sentimental old sausage,' said Mum, but she gave him a quick peck on the cheek.

Dad grabbed her and pulled Jodie and me into the hug too. We all clung together tightly for a moment. Jodie's shoulders started shaking. I thought she might be laughing, but when I wriggled sideways to take a good look at her, I saw she was crying.

'Jodie!' I said, stricken, because she hardly ever cried.

'What's up *now*?' said Mum. 'Jodie?'

'I wish we weren't going. Dad's right, we *have* been so happy here. I don't *want* to go to Melchester College.'

'Don't be so silly,' said Mum. 'We'll be much happier there! It's our golden opportunity. Now, dry your eyes and pull yourself together, you daft ha'p'orth.' Mum looked at me. 'Oh, for pity's sake, Pearl, don't you start blubbing too!'

I was crying because I felt so guilty. I knew Jodie had only agreed to go to Melchester College for my sake. Maybe I didn't want to go there either now.

We all cheered up when we were in the car actually on our way. Mum had packed a picnic. We expected another round of marmalade sandwiches, but there was a surprise home-made chicken and ham pie, Scotch eggs and cheese straws and a tomato salad, and then Mum's special pink iced fairy cakes studded with little silver balls. She always made them for our birthdays, and the birthday girl had to make a special wish, eating her cake with her eyes closed.

'We can *all* make a wish today,' said Mum, feeding Dad as he drove.

'Well, I don't think *I'd* better close my eyes,' said Dad, chomping happily. He pretended he thought Mum's fingers were the icing and licked them appreciatively.

'Get off, you sloppy devil, you're making me all slurpy,' said Mum, but she was giggling.

Jodie wolfed down her own cake, eyes squeezed

40

shut, her long lashes fanned out. Then she swallowed, opened her eyes and smiled.

'What did you wish for?' I asked.

'It won't come true if I tell you,' she said.

'Oh, go on, please,' I begged her.

'Absolutely not,' said Jodie, licking her lips.

'I'll tell you what *I* wished,' I said.

'I *know* what that will be,' said Jodie. 'I won't say it properly because then your wish won't come true either, but I bet it involves you and me, and Melchester College, and I expect there's a "happily ever after" at the end.'

She'd guessed my wish, word for word.

'Oh, you!' I said. 'So is that what you wished too?'

Jodie smiled mysteriously. I could never get her to tell me anything if she didn't want to. No one could ever guess what Jodie was thinking.

She started singing some silly love song about wishes, and then we all joined in, singing old Abba and Beatles and Queen songs, all Dad's favourites, and Mum joined in too, jiggling up and down in the car, doing arm gestures.

'Mum!' I said. 'You're good at it!'

'She was always a right little raver on the dance floor,' said Dad.

'We'll have to go dancing again sometime, Joe,' said Mum. 'You're not a bad dancer yourself.'

Jodie and I groaned. Dad was a seriously *embarrassing* dancer. He waved his arms like a windmill and kicked his legs out sideways.

'Maybe Melchester College will have a ball,' Jodie joked.

'I think they have a leavers' dance,' said Mum. 'There was a photo in the brochure.'

'Well, we're not leavers,' said Dad. 'We're *joiners*. Now, I think we come off the motorway soon, at junction thirteen. You'll have to have a squint at the map and help me, Sharon.'

Mum was generally good at navigating, but this time we got hopelessly lost. We drove down one country road after another, sometimes passing a village shop or a converted church or a row of cottages, but then we were into true countryside, with isolated lonely lanes, tangling branches over our heads, a thick leaf canopy casting us into an odd green bloom.

'It's like the picture of a fairyland in one of my books,' I said. 'Look, even the trees have got all knobbly bits so that they look like weird faces.'

'Watch out for their roots, they're reaching out to *grab* us,' said Jodie, turning her own arms into tree roots and snatching at me. 'Ooh! What was that? Did you see that little greeny-blue thing flying past? Watch it doesn't get in the window. Its little face was all squinty and evil. Maybe it's going to *sting* you.' She nipped at me now, making me squeal.

'Stop it, Jodie. You're scaring your sister,' Mum said sharply.

'I'm not really scared. It's just fun, Mum,' I said.

'Well, give over, both of you, you're getting on my nerves,' said Mum. 'Joe, it looks like we're driving to the ends of the earth. This can't be right. It's not even a real *road*, it's more a grass track. I think we'd better turn back.'

'Let's see where we get to,' said Dad. 'Anyway, we can't do a U-turn, there's not room. We'll end up in the ditch.'

42

'And so the intrepid family drove on and on into the gloom, on through the night, on through the next day, further and further and further down the long and winding road, until it dawned on them they were never ever going to come to the end,' said Jodie dramatically.

'Shut *up*,' I said, giving her a little shove.

I knew she was joking, of course, but she had a way of making it all seem horribly real.

'Don't say "Shut up", Pearl, it sounds so coarse. Say "Be quiet". And Jodie, you *be* quiet. We've all had enough of you.'

Jodie did a silent pantomime of being quiet, pretending to tie a gag around her mouth, making her eyes pop.

We turned down yet another lane, and then another, and then a very windy one up a hill, so we were thrown this way and that, like a fairground ride.

'We'd better have another squint at the map, Shaz. You're right, we've gone wrong somewhere,' said Dad.

'I can't look at the atlas, I'm feeling sick from all these twists and turns,' said Mum.

'You take a look then, Jodie,' said Dad. 'Are you a hot shot at map-reading, pet?'

'Jodie! Jodie, your dad's *talking* to you.'

'Mmm,' said Jodie, pointing to her lips.

Mum had forgotten all about telling her to be quiet. She reached round and flapped the atlas at Jodie, tapping her about the shoulders.

'Don't be so cheeky, miss! Oh God, I feel so sick. Joe, you're going to have to stop the car.'

Then Jodie yelled and pointed.

'For pity's sake, what now?' said Mum. 'Joe, *stop*. I'm going to throw up any minute.'

Dad stopped the car at the top of the hill. He pointed too. 'Oh, my!' he said.

I craned forwards in the gap between Mum and Dad and saw for myself. There, below us, was Melchester College.

She kept giving us odd waves, turning her hands.

4

It shone in the sunlight like a true fairytale palace. There were houses to the right and left of the vast green grounds, but the college itself towered above them all, its domes and pinnacles and turrets and tower etching a complicated pattern in the air.

'Oh, glory!' said Mum. She took deep breaths, her hand over her mouth.

'You're not really going to be sick, are you?' said Dad.

'I wouldn't dream of it,' said Mum. She gave a little belch, though she tried hard to smother it. 'Pardon me! This is the start of our whole new life.'

'It's *better* than Mansion Towers,' I said to Jodie. 'Oh, it's so *lovely!*'

Jodie reached out and held my hand tight. 'I'm glad you like it, Pearl,' she said.

'You like it too? You *must* do.'

'Yeah, it's great. If you like that sort of thing.'

'Do you think we *really* might have a bedroom in the tower?'

'Let's hope,' said Jodie.

'Don't be silly, girls. We have our own quarters in the basement,' Mum said briskly.

'The servants' quarters?' said Jodie.

'No, it's a properly converted flat. And we're not *servants*, we're management,' said Mum.

'You what?' said Jodie. 'Come off it, Mum!'

'Joe, what is your official title?' said Mum.

'I'm the Site Manager,' said Dad. He nodded at Jodie, sticking his tongue out. 'There, miss! I'm one of the posh nobs now.'

'And I'm the Food and Beverage Manager,' said Mum. She enunciated the word *Manager* with particular emphasis. 'So we're management, Jodie, do you understand? I shall even have staff under me – two girls to help with the cooking and cleaning.'

'You're got them already – us!'

'No, your job is to pull yourself together, make the most of this golden opportunity, adjust your attitude, mind your manners and work hard,' said Mum.

'Aye, aye, F and B Manager,' said Jodie, saluting. She spluttered with laughter.

Dad gave her a look. 'You're overstepping the mark, my girl,' he said. 'Still, we're all in a bit of a tizz. OK then, my three girls – wagons roll!'

He started up the car and we drove down the steep hill towards the college. I held onto Jodie's hand as we got nearer and nearer. There was just one road lined with trees – no sign of any other houses.

48

'I wonder where the nearest village is,' said Dad. 'Not much chance of me nipping down the pub. And what about all your food supplies, Shaz?'

'I wish you wouldn't call me that. It's an awful nickname. Call me by my proper name now, Sharon. And there's no worries about food, they'll deliver, silly,' said Mum.

'But where will we *go*?' said Jodie.

'What do you mean?' said Mum, gazing ahead. She was staring at Melchester College as if it was a heavenly vision. She was still very pale from feeling carsick. She mopped her forehead with a tissue.

'What about going to films? Going to Mc-Donald's? Going shopping?' said Jodie, her voice high and piercing.

'I expect I can run you into the nearest town on Saturdays,' Dad said quickly.

'But how will I meet up with *friends*?' said Jodie.

'Your friends will be here,' said Mum serenely. 'You'll make lovely new friends in Melchester College.'

'No I won't,' Jodie muttered. 'I don't want to be friends with all the baby posh nobs.'

'*Jodie!*' said Mum.

'Hey, hey, she's just a bit anxious, that's all. It's going to be a big change for all of us,' said Dad. he sounded a bit anxious himself. 'I didn't realize it was going to be quite as isolated.'

'I think it's beautiful,' said Mum.

'Well, yes, it *is*,' said Dad.

We got to the great gates at the head of a long gravel driveway; elaborate wrought-iron gates just like the ones in my fantasies of Mansion Towers.

'Open sesame!' said Dad.

The gates stayed closed. Dad tried giving a tentative *peep* on his car horn, as if he thought some magic gatekeeper would appear out of thin air and open them. We all peered up at the gates. They were attached to very high railings with sharp spikes at the top.

'Maybe it's a sign, a dire warning. We're not supposed to come here. Let's go back home,' said Jodie.

'Don't be so silly, Jodie. This *is* home now,' said Mum.

'Well, we're clearly locked out. Unless we climb the railings. Which would be very painful. Why have they got those vicious spikes?'

'It's a *school*,' Mum said impatiently. 'It's for security. They don't want anyone dodgy getting in.'

'Or maybe they don't want any pupils escaping,' said Jodie. 'It's like a prison.'

'Well, whatever, how are we going to get *in*?' said Dad. He tooted the horn again, sighed and got out. He walked over to the gates and tried pushing them. They rattled but didn't budge. The big padlock jangled.

'They're locked,' said Dad.

'We'll phone the school and then someone will come,' said Mum, reaching for her mobile.

'But they're shut for the holidays. It doesn't look as if anyone's here,' said Jodie.

The grounds stretched out as far as we could see, completely empty.

'There are lots of people still here. I spoke to the secretary only yesterday,' said Mum. 'She said she'd be here to welcome us. She knows we're coming – *and* our removal van, for heaven's sake.' She fumbled in her handbag and found a letter with the school heading.

'Maybe Big Alf and Young Bernie got here ages ago, when the gates were open. *We* thought they were simple removal men, when in reality they were crazed homicidal maniacs. They parked their van and ran amok with our kitchen utensils, striking deadly blows with frying pans and carving knives. There may be little boys bleeding to death in the bushes, secretaries strangled with their own scarves, the headteacher beaten to a bloody pulp with his own cane,' Jodie gabbled.

Mum sat with her phone pressed to her ear, flapping at her to make her shut up. Then she switched it off, sighing. 'There's no answer!'

'See!' said Jodie.

'Will you button that lip of yours!' said Mum. 'And stop that swearing – I heard you say the b-word.'

'*What* word? I said *bloody*, but that wasn't swearing, it was an accurate description,' said Jodie. 'He heard your phone call, he struggled manfully to answer it, crawling stickily through a pool of his own *blood*, OK? He reached up desperately, seized the phone cord, tugged with the last of his strength and then collapsed, blood spouting from his mouth like a scarlet fountain.'

'Jodie!'

'It gushed all the way down the stairs and it flooded the corridors until it lapped at the stout portals of the front door and then seeped out over the white marble steps.'

I shivered, squinting into the distance, trying to make out the steps. I knew Jodie was talking total nonsense but I looked for the blood even so. Then the door opened – but there was no dying headteacher, no blood, just a stout woman with a very large dog.

Dad saw her too and pressed his car horn hard.

'Don't, Joe! For pity's sake,' said Mum, her hands over her ears.

'It's that secretary! Miss French, the one who interviewed us! I've got to make her hear,' said Dad, tooting again.

'She'll think you're being so rude, tooting at her like that. I'll call her,' said Mum, scrambling out of the car. 'Miss French! Miss French! So sorry to trouble you, but we need you to unlock the gates!'

Mum was shouting at the top of her voice, but trying to talk in her poshest accent, so that it sounded as if she was being strangled.

Jodie giggled. 'Miss French and her hound from hell! We'll hear it howling as it's chained up at night. It will smell our fresh girly smell and break free of its chains. We'll hear its clawed feet padding along the corridors.'

'It'll have to *swim* along the corridors through the river of blood,' I said, trying to shut her up.

I thought I loved dogs but this one looked enormous, even from a distance. Miss French must have heard Mum and Dad because she started striding towards them, her dog bounding along ahead of her. She had a long, long way to walk. She kept giving us odd waves, turning her hands.

'It's like she's going, *Dodgy*,' said Jodie.

When she got a little nearer, we heard what she was shouting.

'Just *turn*!' she bellowed.

'Turn?' said Mum, and she turned uncertainly, spinning right round, looking foolish.

'*Turn?*' said Dad. 'Oh, Lord!'

He pulled the padlock and chain. They swung down, only attached to one of the struts. Dad reached up to the ornate metal handle on the gates. He turned it and pushed hard. The gates opened! Dad went bright red and hit his head with the palm of his hand.

'Oh, for pity's sake, Joe!' said Mum. 'What will she think of us!'

'How could I have been such a *noodle?*' said Dad.

Miss French carried on striding, shaking her head now.

'Oh, Miss French, we're so sorry! You must think us idiots!' Mum burbled.

'Not at all,' she said, though she didn't sound convincing. 'Down, Shep, down!'

Shep the dog was leaping *up*, barking at Dad for all he was worth. His lips were bared, showing his sharp teeth.

'Hello, boy. Good dog!' Dad said nervously.

I cowered in the car. Shep seemed as big as me and fifty times as fierce, more wild wolf than pet. But Jodie shot out of the car and bent down, holding out her arms. Shep veered crazily round and round Dad and then ran headlong at Jodie. He hurled himself into her arms, slobbering all over her as if she was a plate of pork chops.

'*Down*, Shep,' said Miss French. 'Are you *deaf*, mad dog?'

'Watch he doesn't bite, Jodie!' said Dad.

'He's not going to bite, are you, pal?' said Jodie, happily wrestling with him.

'Don't let him lick your *face*, dear,' Mum said tensely.

'He's just giving me a good wash,' said Jodie.

'Shep's clearly fallen for you, young lady,' said Miss French. 'He can be a bit overwhelming if you're nervous of dogs.' She looked at me. I was still in the car. She could only see my face and my velvet Alice band. I think she misjudged my age.

'Come and say hello to Old Shep, poppet. He's a *friendly* old doggie,' she said in that loud bright tone people use to toddlers.

'Out you get and say good morning to Miss French, Pearl,' said Mum.

I got out, feeling shy and silly – and still scared of Shep. He started barking at me, straining to jump out of Jodie's arms. I felt my heart going *thump thump thump* underneath my T-shirt.

'It's OK, Pearl, he's not going to hurt you,' said Jodie. 'Well, he might *lick* you to death.'

Miss French laughed. Mum and Dad laughed too, a little uncertainly. It felt as if they were all laughing at me. I tried to pull myself together. I reached out a trembling hand to pat Shep. He bared his big teeth again and growled. I squeaked and jumped backwards.

'He's only teasing you,' said Miss French.

He looked deadly serious to me.

'Your sister's not a *bit* scared of him,' said Miss French.

'Better both hop back in the car, girls,' said Dad. 'We've got a lot of sorting out to do, and the removal van will be here soon.'

'Oh, it got here over an hour ago,' said Miss French breezily. 'They've nearly finished. If you drive down round the big house, you'll find the van at the back, just by the door to your flat.' She looked at Jodie. She was trying to peel Shep off her but he nuzzled up close, butting her affectionately with his head. 'How about you taking Shep for a walk with me while your mum and dad get settled in? Are you any good at throwing balls?'

'I'm only the *best*,' said Jodie.

'Don't boast, Jodie!' said Mum.

'Well, you can throw for Shep. See if you can wear him out for me,' said Miss French. 'Come on.'

She fished out a chewed-up old ball from the pocket of her quilted waistcoat and tossed it to Jodie. She caught it one-handed and threw it way into the distance. Shep reared up excitedly and hurtled after it.

'You behave yourself, Jodie,' Mum called as Jodie set off after Shep. 'Don't you go bothering Miss French if she's busy.'

Jodie waved in acknowledgement but didn't turn round. Miss French didn't even bother to do that.

'Well,' said Mum. She shook her head.

'Our Jodie's obviously made a big impression,' said Dad.

'Yes, I suppose so,' said Mum. 'She's a *strange* woman, that Miss French.'

'I think she's OK,' said Dad. 'Seems quite friendly.'

'Mmm,' said Mum. 'She's a bit full of herself. Bossing us about when she's only the secretary, after all.'

'Still, she's that type, isn't she?' said Dad, getting into the car and switching the engine back on. 'I feel a total idiot, not sussing out how to open the gate. What will she think of me, when I'm supposed to be the general handyman?'

'We weren't to know,' said Mum. 'I don't appreciate her dragging Jodie off like that. When is she going to deliver her *back*?'

'Maybe she's some weird alien in disguise and Shep is an alien pet robot programmed to capture Jodie, and the moment they're out of sight they'll transform her and she'll be an alien too,' I said.

Dad chuckled as he started driving, but Mum glared at me.

'Don't you start on those silly horror stories, Pearl. We hear enough of that nonsense from Jodie.'

'She's only making up a *story*, Shaz – Sharon. Go on, Pearl, tell us more.'

'No, don't encourage her. You make up something *nice*, Pearl, if you really have to start telling stories.'

I hunched up in the back and made up my own story inside my head about a girl called Pearl who used to get scared of stuff all the time, but then she found a special pearl ring, and the moment she slipped it on it gave her super powers and she was never scared of anything again, especially not animals. Lions fawned at her feet, tigers rubbed round her legs, elephants nuzzled her neck with their trunks – and howling werewolves whimpered plaintively for her attention.

I got distracted as we got closer and closer to Melchester College. The gravel crunched and crackled as Dad drove the car slowly past the front while Mum and I craned out necks sideways, staring up at the great grey gothic building, awestruck. Then we turned round the corner, and immediately the house lost some of its splendour and dignity. There was scaffolding and piles of bricks and several boarded-up windows. Portakabins stood in a row and there were little sheds and huts in odd corners. Several cars were parked in a little bay, and there was our furniture van, doors open, with Big Alf and Young Bernie balancing down the ramp, holding Mum's dressing table.

'Mind those gilt handles!' said Mum, rushing out of the car.

Dad and I followed her, staring round, bewildered. In such strange surroundings Big Alf and Young Bernie seemed like old friends.

'You took your time, mate,' Big Alf yelled jovially to Dad. 'Did you go by the scenic route? Like, via Scotland?'

'Ha ha, very droll,' said Dad. 'No, we thought we'd let you chaps have a clear run without us getting in your way.'

Mum was getting very much in their way now. She followed them down the narrow steps to the basement.

'You're not putting that in the living room, are you? It goes in the *bedroom*, it's part of my bedroom suite. Dear, dear, you've put the good living-room cabinet in the *kitchenette*!'

'We thought it was your kitchen dresser, love,' said Young Bernie. 'Looks good in there.'

None of our furniture looked good anywhere, even in the right rooms. Our flat wasn't a proper flat at all. It was a series of small rooms down a long dark corridor. There were windows in the

57

rooms, but they didn't let in much light. When Big Alf and Young Bernie struggled past, we could only see their shoes. There was old grey-green mottled lino on the floor, and the walls were painted cream, just like a hospital. The biggest room was still on the small side. Our sofa and chairs were squashed in around the television. The table was piled high with boxes containing our books and DVDs and pictures and ornaments. There was an alcove at the back with a cooker and a little sink.

'How can Mum cook for everyone *here*?' I said.

'Don't be silly, Pearl. I'll have a proper big professional kitchen. This is just for us,' said Mum.

It looked too poky, even for the four of us.

'It'll look much bigger without the cabinet crammed in like that,' said Mum. 'Alf, Bernie, can you possibly move the cabinet over to the other side of the living room?'

'We could – *possibly*,' said Young Bernie.

'It's a bit of a liberty,' said Alf. 'You didn't let us know that your gaff was down all them stairs in the basement. It's a bit much expecting us to play musical chairs with your furniture. It's our job to deliver it all in one piece. We've just about done that. It's *your* job to rearrange it if you don't like the way we've set it out.'

'Now be a sport, lads. I've got a bad back,' Dad wheedled. 'Just the cabinet? You can see it's fretting her. You know what women are like – she'll try to move it herself and do herself a mischief.'

Mum glared at him furiously, even though Alf and Bernie started moving the cabinet for her, sighing heavily. She didn't thank them, she simply stuck her head in the air and dragged me off by the scruff of my T-shirt to investigate the bedrooms with her. They were very close together. Jodie and I would have to whisper right in each other's ears if we wanted to share secrets.

Both bedrooms had yellowy-cream wallpaper and ugly green and yellow curtains. They reminded me of a silly song they sang at school: *Green and yellow, Green and yellow, Oh Mum be quick, I'm going to be sick.* The carpet was green too, but a different dark olive shade. Mum rubbed at it with her foot as if she could change its colour with a little determination.

'We'll get new curtains and stuff,' she said, fingering them. 'They'll be easy enough to run up on a sewing machine. I'm sure the school will have one.'

I stared around the little room. It didn't look as if it could ever be even half as nice as our bedroom at home. I was so disappointed. I'd been crazy enough to imagine us living in splendour, in great airy rooms with flock wallpaper and big casement windows with velvet curtains. I'd even wondered if we might have chandeliers.

'We'll brighten it all up for you,' said Mum. She tried to keep her voice bright too, but she was looking around as if it was all too much for her. She rubbed her lower lip anxiously, suddenly looking like a little girl.

'Yes, it'll be fine, Mum,' I said quickly. 'Shall I start unpacking our stuff then?'

'That's my good girl,' said Mum. She turned round again, doing her best to smile – but her nose was twitching. 'Does it smell a bit funny in here?'

'What sort of funny?'

'Dusty? Damp? I think we'll give everywhere a good scrubbing first.' Mum went to the window. 'Look, all smeary!' She put her head to the curtains and sniffed. 'These are going straight in the washing machine! Dear goodness, the couple before us have really let the side down. We'll spring clean from top to bottom, get everything fresh and ship-shape. Good job we've got the whole summer to get organized.' Mum gave me a sudden fierce hug. 'We'll be happy here, Pearl, you and me and Dad and Jodie. I hope she comes back soon, we need every pair of hands we can get.'

Jodie didn't come back for ages.

Big Alf and Young Bernie finished heaving the last of the furniture around. Dad gave them what he thought was a big tip. Big Alf looked at the money in his palm disdainfully.

'Gosh, thanks, gov. Sure you can spare it?' he said sarcastically.

'What have you done with that sister of yours?' Young Bernie said to me.

I shrugged my shoulders.

'I bet she's run away already,' said Young Bernie. 'She's a bit of a live wire, your Jodie. God knows what she'll do in a dump like this. You folks must be mental.'

Maybe he wouldn't have been so rude if Dad had given them a larger tip. Dad looked as if he'd like to snatch it straight back. Mum was outraged.

'I'll thank you not to make personal comments about my daughter,' she said. 'And you're simply showing your ignorance if you refer to Melchester College as a dump.' She said it as if it was her own property and she was the lady of the house.

Young Bernie made a silly *'Ooooh!'* noise, wiggling his eyebrows, but he looked uncomfortable.

'Come on, mate,' he said to Big Alf, and they went without saying goodbye.

'What a pair of ill-mannered louts,' said Mum.

'I told you we'd be better off hiring a van and doing the job ourselves,' said Dad.

'You'd do your back in,' said Mum.

'Even so. The way he looked down his nose at my tenner! Who does he think he is, eh? And how dare he talk about Jodie like that?'

'Where's she got to, then? You'll have to go and start looking for her soon, Joe. That Miss French is probably dying to get rid of her. She must have finished walking the dog by now.'

'That dog wouldn't tire if you took it on a fifty-mile hike,' said Dad. 'Old Shep! That's an Elvis song. Do you think Miss French is an Elvis fan?'

We all sniggered at this. Miss French looked very much a lady for classical music, with her sensible grey bob and her navy waistcoat and pleated skirt and silk scarf – but when Jodie came back, we found it wasn't a joke.

'She's got this amazing Elvis card on her mantel-piece, and when you press his lips, his voice sings, *'Can't help falling in love with you,'* and his heart lights up inside his white sparkly suit – it's so cool!' said Jodie, jumping around and demonstrating.

'Don't start one of your silly stories, Jodie,' said Mum.

'It's true, totally one hundred per cent true,' said Jodie, peering around our flat, running in and out of rooms. 'It pongs a bit, doesn't it?' she said, holding her nose.

61

'Don't use that word! We'll give everywhere a good spring clean tomorrow – and you can help, madam,' said Mum.

'Where are Big Alf and Young Bernie? Have they gone already? Oh, I wanted to say goodbye!'

'It sounds as if you've said quite enough to them already,' said Mum. 'You're not to chat up workmen like that, do you hear me?'

'Dad's a workman. Can't I chat to him?' said Jodie, reaching up to put her arms round Dad.

'You chat all you like, sweetheart,' said Dad, giving her a cuddle. 'Where did you get to, then? How could you walk far in those crazy shoes?'

'We weren't just walking. We went back to her house and she gave me a cup of tea. That's how I saw her Elvis card. And her aquarium with bright blue fish – they were so pretty. And her rude painting of a great pink naked woman.'

'I've never heard such nonsense!' said Mum.

'You wait and see. We're all going to have supper together so maybe she'll ask you back to her house after for coffee.'

'What do you mean, supper?'

'With Mr and Mrs Wilberforce, the headteacher and his wife. Us and Miss French.'

'Us?' I said.

'Are you sure, Jodie?' said Dad. 'They wouldn't ask us for supper, would they?'

'They haven't asked! We haven't had an invitation or anything,' said Mum.

'I'm telling you, Miss French *said*. Tonight, half past seven, at the Wilberforces' house. They live down the drive at the back. Miss French does too.'

'They've got their own houses?' said Dad,

glancing around our room. 'What, modern ones?' He sounded envious.

'It's *much* better living in a real Victorian mansion,' I said quickly, though it was hard to remember we were in Melchester College in these dark basement rooms.

Mum seized hold of Jodie. 'Are you still just kidding us?' she said.

'Mum, what's your *problem*? Why would I make it up?'

'Oh *God*,' said Mum. 'Well, we'll all have to have a bath; we're filthy. I wonder what the hot-water situation is like? Then we'll have to get the cases unpacked, find some decent clothes – and where on earth are the iron and ironing board?'

'Don't fuss, Shaz. No one's going to expect us to look spick and span when we've only just got here,' said Dad, but he was anxiously trying to clean his nails as he talked.

'*Don't* call me Shaz, you know I hate it. Sharon. Jodie, Pearl, don't stand there like lemons. Go and get your clothes unpacked. Pearl, you wear your pretty embroidered skirt, and Jodie, you'd better wear your trousers – *your* skirts are way too short and tight. And you're *not* wearing those shoes, do you hear?'

'Miss French likes them. She says they're saucy,' said Jodie.

'She's the *secretary*,' said Mum, as if it meant lavatory cleaner. 'She's not the head of the school. Mr Wilberforce will *not* be impressed by ridiculous tacky high heels on a young girl. Now find your good trousers and your black shoes and put them on, and *no arguing*.'

None of us dared argue with Mum when she used

that tone of voice. We scrabbled around looking for our clothes while Mum had the first bath. Dad rolled his eyes at us.

'I wish she didn't get in such a huff,' he said. 'I'm sure the Wilberforces are simply trying to save us trouble our first night.'

'What's he like, Dad? You met him at that interview. Is he dead posh?' I asked.

'Ever so, but he seems a very nice bloke,' said Dad. He rubbed the bridge of his nose with his fingers. 'It's peculiar, all this. It all seems to have happened so quick, like. We're bound to feel a bit fish-out-of-water at first. But it will be worth it. We just want to do our best for you girls.' Dad put his arms round us.

'Joe!' Mum called urgently from the bathroom. 'Joe, come here!'

'Oh Gawd, what now?' said Dad.

'I've just thought,' said Mum. 'I'm the cook. What if they're expecting *me* to do the supper?'

'Don't be daft. You're here to cook for the children, not the Wilberforces,' said Dad. 'Don't look so worried, Shaz – *Sharon*, sorry sorry! You're my girl too, you know. Come here, give us a cuddle.'

Mum protested, but we heard splashing and then a kiss. Jodie pulled a face at me and I giggled.

'This isn't such a bad place, you know,' Jodie said softly.

I glanced at the bleak wallpaper and the bile-green and vomit-yellow curtains.

'Not *here*. Though we'll make it look better, you'll see. No, I meant outside, all the grounds. Miss French showed me around the garden bit. There are kitchen gardens with heaps of fruit, and this funny old gardener let me pick a whole handful of raspberries. There are huge great woods too. It's like we're in one of those old-fashioned storybooks, *Two Have Fun at Melchester College*.'

'So you don't mind us being here?'

'Well, I hate being stuck in the middle of nowhere. I'm going to go mad not being able to go out anywhere. But it might be all right while it's just us. We'll make the most of the summer, OK?'

'A very good choice', said Mrs Wilberforce.

5

We stood outside the Wilberforces' house. It was technically a bungalow rather than a house, but very grand and spacious, with white walls and scented jasmine in terracotta pots on either side of the green front door. We stood outside the wrought-iron gate, Mum and Dad and Jodie and me. We were still pink from our baths and in our best clothes. Jodie had even been persuaded out of her red shoes.

Mum inspected all three of us anxiously and had a little peep at herself in her powder compact. Then she checked her watch.

'It's only twenty-six minutes past,' she whispered. 'Perhaps we'd better wait till half past.'

'Why, are you worried we'll catch Mrs Wilberforce in her knickers?' said Dad.

Jodie and I snorted with laughter.

'Ssh!' Mum hissed. 'For pity's sake, they'll hear you. Don't you start larking around, Joe, it won't go

67

down well at all. You too, Jodie. None of your nonsense.'

We stood there, waiting, watching Mum's wristwatch.

'Oh dear, are you locked out again?' said Miss French, walking up behind us in her soft rubber-soled shoes, making us all jump.

'No, no!' Mum said quickly. 'No, we didn't want to arrive too early, like.' The 'like' jumped out of her lips before she could stop it. She clamped her mouth shut, going red.

'I think we're all spot on time,' said Miss French, opening the gate and marching up the wide pathway.

We followed along behind her. Miss French rapped hard at the door. Mum took a step backwards, obviously worried the Wilberforces would think it was her hammering at their front door. It opened almost immediately, as if someone had been crouching on the other side. Mum went redder.

'Hello hello hello,' said a tall man with a beard. He was wearing a very grubby yellow cardigan with leather buttons, two of them missing, a checked shirt with a frayed collar, very baggy corduroy trousers and slippers.

'How do you do, Mr Wilberforce,' said Mum, sounding strained. 'Girls, this is the head of Melchester College.'

Jodie burst out laughing, startling us. 'Don't be daft, Mum, he's the gardener,' she said.

'Jodie!' said Mum, giving her a little shake.

'Button it, Jodie,' Dad whispered, looking agonized.

'No, no, I *am* the gardener. Your daughter and I

met up earlier in the kitchen garden. I am *also* the headmaster here at the college, but that's just the day job. I'm only really happy rootling away like a pig in . . . whatsit. Isn't that right, Frenchie?'

'Absolutely,' said Miss French, chuckling.

'Do come in, Mr and Mrs Wells. It's wonderful to see you. I hope you're settling in nicely. Now, I've already met you, Little Miss Raspberry Guzzler. And you must be . . .?' He bent towards me.

'This is Pearl,' said Mum. 'Say how do you do to Mr Wilberforce, Pearl.'

I mumbled it foolishly, wishing I wasn't so shy. Jodie had already bounded inside. Then she stopped so abruptly that I bumped into her. There was a woman in a wheelchair in the hallway. She had an embroidered Spanish shawl wrapped round her legs. She was quite old, her face wrinkled under thick make-up, her ash-blonde hair falling in soft waves past her shoulders. She was wearing a loose floaty lilac dress, with big amethyst beads round her neck and several huge rings on her small white hands. Only one of her arms worked. She gestured with it, while the other arm hung down, the hand clenched.

'Are you Mrs Wilberforce?' Jodie asked uncertainly.

I think we were both scared she couldn't talk properly. She hesitated, and then took a deep breath. She smiled politely, though her eyes didn't light up.

'Yes, I am, my dear. And you are . . . Josie?'

'Jodie. And this is my sister, Pearl.'

'How lovely to meet you both, Jodie and Pearl. Come into the sitting room. Make yourselves comfortable on the sofa.'

69

We sat down obediently, Jodie stroking the slippery satin cushions and saying how pretty they were.

'Hey, hey, off that sofa! You two sit on the little chairs,' said Mum, bustling into the room.

'Mrs Wilberforce *told* us to sit here,' said Jodie. 'Didn't you?'

'Indeed I did,' she said. 'Please, all of you, come and sit down. Harold, darling, would you pour everyone a drink? What would you like, Mrs Wells?'

Mum hesitated. She didn't drink anything alcoholic at home, and the rare times we all had lunch in a pub garden Mum had a lemonade shandy.

'I'd like a sherry, please,' she said, rather desperately.

'Certainly. Amontillado coming straight up,' said Mr Wilberforce. 'Frenchie, you'll have your usual G and T? And what about you, sir?' He looked at Dad.

'Don't suppose you've got a beer . . . sir?' said Dad.

Mum glared at him, but Mr Wilberforce grinned.

'You bet I have. Bottle for you, bottle for me. Cynthia, wine? And what about you two young ladies?'

'We're not fussy,' said Jodie. 'I'd really like a beer, but wine will be fine.'

Mum opened her mouth but Mr Wilberforce was rocking with laughter.

'You'll have half a thimble-full of wine and count yourself lucky, Miss Cheeky,' he said. 'What about you, little Pearl? Don't tell me you're a beer girl too.'

'She'd like an orange juice, please,' said Mum.

I felt like a ventriloquist's dummy, unable to

70

answer for myself. Jodie chatted away to everyone and they all laughed at her. Mum kept giving her warning looks but Dad beamed at her proudly. I sat on the edge of the sofa, legs dangling, sipping my orange juice carefully. I peered all around the room. There were paintings of ballet dancers in fluffy tutus exercising at the bar, and white china dancers pirouetting, permanently poised on one toe. I wondered if Mrs Wilberforce had been a ballet dancer herself and had had some tragic accident on stage, leaving her crippled in her chair. I pointed my feet this way and that, copying the dance positions.

'Pearl! Stop fidgeting! And mind you don't mark the sofa!' Mum hissed.

Mr Wilberforce and Miss French and Dad were all chatting about the garden and the grounds and playing fields and then cricket, with Jodie cutting in and saying funny stuff. Mum was a bit left out of the conversation. She turned towards Mrs Wilberforce, who was staring into space, making no attempt to be a hostess.

'Can I help with anything in the kitchen, Mrs Wilberforce?' said Mum. 'Seeing as you're . . .'

Mrs Wilberforce raised her eyebrows. 'No, no, it's fine,' she said firmly. She saw me looking agonized. 'Are you all right, Pearl?' she asked.

I nodded, ducking my head.

'You're very quiet!' said Mrs Wilberforce.

'It's our Jodie who's the chatterbox,' said Mum.

'Perhaps this one can't get a word in edgeways,' said Mrs Wilberforce. She nodded at me, tossing her long pale hair. 'Tell me all about yourself.'

My mouth went dry. I tried to swallow.

'She's a bit shy,' said Mum.

'Come on,' Mrs Wilberforce commanded.

'Well,' I said. Everyone else had stopped talking. 'Well,' I repeated. The silence was unnerving. 'Well.'

'*Wella wella wella,*' sang Jodie, starting the old *Grease* song, jogging up and down on the sofa.

Everyone laughed, but Mrs Wilberforce wouldn't let me off so lightly.

'Ssh!' she said to Jodie, her fingers to her lips. 'Let your sister talk.'

'Well, my name's Pearl and I'm nearly eleven though I know I look heaps younger,' I said in a rush. They were all looking at me. I looked down at my lap, my hands clasped tight. I waited. It wasn't enough.

'Talk about school, Pearl,' Mum prompted. 'She's very bright, even though she's so quiet. Always top of the class.'

'Mum!' I said. It sounded such awful showing off.

'Which subject do you like best?' said Mr Wilberforce.

'Well . . . literacy. And art,' I said.

'So you like reading?'

'Never got her head out of a book,' Mum said proudly, though she often told me off for reading so much, saying I'd strain my eyes and develop a squint.

'Good to hear it,' said Mr Wilberforce. 'Cynthia's a great reader, aren't you, darling?'

'Come with me, Pearl,' she said.

She wheeled herself out of the living room, bracelets jingling. Mum gave me a little push. I didn't *want* to follow her, but I shuffled obediently in her wake. We went down a corridor and then she opened a wide door and wheeled herself inside. I

72

breathed in the strange musty smell of old books.

It was a real library, with shelves on every wall, though they only came up to my head. They'd obviously been specially made so that Mrs Wilberforce could comfortably reach all her books from her wheelchair. There were paintings hung at the top: more ballet dancers, women in long dresses, children playing in gardens. It was hard making them out because the room just had one light, a very pretty stained-glass lamp in the shape of a big flower.

'Do you like my library?' she asked.

'It's lovely,' I whispered.

'Have a little browse,' she said. 'You can borrow anything you fancy. You look a very careful girl. There are children's books over on that wall.'

I was used to bright little paperbacks. These were big blue and green and crimson storybooks with gilt decorations on the spine, and very large leather-bound fairytale picture books. I ran my finger very lightly along their curves.

'Take them out and have a look at them,' said Mrs Wilberforce. 'Choose one to take home. But don't read it at the table. I don't want any sticky finger marks or grease spots on my books.'

'Oh no, I promise,' I said. 'Mum doesn't let me read at the table anyway. Were these your books when you were a little girl?'

'Yes, and they were mostly my mother's books, my grandmother's too. They used to be in the proper library in the big house.'

'So was Melchester College *your* house?'

'Oh yes. But my father turned it into a school many years ago – and now, of course, my husband runs it. I used to teach the little ones dancing and music but now . . .' She gestured down at her legs under the shawl, bangles jingling.

I wanted to ask what had happened to her but didn't want her to think I was being rude or nosy. I just made an odd mumbling noise which I hoped sounded sympathetic.

I picked out *The Secret Garden* because I'd seen the film on television and loved it.

'A very good choice,' said Mrs Wilberforce, smiling at me as if I'd passed an exam. 'There's a big house called Misselthwaite Manor in that book and it has one hundred rooms. I remember walking all over Melchester when I was a little girl, starting right up in the attics, counting each room in turn to see if I could get to a hundred.'

'And did you?'

'No, sadly not. I can't remember how many there were. You'll have to count them for me and see. I don't suppose I'll ever be able to get up there myself.' She pressed her lips tightly together – but then managed a smile. 'Now, we'd better not neglect our guests. I shall nudge Harold into the kitchen. I'm sure you're all starving.'

'Can I help?' I said. 'Or maybe my mum?'

'Oh no, Harold has two stalwart helpers already – Mr Marks and Mr Spencer. They do all the hard work.'

I imagined two men in white chef's hats whisking and stirring in her kitchen – and then the penny dropped. We enjoyed a Marks and Spencer supper: wonderful luxury ready-prepared food we were never allowed at home. The grown-ups drank wine, and Mr Wilberforce really did pour Jodie a

74

tiny glass, though Mum frowned. I had red cranberry juice and pretended it was wine. I had glass
after glass, washing down the delicious food. We
had tiger prawns to start with, great juicy monster
prawns, not the weeny pink slithers Mum cooked.
Then we had chicken Kiev with broccoli spears and
fancy mashed potato, and *then* we had enormous
strawberries with dollops of double cream.

It was the most glorious meal I'd ever eaten.

There were even chocolate truffles and Turkish
delight when the grown-ups drank their coffee. I
ate and ate and ate, very happy to be ignored again,
though Mrs Wilberforce smiled at me every now
and then. She spread her huge napkin carefully over
her lap but ate very neatly and nimbly with one
hand, not spilling a morsel. When we'd all finished,
Mum started stacking our plates, determined to
help at last, but Mr Wilberforce took them from her.

'No, no, you're a guest in our house tonight, my
dear. Your culinary duties don't start until
tomorrow. There's just a handful of sad little
Orphan Annies who don't get to go home for the
hols. You'll cook for them, and rustle up a spot of
breakfast and lunch for the under-matron and
Frenchie and me too, if that's OK – but you won't
find yourself too stretched until term starts. But
I'm afraid *you* won't get off so lightly, Joe. There are
any number of urgent jobs. The college is getting
very old and cracked and leaky and creaky, like me!
We'll have a quick recce of the house and grounds
after breakfast tomorrow and work out which jobs
to tackle first.'

'But *we're* on holiday,' Jodie said happily, winking
at me.

'No, no, you two need to give me a hand,' said Mum. 'Don't worry, I won't let them run wild.'

'Well, Jodie can run wildly if she takes Shep along too,' said Miss French. 'He needs all the exercise he can get.'

'And *your* job is to come and visit me, Pearl, and confer with me in my library,' said Mrs Wilberforce.

Mum frowned, irritated that they were telling us what to do, but she didn't like to object. She kept looking at her watch, fussing about our bed time. It was half past ten by the time we got away. I was dying to have a wee after four glasses of cranberry juice but I didn't like to ask to go in front of everyone.

I whispered to Mum as we set off down the path. 'Why didn't you *say*?' she said, exasperated. 'Well, you'll just have to wait. It's not far.'

'I don't think I *can* wait,' I said.

'Don't be silly, Pearl. Think about something else,' said Mum. 'I wish they had proper lamp-posts, it's not very safe when it's so dark.'

'I've got you safe, Shaz,' said Dad, putting his arm round her. 'And my girls,' he added.

'*The father did his best to protect his little family on their perilous path home, but as they approached the dark mansion, they heard a baying in the distance*,' said Jodie.

'Jodie! Don't start now!'

'Don't make me scared, I'll wet myself!'

She threw back her head and howled like a werewolf, but then got distracted. 'Look at the *stars*,' she said, reaching for my hand.

We stared up at the sky, heads tilted right back. 'They're so big and bright and there are so *many*

76

of them. That's the Pole Star, the big brightest one, but what are all the others?'

'I don't know. There's meant to be a Great Bear and a Little Bear – and a Goldilocks eating their porridge,' said Jodie.

'Rubbish! I'll have to find a book about stars,' I said.

'Your new pal Mrs Wilberforce can lend you one,' said Jodie.

'She's a bit odd, that one,' said Mum. 'I don't mean because she's, you know, in a wheelchair. It's just like she's in a daydream all the time. Maybe she's not quite right in the head.'

'She seemed fine to me,' said Dad. 'It must be awful for her, being so helpless.'

'I wish she'd let me lend a hand. It seemed dreadful that *he* had to do all the cooking. Well, not that you could *call* it cooking. Imagine, inviting us to dinner and just giving us a ready meal.'

'Oh, come off it, Shaz, they did their best.'

'Sharon! No, it's madness. I bet they paid a fortune for all that chicken, when I could have bought a couple of birds and done them a lovely fancy *coq au vin*.'

'I thought the chicken was *lovely*. Much much better than anything we ever have,' said Jodie tactlessly. 'Pearl, what's up, you're walking funny.'

'I'm very nearly wetting myself,' I said desperately.

'Really! You're not a baby,' said Mum. 'Look, nip into the bushes and have a wee there.'

'I can't!' I said, but I realized I'd *have* to, or I really would disgrace myself.

I dashed into the bushes, praying there wouldn't

77

be any werewolves lurking. I fumbled in the dark, just about managing, and then pulled my knickers up. I stepped sideways, caught my foot in a bramble and slipped down a sandy bank. I flung my arms out – and caught hold of someone!

I opened my mouth to scream.

'No, please, ssh, you'll scare him!' someone whispered.

He loomed way above me but his voice was light and high, a boy's voice.

'Scare who?'

'The badger! Look!' he hissed.

I opened my eyes wide and stared around.

'There!'

I could just make out a big mound with tree roots sticking out. There was a dark hole and a face peering out, a long face with a white stripe.

'I see it!' I whispered, transfixed.

We crouched, watching. My heart thumped wildly, wondering who this great tall boy was and whether he'd heard me having a wee. Then the badger ambled right out, its head going from side to side. It was bigger than I'd thought, with a stocky chest and powerful paws. It was the strangest, most magical animal I'd ever seen. I breathed in sharply and heard the boy do the same.

'Pearl! Where *are* you?' Jodie shouted, crashing through the bushes.

The badger retreated rapidly into its burrow.

'Blast!' the boy whispered. 'Who's that idiot?'

'It's my sister,' I said.

Jodie yelled for me again, louder now.

'Oh well. You'd better go to her. What are you doing here anyway?'

'Our mum and dad are going to be working at Melchester College.'

'Oh. Right. I'm at the school too. I'm Harley. And you're . . . Pearl? Look, don't tell your sister about the badger set, OK? She sounds much too noisy and shouty, she'll scare them all away. Keep it a secret, yeah?'

'OK,' I whispered.

'Thanks. You're a pal,' he said, and he squeezed my hand.

Three little ones were sitting in a row on a bench.

6

I woke up very early the next morning and lay listening to all the birds. We never saw so much as a sparrow at home, but here there seemed to be great flocks of swallows and starlings, blackbirds and blue tits, all trilling and chirping outside the window.

This was home now. I leaned up on one elbow and peered around the poky little room, wondering how Jodie and I could fix it up. I traced the bobbly pattern on the wallpaper with my fingertips. It was partly peeling away. I edged my fingers underneath and found layers of paper and then plain white-washed wall. There was a little dent, a hole for a nail.

I wondered if some small kitchen maid had once slept in this room. Perhaps she had a little looking glass hanging on the wall. Or maybe she kept an old brown photo of her parents and all her brothers and sisters to remind her of home. Maybe it was a religious picture, a guardian angel spreading feathery white wings above a little child in a pinafore and button boots.

I played *I* was the kitchen maid – Flossie? Mary-Ann? *Kezia!* – lying on one side of the little iron bed, with my best friend Pansy, the parlour maid, curled up close beside me. We had to scramble out of our nightgowns as soon as the grandfather clock in the corridor struck six. We stood shivering in our shifts, sponging our faces with cold water, and then struggled into our ugly uniforms and starched aprons.

I wanted Jodie to wake up and play Servant Girls with me. I crawled into her bed. She cuddled me sleepily but wouldn't even open her eyes.

'Play with me, Jodie, please! I want you to be Pansy the parlour maid.'

'*Who?* Give it a rest, Pearl. It's way too early, too early,' she mumbled into her pillow.

I picked up Mrs Wilberforce's beautiful copy of *The Secret Garden* and lay on my tummy reading instead. I wasn't sure I really liked Mary but she was very interesting. I *loved* her sweet maid, Martha. I muttered her words out loud, not quite sure what a Yorkshire accent sounded like.

'What are you muttering about?' said Jodie.

'I'm reading *The Secret Garden*. Do you think there might be a secret garden here? There are lots of high walls overhung with ivy. Maybe we'll find a locked door and then a key and we'll have our own secret place?'

'Yeah, yeah, whatever,' Jodie mumbled. 'You and your boring old books. What time is it? Do you think Mum and Dad are up yet? I'm absolutely *starving*.

You wouldn't go and make some toast for us, would you, Pearl? And a cup of tea?'

I crept off to the kitchenette obediently, like a real Kezia the kitchen maid, and started making breakfast. I found a kettle and all the cups and plates in a cardboard box.

Mum had already stowed the bread in its enamel bin and put the milk and butter in the tiny fridge. I wondered whether to take Mum and Dad a cup of tea too, but I wanted to savour this special time with Jodie. I always liked it so much better when there were just the two of us. I dug my finger into the butter and then the sugar while I was waiting for the kettle to boil. I licked the lovely big dollop of sugary butter and then started guiltily when I heard the floorboards creaking in the passage.

'Naughty naughty!' said Dad, bursting in on me. 'Lucky your mother didn't catch you!'

'You won't tell her, Dad, will you?' I said, giving him a hug.

'Well, I won't *have* to tell her if you leave the butter all over poky little holes! Smooth it over, lovey. With a knife, not your finger! And is that toast? Don't fill yourself up too much. Your mum's going to be making eggs and bacon in the big kitchen and then we'll all eat in the dining room.'

'With the other children?' I said.

'Yep, though there's only a handful still here. Imagine keeping your kids at school all through the holidays!' Dad tutted and shook his head. 'Make your mum and me a cuppa too, sweetheart.'

Dad went off to take Mum her tea in bed. I carefully carried our two cups back to our bedroom.

Jodie had gone back to sleep, curled up in a little ball under the duvet.

'Jodie? Jodie!'

She played dead, eyes closed, utterly still, even when I tickled her. I *knew* she was playing but I panicked all the same, shaking her frantically.

'*Jodie!*'

'Yeah?' she said, opening her eyes and grinning.

'Don't *do* that!'

'Sorry, sorry, just kidding.' She sat up and drank her tea and ate her toast. She ate mine too because I was too het up to be hungry. I'd see Harley at breakfast, the strange badger boy. We had our special secret.

'Jodie, can I wear your red shoes today?' I asked.

'No, I'm wearing them.'

'Just at breakfast, for a treat.'

'They're way too big for you.'

'I could stuff the toes with tissues. *Please.*'

'OK, OK, so long as you'll be my willing slave for the rest of the day.'

'I'm always your willing slave,' I said, thrusting my bare feet into Jodie's shoes and tottering around in my nightie.

'You look like Minnie Mouse,' said Jodie. 'You're not meant to stick your bum out like that. Sort of *swish* your way along, like this.' She jumped out of bed and demonstrated a model's walk, though she had to zigzag nimbly around all the cardboard boxes.

'Should we start getting everything unpacked and sorted?' I said.

'No! Not *yet*. Come on, let's get dressed.'

'Can I borrow one of your skirts too?'

She peered at me. 'What *is* this, Pearl?'

'I'm just sick of looking babyish.'

But I looked even *more* of a baby in Jodie's clothes, like a little girl dressing up. I gave her back her red shoes, sighing, and got dressed in my own skirt and top and sandals.

Dad was wearing a bright checked shirt and denim jeans so stiff and new he could barely bend his legs. He had his workman's belt buckled round his waist, its leather pouches filled with wrenches and hammers and screwdrivers. He had his new working boots on too, very big and purposeful.

'Oh, Dad, you look like Bob the Builder!' said Jodie, laughing at him. Then she saw his face and realized she'd hurt his feelings. 'Only teasing! You look way cool, ever so hunky. Watch out for that Miss French. She'll be nudging up to you and pinching your bum.'

'You stop your nonsense, saucebox,' said Dad. He gave her a kiss and blew me one too. Then he sniffed the air. 'Can you smell bacon? Come on then, girls, let's go and eat.'

We went down the corridor and turned the corner. There was a big panel of bells set into the wall with copperplate handwriting underneath: *Drawing Room; Sitting Room; Master Bedroom;* room after room after room.

'There's nowhere near a hundred rooms though,' I said.

'What *are* all the bells?' said Jodie.

'It's the servants' bells. They ring in the rooms and it rings here.'

'*Still?*' said Jodie. 'So will they ring for Mum and Dad?'

'Who knows?' said Dad. 'Still, it's not like Mr Wilberforce treats me like a servant. I don't have to bow and scrape to him.'

'Oh let's, it'll be fun,' said Jodie, bowing extravagantly.

She pushed open the door. We stepped into a vast kitchen with a stone-flagged floor and a big wooden table and a huge dresser with shiny pans hanging off hooks, just like the picture of a Victorian kitchen in my history book.

Mum was turning eggs in a sizzling frying pan on the vast kitchen range. Her white nylon overall and white cap and black and white trousers looked far too modern.

'You should be wearing a long dress and a big starched pinafore, Mum,' I said.

'What?' said Mum, checking another pan of bacon. 'Come on, crisp up, you devils.'

'Is that burning smell the toast?' said Jodie.

'Oh no!' said Mum. She pulled the smoking grill pan away from the heat, glaring at Jodie as if it was her fault. 'Look, clear off into the dining room, you two, and let me concentrate. Joe, give me a hand, for pity's sake. I've gone all to pieces. I can't seem to manage a simple fry-up for a dozen. I'll be given the sack before the week's out at this rate.'

'Now, keep your hair on, sweetheart, it looks absolutely delicious. No one does a fry-up like my Shazza.'

'Sharon,' Mum said, but she gave him a quick smile. Then she gestured at us. 'Go on, scat. See that everyone's helped themselves to cornflakes and juice. I laid it all out on the side table.'

I followed Jodie to the end of the kitchen, up a

flight of stairs and out through double doors into the main Melchester College dining hall. It was a very big room of benches and long trestle tables, with one separate table right at the other end. I tiptoed along as if I was in church. Jodie strode forward confidently, swinging her arms. There were four grown-ups sitting at the separate table: Mr Wilberforce, Miss French and two strangers, one a young man and one a young woman.

Miss French waved to us cheerily. 'Good morning, girls!' She breathed in appreciatively. 'Mm, I can smell that bacon sizzling!'

'Jodie, Pearl, this is Miss Ponsonby, our under-matron. We all call her Undie here,' said Mr Wilberforce.

We tried not to snigger.

'She keeps a kindly eye on our resident young-sters during the holidays,' said Mr Wilberforce. 'And this is our gardener, Jed Breaksmith.'

'I thought *you* were the gardener, Mr Wilberforce,' said Jodie.

'It's my hobby. It's young Jed's daily grind,' said Mr Wilberforce.

'I keep him in his place. I have to stop him going crackers with the pruning shears,' said Jed, grin-ning. He barely gave me a second glance but he looked Jodie up and down.

'Hello there!' he said. He was very good looking in a weird wild way. His black hair was long and tangled, several strands threaded with silver and glass beads. I thought he looked like a pirate, dark and threatening, and ducked my head. Jodie smiled straight back at him.

'Hi, Jed,' she said, like they were the same age.

'Hello, Jodie, hello, Pearl,' said Miss Ponsonby, nodding at us the wrong way round. *Undie!* She was less interesting than Jed, a pale young woman with straight mousy hair and an anxious expression. 'Perhaps you'd like to sit with the other children?'

There were four of them. Three little ones were sitting in a row on a bench, kicking their legs. Harley was hunched up on the opposite side of the table. He still seemed extraordinarily tall, even sitting down. The sleeves of his shirt showed a lot of long thin wrist. His hair was thick and bushy and stood out around his head like a mane. His face was long and thin and pale and serious. He was reading a book and eating cornflakes. His eyes darted across the page while he chewed thoughtfully. He didn't look up.

Perhaps he was deliberately ignoring me. I swallowed hard and went and sat beside the three little children. We nodded at each other shyly. They looked too young to be at any school, let alone boarding school.

'Hello,' said the biggest. He was a little boy with big brown eyes and the longest lashes I'd ever seen. His skin was ebony, with a beautiful sheen.

'I'm Zeph,' he said.

I smiled at him timidly. The next child was even shyer than me. She bent her head, her glossy black hair falling in her eyes.

'She's Sakura,' said Zeph. 'And that's Dan.'

Dan was so small he could barely sit up straight on the bench. He rested his chin on the tabletop, his blue eyes solemn, milk all round his mouth.

'Yes, I'm Dan. Actually Daniel. The *real* Daniel

went into a lions' den and he was very brave and I'm a *bit* brave. I don't cry hardly at all,' he said in a high reedy voice.

'I'm Pearl. I'm not even a little bit brave,' I said.

Harley looked up. He seemed genuinely surprised to see me there. He waved his long fingers and pointed to the bench beside him. But Jodie got there first, slotting herself neatly into the space with one swing of her legs. She slid a juice down to me at the litties' end and kept one for herself.

'Hi, I'm Jodie. Who are you?' she said.

'I'm Harley.'

'Your first name, silly!' said Jodie.

'It *is* my first name.'

'So what's your last name? Davidson?' said Jodie, cracking up laughing.

'Oh, you're so incredibly amusing. Like that's the very first time anyone's made that joke,' said Harley.

'Hey, hey, she's just being friendly,' said Dad, hovering near us. It was obvious he wasn't quite sure where *he* should sit.

'Dad!' said Jodie, jerking her head, making it obvious he should go and sit with the grown-ups. She smiled at Harley. 'Hi there, Harley Not Davidson. OK, that's my dad, and my mum's cooking our breakfast, and that's my little sister, Pearl.'

'She's not that little,' said Harley, nodding at me.

'Well, you're certainly not little,' said Jodie. 'How tall *are* you.'

Harley swallowed the last of his cornflakes. He looked weary. 'Six foot four,' he said.

'Wow! And how old are you?'

'Thirteen.'

'So you're still *growing*?' said Jodie.

'Unfortunately.'

'*Guinness Book of Records*, here we come!' said Jodie. 'Are your mum and dad giants too?'

'Shut up, Jodie!' I hissed.

She blinked at me in surprise. 'Why?'

Harley sighed. 'OK, life history: I don't really know about my dad. He cleared off when I was three. He *seemed* tall, but all dads do when you're that age. My mum's five seven, five eight. That's tall for a woman, I suppose.'

'So why aren't you staying with your mum for the holidays?' said Jodie.

'Jodie, stop *badgering* the lad!' Dad said.

Harley and I looked at each other. He smiled. I smiled too.

'What?' said Jodie.

Harley shrugged his shoulders. They looked as thin and spindly as a wire coat-hanger. 'Maybe I'm not quite ready to tell you my life history,' he said.

'Oh, I'll tell you mine,' said Jodie.

She started yacking away, telling him about Moorcroft, boasting about the times she bunked off and all the different things she did with Shanice and the others. Dad frowned at her. Zeph and Sakura and Dan stared at her round-eyed. Harley seemed to be hardly listening, glancing wistfully at his book. Then Mum came swinging through the doors with her big tray, and Jodie had the sense to shut up at last.

Mum waved her hand at Dad, almost pushing him to go and sit at the top table with the others.

She served them first, each plate a work of art: egg, bacon, sausage, tomato, fried bread and mushroom. Miss Ponsonby looked fussed and said she really couldn't tackle a big cooked breakfast and could she just have a boiled egg please? 'Of course,' said Mum, but she looked daggers at her. However, Dad and Miss French and Jed and Mr Wilberforce all tucked in enthusiastically.

'I've already had my bowl of rabbit droppings – ha ha, *muesli* – at home, but I feel I'm duty bound to try out your home cooking, Mrs Wells,' said Mr Wilberforce, happily stuffing a sausage into his mouth. He peered over at the plates Mum was serving to us children.

'Good heavens, I'm not sure the budget will run to such gorgeous big grills for the little ones,' he said.

'I'd like to feed them up and make a bit of a fuss of them during the holidays,' said Mum, putting vast plates in front of all of us.

I got one too, even though Mum's always despaired that I'm finicky with food, unable to swallow runny egg or bacon fat or tomato skin. Sakura looked equally wary. She sat staring at her food for a long time until Jodie slid along the bench and cut it all up for her in case she couldn't manage it herself.

'Eat it all up now, yum yum!' Jodie commanded.

Sakura picked up her fried bread with her thumb and forefinger, smeared the tip with yellow yolk and nibbled at it delicately. Dan was anything but delicate. He held his fork in one hand but ate determinedly with the other, shovelling it up and aiming at his mouth, not always accurately. Zeph

91

ate properly with a knife and fork but played his own little game with his meal, separating each sort of food so that they didn't touch. He finished one before starting the next. I imagined his stomach with a layer of dark brown mushroom, light brown fried bread, red tomato, pink bacon and yellow egg, like those tubes of coloured sand you get from the Isle of Wight.

Harley wolfed his own plateful. Mum glanced at him approvingly as she doled out racks of toast.

'That's right, lad, you set them a good example,' she said.

She gave him a second glance, taking in his length, and looked astonished. I frowned at her, willing her not to say anything about him being a growing lad. Mum frowned back at me, taking in my still-heaped plate.

'Come on now, Pearl, you're not a baby. Eat up, dear. Don't let me down.'

I cut my bacon into tiny pieces the size of my thumbnail and balanced one on the end of my fork. It looked horribly fatty. Dad was watching me. When Mum had turned her back, I made out my fork was an aeroplane, flew it through the air and made it land in Dan's mouth. He swallowed happily and opened his mouth for more. I got rid of half my breakfast before Miss Ponsonby clacked over to our table in her flip-flop sandals.

'Don't give him any more, dear, or he'll be sick,' she said, attacking Dan's face vigorously with a wet wipe, as if she was cleaning a window. He squirmed and whined but didn't put up much of a struggle. I felt sorry for Sakura, who got the wet wipe next. Her face was pristine before and ended up smeared with Dan's slurpy crumbs. Zeph ducked his head out of the way.

'I'm not a baby. I'm absolutely *clean*,' he said, folding his arms, his lower lip sticking out.

'OK, Zephaniah,' said Miss Ponsonby, knowing when she was beaten.

I folded my arms too, just in case she thought *I* was a baby. She smiled at me.

'I wonder if you'd like to join the others for our holiday play club?' she said brightly. 'We do all sorts of craft work. We made puppets yesterday, didn't we, children?'

'My puppet *died*,' said Dan mournfully.

'His head just fell off, darling. We'll fix it back on today,' said Miss Ponsonby.

'No, keep it off, then he could be a headless ghost,' said Zeph. 'Yeah, and I'll make a skellington and then they can fight each other.'

'No fighting, Zeph, you know the rules,' said Miss Ponsonby. She looked entreatingly at me. 'The boys get a little boisterous at times. It would be lovely for Sakura to have another girl around. You could paint together or do some sewing or knitting, or perhaps you could do a little sculpting with clay, Jodie?'

I fidgeted on the bench, trying hard to think up a polite excuse. I didn't want to go off with all these strange children!

'She's Pearl. *I'm* Jodie,' said Jodie. 'It's lovely of you to invite Pearl, Miss Ponsonby, but I'm afraid she can't. We have to help our parents with all sorts of stuff, and we're decorating our new bedroom, and Pearl had this very important reading project set by Mrs Wilberforce so she's going to be *ever* so busy for the next few weeks. Still, thank you very much indeed for asking her.'

I smiled up at Jodie, my sister, my saviour. Miss Ponsonby led Zeph and Sakura and Dan away and I was left with Jodie. And Harley.

'OK,' said Jodie, grinning. 'So what are *we* going to do today?'

'Don't you have to help your parents and decorate and all that stuff?' said Harley.

Jodie peered over at the end table. Dad was talking to Miss French. Mum had poured herself a cup of tea and was sitting at the end, in Miss Ponsonby's place, deep in conversation with Mr Wilberforce.

'Not if we clear off sharpish!' said Jodie. 'Come on, quick, while they're not looking!'

The three of us slid off the bench and made it out of the main door without being spotted.

**The cupboard made a great groaning sound
as we shoved at it.**

7

We stood in the middle of the main hallway, portraits peering down at us. Grim men with jutting chins and women in profile with long noses.

'God, who are they? Old teachers?' said Jodie.

'They look like relatives. I suppose they're Mrs Wilberforce's ancestors. This used to be her family house,' said Harley.

'Wow, some family! Like they go back centuries! They must be really really rich and posh.'

'Posh, yes. Rich, mm, maybe not any more. Melchester College is falling to bits.'

'But my dad can fix it up now,' said Jodie.

'You'd need a hundred dads to fix this dump,' said Harley.

'You call this a *dump*?' said Jodie, gesturing at the chandelier above us.

'You wait till you see behind the scenes,' said Harley.

'Well, come on, then. Show us around,' said Jodie. Harley hesitated. He looked down at his book.

'You don't have to,' I said quickly. 'You probably want to get on with stuff.'

'No, it's OK,' he said.

'What's your book?' Jodie asked.

'Oh.' Harley looked embarrassed, going pink.

'Hey, is it a dirty book!' said Jodie.

'No, it's a classic. You'd hate it,' he said.

'Let's see, then.' She squinted at the spine. '*Jude the Obscure*. Have you read that one, Pearl?'

I shook my head.

'It's not a children's book,' said Harley.

'Pearl's a great reader – she reads all sorts, *lots* of classics,' said Jodie loftily.

It was my turn to blush now.

'No I don't,' I mumbled. 'Just one or two easy ones.'

'I'll show you the library if you like,' said Harley. 'Don't get excited, it's pretty crap though.'

He led us along the corridor into a big room with handsome wall-to-wall shelving. The books themselves looked sparse and flimsy on the deep shelves, mostly cheap tattered paperbacks mixed up with old Enid Blytons and Biggles and mock-leather children's encyclopaedias. Jodie wrinkled her nose and sat down at one of the computers, starting to fiddle.

I peered at the books.

'See, I told you,' said Harley. 'I thought there'd be wonderful old leather-bound volumes going back donkey's years.'

'There are!' I said shyly. 'But not here. They're in Mrs Wilberforce's house.'

'So you've been in there? I haven't! She's got lots of books, has she?'

'She says I can borrow some,' I said. I took a deep breath. 'I could ask if you could borrow some too if you like, Harley.'

'Cool,' said Harley.

He was flipping his way through the books. 'Have you read this?' he asked, holding up *The Wind in the Willows*.

'Yes, it's great,' I said. 'I like Moley.' I paused, glancing at Jodie. She was frowning at the computer keyboard, tapping keys impatiently. 'And Badger,' I added.

Harley smiled at me. It was as if we were talking in our own secret code.

'You haven't told her, have you?' he mouthed at me.

I shook my head.

Harley put his head very close to mine. 'We'll go and watch again, at night. You and me. OK?'

'OK!' I said.

'What are you two whispering about?' Jodie called. 'Hey, this is a totally rubbish computer, you can't access anything.'

'They don't want to enlighten the kiddywinks,' said Harley. 'Keep them ignorant and unsuspecting.'

'Is that what you are, Harley Not Davidson?' said Jodie, shutting the computer down in disgust.

'No, no, I'm very knowledgeable and highly suspicious,' said Harley.

'That's cool,' said Jodie. 'Come on, then, the library's boring. Show us the rest of this place. How long have you been shut up here?'

'Only since last year. I get moved around a lot.

I've been to so many schools I've lost count,' said Harley.

'Why?'

'I don't fit in.'

'We don't fit in either,' said Jodie. 'Pearl gets teased because she's so weirdly brainy—'

'I'm *not*,' I said, squirming.

'And I'm the bad girl,' said Jodie, spinning round on one foot and throwing her arms out, going, '*Ta da!*'

'Maybe you'll both fit in here. Most of the kids are weird or bad,' said Harley.

'Aren't they all little posh-nob boffins?' said Jodie.

'No, this is a kind of last-ditch dumping ground for kids no one wants,' said Harley.

'You're kidding,' said Jodie. 'This is dead posh, anyone can see that.' She gestured to the cream walls in the corridor. 'Look, no graffiti! You should see the walls of my old school. Kids sprayed their tags all over, and wrote dirty stuff about the teachers.'

'Oh well, at least it showed they were literate. Half the kids at Melchester are so dyslexic they can't even spell four-letter words,' said Harley.

'Don't be so snotty,' said Jodie. 'Just because you're obviously a goody-goody brainbox.'

'I'm hopefully a brainbox but I'm considered a baddy-baddy,' said Harley. 'I've been expelled twice. And the last school I was at said they thought I'd be happier elsewhere so that's almost an expulsion too.'

'What did you *do*?' I asked, staring up at him.

'He didn't do anything, he's just kidding,' said Jodie.

'I'm not,' said Harley. 'Though I didn't do anything interesting. One time it was for insubordination. The headteacher kept yelling at this sad little kid so I yelled back on his behalf. I wouldn't apologize because I felt I was in the right, so eventually they expelled me. And the other time it was supposedly arson—'

'Wow!' said Jodie. 'You set the place on fire?'

'I didn't mean to. I was just trying out a pack of cigarettes, seeing if I could acquire a decadent illicit habit, and I failed to stub one out properly and it set fire to my wastepaper basket and then the whole wretched bed caught fire. No one was *hurt* but the school decided to get shot of me all the same.'

'That figures,' said Jodie. 'So, have you got any fags on you now?'

'I gave it up. Not good for my general fitness,' said Harley, flexing his long spidery arms.

Jodie laughed. 'You *are* joking, I take it? You're not exactly the spitting image of a sports jock, are you, mate? What do they do for sports here, anyway?'

'There's a gym. I'll show you.'

'I *hate* gyms,' I said.

'Me too,' said Harley.

'Wimps!' said Jodie.

When Harley led us inside the Melchester College gym, Jodie let out a whoop at the sight of the ropes and the wall bars and the horse.

'Yeah!' she said, unhooking the ropes and letting them swing. She leaped onto one and swung herself backwards and forwards.

She made it look so easy, I tried too. I couldn't

climb up high enough and bumped back to the floor, looking a fool. Harley was sensible enough not to try. Jodie swung wildly above us, her thin legs wrapped round the rope.

'Wheeee!' she sang.

'We hear you, Tarzan,' said Harley. He looked at me sympathetically. 'You're not sporty, Pearl?'

'No. Absolutely not.'

'Me neither. Apart from basketball. I just reach out and dunk the ball through the hoop.'

'Will I have to do basketball here?'

'Maybe. You get a choice of three different sporty things, winter and summer.'

'Can't you just choose not to?'

'I wish.'

'Hey, you two down there! Look at me!' Jodie called.

'I can't or I'll be staring straight up your skirt,' said Harley.

She stuck her tongue out at him. 'Do you think I could jump from one rope to the other?'

'No.'

'I bet I can. Watch!'

'No, don't, Jodie, you'll fall!' I shouted.

'Come down, crazy girl, you'll break your neck!' said Harley.

Jodie laughed, lunged forward, reached for the neighbouring rope and grabbed hold. She spun round, the rope juddering, but she kept her grip, though one of her red high heels fell off. She kicked the other one off too and then climbed down monkey-fashion, landing lightly on her bare feet.

'Just throw roses at me, folks, I know I'm

brilliant,' she said, throwing her arms out and curtsying.

'Watch out we don't throw rocks at you,' said Harley. He looked at me. 'Is she always this mad?'

'Yes.'

'Oh well. Maybe she'll liven things up at Melchester.'

'I'm great at livening things up,' said Jodie, stepping back into her shoes and giving a little wiggle.

'I bet you are,' said Harley. 'OK, have you seen enough of this scholastic dump, because I've got things to do.'

'No, no! Come on, Harley, show us *all* of it!'

'Well, the science labs are along here too. You can always have fun blowing yourself up.'

He showed us the science labs. Mercifully the equipment was safely locked away.

'Anywhere you want to see, Pearl?' Harley asked.

'Is there a special art room?'

'Yep. Come on then.'

All the art materials were locked away too, but there were paintings pinned up all over the walls. The artwork was mostly uninspiring, copies of famous paintings like Van Gogh's *Sunflowers* and Picasso's *Child with a Dove*. There were some self-portraits too, all very stiff and self-conscious. The only painting I really liked was an animal painting, a very long thin wistful giraffe on four sheets of paper sellotaped together.

'I like the giraffe!' I said.

'Ah! My self-portrait. I'm glad you like it,' said Harley.

'Did you really do it?' I said.

I peered at it closely. There was Harley's signature at the bottom.

'I can't believe I picked it out!' I said, thrilled. 'What a coincidence!'

'Come on, you *knew*,' said Jodie. 'Great long tall weirdo creature. Great long tall weirdo boy. Doesn't take much power of deduction.'

'I *didn't* know,' I said. 'Which do you like, Jodie?'

'They're all a bit rubbish,' she said. She grinned at Harley. '*Especially* the giraffe. Show us something else. Where are all the ordinary classrooms?'

They were up the big flight of stairs to the first floor. Each classroom was pretty much the same, dull and a little dusty, with old-fashioned ink-stained desks and revolving blackboards on one wall.

'No whiteboards? *Chalk?*' Jodie picked up a white stump of chalk and started drawing a cartoon version of herself, all big eyes and spiky hair and wide grin. She printed underneath *Jodie was here!!!*

'Very artistic,' said Harley sarcastically.

The junior school classrooms up on the second floor were more interesting, with a Wendy house and floppy teddy bears and a set of enormous building bricks in red and blue and yellow. I'd have liked to play at building my own house but we had to be very quiet. Miss Ponsonby was in the junior art room with Zeph and Sakura and Dan. We tiptoed past the open door, peeping in at them. Zeph was painting in a careless splashy manner, waving his paintbrush around as if he was conducting an orchestra. Sakura was painting very delicately indeed, her tongue sticking out in concentration. Dan wasn't painting at all. He was stirring a saucer of red paint with his finger and then dabbing himself experimentally. He looked as if he had a bad case of measles.

'Poor little kid,' Jodie whispered, when we were down the end of the corridor. 'What is he, *three?*'

'He's five. He's ever so bright but he somehow seems a bit backward,' said Harley.

'No wonder! How could anyone send such a baby to boarding school?'

'He cries a lot. They all do, especially at night,' said Harley. 'Well, I don't know about Sakura. She sleeps in the girls' dormie. Zeph and Dan are in the boys' dormie with me.'

'So what do you do when they cry?' Jodie asked. 'Do you give them a cuddle?'

'I read to them,' said Harley.

'Oh, *sweet*,' said Jodie. 'What, like, you read them *Little Noddy* and *Thomas the Tank Engine?*'

'No, if you really must know, I'm reading them *The Hobbit*.'

'Is that one of those hairy little dwarfy guys with big feet in that wizardy film?' said Jodie. 'They're way too young for that.'

'*They're* not reading it, *I* am,' said Harley. 'Zeph likes it because he's seen *The Lord of the Rings* on DVD. And Dan likes the name Bilbo and laughs every time I say it, so we're all three happy.'

'Where's this boys' dormie then?' said Jodie. 'Is it along here or upstairs?'

'The dormitories aren't in the main building. There's a boys' house and a girls' house, near the bungalows.'

'So what's upstairs?' said Jodie.

'There isn't really an upstairs,' said Harley.

'Yes there is!' said Jodie, running down the corridor to the end.

There was a big store cupboard standing there, but Jodie peered round it.

'Stairs!' she said.

'Yes, but as is obvious, we're not allowed up there,' said Harley.

'Then surely it's *equally* obvious there must be something exciting hidden away!' said Jodie. 'Come on, help me shift the cupboard till we can squeeze past.'

'It's strictly out of bounds,' said Harley.

'So what are they going to do? Kill us?' said Jodie.

'Old Wilberforce is quite inventive when it comes to punishments,' said Harley.

'Well, he can't punish us *now*. It's the school holidays. We can do what we like,' said Jodie.

'I'm still in his care,' said Harley.

'Well, *we're* not,' said Jodie. 'Come on, Pearl, help me!'

She tugged hard at the cupboard, going red in the face with the effort.

'You'll hurt yourself, Jodie!'

'So give me a hand!'

I scrabbled at the cupboard too. We could barely budge it an inch. We looked at Harley.

'It's not worth the effort and the potential aggro. There's nothing *up* there,' he said, but he came and stood beside us and heaved too.

'I think there are attic rooms,' I said. 'Mrs Wilberforce told me about them. She said she tried to count them all once. She said I should have a go.'

'There! She's given us her permission to have a

peer round,' said Jodie. 'Come on, use your shoulders. One, two, three, *push!*'

The cupboard made a great groaning sound as we shoved at it.

'Ssh, we don't want Miss Ponsonby to come running,' said Harley.

'She's miles up the other end. She won't hear a thing. Come on, one more go.'

We hauled at the great cupboard and it suddenly budged and shifted sideways, toppling alarmingly

'Watch it! It'll fall on top of us if you're not careful,' said Harley.

'It's fine, it's fine,' said Jodie. 'Look, we can just about squeeze through. Lucky job we're all thin. Let me go first!'

She hunched her shoulders up, stood sideways and wriggled slowly through the gap.

'It looks horribly dark through there. Are there any spiders?' I asked anxiously.

'Ooooh! Tarantulas! Help, help, killer tarantulas as big as beach balls! They're jumping all over me with their hefty hairy legs!' Jodie called.

'She's such a pain, your sister,' said Harley, sighing. 'Are you going next?'

'All right.' I paused. 'Will you come too?'

'What do you think I'm going to do? Shove the cupboard back and wall you both up for ever?'

'Stop it! You're as bad as Jodie!'

'Never,' said Harley.

I still hesitated, looking at the gap.

'She's joking about the spiders,' said Harley.

'I know she is. It's just the moment she says it I can kind of *feel* them,' I said.

'Here,' said Harley. He held out his hand. 'Hang

onto me. If you feel anything at all spidery, just give a yell and I'll yank you straight out.'

I smiled at him and then squeezed through the gap, hanging on tight.

'Oh, it has to be a wedding dress,'
said Harley.

It was like squeezing into a different world. It smelled damp and musty, and it was much dustier. The narrow stairwell was very dark.

'I don't like it!' I said. 'Jodie, let's go back!'

'Don't be such a wimp. Here, hold my hand. Is Harley coming?'

'Give us a chance,' Harley called.

He stuck his arm through the gap, then squeezed his long lanky body through, limb by limb. Then we stumbled up the murky stairs, coughing as we breathed in the dust. There was a long corridor with *lots* of spiders' webs dangling down from the ceiling.

'Look!' I said, pointing at them.

'They're just little baby spiders,' said Jodie. 'Isn't this great? It's like we've found our own secret passage.'

We stood peering along the long corridor. There were buckets and basins all the way up it, half full of dank water.

'I think the roof's leaking big-time,' said Harley.

Jodie was dodging around them, trying doors. Some were locked, without any keys.

'What's going on? What's in here? Why has Mr Wilberforce blocked the way with that cupboard? Perhaps we'll find the bodies of all his former wives, like he's a Bluebeard and he's murdered them all. Maybe he even had a go at murdering the present Mrs Wilberforce by shoving her out the tower window but she miraculously survived, though of course tragically maimed.'

'Don't, Jodie!' I said. 'That's horrible!'

'She *did* fall. Someone told me in the village. It was years and years ago, before she was married,' said Harley.

'Truly?' I said. 'How awful! I wonder *how* she fell? You don't think someone really pushed her, do you?'

'Maybe we'll try to find out. We'll solve the Mystery of Melchester,' said Jodie.

She wandered along the corridor. One of the doors was off its hinges, but we didn't spot any dead wives when we peeped in, not a single coffin. It was just old school junk: broken computers, wobbly desks, and stacks of cheap plastic chairs, big ones, medium-sized ones and little ones.

'*Oh, it's too big. Oh, it's too soft. Oh, oh, oh, it's just right!*' said Jodie in a funny Goldilocks voice, trying out all three sizes.

She tried another room while Harley and I stacked the chairs back neatly. She just took a running push at the door and it creaked open.

'Jodie! Don't! You mustn't break the lock!'

'It was broken already. Come and look!' she called.

112

We found her kneeling amongst big cardboard boxes and battered trunks, pulling out limp paper-chains and tinsel and winding them round her neck like garlands. One of the trunks had old costumes from school plays.

'Now you have to admit, this is seriously cool,' said Jodie. She snatched up a white veil and a long blue dress. 'Oh, wow, I've always wanted to be Mary,' she said, still rummaging. 'No, no, look, even better, *white feathers*! Blow Mary, I'll be the Angel Gabriel, then I can wear wings.' She pinned them on her back and flapped around the room.

I fingered the fruit-gum jewels on the three cardboard crowns wistfully. I wanted to play at being a queen but I'd feel too silly in front of Harley. Then I found a lovely smooth black velvety coat and I slipped it on, stroking the sleeves.

'I like your coat, Pearl! What else is there? What's that brown furry one? Are these the Three Wise Kings' robes?' Jodie put on the brown fur and tried to tie the long thin belt round her waist.

'Weird belt! It's more like a tail,' she muttered.

'It *is* a tail!' said Harley. 'You're Ratty! And you're Mole, Pearl.' He delved into the trunk and found a large coarse black fur coat with a white streak down the front. He tried it on, grinning. 'Who am I, Pearl?'

'*Badger!*' I said.

There was a bright green spotted mac at the bottom of the trunk, a perfect Toad outfit.

'You'd make a great Toad, Jodie,' said Harley. 'Leap around going *Parp-parp.*'

'*Parp-parp! Poop-poop!*' said Jodie, flinging the Toad mac over her head and doing little froggy leaps around the room. She tripped in her high heels and ended up sprawling on the floor, laughing.

'How old are we? Mucking around like little kids!' she said breathlessly.

'You're the number one mucker,' said Harley.

'Charmingly put! I wonder if they'll do a play this year? I want to be in it. Is there a proper stage here, Harley?'

'Of sorts. So, Dame Jodie, this is presumably the start of your acclaimed acting career?' said Harley.

'Do not mock! My moment of fame will come, you'll see,' said Jodie. 'I'm going to be a mega star.'

'Do you want to act too, Pearl?' Harley asked.

'I like dressing up and pretending, but not in front of people!' I said.

'So what do you want to do?'

'I think I want to write,' I said shyly.

'She's written heaps and heaps. You should get her to show you. Some of her stories are brilliant,' said Jodie.

'No, they're not, they're rubbish,' I said, blushing. 'And my stories aren't anywhere *near* as good as yours. Tell Harley some of your stories, the really creepy, bloody ones.'

'He thinks we're weird enough already,' said Jodie.

'I *like* weird! I positively celebrate it,' said Harley. 'I *have* to take that standpoint as you don't get much weirder than me. I'm going to earn a fortune exploiting my own weirdness. I shall do my best to keep on growing and be a living freak in a circus – Harley the Hundred-Metre Man. They'll have to construct an enormously tall tent to exhibit me,

114

with staircases and balconies so that people can climb up and gawp at me eyeball to eyeball.'

'Yeah, you're weird all right,' said Jodie. She rattled ten or twelve walking sticks in a wonky umbrella stand. 'Hey, are these *canes*? Does Mr Wilberforce whack you on the bum when you've been bad?' She took two of the canes and hobbled backwards and forwards with them. Then she pressed down hard on them, balancing, and swung between them. There was a hatstand too, with bowlers and trilbys and caps, even a battered grey top hat. Harley put it on and then draped a long black cape over his shoulders.

'Hey, it fits, more or less,' he said, swaggering about, doffing his hat to us.

'Are they costumes for some old-fashioned play?' said Jodie.

I picked up a moth-eaten fur stole with two creepy little animal heads at one end. They had staring glass eyes and glinting teeth.

'Yuck, they're real furry creatures,' I said, dropping it on the floor. 'I don't think they're dressing-up costumes, they're real Victorian ones. I drew some like this for my Victorian project at school.'

'*This* isn't Victorian,' said Jodie, hauling a heavy mink coat round her shoulders. She tossed her hair and struck a film-star pose.

'And what about this?' said Harley, slipping his long arms into a soft white fur jacket.

It looked ridiculous on him, his wrists and splayed hands sticking out miles below the cuffs.

Jodie laughed. 'You look like a half-skinned rabbit.' She stroked him mockingly. 'Good

115

bunnykins. Hey, I think that jacket *is* rabbit. Oh dear, it's so sad. Yet it's so soft too. Let *me* try it on, Harley.'

'It's like all the people who ever lived here left their coats behind,' I said.

'Perhaps that's why they're here. Maybe these all belonged to Mrs Wilberforce's family, her parents and grandparents,' said Harley, wriggling out of the jacket and letting Jodie try it on.

It looked lovely on her. She kept it on while we went on to the next room. Jodie was an expert at getting in now. We couldn't find any more clothes, apart from a splendid crimson smoking jacket with a matching tasselled fez and a half-finished long white dress still pinned on a dressmaker's dummy.

'Oh, it has to be a wedding dress,' said Harley. 'This is too Miss Haversham for words!'

I'd seen the film of *Great Expectations* on television and remembered Miss Haversham was the old lady who'd been jilted on her wedding day, so I could nod intelligently.

Jodie pinched the waist and held out the long skirts. 'Yes, it's definitely a wedding dress, a total white meringue,' she said. 'Sooo, was it going to be Mrs Wilberforce's dress? And then some guy jilted her, so she threw herself from the tower in deep despair.'

'Sherlock Jodie,' said Harley. 'Though I doubt it's as elemementary as that.'

'Poor Mrs Wilberforce,' I said.

'You can ask her all about it when you take her book back,' said Jodie.

'I can't do that! She might not like me talking

about it. How awful if something like that really *did* happen,' I said.

'It's not real, we're just making it up,' said Jodie. She took the white rabbit fur coat off and draped it tenderly round the dummy's shoulders over the long white dress. 'There now,' she said softly.

She went on to explore the next room. 'Pearl! Pearl, come and look at this!' she called.

I went running. I stared around the room, my mouth open. It was like a nursery, with a beautiful Victorian scrap screen, four panels of plump-cheeked pouting children, overblown roses, little bluebirds with beady eyes, and flying fairies with spotted butterfly wings. There were old wooden chairs painted with hearts and flowers, a wobbly washstand, an old clothes horse, a misshapen fire-guard and a big leather trunk.

Jodie tried to prise it open but she was a nail biter and couldn't get a proper grip.

'Go on, Pearl, you do it,' she said. 'I don't think it's locked, it's just stiff.'

I bent over and tugged hard, using my hands like hooks. The lid gave a little and I started levering it up.

I peeped inside.

'Oh!' I said, sitting back on my heels. My arm trembled as I eased the lid right up. 'Oh!' I said again. 'Oh, oh, oh!'

'You sound like a session singer, Pearl,' said Harley, standing in the doorway. 'What's in the trunk? Diamonds? Gold bars? Rubies big as gravel?'

'Better better better,' I said. 'It's *toys*.'

The trunk seemed full of old stuffed animals

117

carefully swaddled in scraps of white silk, laid end to end.

'I though you said you were too old for toys now?' Jodie teased. 'Go on, get them all out so we can see what's there.'

I didn't like to disturb them. They looked as if they were in little silk shrouds in a communal coffin.

'Maybe we should just leave them exactly as they are,' I said.

'Nonsense,' said Jodie, leaning over, prodding this one and that one. She found a brown furry arm and pulled. 'It's a *monkey*!' she said. 'Look, a chimp in blue trousers with a red bow tie. Isn't he cute!' She pulled him out and then shrieked when his big beige rubbery foot slithered down her front and fell to the floor. 'Oh, *gross*! He's gone rotten, he's all warped and manky.'

She dropped him so that he fell beside his severed foot. He went on gamely grinning with his orange mouth.

'Poor manky monkey,' said Harley.

I went and picked him up, feeling sorry for him. His foot was horribly wrinkled and spongy. I didn't like touching it, but I tried poking it back into the monkey's hollow leg. It fell straight off again, flopping into my lap.

'Perhaps we could glue it on?' I said, smoothing his fur and pulling up his trousers, trying to comfort him.

Jodie was poking further into the trunk. 'God, there's a whole *family* of rotting monkeys incarcerated in here, look!' She held up a girl monkey in a blue dress and pinafore. She had little earrings piercing her crumbling ears.

'Hey, I like her little starry studs,' said Jodie, trying to pick them out.

'Don't take them away from her!' I said.

'Look, she's only got half her ears left. She doesn't *need* earrings.'

'Yes she does!' I tried to think of a way of getting Jodie to back off. 'Maybe the earrings made her ears get all infected and that's why bits have dropped off. If you take the earrings, then your ears will go like that, too,' I said, taking the girl monkey and rocking her in my arms.

'You two are so seriously mental,' said Harley. 'So, we've got Hop-along and Nibble-ear. Anyone else?'

Jodie found a baby monkey in a long white dress. She had a bonnet pulled very low over her eyes, which was just as well, because half her face had peeled away. Then we found her big brother in a red waistcoat and black cord trousers. He was in better condition, but he'd lost one thumb.

'So, we have Little Faceless and Greedy Suck-a-thumb,' said Harley, settling them in my lap. 'There you are, Nurse Pearl, a set of little simian patients for you to put to rights. And when you're done doctoring them, you can do a dormie round. Zeph's teddy has suffered a serious amputation.'

'Do they all have teddies?' said Jodie, fiddling with a doll. She had a pretty face and long fair hair but her arms and legs dangled dejectedly, her internal elastics rotted away.

'Dan has his Man,' said Harley.

'What, Action Man?' I said.

'No, it's one of those creepy biology kits where you see inside this transparent man to all his heart

119

and lungs and liver. He has no willy though. I wittily suggested calling him Willy-Nilly but Dan insists his name is simply Man.'

'How come he's got one of those things? He's only a baby,' said Jodie.

'I think he's got these weirdo parents who want him to be an infant phenomenon,' said Harley. 'He's also got a Peter Rabbit cuddly toy but he never plays with it. I read him the *Peter Rabbit* story, and then I took him out to the vegetable garden and we played Peter Rabbit eating all the lettuces but Dan was rather half-hearted about it and poor old Peter got a bit muddy burrowing in the cabbage patch. His paws have never been the same since.'

'You call *us* weird!' said Jodie. 'Do you think the kids would like to play with the monkeys? Or do they have to stay chained to that Miss Ponsonby all day?'

'Pretty much,' said Harley. 'I think they'd love to come up here, but I'm not sure we could trust them to keep quiet about it. If anyone finds out, we're in *big* trouble.'

'OK, this is our secret,' said Jodie. 'So what else is along here? We might as well take it all in while we can.'

We found a room with an open door full of old bedroom furniture – dressing tables and spotted mirrors and a large wardrobe.

'Hey, let's go to Narnia!' said Harley, opening the wardrobe door a crack.

'Idiot,' said Jodie, but she got right in the wardrobe.

I got in too. Harley squeezed in beside us, bending his head right down, and pulled the door shut. It was so dark inside that we couldn't see a thing. We stood squashed up together, giggling a little hysterically. I wanted to hold Jodie's hand but worried that I might grab Harley by mistake.

'So where's Narnia, then?' said Harley. 'Let us in, Wicked Queen. I want to ride on your sleigh and nibble your Turkish delight.' He banged his fists on the back of the wardrobe.

'There's no Narnia,' said Jodie. 'No way out the back of the wardrobe. And no way out the front either. You've shut the door and the handle's on the outside. We can't get out! We're entombed here for ever! We can shout and yell and hammer with our fists, but we're way at the end of the forbidden corridor and no one will ever hear us. We're stuck in this wardrobe like three corpses in a coffin—'

'Shut *up*, Jodie!' I said, panicking, pushing on the wardrobe door.

It gave easily and I tumbled out into the room again, landing on my knees. Jodie jumped out after me, laughing her head off. Harley unfurled himself after her, laughing too.

'That was *horrible!*' I said. 'Don't make stuff up like that, Jodie, you make it too real.'

'It was just a silly joke, babes,' said Jodie. 'We were only in a *wardrobe*.'

'Yes, but you made it seem like it was a real coffin.'

'I quite fancy the real coffin idea,' said Harley. 'It would be cool to have your own comfy coffin to curl up in, only emerging by the light of the full moon, teeth bared, ready for a little snack.'

'If you keep on growing, they'll have to make you a special long long long coffin, like those long black boats you get in Venice,' said Jodie.

'Gondolas? Yes, even better. I could float down some murky Venetian canal, ferried by a mournful-looking black-robed gondolier.'

'Have you even been to Venice, Harley?' I asked shyly.

'Yes, I went with my ma, when she was temporarily between men, just before she met my current stepfather.'

'I suppose you've been to lots of places abroad?' Jodie asked.

'Some. Paris, Amsterdam, Vienna, Florence, America lots of time – just the usual,' said Harley.

'That's maybe *your* usual, matie. We haven't been anywhere, have we, Pearl? We went to Spain once but Mum got all fussed about the noise from the nightclub and Dad didn't like the food. Honestly, they're a joke, our parents.'

'Not as jokey as mine,' said Harley. 'I'll swap you.'

'Sure!' said Jodie.

'You don't know what they're like.'

'I'll take a chance. It'll give Mum a break. She's desperate to get rid of me.'

'She is *not*!' I said.

'Oh go on. You know perfectly well you're Mum's favourite, Pearl,' said Jodie.

'Well, you're *Dad*'s favourite. And you're *my* favourite too,' I said.

'Really, Pearly? Even though I scare you rotten?' said Jodie, suddenly clasping her hands round my neck, pretending to throttle me.

I started tickling her in retaliation and she shrieked.

'Ssh! Shut up, Jodie. I will get in *so* much trouble

if we're caught,' said Harley.

'Oh, for heaven's sake! We're not doing any *harm*,' said Jodie. 'Why are they so fussed about all these attic rooms? It's not like any of this stuff is really *worth* anything. No one would want it, ugly old stuff,' she said, kicking the massive wardrobe. She kicked too hard and hurt her foot.

'Ow!' she moaned, hopping on one leg. She wasn't good at balancing on just one high heel and nearly toppled over. She grabbed hold of Harley. 'Whoopsie!'

He sighed. 'No wonder you're falling over. Look at your stupid shoes,' he said irritably.

'You sound like my *mother*,' said Jodie, tossing her ponytail. She marched out of the room, exaggerating each step. '*Wibble-wobble, wibble-wobble,*' she chanted, making her ankles do just that.

Harley raised his eyebrows at me. I shrugged, grinning. I felt guilty. It was as if we were ganging up on Jodie, but it was exciting all the same. Whenever we'd ever met anyone new before, they'd always wanted to be Jodie's friend, not mine. But Harley definitely seemed to want to be *my* special friend. Seeing the badger together had been like a magic enchantment.

We heard Jodie tapping down the long corridor, trying more doors.

'Come *on*, you guys,' she called.

'She's an old bossy knickers, your sister,' said Harley. He was busy rearranging the mirrors, adjusting them carefully. 'Here, Pearl, take a look.'

I bent down and saw myself reflected in the mirror – and then again and again and again, multiple Pearls endlessly smiling and smiling, until

I felt dizzy, not sure which one was *me*.

'*Hey!*' Jodie called. 'Come here! Wait till you see what *I*'ve found!'

'Oldest trick in the book,' said Harley, pulling faces in the mirror beside me. 'Don't take any notice, Pearl.'

Jodie kept calling, sounding really excited.

'I don't think she's kidding us,' I said. 'Let's go and see, Harley.'

I ran out of the room and down the corridor. Jodie was right at the end, standing in front of a door.

'Look!' she said, leaping up and down.

'Look at *what*?' I said. 'It's just another door.'

'It's right at the end of the corridor! Can't you guess which door it is!'

'I don't know.'

'It's got to be the door into the tower!' said Jodie. 'Oh, wow!'

'But it's properly locked, see,' said Jodie, pointing upwards at the bolt. She jumped up but didn't get anywhere near it. '*Harley!*' she hollered. 'We *need* you. Come on, Daddy-Long-Legs, this is a job for you.'

Harley strolled slowly along the corridor, refusing to hurry.

'Come *on*! We need you to undo the bolt!'

Harley reached up and grappled with it. It had been partly painted over. At first it looked as if it wouldn't budge at all, but Harley kept pulling at it.

'Lift me up. *I*'ll do it,' said Jodie, tugging at him.

'Just give me a chance, will you?' he said. He bashed at the bolt with the side of his hand. It seemed to give a little.

'Do it again!' said Jodie.

'It bloody *hurts*,' said Harley, but he went on bashing until the bolt slid undone.

'Hurray!' said Jodie, rattling the door handle.

It still wouldn't open. Jodie pushed and shoved it. She even tried kicking it.

'You can't get in, Jodie,' said Harley.

'I *will* get in,' she said. 'You'll see.'

Mum was red in the face, tears spurting down her cheeks.

9

'We'll have to find the key,' said Jodie. 'We've *got* to get into the tower.'

'I think it's all blocked up anyway,' said Harley.

'Well, we can *un*block it,' said Jodie. 'There's definitely a room up there because you can see a window on the outside. Maybe the really really naughty Melchester College pupils are shoved into the tower and languish there. Hey, I can hear someone calling. It's very faint, very hoarse, very desperate – listen!'

We knew she was kidding, of course we did, but we still listened. Then I heard someone calling, very faint and far away but still distinct. Harley and I stared at Jodie's mouth as if she was performing some clever act of ventriloquism. She looked taken aback.

'I *did* hear something,' she said.

We listened again. There was another faraway cry.

'*Jodie! Pearl!*'

'Oh God, it's Dad,' said Jodie. 'Quick, we don't want him catching us up here!'

She slipped off her red shoes and we started running madly down the long corridor, past all the attic rooms, towards the stairs. Harley ran awkwardly alongside us, lifting his legs up oddly, knees high, like a galloping pony. We got to the stairs at last and skidded down them, sliding on the old lino, green and slippery as seaweed. Then we squeezed back through the gap by the big cupboard.

Dad's voice was much louder now.

'Quick, don't let's hang round in front of the cupboard, it'll look way too suspicious,' said Jodie.

'In here,' said Harley, shoving us into a class-room. We stood still for a moment, trying to catch our breath.

We heard Dad calling again, louder now.

'We're in here, Dad!' Jodie yelled. She nodded at us. 'Act like we've been here ages,' she hissed.

She sat at a desk, slipped her shoes back on and put her feet up on a chair. I sat beside her. Harley started a chalk drawing on the old-fashioned black-board. He drew a broad head with a long snout.

'What's that? A dog?' said Jodie.

'I bet Pearl can guess,' said Harley.

'It's a badger,' I said proudly.

Then Dad came into the classroom, dirt and oil already smeared on his new work clothes. '*There* you are!' he said. 'I've been looking all over for you. Where have you been?'

'Just hanging out here, Dad,' said Jodie.

'I came looking for you along here only ten minutes ago,' said Dad.

'Oh well, we've been in some of the other class-rooms too. Harley's been showing us around, haven't you, mate?' said Jodie.

'That's me, utterly matey,' said Harley. 'Always ready to oblige.'

'Well, lad, Mr Wilberforce wants you to oblige him. He wants you to help him lop his hibiscus.'

'Isn't that Jed's job?' Harley asked mildly.

'Let's all go and help Jed!' said Jodie.

'No, no, you need to help your mother, Jodie. You too, Pearl. What were you thinking, sloping off? There's so much work to be done. You two go back to our flat pronto and get cracking.'

'Yes, Dad, no, Dad, at the double, Dad,' said Jodie, saluting and clicking her high heels.

He pretended to take a swipe at her. She dodged, laughing. Dad shook his fist at her but he was grinning. Harley was watching, looking wistful. I wondered what it would be like not to have a dad. My sympathy made me brave.

'Maybe see you later, Harley?' I said.

'Sure,' he said, smiling at me.

'Oooooh!' Jodie squealed when we were going along the basement corridor together. '*Maybe see you later!*' she repeated, in my voice. 'You bold girl. Practically making a date with old Harley Not Davidson!'

'I wasn't!' I said, going red.

'You're blushing. Fancy, you've only been here five minutes and you've got yourself a boyfriend.'

'He's not my boyfriend!' I protested, shoving her. 'He's just a *friend* friend.'

'You've really got a thing going between you, what with all this booky-booky talk, and little smiles like you've got a big secret together.'

'Shut *up*. It's not like that. He's just being kind to me, the way he's kind to Dan and Zeph and Sakura.' I paused. 'Isn't he?'

'He *likes* you, stupid. It's obvious.'

'Well, he likes you too,' I said.

'No, he doesn't. I irritate him,' said Jodie. 'Still, I intend to have my pick of all these posh guys when the term starts. And I *might* just click with old Jed.'

'Jodie, he's much too old!'

'I like older guys. And they like me. Look at Bernie. He really fancied me.'

'Oh, Jodie, he was just kidding around. *You're* kidding, aren't you?'

'Maybe,' said Jodie. 'I do reckon Jed though. His *eyes*! And that grin of his – wow!'

She burbled on about him for ages while we were sorting our bedroom. I couldn't work out if she was serious or winding me up. She kept teasing me about Harley too. It made me feel important, grown up, on a par with Jodie herself.

I unpacked my boxes, arranging my real doll's house and my shoebox Mansion Towers and my snow globes and my little plaster poodles and my scrapbooks and my jars of beads and my fairy lamp and my three little black teddy bears. I looked at them without enthusiasm. I flicked Edgar, Allan and Poe with my fingernail so that they fell over on their backs, furry paws in the air.

'*Ouch! ouch! OUCH!*' said Jodie, pretending to be the bears.

'They look a bit silly, don't they? All my stuff is so babyish. Shall we make our bedroom really stylish and sophisticated, no girly stuff at all?'

'You're one hundred per cent girly, Pearly,' said Jodie, laughing at me.

'Yes, but I don't have to stay girly for ever,' I said.

'True,' said Jodie. 'Though I *like* you girly. I had plans to make this a lovely pretty pink room for you, with ruffled curtains and satin ribbons. We could scrape off all this scuzzy wallpaper and paint it white and you could paint little roses all over, you're good at them. You could paint little pink poodles too, yeah? And what else could we paint? Pink fairies with their own fairy palace? Yeah, *loads* of fairies like those soppy books you used to read, a whole flock of fairies. You could have a fairy dress with little net wings—'

'And a fairy wand, and I could poke you in the tummy whenever you teased me,' I said.

'I'm *not* teasing,' said Jodie.

She saw the little torn piece of wallpaper by my bed and pulled it. A big strip came away, exposing the whitewashed wall.

'There! It comes away easy-peasy. We can strip it all off and get it painted in no time.'

'Jodie! Don't! You're tearing it all!'

'Of course I am. It's all got to come off, dopey. We can't paint on top of this old wallpaper.'

'But what will Mum say?'

Mum said a great deal when she came in to check on us. She seized hold of Jodie, hitting out at her.

'How *dare* you! Look at the mess you're making! You're wrecking your whole room!'

'*Ow!*' Jodie screamed. 'Don't you *dare* hit me!

You're not allowed to hit kids. If they found out here, they'd sack you. Stop it!'

'*You* stop it then,' said Mum, her arms swinging at her sides. 'And I didn't *hit* you. I smacked you, like any good parent.'

'*Bad* parent. You could be prosecuted,' said Jodie. 'Better watch out I don't tell on you to Mr Wilberforce, Mum.'

'Don't you dare try to blackmail me, young lady. Look, for pity's sake, can't you try to *help*, not hinder? You too, Pearl. Why didn't you try to stop your sister making such a terrible mess?'

'We're sorry, Mum, I said.

'No we're not! We *are* helping. You said we could redecorate the rooms and that's just what we're doing. You *said*, Mum.'

'Later, once we're all straight. We haven't even unpacked yet, and I'm trying to give everywhere a good scrub. I've been down on my knees on that kitchen floor. I don't know who the cleaners are but they deserve to be sacked. There's grease an inch thick around that cooker. We'll have cockroaches if we don't watch out, and I've found mouse dirt in the pantry. It's disgraceful, a total health hazard. The very least you two could do is give me a hand with the cleaning, but you run off and play flipping Hide and Seek with that great gangly boy, and *then* you rip your room to shreds!'

Mum was red in the face, tears spurting down her cheeks. We'd never seen her so worked up before. I felt tears pricking my own eyes. Even Jodie looked worried.

'Mum? Hey, don't cry,' she said, giving her a hug. 'Look, we can always stick the wallpaper back on

132

the walls if that's what you want. And you can smack me all you like if it makes you feel better. Go on, have another bash, feel free!'

'Shut up, you bonkers banana,' said Mum, hugging her back. She sniffed and absent-mindedly wiped her nose on her sleeve, though she'd have been outraged if either of us had done the same.

'Shall we come and help you scrub your kitchen floor, Mum?' I said.

'Well, I've broken the back of it now. Broken *my* back too, I dare say.' Mum sniffed again. Her eyes were still brimming. 'I need a decent cleaner, but where am I going to find anyone in the middle of nowhere? I didn't realize it would be *so* isolated here, and the Wilberforces and that Miss French, they're not really what you'd call friendly, and the children all seem such an odd bunch.'

'Harley's not odd,' I said.

'Yes he is,' said Jodie.

'I thought they'd all be . . .' Mum waved her hand in the air, trying to find words to describe angelic well-mannered children with neat uniforms and posh voices. 'The little ones look pathetic and that Harley's a ragbag. His sleeves end halfway up his arms!'

'He can't help being tall,' I said.

'He's not tall, Pearl, he's incredibly freakily gigantically elongated,' said Jodie.

'Shut up,' I said.

'Pearl, don't use that expression, it's horrible. And I don't know why you're arguing. He *is* a bit freaky looking.'

'You shut up too!' I said.

'*Pearl!*' Mum looked astonished.

133

Jodie clapped her hands, roaring with laughter.

She got told off too, but Mum didn't put her usual energy into it. She kept nibbling at her lower lip, looking all around the room. She fiddled with the tattered strips of wallpaper.

'You've made such a mess of it, girls,' she said. She paused. 'It looks like I've made a mess of things too. Maybe we'd have been better off staying where we were. Everything's gone topsy-turvy. I thought it would be such a step up for us all, a chance for you girls to turn into little ladies, but look at you! You're already running wild. Even you, Pearl. Imagine, telling me to shut up!'

'I'm sorry, Mum,' I said.

'She was just upset because you were having a go at her Harley,' said Jodie.

'He's not *my* Harley,' I said hotly.

'Then why are you blushing? He's your boyfriend!'

'Stop teasing her, Jodie. You're being silly. *You're* too young to have a boyfriend, let alone our Pearl.' She looked at us both. 'So, what do you think? Is it a mistake, our coming here?'

'Of course not. It's *lovely* here,' I said.

'You really think so, Pearl?' said Mum. 'You're such a bright girl. I wanted to give you the chance I never had. And this *is* a good school, and you'll be able to be taught properly and you'll talk nicely and have good manners – and never ever say shut up to your mother!'

'*I'll* say shut up,' said Jodie. 'Excuse me, Mum, you've got two daughters, you know.'

'Yes, I do know, and one of them drives me completely crackers,' said Mum, pulling Jodie's spiky ponytail. 'So? What do you think, Jodie? Are you happy here?'

Jodie frowned. Then shrugged. 'It's a laugh,' she said lightly. 'So, can we get on with our wallpaper stripping?'

'If you do it properly. I want every little scrap off. You need to soak it and use a scraper. Then I'll see if Dad's got time to give it a quick coat of emulsion.'

'No, we'll do it,' said Jodie. '*Please*, Mum.'

'We'll see,' said Mum. 'Get it all stripped first. Don't you dare leave it looking such a mess.'

'We'll do it all, Mum, promise,' I said.

It took much, much longer than we thought. Jodie got fed up after a while and flopped down on her bed, her legs in the air, turning her feet at different angles to admire her high heels. I wanted to flop too but I kept patiently stripping. I hoped I might find more signs of the little servant girl – a scrap she'd stuck on the wall, her height marks, a little scribbled heart with the initials of her sweet-heart – but there was nothing. I had to make her up. I started telling Jodie the story but she kept yawning.

'Your stories are so *girly*, Pearly. Look, let *me* tell it.'

I didn't like the way she told it at all. She made the cook get more and more angry with the little servant girl, beating her with a wooden spoon, tapping her hands with her ladle, whacking her about the head with her saucepan . . .

'Until one day little Kezia the kitchen maid got soooo fed up, she crept up behind the mean old cook, throttled her with her own apron strings, and then stuffed her in a giant pot and boiled her in a great soup. Everyone feasted royally on the cook for a fortnight, smacking their greasy lips with pleasure.'

'No they *didn't*,' I said. 'Why do you always have to muck the story about, Jodie? It's silly always making it creepy and weird. You always *spoil* stuff.'

Jodie sat up. 'OK,' she said. 'I won't tell you any stories any more.'

My stomach knotted. 'I didn't *mean* it,' I said quickly.

'Yes you did,' said Jodie. She jumped to her feet. 'I'm bored anyway. See you.' She walked to the door, humming a little tune.

'Jodie! Don't go! Look, you *can't* go. We promised Mum we'd finish scraping off the wallpaper,' I said.

'*You* promised. So *you* finish it,' said Jodie. 'I've got better things to do.'

'But that's so mean! You can't just leave me,' I said.

'Yes I can,' said Jodie. She waved her hand in the air and went out of the door.

'Come back!' I called. 'Don't be like that. You know I love your stories. Jodie? Jodie, *please*.'

I waited, my heart pounding. I hoped I might hear her shoes clip-clopping back along the corridor. She might just be playing a joke on me. She'd come bursting into the room any minute, laughing at me.

But she didn't.

**I sat where I was, savouring every second
of my happiness.**

10

I didn't know what to do. I wondered about running after her, but I knew Mum would be *so* cross if we left the wallpaper half stripped. I couldn't blame her. It did look very ugly with tatters hanging everywhere.

I carried on for five minutes, scraping, picking, pulling. It was so much worse doing it all by myself. I felt more and more worried about Jodie. Maybe she'd be furious with me for not following her. I couldn't stand the rare times when she was in a sulk with me. I flung my scraper down and went running after her, hoping she might be mooching about just outside the back door. There was no sign of her. I looked all around the back courtyard, then right round the front of the house. I still couldn't see her.

'Jodie?' I called. 'Jodie!'

There was no answer. There was no point running all over the grounds when I had no clear idea where she'd be. I ran back to the house, thudding along the gravel path, and then in through the back door. I wondered if she'd somehow crept back inside. She might be there in our bedroom, waiting for me. But the room was empty, looking uglier than ever.

I felt like bursting into tears. I squeezed my eyes shut. 'Don't be such a *baby*,' I whispered to myself.

I picked up the scraper and started all over again.

'I'll show her,' I muttered. 'Why should *I* feel so bad? *She*'s the one who's being mean. Mean mean mean. Why should I always do what she says just because she's my sister?'

I scraped scraped scraped. I felt as if I was scraping myself free from Jodie.

I told my Kezia story to myself. Poor Kezia was feeling miserable because Pansy was mean to her, making her do half her work as well as her own. I scraped with renewed vigour, and when I'd got the last little shred of wallpaper off, I squatted down in the soft damp crinkled mound. I drew a tiny pencil portrait of Kezia, looking forlorn in her ugly uniform, her dress drooping down to her ankles, her boots much too big and sticking out sideways.

Then I heard footsteps and jumped up hopefully – but it was Mum.

I dropped the pencil on the floor and sat in front of my tiny drawing.

'Good heavens, what a mess!' said Mum, kicking the wallpaper with her toe. 'Still, you've done a magnificent job, girls.' She looked round. 'Where's Jodie?'

'She's . . . she's just gone out for a little while,' I said.

'Well, I'm dishing up lunch at one sharp,' said Mum. 'Right, dear, I'll find you some black plastic rubbish bags and you can pick all the wallpaper up. We'll speak to Dad about that emulsion. What colour would you like? A nice sugar-pink?'

'Pink's too little-girly,' I said.

'You *are* a little girl!' said Mum.

'No I'm not. I'm nearly eleven.'

'Oh yes, practically middle-aged.'

'Don't laugh at me, Mum!'

'Well, honestly, pet. Don't you grow up too soon. I don't know how I'm going to cope when there are two teenagers in the house. What do you want for your birthday, dear? Come on, anything you like.'

'Books.'

'You *always* choose books! Can't you think of something else? Give it some thought. Now, I'm going to put the veg on. I've got two lovely big dishes of toad-in-the-hole coming along nicely. You be in the dining room by one o'clock, OK?'

I stuffed the wallpaper into the plastic bags, even clearing up the last shreds with a dustpan and brush. Then I went through our flat, along the dark corridor and into the steamy kitchen. Mum was hovering over the pans on the range, red in the face.

'Where's Jodie?'

'She's just coming,' I said.

I wanted to be in the dining room early so I could maybe have a minute or two with Harley. I was there *too* early. I wandered up and down the empty room, round and round each table and bench, wondering what it would be like when all the children were there. These magic summer holidays

141

wouldn't last for ever. The school would be crowded with strangers at the start of term.

I'd been so excited at the idea of living in such a beautiful gothic mansion as Melchester that I hadn't thought properly about the children. I'd read the Harry Potter books, but obviously the pupils wouldn't be trainee wizards. I'd had a hazy picture of jolly girls playing tricks on the French mistress and having midnight feasts. I hadn't got as far as imagining boys. Harley was totally unexpected. What would the other boys be like? I didn't mind *little* boys like Zeph and Dan but I hated big boys. I'd once seen an old film of *Tom Brown's Schooldays* on the television. Tom was horribly bullied. He'd even been hooked above the open fire and roasted like a rack of lamb.

I stared at the big fireplace at the end of the room. The grate was full of pine cones. It didn't look as if it was ever lit, which was a relief.

I wondered if Harley was bullied at all. He was so tall he'd tower over all the other boys, but he was also very thin and spindly. I wasn't sure he'd be much use in a tussle or an outright fight. Maybe he kept to himself, hiding away from trouble, like a badger.

I thought about that magical shared moment, shutting my eyes to see the strange night-time animal standing still in the moonlight.

I felt bad not telling Jodie, but Harley was right. She couldn't keep quiet and still for more than a few seconds. Besides, she'd been mean to me, very mean, leaving me to strip all the wallpaper myself. My arm and shoulders ached and I had blisters on my fingers and thumb. I felt proud of myself.

I swung my arms round and round to ease the ache and then felt foolish because Miss Ponsonby and the three little children were filing silently into the dining room and saw me doing my windmill impressions. Zeph laughed at me. Dan copied me, flinging his own arms about, and his legs too. Sakura simply stood still, blinking timidly. She was wearing an old-fashioned smocked dress that was much too big for her. The short sleeves hung like bells past her sharp little elbows and the skirt hem brushed the top of her white socks. She looked pathetic, but her small hands were stroking the soft cloth proudly.

'That's a lovely dress, Sakura,' I said. 'Don't you look pretty!'

She smiled radiantly, her big black eyes glowing. 'My daddy sent it to me. It's my new summer dress,' she said proudly.

'You're very lucky,' I said. I paused. 'Are you going to see your daddy this summer?'

'Oh no. He's in *Tokyo*,' said Sakura, as if it was a different planet altogether.

'I haven't *got* a daddy,' said Dan, making his transparent man walk along the tabletop.

'Have you got a mummy?' I asked.

'I don't think so,' said Dan. 'I have a granny but she's not very well.'

'I've got a mummy and I've got a different daddy now and I've got to stay at school until I'm a good boy,' said Zeph. 'I'm bad.'

'I think you're a *very* good boy,' I said.

'I'm not. I threw paint on the floor, didn't I, Undie?'

'I think it was an accident,' said Miss Ponsonby kindly.

'It wasn't,' Zeph muttered. 'I just felt like doing it.'

Miss Ponsonby chose not to hear him. She settled the three children on the bench. I poured them all glasses of water which they lapped at furiously, like camels. Dad came strolling in, his toolbelt dragging on his hips like a gun holster. Zeph and Dan clamoured for his attention, wanting to see his hammer and chisel and screwdriver. Dad let them pull them out of their pouches. Zeph immediately started hammering the table, while Dan aimed the screwdriver at him like a gun, going *Bang bang!*'

'I think they're too little for real tools, Mr Wells,' said Miss Ponsonby, wrenching them out of their fists.

'I'll see if I can find you some plastic tools, boys,' said Dad. 'Didn't you use to have a toy set, Pearl?'

'I don't want a toy hammer, I want a real one,' said Zeph.

'I want a real gun and then I could really shoot you,' said Dan.

'Now, now, that's not very nice,' said Mum, coming into the dining hall with the first trayful of food. She raised her eyebrows at Miss Ponsonby. 'Kids, eh?' she said. Then she looked round. 'Where's our Jodie?'

Jodie burst into the room, *hanging on Harley's arm*. Mr Wilberforce and Miss French and Jed were with them. Jodie muttered something and they all burst out laughing.

'Oh dear, we've been keeping you waiting, Mrs Wells,' said Miss French.

'That's quite all right,' said Mum stiffly.

'Blame it all on me, please!' said Mr Wilberforce.

144

'Me and my hibiscus. I had young Harley here clipping away and Jodie sweetly came to lend a hand. Then Frenchie strolled along to see what we were up to and that dratted mutt of hers ran riot, knocking the stepladder over and chasing all through my flower beds.'

'I'm *so* sorry, Harold,' said Miss French. 'It's appalling, I simply can't get him to behave.'

'Jodie had the devil of a job catching him, didn't you, dear?' Mr Wilberforce nodded at Mum. 'She's a sparky kid, your Jodie.'

Mum smiled and fiddled with the hot plates on the trolley. Mr Wilberforce sat down, breathing in appreciatively.

'Something smells totally delicious. What are you spoiling us with today?'

Mum lifted the lid of her big serving dish with a flourish.

'Oh my! Toad-in-the-hole! What joy!' said Mr Wilberforce.

'How totally gorgeous!' said Miss French, smacking her lips together.

They sounded so over-the-top I wondered if they were teasing Mum, but she took their compliments at face value.

'I've always had a light touch with my Yorkshire pud,' she said proudly.

'So the brown bits are toad, are they?' said Jed. 'Do you roast them or fry them?'

Mum knew *he* was teasing, and gave him a quick rap on his knuckles with her serving spoon.

Jodie and Harley came over to my bench. I turned to Sakura and started complimenting her on her dress all over again. I saw Jodie sit right up the other end of the table. She still had a firm hold of Harley. My friend Harley. The first real friend I'd ever had.

'Hey, sit down, Harley! I'm starving, aren't you? My mum's toad-in-the-hole isn't bad nosh, actually, but isn't there anywhere round here where you can get decent food – chips and pizza and stuff? Don't you get McDonald's in the country?'

'There's a chip van on Friday night in Melchester village, but that's two miles away,' said Harley.

'Oh, wow, wild night life, a chip van once a week,' said Jodie. 'Pity you haven't got a real Harley. We could be out of here like a shot.'

'Yeah, like I'm old enough to have a motorbike licence,' said Harley.

'You're so tall lots of people would think you're sixteen or seventeen,' said Jodie.

It was almost as if she was flirting with him. It was so mean of her. She didn't even like him that much. She carried on chatting, quieter now, so I couldn't hear what they were saying. I chewed a piece of sausage over and over again, unable to swallow. Harley was probably telling her about the badgers right this minute. He was obviously fed up with me already. He had Jodie for a new best friend.

I spat a mouthful of sausage gristle into my hankie. I fed the rest of my meal to Zeph. Sakura wasn't eating hers either, prodding her sausages gingerly, as if they might leap up and croak at her.

'They're not *real* toads,' I said.

'I know,' said Sakura, but she still inspected each one, on the look-out for bulbous eyes and warts. Dan got tired of eating halfway too, and took his

146

man for a hike up his mashed-potato mountain.

'Come on, eat up nicely, children, or you won't get any pudding,' said Mum, bustling past. 'It's spotted dick and custard.'

Jodie and Harley cracked up laughing. Mum glared at them and patted me on the back.

'Eat up, chickie. You've worked really hard this morning. Good girl!'

She was treating me as if I was one of the little ones. I *behaved* like one too, messing around with my food, squashing it all up to make it look smaller. Mum sighed and tutted at me. I couldn't even eat the silly spotted dick dish either. I just sat and stared at it.

'Hey, don't you want your pudding, Pearl?' Harley called.

I shook my head.

'Can I have it then? Your mum's a brilliant cook,' said Harley.

I pushed the plate towards him. I pushed a little too hard, so that the full plate nearly whizzed straight past and launched itself into mid-air like a flying saucer, but he caught hold of it in time.

'Here, have mine too, Harley,' said Jodie. 'Hey, roll up, roll up, watch the Incredible Hurling Harley eat three puddings in one go, and then he'll *explode*, custard spouting from every orifice, spotted dick spattering everything in sight.'

Harley waved his spoon in the air and golloped the pudding in three mouthfuls.

'God, you're incredible. I'd have to walk bent for a week if I noshed that lot,' said Jodie. 'You'll have to walk it off. Let's take Old Shep for a long walk, eh?'

'You take him. I'm busy this afternoon,' said Harley.

'Doing what?' said Jodie.

'Doing my stuff,' said Harley.

'OK, suit yourself,' said Jodie. She got up off the bench and nodded her head at me. 'Come on, Pearl.'

She had such a nerve!

'Come on what?' I said.

'Come on, let's take Old Shep for a long walk.' She frowned at me. 'You're not really scared of him, are you? He won't hurt you, he'll just lick you to bits.'

'I'm not the slightest bit scared of him,' I lied. 'But I don't want to go for a long walk. I'm tired. After stripping the wallpaper from our bedroom.'

Jodie stood staring at me. Then she shrugged. 'OK, Miss Goody-goody Two Shoes. I'll take Old Shep for a walk by myself.'

'I'll come!' said Zeph. 'I'd much sooner walk Old Shep than do more sploshy old painting.'

Miss Ponsonby didn't object. Maybe she was glad to be free of him for a bit. She took Sakura and Dan off with her. Jodie went off with Miss French to collect Old Shep.

'What are *you* going to do, pet?' Dad said to me. 'Mum says you've made a grand job of your bedroom. You have a think what colour you want it painted – though you'll have to wait a bit, I've got that many jobs to do.'

'That's OK, Dad. I'll read for a bit,' I said.

'You and your books,' said Dad.

I went down the hall towards the kitchen. I think Harley might have called after me. I didn't turn round.

148

I went to my room. The stripped wall looked very bare and ugly, with scrape marks all over it. I felt sore and scraped too. I lay face down on my bed, trying not to worry about Jodie. I didn't see why I had to run after her and take that scary werewolf for a walk, especially when she'd been so mean about the room. *She* was the one who should be feeling bad, not me. Everyone always said I should stand up to her, not let her boss me around so much. I'd done just that but now maybe she'd stay cross with me. I dreaded it when she went all sulky and wouldn't talk to me.

I hated it that she'd talked to Harley all lunch time. Jabber-jabber, whisper-whisper, chuckle-chuckle. They were probably laughing about *me*. I didn't want to think about it. I sat up and reached for Mrs Wilberforce's copy of *The Secret Garden*. I couldn't concentrate for a page or two but then I got sucked into the story. I read solidly for more than an hour, lost in Misselthwaite Manor with Mary. Then I started glancing at my alarm clock, wondering when Jodie was coming back. She'd said she'd take Old Shep for a long walk. Surely this was a very very long walk?

Mum was concerned too. She put her head round the bedroom door. 'Where's that sister of yours?'

'I don't know, Mum.'

'I want her back here where I can keep an eye on her. She's running wild already. What do you think she's up to now?'

'I don't *know*, Mum.'

'I'd send your dad after her but he's busy banging a banister back into place. Dear, dear, it might be grand, but I'm telling you, the whole place is falling to bits. Pearl, do get your head out of that book. You'll strain your eyes.'

'I'm fine, Mum.'

'No you're not, you're all red-eyed and frowny. Look, *you* nip out and see if you can spot your sister. You can get a bit of fresh air at the same time.'

'Oh, Mum! I don't know where to look.'

'Don't be so wet. Just trot up the lane to Miss French's house. I'm sure our Jodie will be hanging round there. And you can always pop in on Mrs Wilberforce, tell her you're enjoying her book.'

'No, Mum!'

'Yes!'

'I'm too shy.'

'Don't be so soppy. Think how horrible it must be for poor Mrs Wilberforce, stuck in that wheelchair of hers, unable to get out and about and see folk. You go and have a little chat with her.'

'Please don't make me. Can't I just stay here?' I begged.

'Oh, for pity's sake! I've got one daughter who clears off Lord knows where, while the other one wants to hide away in her bedroom all day, mouldering.' Mum gave me a light tap on my bottom. 'Come on, up you get and do as I say, chop-chop.'

So I got up and set off, clutching *The Secret Garden* to my chest. I went past the outbuildings and then turned down the sandy lane, trees crowding in on either side. There was no sign of Jodie and Old Shep. I didn't feel brave enough to go and bang on Miss French's door. I rehearsed what to say inside my head. I even rehearsed what I was going to say to Old Shep – *Here, boy, there's a good boy, down, boy* – in a firm, friendly voice so he wouldn't bite me.

I was trembling by the time I knocked on the door. It was a waste of time anyway, because no one was in. I thought of going to Mrs Wilberforce's bungalow as Mum had suggested, but that seemed scary too. I wasn't at all sure what to *say* to her. I was only halfway through *The Secret Garden* anyway so I didn't want to swap it just yet.

I wandered along to her house all the same. I even tiptoed up the garden path and breathed in the sweet jasmine scent. I put my hand out – but didn't knock at the door. Her house was very silent. Maybe she was having a rest after lunch. If so, it would be unkind to disturb her. I'd come back tomorrow or the day after, whenever I'd finished the book.

I backed down the path again and started trailing back to the school. I decided to find a quiet little grassy patch to tuck myself away where I could read my book. I tried to remember where the badger set had been. I'd got about halfway down the lane before I'd had to rush off to have a wee. I was sure it was the left-hand side somewhere . . .

I wandered in and out of the trees, peering round every likely bush, when I suddenly stumbled, tripping over Harley's leg. He was lying on his stomach, stretched out in a long line, reading his book. I gasped, but managed not to scream, because I saw the badger set behind him.

He smiled at me. 'Hi,' he said quietly. 'Don't look so worried, like you're Little Red Riding Hood and I'm the Big Bad Wolf.'

'Sorry!' I said foolishly. 'You'll think I'm stalking you or something. I'll leave you alone. I know you've got stuff to do. You need some peace.'

'I said that to *Jodie*. Come on, keep me company. I don't think we'll see any badgers, they're mostly nocturnal, but we could get really lucky. One time I saw a mother with a cub.'

'Oh, I want to see a baby one too!' I said, squatting down beside him.

'Typical girl,' said Harley, but he was just teasing.

We sat together, staring at the dark entrance to the badger set. We waited expectantly. Nothing happened.

'I wish we could magic ourselves small enough to walk in,' I whispered.

'I wish I could magic myself small, full stop,' said Harley.

'Oh no, it's great to be tall because . . .' I tried desperately to think of something. 'You can reach things.' This sounded so limp that Harley laughed at me.

'As in, *Oh dear, we've kicked our ball on the roof, let's send for Harley the Human Crane to reach it for us?*'

'Or, *Oh dear, the giraffe's got an itch on his head, let's send for Harley the Human Crane to scratch it for him,*' I suggested.

'*Nice* one. OK, OK – *Oh dear, the weathercock's stopped spinning on the church spire, let's send for Harley the Human Crane to twirl it for us.*'

'Not bad. What about, *Oh dear, King Kong's jumping about on top of the Empire State Building, let's send Harley the Human Crane to snatch him off,*' I said.

We played the game until we were snorting with laughter, our hands over our mouths so as not to alarm the dozing badgers. Then we reversed it, and I was Pearl the Mouse Child, scampering in and out of burrows and rescuing dropped coins and diving in and out of cat flaps.

'You'll be like a little Borrower,' said Harley. 'Have you read that book? It's great, you'd love it, Pearl.' He looked at the lovely old copy of *The Secret Garden*. 'Is that from Mrs Wilberforce? Hey, it's a first edition! You'd better be extra specially careful with it. Put on your kid gloves before turning each page.'

He started reading a few paragraphs and then swapped back to his own Hardy book. He lay on his stomach again. I hunched up beside him, leaning against the mossy bank. The sun came through the leaves of the trees and shone warmly on us, making my skin glow. It gently dappled the pages of my book, so I undid my hair and let it swing forward like a curtain, shading it.

'You've got lovely hair, Pearl. You should always wear it loose like that,' said Harley, looking up.

He went back to his book, frowning a little as he read, but every now and then he glanced up and gave me a grin. I smiled back shyly, as warm inside as out, feeling happy happy happy. Then I went back to Misselthwaite Manor and wheeled Colin to the secret garden while the robin flew over our heads.

A real bird sang on a branch above us, and when it flew off, I was sure its chest was red. I felt as if I was straddling two worlds at once, not quite sure what was real and what was imaginary. I'd stepped into a real world better than any fantasy. I hoped the badger would come and peer at us. I especially longed to see the baby badger. I imagined it scampering out on little legs, pink snout quivering in the sudden sunlight. It stayed tucked up in its set.

I knew I should be getting back to *my* home. Mum would have long since started panicking. She fussed enough when Jodie went missing, but she went into full-scale shrieking-alarm alert if I ever disappeared. But I sat where I was, beside Harley, savouring every second of my happiness.

When I went back at last, Mum was in tears again and I felt dreadful. I didn't tell her I'd been with Harley. I didn't exactly lie, I just said I'd gone looking in vain for Jodie, and then sat reading my book. Jodie had long since returned and was now off again, supposedly gardening.

'Though it beats me why she's so keen to work with Mr Wilberforce in the garden when your dad and I could badly do with a helping hand. What is it about this gardening? Our Jodie's never so much as planted a bulb in her life.'

I was pretty sure Jodie still didn't care about planting or pruning – or even Mr Wilberforce. She just wanted to hang out with Jed the gardener.

She still seemed to be steering clear of me, but when I went back to our bedroom, I found Kezia the kitchen maid had company. There was a little pencilled drawing of Pansy the parlour maid standing beside her. She had a speech bubble saying, *Kezia is just like a sister to me and she'll always be my best friend, no matter what.*

**Harley dabbed her back, giving her
a purple beard.**

11

Dad drove Mum and Jodie and me into Galford the next morning. It was Melchester's nearest town. Melchester village only had one general store. Dad needed to buy any number of items from a DIY shop and Mum needed new kitchen equipment, so it was an official trip. Jodie and I went along for the ride. It was a *long* ride, a good twenty miles or more.

The town itself was a shock, with its ugly concrete car park and shabby 1970s shopping centre. It was really only one high street with a few smaller streets leading off it, but it seemed like a huge city centre after the isolation of Melchester. Dad parked the car and we wandered around a little, aimless and dazed, before Mum got us organized. Jodie wanted to go off and find a McDonald's but Mum wouldn't let her.

'We're all going to stick together. I've had enough of you girls wandering off.'

'We'll have to get them reins, you know, like toddlers. That way we'll drag them round with us all the time,' said Dad. 'Now, where do you think the B and Q might be?'

He found an old-fashioned hardware shop instead, and spent ages happily fingering nails and screws and locks, ordering all sorts of stuff. We chose the paint for our bedroom quickly enough. Mum wanted us to pick pink or pale primrose or light blue. We groaned in unison and decided on deep purple.

'But it'll look so *dark*,' Mum said. 'You want something fresh and light and pretty for a bedroom.'

'Let the girls choose what they want,' said Dad. 'And you can choose what you'd like for *our* room, Shaz. Any colour, even shocking pink.'

Mum chose china blue, and picked out chintzy white curtains decorated with little blue eighteenth-century people in the fabric shop down the road.

'It's a French design. So classy!' she said.

She wanted us to pick something similar but Jodie found a roll of cheap black velvet.

'You *can't* have black, Jodie. And that isn't even curtain material, you noodle.'

'It'll make glorious gothic curtains, Mum. And look, we could have a black fur rug on the floor. It would look so great. Oh please please please,' Jodie begged. She lay on the fun fur rug, batting her eyelashes hopefully.

'Now stop that. Get up! You can't have a whole new roomful of stuff. We're not made of money,' said Mum.

158

'Couldn't I have that black rug as my birthday present?' I said.

'You don't want *black*, Pearl. Maybe a nice *white* furry rug? Or there's a pink one with a teddy?'

'Mum! I'm way too old for teddies,' I said. 'I'd like black. *Please.*'

Mum eventually gave in. When we got back to Melchester College, Jodie and I started painting our room straight after lunch. Most of our stuff was still in boxes so it was easy enough to pile them out of the way and cover our bed with an old sheet. We wore our oldest clothes too, but Mum still fussed, so Jodie had the brilliant idea of stripping off to our underwear.

We were happily sloshing paint around in our knickers, both of us speckled all over in purple, when Mum came in – *with Harley*!

Mum gasped, Harley groaned, I yelped, and Jodie roared with laughter.

'For pity's sake! Put your clothes on, girls! What are you thinking of!' Mum hissed, outraged.

She bustled Harley out of the room so quickly he forgot to duck and bumped his head on the door frame. Jodie carried on laughing, staggering about, clutching her stomach. It was all right for her. She was wearing matching underwear for once, her black bra and little black briefs. She looked gorgeous. I looked awful in dreadful baggy big white pants. I wanted to *die*.

'Come into the kitchen the minute you're decent,' Mum called.

'Oh *God*,' I moaned. 'I feel so awful! Harley saw my *knickers*!'

'Well, don't worry, Pearly, they're hardly likely to

inflame him,' said Jodie, stepping into her jeans. 'Hey! Don't look so woebegone, it's *funny.*'

'No it's not. It's the most embarrassing thing *ever,*' I said. 'I can't ever face him again.' I threw myself on the bed, crawling under the cover.

'So what are you going to do? Hibernate under your duvet? Don't be so daft. Come on, get dressed.'

Jodie threw my jeans and T-shirt at me but I cowered where I was.

'Idiot,' she said, and went off whistling towards the kitchen.

I lay on my bed, hands over my face, heart thudding. Then Mum came back into the bedroom.

'Pearl? What are you doing, you silly girl? Get up!' she said tugging me out from under the duvet. 'Come on. Harley and Jodie are eating my butterscotch cookies in the kitchen. You come and have some too.'

'I can't come,' I said, starting to cry.

'Don't be such a silly baby,' said Mum.

'Harley saw my *knickers,*' I wailed.

'Well. They're clean, and they're perfectly decent. It doesn't really matter, you're only a little girl. It's much worse for Jodie but she doesn't seem to care. Typical!' said Mum. 'Now come on, Pearl, stop making such a silly fuss.'

I had to do as she told me. I pulled on my clothes, tugging hard at my horrible knickers, shoved my feet into my sandals and then stomped after Mum into the kitchen. Harley and Jodie were sitting swinging their legs on the edge of the big table, eating their cookies. Jodie was wearing her high heels with her jeans. Harley's legs were so long they hovered an inch above the ground. He looked

160

at me. I felt as if Mum's oven was switched on inside me.

'Hey, Pearl, you're as red as my shoes!' Jodie laughed.

I could have hit her.

Harley nodded at me. 'Hi, Pearl,' he mumbled. He was a little red too. 'Sorry to burst in on you like that. I was just offering to help with your decorating. Not that I've ever *done* any so I'm maybe not much cop at it.'

'You'll be great, Harley,' Jodie interrupted. 'You can do the ceiling. We won't need to bother with a stepladder!'

I wished Jodie wouldn't always tease him about his height. He made sarcastic *ho ho ho* noises but it was an obvious effort. I suddenly stopped fussing so about making such a fool of myself and thought about Harley instead.

'We'd love you to help, Harley,' I said. 'Don't worry, we don't really know what we're doing either.'

'Well, don't make too much of a mess,' said Mum. 'And for pity's sake watch what you're doing. I don't want purple smears all over everywhere. Why ever did you have to pick purple? It's such a harsh colour.'

'You've got harsh girls, Mrs Wells,' said Harley. 'They certainly keep me in line. Especially Pearl – she's *so* fierce.'

Mum blinked at him, taking him seriously.

'Yeah, too right,' said Jodie. 'She's been bullying me for years. Burly Pearly! Watch out, one kick from her little black patent shoe can send you flying.'

161

I stuck my tongue out at Jodie.

'Hey, watch out! See the deadly venom sac in her pretty little neck! One strike of that pink tongue and you've had it, dead within five seconds,' said Jodie.

'Stop being silly, girls,' said Mum. 'Would you like milk or juice with your cookies? Or maybe a cup of tea?' She looked at Harley. 'I've got Earl Grey tea,' she said proudly.

'Thank you very much, Mrs Wells,' he said. 'That would be lovely.'

Jodie rolled her eyes. 'Coo, what's this Earl Grey, Mum?' she said, putting on a funny mock-Cockney accent. 'What d'you mean, it's tea? What's up with good old PG Tips, eh?'

Mum glared at her, sighing heavily. We drank our posh tea and ate our cookies and then set off to do more painting.

'Are they your really old clothes, Harley?' Mum said doubtfully.

They were too small for him, the jeans ankle high, but they were still bright blue, and his skimpy sweatshirt looked pristine.

'Don't worry, Mum, Harley can strip down to his underpants like us,' said Jodie.

Mum's head jerked in horror.

'Joke!' said Jodie.

'One day you'll go too far, young lady,' said Mum.

'Not far enough,' Jodie muttered.

We spent hours and hours peacefully painting. Jodie played her favourite CDs very loudly, singing along, painting in time to the music. She waggled her bum too and did a little tap dance in her red shoes. Harley painted with great sure wide strokes,

162

up and down, up and down, but when he came to the pencilled drawings of Kezia and Pansy, he made a little purple arch round them. He bent right down and pencilled in a gangling boy in livery saying, *'I am Frederick the footman. I am friends with Kezia.'*

'And Pansy!' said Jodie.

'Yeah, OK.'

'Well, write it in!'

Harley started writing. *'And bossy-boots shouty-pouty Pansy is my worst enemy,'* he said slowly, as if he was printing it.

Jodie charged over indignantly but saw he'd simply added *'and Pansy'.*

Harley winked at me.

I painted with careful, finicky little strokes. My hand was steadiest so I painted right along the skirting board. Then I got my own box of paints and coloured Kezia and Pansy and Frederick in very carefully.

We were nearly finished by the time Mum sounded the gong for tea. The smell of paint had made me feel a bit sick, but as soon as I sat down at the table between Harley and Jodie I was suddenly ravenous. I wolfed down my tuna and sweetcorn sandwich and my egg and tomato roll, I crunched all my carrot sticks, I slurped up my yoghurt, I golloped down my grapes, and I ate *three* of Mum's home-made cookies, oatmeal, chocolate and almond.

'Well done, dear!' said Mum, patting my shoulder as she passed. 'It's lovely to see you with such a healthy appetite.'

Dan looked at me mournfully. 'You could share your cookies with me,' he said. He made his man stomp over to my empty plate. *'Dan and me are still hungry. Feed us!'* Dan made him say in a funny fierce voice.

I fed them both pretend mouthfuls.

'No, no, we want *real* food!' they insisted.

'You'll have to ask my mum. I'm sure she'll give you more,' I said.

Dan blinked over at Mum in her white overall and checked trousers. 'That's not your mum!' he said, giggling. 'That's Mrs Wells, the new cook lady.'

'I know, but she's my mum as well,' I said.

'She's my mum too,' said Jodie, giving the last cookie to Dan.

Dan munched, considering. 'She's *my* mum too then,' he said happily.

Jodie laughed at him but it made me want to cry.

'Imagine, poor little Dan thinking our mum is his mum,' I said when we were back in the bedroom, finishing off our beautiful purple room. Harley was still with us, doing the finicky overhead corners.

'Perhaps she can be a communal mum,' he said. 'I'd like to appropriate her myself. She's very kind, very patient, and she makes excellent cookies.'

'You're nuts!' said Jodie. 'Our mum's a good cook, I grant you that, but she's ever so *un*kind and *im*patient.'

'Oh, Jodie, she's not,' I said.

'She might seem like that to you because you drive her mad,' said Harley. 'I'm sure she's sweet to Pearl.'

'*Everyone's* sweet to Pearl,' said Jodie. 'Even me! So what's *your* mum like, Harley?'

'Don't be so nosy, Jodie,' I said, though I badly wanted to know too.

'She's a cow,' said Harley matter-of-factly.

164

'What?'

'You mean she's horrid to you?'

'She's always perfectly civil. In fact she goes out of her way to take me out for posh lunches and gives me elaborate presents, but her heart isn't in it. I don't think she even *has* a heart. If she was transparent like Dan's man, you'd see a big empty space between her lungs and her liver. She doesn't love me, though she smarms all over me. I embarrass and irritate her. I don't think she's ever loved any of her boyfriends. She's stuck with this last one the longest, but then he's the richest. A shipping magnate, no less.'

'Are you making this up, Harley?' I asked uncertainly.

'Oh no, this is way too banal and boring. I could invent *much* better bad family backgrounds. There! Look, I've painted that corner to perfection. I think my extremely expensive education is wasted. I'd be a brilliant painter and decorator.'

'Is your stepfather horrible to you?' I asked.

'Not particularly. He tried hard with me at first. He even took me to a football match. We sat in the manager's box. But I hate football. I haven't got a clue who any of the players are, so it was all a bit wasted on me. He still tried though. He took me to cricket, which was like watching this purple paint dry, and he wanted me to take up basketball training because of my height. He just couldn't seem to get the fact that I'm not a sporty type. He only stopped trying when I stole his credit card.'

'You did *what*?' said Jodie, eyes big.

'You didn't!' I said.

'Yes I did. Well, he's rich. He wasn't going to miss

it. So I ordered all sorts of stuff online – not even stuff I really *wanted*; mainly stuff for the sheer hell of it. I set myself a task of doing it alphabetically, so I ordered an apple tree and a whacking great Victorian birdcage and a set of china and fifty pairs of Damart underpants. It was great fun – it took hours and hours – and then the stuff kept arriving for *weeks*.'

'Did he know it was you?'

'Oh yes.'

'So what did he *do*?'

'He said I was warped and twisted and a stupid berk but he was more baffled than angry. My mum sent me to an extremely expensive psychiatrist and I made up all these bizarre fantasies just to wind him up. *Any*way, they couldn't work out why I was so mad or bad or whatever, so they sent me off to boarding school.'

'Yeah, yeah, loads of parents do that, but how come you're here in the holidays?' Jodie asked. 'Did they just, like, *dump* you?'

'On the contrary. I dumped them,' said Harley. 'I couldn't stand the idea of going home. Well, there isn't a home any more. My ma's rented out her London flat. She and the moneyman are spending their summer on a bloody great yacht in the Greek islands. I get seasick in a rowing boat on the Serpentine, and even if I didn't, their uninterrupted company would make me puke. So I opted to stay put here. They could hardly contain their joy and delight.'

'I think you're a bit cracked,' said Jodie. 'I'd fancy life on a luxury yacht, wouldn't you, Pearl?'

I shrugged. 'It depends who with.'

166

'Hey, pity you didn't make it right through to Y with your internet shopping, Harley. You could have bought your own yacht, then we could sail round with you. We wouldn't make you puke, would we?'

'Well, Pearl's OK. You'd maybe make me retch a little bit every now and then,' said Harley.

'Cheek!' Jodie took her paintbrush and dabbed it up at him, streaking his nose purple.

'Jodie!'

Harley dabbed her back, giving her a purple beard.

'Stop it, you two!' I shrieked.

They turned to me, and I ended up with two purple ears and a long purple streak in my hair.

'Oh God, I didn't mean it to go in your hair, Pearl. I do hope it washes off, babe,' said Jodie, looking worried. 'Still, purple's a cool colour. Maybe I should have a streak too. Do you think it would clash with the orange? Let's be the Purplehairs. Come on, Harley, join the club. I'll paint your curls. It'll give you a punky kind of edge.'

Mum went crazy when she saw us. She sent Harley off, and then scrubbed my ears with white spirit until I thought they would fall right off. She washed my hair with it too, sitting me in the bath and attacking me with a flannel as if I was a baby. She couldn't quite haul Jodie into the bath too, but she made her wash her own hair.

Dad thought it funny, which made Mum even madder. When she left me alone at last, my ears were no longer purple, they were dark red, like raw meat. I put my hands over them, my head still ringing.

'I'm sorry, Pearl,' said Jodie. She sat on my bed

and gave me a cuddle. 'I know I started it.'

'You *always* start it,' I said, sighing.

'I know, I know. I'm a meany old sister. No wonder you're fed up with me.'

'What makes you think I'm fed up with you?' I said.

'Well, you just want to go round with old Harley Not Davidson now,' said Jodie.

'No I don't!' I said, though I could feel myself going red.

'It's OK. *He's* OK, in a weird geeky kind of way. So what does it feel like to have a boyfriend?'

'He's not my *boyfriend*,' I said, going even redder.

'Yes he is! You cheeky little squirt – *I* didn't have a boyfriend when I was ten.'

'I'm very nearly eleven. And he's *not* my boyfriend. He's just my friend.'

'So what sex is he? He's a boy, right? So that makes him a boyfriend by my reckoning. And this from the girl who said not so long ago that she didn't ever ever ever want a boyfriend.'

'You said it too!'

'Yeah, well, I haven't *got* a boyfriend yet. Though I'm working hard on Jed.'

'You're joking, aren't you?'

'Don't you think he's really good looking?' said Jodie.

'Yes, but he's grown up, Jodie!'

'So am I, nearly,' said Jodie, unpinning her hair and shaking it out in a little red cloud around her head.

'Yes. Exactly. You watch out,' I said. I thought of Jed and his dark gypsy eyes and his wild hair and his swagger. 'I don't like him, Jodie. He's kind of creepy. He makes me go all shivery.'

'He makes me go shivery too,' said Jodie, running her fingers through her hair, pretending to act sexy.

'Stop it,' I said, giving her a little push. 'You watch out. Don't do anything with him, will you?'

'Like what?' said Jodie.

'*You* know. Kiss him.'

'I bet he's a seriously great snogger,' said Jodie. She started kissing her own arm in a slurping sort of way, murmuring, '*Oh, Jed, oh, Jed.*'

'You are *bad*,' I said.

'No, *you*'re the bad girl. At least I keep my clothes on when I'm around Jed. *You*'re the girl who strips off and flashes her knickers at her boyfriend.'

'I didn't mean to! Stop teasing me,' I said, giving her another push.

She pushed me back and we ended up having a push-and-shove wrestling match on the bed. Jodie was stronger than me but I managed to get one arm free and started tickling her. She creased up laughing and we both rolled over and giggled like crazy, lying on our backs. Jodie took hold of my hand.

'You still love me best though, don't you, Pearl?'

'You know I'll love you best for ever and ever and ever,' I said.

It was a real Japanese gown in red silk.

12

When we woke up, Mum was hanging our black velvet curtains at the window.

'Oh, Mum! Have you made them already?' I said, sitting up and hugging my knees.

'Well, I don't know who else would have been fool enough to stay up till past midnight stitching away at the damn things. Black velvet! I've never heard of such a thing. You could have made this room so fresh and pretty and yet you've turned it into a funeral parlour,' said Mum.

'OK, start mourning your little corpse daughters,' said Jodie, crossing her hands on her chest and lying back on her bed. She rolled her eyes up and opened her mouth slightly, looking so alarmingly dead I hit her with my pillow.

'Stop messing around, you pair of idiots,' said Mum. 'There! Well, they drape nicely, I'll say that for them. You might as well have the black rug now, Pearl, to set them off.'

'Is it still my birthday present?'

'Well. Part of it. I was thinking, maybe you'd like a little party,' said Mum, sounding hopeful.

She'd always longed to give Jodie and me a proper girly party, where we wore pretty dresses and played old-fashioned games like Musical Bumps and Pass the Parcel and ate sausages on sticks and trifle and fairy cakes. Jodie had always been up for a party, especially her own, but she'd wanted to wear her jeans and play Murder and eat takeaway pizzas. The last time she'd had a party she'd started a mad game of football in the living room and broken Mum's Lladro china lady. That put an end to Jodie's parties.

Mum had tried hard to encourage me along the party route but I was always far too shy.

'You know I don't like parties,' I said now. 'Can't I just have a birthday tea?'

'We could turn it into a *little* party,' said Mum. 'We could ask those three poor little moppets. I bet they've never been to a party in their lives. Think how they'd love it.'

I imagined Zeph jumping up and down for Musical Bumps, Sakura delicately opening a parcel, Dan with trifle all round his mouth, and I couldn't help smiling.

'All right, if it's just them,' I said.

'Don't you want that Harley to come too?' said Mum.

I swallowed. 'I don't think he'd want to come to a party,' I said.

'Rubbish!' said Jodie. 'He'd want to come to *your* party, Pearl. OK, so your party guests are the three

172

littlies and long tall Harley and me. Do I get to invite someone too?'

'It depends,' said Mum. 'Who do you want to invite? Not that Miss French and her wretched dog!'

Jodie spluttered.

'Well, you've got very thick with her. I dare say she's a perfectly nice lady but she's a bit full of herself, if you ask me. And I'm not having that Shep. He'll wreck the place, and anyway, Pearl's frightened of him.'

'I don't want Old Shep *or* Old Frenchie,' said Jodie.

'Don't call her that!'

'Why not? Everyone else does. No, I was thinking, how about Jed?'

Mum blinked. 'What? No! Don't be silly. You're definitely not asking him!'

'Why not? He's ever so nice. He's teaching me how to garden, him and Mr Wilberforce.'

'You stay away from that Jed, Jodie, he looks a wild lad. I'm not having you hanging round boys like that. Now stop the nonsense. This is Pearl's party, not yours.'

Jodie pulled a face at Mum and turned her back on both of us. 'Pearl Pearl Pearl Pearl Pearl! It's *always* Pearl's party,' she muttered.

I stared at the hunch of her shoulder, astonished. 'No it's not! Look, I don't *want* a party. I won't have one, OK?' I said.

'*Now* look what you've done, Jodie,' said Mum. 'You should feel thoroughly ashamed of yourself, trying to spoil things for Pearl. You should count yourself lucky you've got such a dear little sister.

173

Now up you get, both of you. Breakfast in twenty minutes.'

'Thank you for the curtains, Mum,' I said. '*And* the lovely fluffy black rug.'

'You're welcome, pet,' said Mum, bustling out the room.

'Creep!' Jodie muttered.

'I know. But it *was* nice of her.'

'Mmm.'

'Jodie, I really *don't* want a party.'

'I know. I'm not really fussed, I was just winding Mum up. But it'll be fine. We'll make it a lovely party for Zeph and Sakura and Dan. And Harley will be cool about it. He likes little kids. he likes *you*, doesn't he?'

'Do you think he thinks about me as if I'm *that* little?' I asked.

'Yes. No. *I* don't know. What about Jed? Do you think he thinks *I'm* a little kid?' said Jodie.

'I hope he does,' I said. 'Jodie, if you *really* want to ask Jed to come, I could ask Mum again.'

'No, she'd never budge on that one. And can you really see Jed at a children's party?' Jodie jumped out of bed, grinning at me. 'Maybe Jed and I will have our own private party.' She started doing a sexy dance, running her fingers up and down her own arms and twitching her hips.

'You're *so* bad! Hey, teach *me* how to dance like that.'

I jumped out of bed too and did my best to copy her, narrowing my eyes and pursing my lips in an effort to look sultry.

'You look like a short-sighted goldfish!' said Jodie, rocking with laughter.

At breakfast time she told Zeph and Sakura and Dan that I was having a party.

'I'm *maybe* having a party,' I said. 'I might not really want one.'

'Why wouldn't you want a *party*?' said Zeph. 'Will you have lots to eat?'

'I expect so.'

'I'll wear my party dress,' said Sakura.

'Do I like parties?' Dan said cautiously.

'Maybe. I don't like them much,' said Harley, from up the other end of the bench.

'Oh,' I said, all my cornflakes squeezing tight into a soggy lump in my tummy.

'You'll *love* parties, Dan,' said Jodie. 'And you'll have to come to Pearl's party whether you want to or not, Harley, otherwise she'll sulk big time.'

'No I won't!' I said. 'You don't have to come, Harley.'

'But you will, won't you?' said Jodie.

'Maybe,' said Harley. He winked at Sakura. 'So long as I can wear *my* party dress.'

Sakura looked startled. Zeph and Dan roared with laughter. Sakura started giggling too, her hands over her mouth. The three of them collapsed against each other on the bench, chortling.

'Oh well, we won't need to hire a clown, not if we've got Harley here on tap,' said Jodie.

'Has he *really* got a party dress?' Sakura asked me when she'd stopped giggling.

'Probably not,' I said.

'*I've* really got a party dress,' Sakura confided.

'Yes, I know. You were wearing it yesterday,' I said.

'That wasn't my *party* dress!' she said, giggling

175

again. 'My party dress is much, much prettier. Do you want to see it? I'll show you.' She slipped her hand into mine.

'All right,' I said. 'Though are you allowed?'

'Of course she's allowed,' said Jodie. 'I want to see this dress too.'

We got up off the bench together. Miss Ponsonby stood up over at the top table.

'You're not running off, are you, Sakura? We're going to make our special raffia baskets today,' she said.

'I don't want to make a silly girl's basket,' said Zeph. 'Can I come with you too?'

'Me too!' said Dan.

Miss Ponsonby frowned.

'We're just going to see Sakura's dress, Miss Ponsonby. We'll bring everyone back in ten minutes tops,' Jodie said, smiling. 'You can relax and have another cup of tea.'

'Now there's an offer you can't refuse,' said Mr Wilberforce, eating one of Mum's sausages with great relish. 'So you're a teacher's assistant and general childminder today, young Jodie. You're proving a very versatile member of the Melchester community. You're also a gardener and a dog-walker.'

'I hope you'll take Old Shep for another walk this afternoon, Jodie. He's so much better behaved if he's had some really good exercise. I'm useless. I get worn out long before he does,' said Miss French.

'Of course I'll walk him,' said Jodie. She glanced at Jed. 'And I can help out with any gardening stuff if you like. Any odd job you get bored with. I love gardening.'

176

Jed raised his eyebrows at her, looking amused. Mr Wilberforce was most enthusiastic.

'Do come and help, my dear. There's always heaps to do. Jed and I do our best but the grounds are determined to revert to wilderness. Even the formal garden is a disgrace this year, the lawn especially.' He sighed.

'Don't look at me,' said Jed. 'There's not much point trying to mow it into nice neat stripes when those blooming badgers have been burrowing. Pesky vermin. You should let me put poison down.'

I stiffened. I forgot to be shy. 'You can't poison badgers! They're lovely animals,' I said.

'She's right,' said Harley, behind me. 'Morally and indeed legally. It's totally against the law to kill a badger. You'd be prosecuted and severely fined.'

'You're just a silly townie kid,' said Jed contemptuously. 'No point getting all sentimental over badgers. They burrow all over the shop and they spread TB amongst your cattle.'

'I think you'll find that's heavily disputed,' said Harley. 'In fact some experts think it's the cattle that give the badgers TB.'

'Toffee-nosed twit,' Jed said softly to Harley, turning his head so that Mr Wilberforce couldn't hear.

'Come on, Sakura, lead the way,' said Jodie hurriedly.

We walked out with all three little ones. Harley loped along too, his fists clenched.

'Did you hear what he called me?' he said.

'No,' I lied tactfully.

177

'He called you a toffee-nosed twat,' said Jodie, thinking she was being helpful. 'Nothing to get too steamed up about.'

'What? I'm so steaming I'm boiling.'

'He didn't *mean* it. Or even if he did, so what? You *are* toffee-nosed, Harley. No one could talk posher than you. And you deliberately act like a twat half the time, you must admit.'

'Thanks a bunch,' said Harley. 'So I take it you actually like Jed the badger-baiter, Jodie? I think that makes *you* a bit of a twat.'

'Nonsense! He isn't a badger-baiter.'

'Badger-poisoner then.'

'You've got these really big ears, Harley. Don't you ever use them? He said he'd *like* to poison them, he didn't say he really would. He was just winding you up. He's the guy who does all the real work in the gardens and Mr Wilberforce just takes it for granted, but the moment you and I mosey along and cut off a few fiddly little branches, Mr Wilberforce does his nut praising us. Of *course* we're going to pee him off royally.'

'*You* don't. He seems quite smitten with you,' said Harley.

'*Really?*' said Jodie delightedly.

'*Really?*' said Zeph, imitating her.

She picked him up by the armpits and whirled him round and round until he squealed. Then she gave Sakura a twister, then Dan. I remembered when *I* was little enough to have Jodie whirl me round. I couldn't be cross with her for sticking up for Jed, even though I disliked him more than ever now. I glanced at Harley, who was still stalking along, flushed in the face.

178

'Stop huffing and puffing about Jed, Harley,' said Jodie. 'Come on, lighten up.'

We went along the path, past the spot where our own badgers were hiding in their woodland set. At least they were safe from horrible Jed. Harley glanced at me and we nodded significantly. We walked on, the children hopping round and round us, past the Wilberforces' bungalow.

Mrs Wilberforce was sitting in the window, peering out. She was wearing a flowing purple dress, her hair long and loose so that she looked like a faded fairytale princess. I felt anxious, because I hadn't been to visit her yet. It wasn't exactly that I didn't want to go. I kept thinking about all those lovely old leather-bound books. I'd finished *The Secret Garden* and badly wanted to borrow another book, but I felt stupidly shy of going to see Mrs Wilberforce by myself.

I ducked my head as we walked past, but I could see out of the corner of my eye that she was waving. I half raised my arm awkwardly, as if I was hailing a taxi.

Zeph saw me and peered round. 'You're waving at that spooky lady!' he said, astonished.

'She's *not* a spooky lady,' I said. 'She's Mrs Wilberforce, Mr Wilberforce's wife.'

'She's *ever* so spooky. She can't walk or talk,' said Dan.

'That's silly. She can speak perfectly. She just has to use a wheelchair because she got hurt,' I said.

'Who hurt her?' said Sakura.

'She hurt herself,' said Jodie. 'She was crossed in love, jilted on her wedding day, and so she climbed the steps to the tower, and at midnight she gave

179

one last hopeless howl and cast herself out of the tower window, down down down, tumbling over and over in the air, her nightgown billowing. She should have been smashed to pieces on the hard flagstones below, but see her long hair? Well, it got caught up in all the ivy and her neck snapped. She dangled there helplessly until they cut her down. She couldn't struggle because her arms and legs wouldn't work any more, and ever since she's been like a poor sad broken doll.'

Zeph and Sakura and Dan were all stopped in their tracks, open-mouthed.

'Stop it, Jodie! They're only little. They'll believe it,' I said, though she'd told it so vividly I saw Mrs Wilberforce falling too, long hair flying, down and down . . .

'We won't hurt ourselves, will we?' said Sakura.

'Only if you go up in the tower. Then you might find yourself irresistibly pulled to the window and you wouldn't be able to stop yourself. You'd step out into thin air and then—'

'Don't listen to her, Sakura,' I said, putting my hands over the little girl's ears. Her hair was very thick and silky, soft under my fingers.

'She's telling stories, isn't she?' said Zeph. 'You can't get up into the tower.'

'That's what *you* think,' said Jodie. 'I might find a way.'

We'd come to twin two-storey houses now, mirror images of each other, with white stucco walls and black window frames and bright red doors, with green rectangles of grass in front. All they needed was a smiley sun and a stripe of blue sky up above

180

and they'd look as if they were painted by a giant child.

'That's the girls' house,' said Sakura, pointing to the nearest one. 'And that's the boys' one.'

'Oh, rats,' said Jodie. 'I hoped one would be painted pink and one blue.'

'My party dress is red and gold,' said Sakura. 'Come and see!'

We all trooped into the girls' house, even Harley and Zoph and Dan.

'Though we're not allowed,' said Dan. 'The big girls chase us out if we go in there.'

'They won't chase *me*,' said Zeph, strutting about. 'We're not scared of any silly old girls, are we, Harley?'

'I'm *very* scared of girls,' said Harley. 'Jodie's dead scary. Watch she doesn't kick you with her high heels. And Pearl can pack a hefty punch. But Sakura's the *most* scary. Watch out for her karate! She'll go *whack whack* and chop you into little bits, won't you, Sakura?'

Sakura doubled up laughing, her hands over her mouth. 'You're so silly, Harley!' she said.

She led us to the little girls' dormitory on the ground floor. All the beds were stripped and empty apart from Sakura's at the end, by the far door.

'That's Undie's room,' she said. 'She keeps her door open when it's just her and me so I can hear her going *snore snore snore* so I don't get scared.'

Sakura had dolls and teddies lying in complicated cuddles all over her red duvet. There were so many, there didn't look as if there would be much room for Sakura herself. Zeph picked up a doll in each hand and made them do karate on each other.

181

Dan purloined a baby doll and pulled her knickers off to see if she had a real bottom. Sakura looked understandably anxious.

'Put the dolls back, boys. They're not yours, they're Sakura's,' I said.

They didn't take any notice.

'Hey, hey, Zeph, I'll karate chop *you* if you don't watch out,' said Jodie, miming. 'And as for you, Dan the man, watch out or I'll whip your trousers down and see if *you*'ve got a real bottom.'

All three shrieked at this. The boys threw the dolls back on Sakura's bed. She patted them into place, nodding at Jodie gratefully.

'Come on then, party girl, show us your dress,' said Jodie.

Sakura went to her wardrobe and carefully shuffled through the little outfits. I already had a smile on my face, ready to reassure her that her dress was lovely, though I was sure it was going to be as strange and old-fashioned as her day clothes. But it wasn't really a dress, as such. It was a real Japanese gown in red silk, patterned all over with pale cherry blossom and tied with a wide gold brocade sash.

'Oh, it's beautiful!' I said.

'Fantastic,' said Jodie.

'*Much* prettier than *my* party dress,' said Harley.

Sakura beamed. 'See the cherry blossom?' she said. 'That's what Sakura means in Japanese.'

'You'll be the star of the party, Sakura, apart from the birthday girl herself,' said Harley.

'No, *you*'ll be the star in your party frock,' said Jodie. 'Come on, then, let's see it. Is it hanging in your wardrobe? Show us where you guys hang out.'

The boys' house was pretty similar to the girls'. Apparently Zeph and Dan were usually in different dormitories but they'd been put next to each other for company during the holidays.

'What about you, Harley?' said Jodie. 'You can't tell me you fit into one of these dinky little beds.'

'Harley sleeps upstairs with the big boys,' said Dan. 'He's got a big big big special bed.'

'Oh, let's see, let's see,' said Jodie.

We were both imagining a ridiculously elongated cartoon bed the length of the entire dormitory. It was a bit disappointing to see that Harley's bed was just an average full-size single bed, his navy striped duvet neatly patted into place. There was a *teddy bear* lying on his pillow, furry limbs stretched out, with a straw hat over his face as if he was having a snooze in the sun.

'Has *he* got a party dress, Harley?' asked Sakura.

'No, he hasn't got a party outfit, Sakura. Maybe we could make him one. He'd love a beautiful red Japanese dress just like yours.'

'Maybe we could find a silky scarf and wrap it round him with some ribbon?' said Sakura.

'Good idea. I'll need some help though. Are you any good at sewing?'

'I'm not allowed needles and sharp scissors yet,' said Sakura. 'Undie says I might hurt myself.'

'So what about you, Pearl? You'll help me, won't you?'

I nodded at Harley uncertainly, not sure if this was all a joke or not.

Jodie was more forthright. 'Is the teddy *really* yours? Are you totally retarded?'

'I'm just an emotionally deprived child who's

languished unloved in too many boarding schools,' said Harley. 'I need my little ursine companion.'

'Even Pearl's stopped playing with her soppy little teddies,' said Jodie, shaking her head at him.

'I still have them sitting by my bed,' I said.

'What are their names?'

'Edgar, Allan and Poe.'

'Cool names! So you like reading Edgar Allan Poe?' said Harley, sounding very impressed.

'No, I just saw his name on a book in the library,' I admitted, shame-faced.

'Nothing wrong with appropriating a name, though it can obviously backfire on you. *My* bear is called Mr Rigby Peller, which is *actually* the name of the shop where my ma gets her underwear. I saw the name on a fancy carrier bag and thought it would be splendid for the bear I'd just been given for my fifth birthday. I christened him privately with a bottle of Evian water and we were packed off to boarding school together. I told the other boys his name very proudly, thinking it utterly distinguished, and a cut above all their Eddies and Freddies, but one unpleasant older boy bellowed with laughter and said that was the label on his mother's push-up bra. Rigby Peller and I became the school laughing stock after that.'

I was touched by his story, though I wasn't sure if he was making it all up. Jodie simply laughed at him.

'No wonder, you pathetic little diddums,' she said. 'Come on then, show us this party dress.' She flung open his wardrobe and started clicking his coat-hangers along the rack, rubbishing his long limp trousers and jeans and jackets.

'Stop it, Jodie. Don't be so rude!' I said fiercely. I pushed her hard, slamming the wardrobe door shut so she nearly got her fingers trapped.

'Oh, temper temper,' she said, laughing. 'Come on then, let's get back or Miss Ponsy will be getting seriously narked.'

I wanted to stay longer and look at the books on Harley's shelves. I could see adult books on astronomy and psychology and art and natural history, but there were also old children's stories – *The Wind in the Willows, Treasure Island*, several *William* books, *His Dark Materials*, all the Harry Potters, all the Narnia stories, lots of E. Nesbits, even an *Alice in Wonderland*. I badly wanted to browse and see which were well-thumbed. It would be like peeping into Harley's head. But Jodie had Zeph and Dan by the hand and was already down the length of the dormitory and out of the door. Sakura was trooping after them, looking back at me anxiously.

'Just coming, Sakura,' I said, still squatting by the bookshelf.

I looked up at Harley. He looked down at me.

'We can always come back this afternoon so you can look at my books, Pearl. *Without* the entourage.'

'Thanks,' I whispered.

'Come *on*, Pearl!' Jodie called sharply.

'Why do you let her boss you about so?' said Harley.

'She doesn't really *boss*,' I said.

'Yes, she does!'

'Well, she just looks after me. Because I'm her sister.'

'Yes, but you're not a little kid any more. You

don't *have* to do what Jodie says.'

'You don't understand. You haven't got a big sister.'

'I'm very glad I haven't got a big sister like Jodie,' said Harley.

**Then Mum and Dad came in, singing
'Happy Birthday'.**

13

I hadn't really thought what I was going to wear for
my birthday. I had my pink dress. I'd had it nearly
a year but it still fitted me perfectly and I'd worn it
so little that it looked brand new. I'd liked it last
year. I'd admired the delicate pink-and-white
striped silk, the lace collar, the full skirt. I'd twirled
round and round in it, feeling like a ballet dancer.
Mum had called me her little fairy and had made
fairy cakes for my birthday tea. I blushed at the
thought now.

Mum caught me dressed up in the pink dress
early in the morning, staring in the mirror in
horror.

'I'd have given anything to have a party frock like
that. You look as pretty as a princess,' she said.

'No I don't, Mum. I look *awful*,' I said. 'It's so
babyish.'

'Don't be silly,' said Mum. She gave me a hug.
'You're still my baby, anyway.'

'No I'm not. Eleven's nearly a teenager.' I struck a pose, hands on hips.

'Don't *you* start getting above yourself, missy. I've had enough cheek from your sister to last me a lifetime,' said Mum, looking over at Jodie and sighing.

We'd thought Jodie was still asleep, but a hand came out from under her duvet and waggled its fingers.

'My dress is too small for me now,' I said.

'No it's not. The hem's still just on your knee, though I could let it down if you really want.'

'It's too *tight*,' I said, sticking my chest out as far as possible. 'Here,' I said, pointing.

'Rubbish, you're flat as a pancake,' said Mum.

'It hurts under my arms,' I lied, wriggling.

'Where?' said Mum. 'There's plenty of room!'

'Can't she have a new outfit for her own birthday?' Jodie mumbled. 'Especially as you talked her into having this party.'

'It's not exactly a proper party, it's just a little get-together, a birthday tea,' said Mum. 'But all right, I suppose I could always get Dad to drive me into town this Saturday. I think there's a market where we might be able to buy a length of silk.'

'Can't I have something ready-made, Mum? Not a dress.'

'Well, what?' said Mum.

'I don't know. Something more casual.'

'You're not wearing jeans to a party!'

'Not jeans, then, but something . . .' I looked around wildly for inspiration and saw the curtains. 'Something *black*.'

'Don't be ridiculous, Pearl. You can't wear black at your age!' said Mum.

'Is there any black velvet left over from the curtains?' said Jodie.

'Well, a bit. Not enough for a dress though – and it's summer. You can't wear black velvet in August!'

'A skirt, a little black velvet skirt,' said Jodie. She sat up, waving her hands, describing the shape in the air. 'And then you could wear one of my black T-shirts, Pearl, that would look cool. What do you think?'

'Oh *yes!*' I said.

'Oh *no,*' said Mum, folding her arms.

Jodie knelt up in bed, looking earnest. '*Please* make her the skirt, Mum. *I'd* make it but you know I'm rubbish at sewing. Make Pearl the skirt so she can look the way she wants on her birthday. Go on, Mum, please please please,' she said, nudging forward on her knees, turning her hands into paws and begging like a puppy.

'I'm not your dad. You can't get round me by acting daft,' said Mum, swatting at her with her teatowel.

But that evening after we were in bed we heard her scissors snipping away and then the whirr of her sewing machine.

'There!' said Jodie happily.

'Are you giving me a present, Jodie?' I asked.

'How can I give you a present? I can't just dash out to the shopping centre, can I?'

'Aren't you even giving me a card?' I said.

'Oh sure, like there's a Clinton's round the corner,' said Jodie.

But when I woke up very early on my birthday

morning, I felt paper crackling on my pillow. I rolled onto my tummy and found a beautiful home-made collage card picturing both of us having a big hug. Jodie's hair was tufty orange wool and my hair was a whole skein of pale yellow embroidery thread, obviously nicked from Mum's sewing basket. We were both dressed in scraps of black velvet. Jodie had cut out paper shoes for us from a magazine. She had red high heels, of course, but I had them too, with spiky stilettos almost the length of my paper leg. She'd printed at the top: *To the best sister in the world on her eleventh birthday – Lots of love, Jodie.* She'd given me eleven kisses and an extra big one for luck.

I kissed the little paper image of Jodie and then reached for the little parcel. It was a bead bracelet laid out in an arc on a piece of cardboard. She'd taken a handful of my little glass beads and threaded them into rainbow formation: red, orange, yellow, green, blue, indigo and violet. At one end of the rainbow bracelet she'd sellotaped a yellow pound coin with an arrow saying *Crock of Gold!*

I jumped out of my bed and dived under the duvet beside Jodie.

'Hey! Stop rocking the bed! Mind those sharp little elbows,' she grumbled, but she cuddled me close. 'Happy birthday, little Pearly Girly.'

'I'm not little any more. I'm eleven. I'm big big big,' I said, stretching right out. 'See, feel, I'm nearly as tall as you are now.'

'Oh, so you are. At least as tall as me. Taller. In fact I should say you're very nearly Harley size now. My goodness, you'll make a terrifying pair. You'll be bossing me about left, right and centre.'

'I wish,' I said.

'What will you wish when you cut your birthday cake?' Jodie asked.

'I don't know,' I fibbed. 'Do you think Mum's making me a proper birthday cake then?'

'Oh, come on. How could she resist? It'll be the full works with a piped icing message and candles. Pink and white, most likely, to match your dress – *not.*'

'I wish it was just going to be *us* at this party,' I said.

'And Harley.'

'Not even Harley.' It was easier confiding in the dark under the duvet. 'I like him and I sort of like being with him but I always feel so *shy.*'

'Shy of *Harley?*' said Jodie.

'Don't you ever feel shy of anyone, Jodie?'

She was quiet. So quiet I thought she'd gone back to sleep. I gave her a little nudge.

'I'm thinking,' she said. 'I'm mostly not a bit shy. Not of *boys.* But guys like Jed and that Bernie – I feel a bit weird and wobbly when they look at me. Is that feeling shy?'

'I *hate* that way of looking.'

'I like it.'

'Don't you find it scary?'

'I like being a bit scared, it's exciting,' said Jodie.

'We are so different,' I said, nestling up to her.

'I used to be convinced Mum and Dad had adopted me,' said Jodie. 'Maybe they thought they couldn't have kids so they went along to this children's home. I'd have made a funny face at Dad and he'd have picked me, and then as soon as they'd signed all the adoption papers, Mum would have found she was pregnant after all, but it was way too late to send me back.'

'Stop it! Of course you weren't adopted.'

'I sometimes wish I was. I'd like a totally different mum.'

'You wouldn't ever want to swap Dad.'

'Well. Maybe. But it's not like he's really cool or exciting or important. He's just *Dad*. I'd like a dad who was a rock star or a premiership footballer – yeah, and my real mum was a groupie, say, and he doesn't even know that he's got this secret daughter. But one day he'll find out and fall for me and whisk me away.'

'What about me?'

'He'll whisk you too.'

'No he wouldn't, not if we weren't real sisters.'

'We're *always* real sisters, you and me,' said Jodie. 'I'll always love you best and you'll always love me best, right?'

'Couldn't be righter,' I said.

Then Mum and Dad came in, singing 'Happy Birthday', with presents wrapped in silver paper tied with white ribbon. I stroked them gently and fingered the ribbon. Jodie started prodding and squeezing them until Mum slapped her hand away.

'Get off! They're not *your* presents, Jodie. Let Pearl open her own presents in peace.'

'Well hurry *up*, Pearl. You always take such an age. You'll be twelve before you've opened the presents for your eleventh birthday.'

There was a little oblong package from Dad that I hoped *might* be a mobile phone, though there wasn't really anyone I wanted to ring. It wasn't a phone at all; it was a leather jewellery box containing a string of pearls.

I cupped the pale little beads in my hands. They seemed the sort of jewellery old ladies wore. Dad was looking at me anxiously. I tried very hard to look thrilled.

'Oh, wow, Dad. Thank you so much. Real pearls!' I said.

'Well. they're not *real*, of course, but they're *good* imitation,' said Dad. 'Do you really like them, pet? I so wanted to give my Pearl her very own pearls. Your mum wanted to wait till you were a bit older—'

'Still, she's determined to grow up as soon as possible,' said Mum. She tugged one of my night-time plaits. 'Though bless you, Pearl, you look about six years old right this minute.'

Mum gave me a fluffy pink toy poodle, a bottle of rose toilet water and a big jar of rose bubble bath. There was just one parcel left. I opened it up carefully, my hand shaking a little. There was Jodie's black T-shirt, washed and ironed, with a new black velvet trim round the neck and sleeves. Underneath there was a black velvet skirt, very short, made in ruffled layers.

'Oh!' I said, trembling.

'I didn't have a proper pattern. I had to make it up and hope for the best,' said Mum. 'Try it on then, Pearl. Let's hope it fits.'

I pulled the skirt on under my nightie. It fitted perfectly.

'Hold up your nightie and let's see. Oh dear, it's much too short!'

'No, it isn't, Mum, it's perfect,' said Jodie. 'Give us

a twirl, Pearl. You look fantastic, like you're going out clubbing.'

I ran to the mirror and stared at myself. The skirt really did look wonderful.

'Oh, Mum, *thank* you! It's the best birthday present ever,' I said, dancing around the room.

'Don't talk such nonsense! Think of all the lovely expensive presents I've given you in the past. This is just a tacky little length of velvet,' said Mum, but she looked pleased even so.

The party was due to start at four o'clock. Mum served a very small lunch – tomato soup and sandwiches – so that we could eat a big birthday tea.

'I want a big birthday *lunch*,' said Zeph. 'I'm still starving! I don't want to go to your silly old birthday party, Pearl. I've got to have *another* bath and change my clothes, Undie says.'

'I wish I wasn't having a party too,' I said.

I had only managed two spoonfuls of soup even though tomato was my favourite. I suddenly felt so worried about this wretched party. What were we going to *do* from four o'clock to six thirty? We couldn't eat tea for two and a half hours!

'You'll play party games, silly,' said Mum.

'What sort of games?'

'Blind Man's Buff and Squeak Piggy Squeak,' said Mum, saying the words softly, as if they were magic spells. 'They're party games.'

'How do we play them?'

'*I* don't know. I never got invited to any parties when I was a little girl because I came from such a hopeless family. My brothers were forever nicking stuff right from when they were little, and always fighting – and my sister was a nightmare. I don't blame those mothers for steering well clear of us. But I had this reading book and the children had a party and played those games,' said Mum. 'I'm sure you can make them up. Now don't bother me, dear. I've still got *such* a lot to do. Don't come in the kitchen, I don't want you to see your cake.'

'Do *you* know how to play Blind Man's Buff, Jodie?' I asked.

'Of course not! No one plays those weird old games at parties any more. Little kids have themed parties, swimming or football, and big kids have a ride in a limo and meals at Pizza Express.'

'So what will *we* do?' I asked.

'We'll invent our own party games, Pearl,' said Harley. 'Don't worry.'

I was mostly worried about him. I didn't want him to be bored. I knew he wasn't a party person any more than I was.

'I'll make some up for you,' said Harley.

'I'll make some up too,' said Jodie. 'Hey, how come you haven't got Pearl a birthday card, Harley? She was really hoping you'd make her one, seeing as you're meant to be so dead artistic.'

'No I *wasn't*,' I said, going red. 'Shut up, Jodie.'

'*We're* making you cards,' said Dan.

'Ssh! Undie says it's a surprise,' said Sakura.

'Mine's gone all splotchy,' said Zeph. 'It's a total rubbish card.'

'I'm sure it's lovely,' I said.

It was all such an *effort*. I wanted to slope off by myself and hide until it was party time but I couldn't even do that. Mr Wilberforce came striding down from the top table and gave me a box of choco-late truffles.

'These are for you, birthday girl.'

'Ooh, how lovely of you, Mr Wilberforce. Pearl, what do you say?' Mum hissed.

'Thank you very much,' I gabbled obediently, though I didn't really *like* truffles.

'You're very welcome, my dear. Now, Mrs Wilberforce has a little something she wishes to give you too. Run along to my house and see what it is. If you go straight away, you'll catch her before her afternoon nap.'

I sat on the edge of the bath and started
writing my journal there and then.

14

I asked Harley if he'd go with me to see Mrs Wilberforce.

'Then you could look at all her books. I'm sure she'd let you borrow some yourself,' I said.

'No, I've got things to do, party games to plan,' said Harley.

I turned to Jodie and started begging her in turn.

'No way. I wouldn't even if you'd asked me first. I've got things to do too,' she said huffily. 'Go on. You go. You're the one she wants to see.'

I nudged up close to Jodie. 'I'm *scared*,' I whispered in her ear.

'Look, you're eleven now,' she said. 'Don't be such a baby.'

I thought about taking one of the little ones, but Miss Ponsonby said they all had to go with her. I was on my own.

I fetched the copy of *The Secret Garden*. I'd enjoyed it so much I'd read it all over again. Jodie had flicked through it, keen to pick up any gardening tips to impress Jed. She tossed it to one side after twenty minutes, wrinkling her nose.

'I can't think what you see in it, Pearl. It's written all weird and old-fashioned and it's such a waste. There's this huge creepy house and mysterious crying at night and you think something really scary is going to happen, but it's just this little invalid boy and he doesn't even die to make a good weepy bit. He gets better. How tame is that! And the gardening bits aren't much cop either.'

I hugged *The Secret Garden* to my chest now, protecting it from Jodie's scorn. I played I was Mary talking to Dickon as I walked along the path. The robin came and perched on my shoulder, and I carried the lamb in my arms. Dickon led me to a grassy bank and we sat down beside a badger set, waiting patiently. Dickon played a tune on his pipe and the badgers all came running, big ones, small ones, tiny baby cubs, all playing about our feet . . .

I wanted to stay lost in my imaginary world but I was already outside the bungalow. I gripped my book, looking at the window. I couldn't see any sign of Mrs Wilberforce. Maybe I could tell a little fib, pretend I'd knocked but could get no answer. I'd dawdled on the path. Maybe she was taking her afternoon nap already. Surely it would be rude to disturb her.

The curtains twitched. I blinked anxiously at the window. I couldn't see her, but perhaps she was behind the curtains peering out at me. I wanted to run away, but how would that make her feel? How awful if she thought I was like the little kids, scared because she was in a wheelchair. She wouldn't understand I was so stupidly shy that I was scared of everyone.

But I was eleven now. Jodie was right. I wasn't a baby any more. I took a deep breath, opened the gate and marched up the driveway to the bungalow. I rang the doorbell, pressing it firmly so it rang loud and clear. I waited, my heart beating fast. Then the door slowly opened, and there was Mrs Wilberforce smiling at me.

'Hello, Pearl. Happy birthday.'

'Thank you,' I said.

'You look *much* older today,' she said.

'I wish!'

'It's funny, I always looked young for my age when I was a child. I used to get so cross about it! And yet now I'd give anything to look younger.' She fingered a strand of her long wavy hair. In the daylight I saw that it was snowy-white, not blonde at all.

'I think you look quite young,' I said, though the deep lines on her face made her look ancient. She'd covered her pale cheeks with rouge and dabbed powder everywhere and painted her lips bright pink. The colour had started to run up all the little creases round her lips.

She shook her head at me sadly. 'My hair went white overnight when I had the accident,' she said.

She manoeuvred her wheelchair down the wide hallway and into her library. I took a deep breath. 'The accident?' I repeated in a tiny voice.

'Yes, Pearl,' she said. 'When I fell and broke my neck.' She looked down at her lifeless legs under her long dress.

'When you fell?' I whispered.

'In the tower,' said Mrs Wilberforce. She looked at me. 'Surely someone's told you?'

'Well, I sort of heard stuff, but I didn't know whether it was true,' I said. 'I didn't know whether to believe it.'

'It's true all right,' she said. 'I didn't know whether to believe it either. I still don't sometimes. I wake up, and just for a moment I've forgotten, and I think I can swing my legs out of bed and jump up – and then I try to move . . .' Her eyes filled with tears.

'I'm so sorry,' I said, feeling terrible.

'No, no, *I'm* sorry. What am I doing, getting maudlin after all these years, and on your birthday too! I have a present for you, Pearl.' She handed me an oblong parcel carefully wrapped in swirly marbled paper and tied with a lopsided bow. I thought of the care she must have taken to wrap the present one-handed, tucking the ends of the paper in, maybe tying the ribbon with her teeth. I wanted to cry too. I took the present, forgetting to say thank you. I was trying desperately to think of something positive to say.

'Still, at least you didn't get killed when you fell out of the tower. It's such a long long long way down. It's amazing that you survived.'

She stared at me. 'I didn't fall *out* of the tower! Dear goodness, no one could survive that! I'd have been smashed to pieces on the forecourt.'

'But didn't you get tangled up in the ivy?' I said. 'Jodie said—'

'No, no! Your sister Jodie's got a very gothic imagination. I fell *inside* the tower, down the steps. I used to love to go up to the tower room. It was my own private study. I had it as my bedroom when I was a little girl. It was a little cramped and uncomfortable and always very cold, and I had to go up and up all those winding stairs, but I thought it was worth it to have such a special room, like something in a fairy tale.'

'I'd love it too,' I said.

'I'd go up there most nights even after I was grown up. I kept some of my favourite books up there. Sometimes I just stood at the window looking out at the moonlit countryside. Then one night I lost track of time and then I heard Harold – Mr Wilberforce – calling me. I hurried downstairs, just that little bit too quickly. I'd hurtled down those narrow little steps thousands of times, but this time I slipped. I tried to grab hold of the banister but it broke away and I fell. That's *my* fairy story, where everything ends *un*happily ever after.'

I stood shifting uncomfortably from one foot to the other, wishing I knew what to say. I felt my face going red.

'I'm sorry, I'm sorry! Let's forget all about me. This is *your* special day. Come on, dear, open your present.'

I started carefully undoing the paper. I could feel it was a book. I wondered which one she'd picked out for me. I let the wrapping paper slither to the floor and held it in my hands. It was beautiful, with a greeny-blue marbled cover and an olive leather spine and corners. I stroked it in awe and then opened it up. There was a blank page. I turned it over. Another blank page, and then another and another.

I looked at Mrs Wilberforce. 'Where's the story?' I asked timidly.

'Ah. It's going to be *your* story, Pearl. It's a manuscript book for your own stories. I bought it years ago in Italy but I could never think of anything to put in it. I wondered about keeping a journal, but what would I write now? Every entry would be identical. Got up, sat in my wheelchair, read, went to bed.'

I struggled. 'I could maybe push your wheelchair, Mrs Wilberforce, and take you for walks?'

'Oh, darling, that's a very sweet offer, but I'm far too heavy for a little girl like you.'

'Well, my sister Jodie could push you.'

'Mmm, maybe not! But thank you for the offer all the same.'

'Thank *you* for the lovely writing book.'

'Feel free to borrow lots more storybooks. Did you enjoy *The Secret Garden*?'

'It was wonderful. I read it twice,' I said, slotting it back in its place on the shelf.

'Are you tempted to find a secret garden of your own? Harold – Mr Wilberforce – could give you your own little plot.'

'I'm not very good at growing things. We grew hyacinths at my last school but mine went all wonky. It's Jodie who's really interested in gardening,' I said.

'No, I think Jodie is more interested in Jed the gardener,' said Mrs Wilberforce.

I blinked at her. She might be stuck indoors in her wheelchair but she didn't miss much.

'Did you try and count the rooms in Melchester to see if it measured up to Misselthwaite?' she asked.

I swallowed, pretending to be looking at the books on the shelf, not wanting to look her in the eye.

'I tried counting some of the rooms,' I said.

'But not all of them?'

'Well. We're not allowed on the top floor,' I said.

'Ah. Very wise. There's nothing very interesting up there, as far as I can remember. Flotsam and jetsam from former lives.'

'Flotsam? Jetsam?' I thought hard. 'Are they the names of the monkeys?' Then I clapped my hand over my mouth.

She looked hard at me, the lipsticked corners of her mouth twitching. I thought she might shout at me but she smiled instead.

'So you *have* been thorough in your counting?' she said.

'I – I'm sorry. I know we're not allowed. We just had a little tiny explore,' I said.

'We?' said Mrs Wilberforce.

I blushed. I was terrified of getting Harley into trouble. 'It wasn't anyone's fault,' I said quickly.

'You and doubtless Jodie just happened to find yourselves wandering on the top floor, idly walking straight through the cupboard that I believe blocks the way?' said Mrs Wilberforce, but she didn't sound too cross.

'I'm so sorry,' I said. 'We didn't do any harm. We just peeped into the rooms. We didn't touch anything. Well, if we did, we put it back. We didn't break anything, I promise.'

'I'm more worried about *you* getting broken,' said Mrs Wilberforce. 'I'm not at all sure about those creaky old floorboards. Poor old Melchester is gently rotting away right down to its foundations.' She suddenly looked alarmed. 'You didn't get up in the tower, did you?'

'No.'

'You're sure, Pearl?'

'Yes, honestly. We *wanted* to, but it's all locked up and there isn't any key.'

'Good. You mustn't ever go up there, it's far too dangerous. That door must always be kept locked. I don't really want you making a habit of wandering in and out of the attics either. Still, you seem a careful, cautious child.' She smiled at me. 'So you found my old monkey family. I'd totally forgotten them. I made them all special outfits.'

'A little red jacket and dungarees and a long baby gown and a frilly dress with a pinafore,' I said softly.

'Yes! My dear old monkeys! Fancy them lying up there all these years. Maybe you could fetch them for me? I'd love to see them again.'

'Of course I can.'

She saw me hesitating. 'What is it?'

'Well, they've got a bit broken,' I said. 'We didn't do it, I promise. It's their rubber bits. They've kind of rotted away. The man monkey's feet have fallen off and the baby's lost most of her face.'

'Ugh! Oh God, I couldn't bear to see them. We'll leave them where they are. R.I.P. Rotting In Peace.'

'The costumes aren't rotting.'

'What costumes?'

'Coats and hats and fur things.'

She didn't look very interested.

'And a special dress,' I said.

'Special?'

208

'It's on one of those dummy things. It's not quite finished. It's white and very beautiful. I think it was going to be a wedding dress.'

'My wedding dress,' she said. 'It was going to have a long lace train. I was going to sweep down the aisle with little bridesmaids holding up my train, but then the accident happened and I wasn't up to sweeping anywhere. I wanted to call it all off. It wasn't fair on Harold when I was hopelessly crippled, but he wouldn't hear of it. We were married very quietly six months later, when I was able to use a wheelchair. We lived in the main building at first, but I found it very upsetting being confined to the ground floor. There was no way we could adapt everything to be suitable for an invalid. It seemed easier to have the bungalow built, custom made for me.'

She looked around the room, her expression bleak.

'It's lovely here,' I said politely.

'No it's not. It's hideous. I hate it here. But that doesn't matter, I'd hate anywhere now.' She put her head on one side. 'Hark at me moaning again. I should learn to count my blessings. Play the Glad Game like Polyanna. Have you read that book? It always sets my teeth on edge. Likewise saintly Cousin Helen in *What Katy Did*. Still, I love Katy herself, especially before her accident.'

I blinked at her, confused.

'You haven't read *What Katy Did*? Oh, Pearl, call yourself a bookworm! Let's find my copy.' She wheeled herself rapidly round the shelves until she found it.

'There! Read it and tell me what you think. Call

round any time.' She raised her eyebrows. 'I'm always in.'

I thanked her again for my birthday present and then ran off, clutching both books. I had to get ready for the party, but I peeped at the badger set on the way. I imagined the whole family of badgers got up in their best black-and-white party clothes, ready to wave their paws in a festive fashion and grunt 'Happy Birthday'.

I imagined them so vividly I felt disappointed when there were no badgers in sight, not so much as a nose or a claw. I crept right up close to the set and tried to peer into the hole but I couldn't see anything at all, just dark earth.

I got my hands and knees muddy crouching there.

'What on earth have you been up to?' said Mum when I got back home. 'For pity's sake, you'd better jump straight in the bath. I don't know, you're a great girl of eleven now and yet you've obviously been grubbing around making mud pies. I hope you haven't got Mrs Wilberforce's books all over muddy fingerprints. Has she lent you two this time?'

'One of them is my birthday present,' I said, showing Mum. 'It's for me to write in.'

'Are you sure? It's a beautiful book, much too grand for you to scribble your stories in.'

'I'm going to keep a journal,' I said.

'Oh my!' said Mum, laughing at me. 'Anyway, you go and run a bath – and see what your sister's up to. She's been holed up in that bedroom for ages.'

'Go away!' said Jodie when I went in our bedroom. 'I'm inventing surprise birthday games. Clear off, Pearly.'

I went off to have my bath, filling it with my new

rose bubble bath. While the taps were running, I sat on the edge of the bath and started writing my journal there and then, worried that Mum might confiscate my book until I was older. It was a bit scary starting the first beautiful pale cream page. I wrote lightly in pencil so that I could rub it out if I made a mistake.

My name is Pearl. I am eleven years old today. I'm going to have a birthday party. My sister Jodie and my friend Harley are in charge of the games. I'm not sure I LIKE games but I suppose you have to play them at parties.

Then I closed the book carefully, put it right on the other side of the room so it couldn't possibly get splashed, and jumped in my bath. I lay back in my rosy bubbles, swishing myself backwards and forwards, watching my pale skin glow pink with the heat.

Jodie put her head round the door, sniffing elaborately. 'Mmm, I smell a rosy-posy pong, birthday princess. Want me to shampoo your hair?'

I sat up and she soaped my hair, massaging my scalp with her hard little fingers. She experimented with different hairstyles when it was stiff with soapsuds, twirling it around and sculpting it into place, but when I'd rinsed and dried it, I decided to let it hang down loose.

'No, it's too little-girly,' said Jodie. 'I'll pin it up properly for you.'

'I like it loose,' I said. It felt soft and comforting round my shoulders, like a curtain I could hide behind.

Jodie wanted to put make-up on me but I wasn't sure about that either. I'd experimented myself but I just looked like a little kid playing with face paints. Jodie smeared some shimmery stuff on my eyelids and outlined my mouth with pale pink.

'There! Very pretty. Only watch out – if we see pink smears all over Harley's face, we'll know you've been kissing him,' she said.

'I'm not going to kiss Harley!' I said, blushing.

'Just wait till he sees you in your birthday outfit. He'll be overcome with passion,' said Jodie, snorting with laughter.

'Shut up, you idiot,' I said, trying to stick my nose in the air and act dignified – only I got the giggles too.

I pulled on Jodie's black T-shirt and my new black velvet skirt. They looked fantastic.

I put my long string of pearls round my neck and my rainbow bracelet round my wrist.

'There! You look lovely,' said Jodie.

'Really?'

'Yep. But not quite as absolutely stunningly lovely as *me*.' She struck an attitude, then did a little tap dance in her high heels.

Mum dressed up too, changing from her checked trousers and white top into her best blue dress with the low neck and the tight patent belt, and she even wore her own high heels. We were so used to her in practical work clothes that she seemed like a glamorous stranger.

'You look so pretty, Mum!' I said.

'Don't talk nonsense,' said Mum, but she looked pleased.

'It's not nonsense at all,' said Dad. 'You're as

pretty as a picture. And so are you, birthday girl. And you too, Jodie pet. My three best girls, all of them little crackers.'

'Then you'd better measure up, Joe. You can't come to Pearl's party in your work clothes! Get changed quick – best shirt, and wear a tie.'

'Oh come on, Shaz, it's only a party for the little-uns.'

'*Sharon*! Mr Wilberforce will probably look in, and Miss Ponsonby and that Frenchie, all sticking their noses in.'

'Do we have to have them too?' I asked, horrified.

'If they're coming, then I can't see why Jed can't come,' said Jodie. 'I bet he's good at all sorts of games!'

'Stop that silly talk, Jodie. The others will just be there for the birthday tea. I dare say they'll clear off afterwards while you're all playing.' Mum looked at her watch. 'Right, Pearl. You'd better go into the dining hall. Your guests will be arriving soon.'

My stomach clenched. 'Oh, Mum! I don't want to. I don't know what to say to them. I don't want this party. Please, can't I just stay here till it's over?' I begged.

'Don't be so silly,' said Mum. 'Of course you have to go to your own party!'

'You'll have a lovely time, pet, you'll see,' said Dad.

Jodie put her arm round me. 'I'll come with you, Pearl. It's OK. I'll look after you. You're going to have a great time, I promise you.'

We had to gallop the length of the dining room,
hee-hawing at the top of our voices.

15

I clung to Jodie gratefully. We walked down the corridor, through the kitchen and into the dining room. I stood still, my heart thumping. Mum and Dad had put up a banner saying HAPPY BIRTHDAY PEARL. There were pink and white balloons taped to either end of the long table. The party food was laid out on pink plates. It was old-fashioned storybook party food: tiny sandwiches; sausages on sticks; fairy cakes; gleaming red and green jellies; a big bowl of creamy trifle studded with cherries.

'Ah, bless,' said Jodie, snatching up a sandwich and several sausages.

'We're not supposed to eat anything yet,' I said.

'It's your party. You can eat your own food when you want,' said Jodie, dipping her finger in the trifle and having a big lick of cream. 'Yum! Try a bit!'

'I don't actually feel like eating. I feel sick,' I said.

'You are so weird,' said Jodie. 'Are you shivering?'

She briskly rubbed the goose pimples on my arms. 'There, let's warm you up a bit. Wait till you've played some of my party games. You'll be warm as toast then.'

'I really really really don't want to play party games,' I said.

But then Harley came striding into the dining room, looking astonishing. He was wearing a bizarre black felt wizard's hat, the plum silk smoking jacket from the attics upstairs, and his own too-short jeans, showing his socks, one scarlet, one canary yellow.

'Good God, it's a clown,' said Jodie.

Harley ignored her, took off his wizard's hat with a flourish and bowed low. 'Happy birthday, Pearl. I am Harley, purveyor of excellent, instructive and original party games. This is my magical wizard's hat – and lo and behold, here is your birthday present lurking inside.'

He held the hat out to me. I felt inside the silk lining and found a long narrow package tied up in brown paper and string.

'Fancy party packaging,' said Jodie.

I undid the string, unwrapped the paper and found a long black object inside.

'What *is* it?' said Jodie.

I flicked the switch and it lit up.

'A torch! Well, that's a weird present. Why on earth would Pearl want a torch?' said Jodie.

'I think it's a wonderful present. Thank you, Harley,' I said.

'If you should ever find yourself out in the dark for any reason, I hope the torch will come in handy,' said Harley.

'Oh yeah, that's *so* likely,' said Jodie. 'Look, *I've* got all the party games sussed out, Harley.'

Miss Ponsonby seemed to think *she* was in charge of party games. She was carrying a big basket when she brought Zeph and Sakura and Dan to the dining hall. There were wrapped packages for prizes, a blindfold, and a big painting of a donkey with a separate droopy wool tail.

'I painted the donkey's bottom,' said Zeph.

They'd all painted me cards too. Zeph had daubed me another donkey eating an enormous orange carrot. He had a speech bubble saying, *Hee-haw Happy Birthday*.

'It says *Hee-haw* – *Hee-haw*, you know, like a donkey!' said Zeph.

He was still damp from a scrubbing in the bath, but his hands were still ghostly grey with paint. He wore a white T-shirt, red shorts and red strappy sandals. He also wore a tartan bow tie on a piece of elastic. He kept snapping it proudly.

Sakura had written her 'Happy Birthday' in lettering so little I could barely read it. She'd drawn me a delicate picture of tiny things: butterflies; rabbits; kittens; dolls; necklaces; fans; small smiley suns. She pointed to each object with her finger, explaining them. She looked beautiful in her Japanese costume. She even had a flower clipped above her ear.

Surprisingly Dan wore flowers too, a long daisy chain round his neck like a garland. He had daisy-chain bracelets and even a daisy-chain anklet. His transparent man had his own daisy chain dangling down past his visible abdomen.

'I've learned how to make daisy chains,' he said

217

unnecessarily. 'I'll make you one for your birthday if you like, Pearl.'

'That would be lovely, Dan, but I've already got my new necklace and my new bracelet. But thank you. Your daisy chains look lovely on you.'

He did look very cute, especially as the flowers looked so incongruous with his blue and white striped dungarees. He'd drawn a picture of himself on his card, his blue stripes added so enthusiastically that he'd poked several holes in the paper. He'd drawn daisies at each corner and a carefully crayoned message: *Happy Burday Purl X X X*.

'Undie said I've spelled it wrong. She said I should have waited and asked her,' said Dan.

'I like it spelled just the way it is,' I said. 'It's a lovely card. Thank you for *all* your lovely cards.'

'Can we start eating now?' said Zeph, eyeing the table.

'We're going to play a few party games first,' said Jodie.

'Oh yes, we've got to pin the tail on my donkey,' said Zeph, clapping his stained hands.

'I've got *much* better games,' said Jodie. 'Take your pick: Ghosts or Murder or the Deadly Dare game.'

'Maybe we'll play your games after tea, Jodie,' said Dad, hurrying into the dining room in his best blue shirt and grey trousers. 'We don't want the little ones getting so over-excited they can't eat their tea.'

So we played Miss Ponsonby's traditional party games first. We all took it in turns to be blindfolded and pin the tail on the donkey. The three little ones tried hard, all of them managing to locate the donkey's big bottom. I could have placed the tail in a perfect position, but I stuck it on the donkey's back so that one of the little ones could win.

Jodie and Harley didn't take the game seriously either. Harley stuck the tail behind the donkey's ear so that he looked as if he'd grown a plait. Jodie stuck the tail underneath the donkey, between its legs, so that it stuck out suggestively. Zeph and Sakura and Dan collapsed with laughter. Miss Ponsonby sighed.

'Now then, Jodie, play the game properly,' said Dad, giving her a nudge.

'I *am*,' said Jodie. 'If you can call it a game. *Now* what happens?'

'That's it,' said Miss Ponsonby huffily. 'Dan's the winner.'

'*I* want to be the winner,' said Zeph. 'It's *my* donkey. I painted it.'

'No, look, I'm the closest, *I'm* the winner!' Dan shouted excitedly. He leaped up and down, his daisy chains bouncing on his chest.

'It's not fair though. *I* pinned the tail on the donkey's bottom too,' Zeph said, clenching his fists.

'I really really really *want* to be the winner,' said Dan, his face crumpling.

'I think *you're* the one getting the children over-excited, Miss Ponsonby,' said Jodie.

'I think we'd better have a donkey race to decide who's the winner,' said Harley. 'OK, I'll be your donkey, Dan. Jump up on my back. Zeph, you have Jodie. And Sakura, you have Pearl. OK, folks, Donkey Derby time.'

Harley lined us up, and then when he shouted, '*Carrot!*' we had to gallop the length of the dining room, hee-hawing at the top of our voices. It was so ridiculous that Harley and Jodie and I could barely stagger for laughing, let alone gallop. Jodie fell off her red heels and collapsed in a heap with Zeph. Harley ran on ahead on his great long legs but Dan dropped his transparent man and insisted they go back to retrieve him. So I galloped past them, light little Sakura on my back, and we won!

Miss Ponsonby gave us both a prize – a little bar of chocolate.

'I want some chocolate too because I was the real winner,' said Zeph.

'I think you'll win the *next* game,' said Harley.

'You've all got a chance of winning. It's Pass the Parcel,' said Miss Ponsonby. 'Sit down cross-legged on the floor.'

'Ooh, I'm beside myself with excitement,' said Jodie, but she sat down willingly enough, though her skirt was way too tight and short for her to cross her legs decently.

Dad had his old CD player plugged in and we started solemnly passing the parcel round and round our circle while Abba sang 'Dancing Queen'. Each time Dad stopped the music, the person holding the parcel had to prise off the sellotape and rip away the paper. Jodie got bored and stood up and started jiggling around to the music as she passed the parcel. Zeph and Sakura and Dan copied her, jumping up and down. Harley stood up too and started doing a weird dance himself, thrusting his arms in the air and kicking his legs out sideways. So I stood up too and bounced a little. It was suddenly becoming the funniest game ever.

Miss Ponsonby frowned at the dancing to start

with, but actually joined in herself. Even Dad did a little twirl every time he started playing the track all over again. Mum was darting in and out with more sandwiches and jugs of orange squash. She looked startled to see us all dancing, but when she realized it was a proper party game, she twitched her hips and did a little step-tap routine as she dashed to and fro.

Sakura was the last one holding the parcel, now reduced to a tiny matchbox. It was crammed with little heart-shaped red sweets.

'That's not fair! Sakura won the last game!' Zeph wailed.

'Hand your sweets round, Sakura, that's fair,' said Dan.

'I don't want to hand them round, they're too pretty. I want to keep them,' said Sakura, snapping them shut in the matchbox.

We gave the boys our chocolate bars to shut them up. Then we played Musical Statues to more Abba, all of us leaping about crazily, circling each table. Zeph hovered beside the tea table, his hand darting out every now and then.

'Now, now, Zeph, don't you dare touch until it's properly tea time,' said Miss Ponsonby.

'Yes, naughty naughty!' said Jodie, whirling past, but her hand darted out too and she secretly fed him several sausages.

Mr Wilberforce and Miss French came strolling in and we all froze, even though Abba went on singing *Knowing me, knowing you.*

Aha-aha!' Mr Wilberforce sang, and he joined in jumping.

Miss French jumped too, though she really

needed a sports bra if she was going to leap so energetically. Then Dad stopped the music and we all froze into statues. Miss Ponsonby judged who moved first. She kindly ignored Zeph's wobbles and Dan's wriggles, trying to catch Sakura out, as she'd won all the games so far. But Sakura was a brilliant statue, standing absolutely still, scarcely even blinking. The boys tickled her but she still didn't move a muscle. She was better than any of us, even Mr Wilberforce. She ended up with her third prize, a tiny thumb-sized white statue of a cherub.

'You can play he's a baby and make him a little cot out of the matchbox,' I said.

'My, all that dancing has given me a raging thirst,' said Mr Wilberforce, mopping his brow with a big hankie. 'Do you think I could pour myself a glass of squash?'

'I've put the kettle on for a nice pot of Earl Grey for the grown-ups,' said Mum. 'It'll be ready in two ticks – and then we can start on the birthday tea. Pearl, dear, you sit in the middle of the bench as it's your party.'

I sat down with Jodie on one side of me and Harley on the other. Zeph and Sakura and Dan sat opposite. Zeph reached out both hands and grabbed a fairy cake in each.

'No, Zeph, *wait*!' Miss Ponsonby hissed.

'What are we waiting *for*?' said Zeph. 'I want my cakes!'

'We're waiting for *another* cake,' said Jodie.

Mum came back into the dining room, proudly carrying a big birthday cake on her best pink glass plate. The cake was covered in white icing with *Happy Birthday Pearl* in swirly pink letters, and a pattern of pink and silver balls and little rosebuds – but Mum had tied a black velvet ribbon round the cake as decoration.

She set it in front of me and lit the candles and then started singing, with Dad conducting.

'Happy birthday to you!'

Jodie and Harley joined in. Zeph and Sakura and Dan sang too. Mr Wilberforce and Miss French sang, his voice very deep and hers very high and warbling. I sat still, my heart thumping, hating all the attention and worried that I wouldn't be able to blow the candles out in one go. I took a deep breath and blew hard and then closed my eyes to make a wish.

I wish Harley and I could see a badger again!

'Why have you got your eyes closed, Pearl?' said Dan.

'Ssh, she's making a wish,' said Jodie. 'She can't tell you or it won't come true.'

'Oh go on, tell, tell!' said Zeph.

'She can't. *I* know, but I know everything,' said Jodie. She smiled at me.

She thought I'd wished my usual wish: *I wish Jodie and I stay best friend sisters for ever and ever.*

I smiled back, but my heart was thumping. She *didn't* know everything about me nowadays. I couldn't help feeling guilty that I'd used my wish on Harley. I argued inside my head that I didn't *need* to say the sister wish because of course we'd stay best friends for ever anyway, no matter what.

'Can I have a wish?' said Zeph. 'I wish it's time to eat!'

'OK, son, tuck in,' said Dad, helping him to sandwiches and then passing the plate to the grown-ups.

They stood around snacking on sandwiches and slices of birthday cake while we sat and ate unsupervised. Zeph was in seventh heaven, steadily lobbing cakes, sausages and sandwiches into his mouth. Dan ate more cautiously, peeling back the bread to examine the contents of every sandwich, and then cutting off small square portions for his transparent man. Sakura concentrated on her slice of birthday cake, delicately nibbling the icing, sucking each silver ball and licking the butter cream.

Harley and Jodie ate steadily, both talking to me at once. I tried to keep track of each conversation and nodded at appropriate moments, feeling as if I was at a tennis match.

'Eat up, birthday girl!' said Mum, darting over to pour more orange squash. 'Do you like the cake, darling?'

'It's lovely.'

'There! And you're enjoying your party, aren't you? I knew you'd have fun playing all the party games,' said Mum happily.

There were more games after tea but these were more of a trial. Mr Wilberforce and Miss French wandered off and Miss Ponsonby went into the kitchen with Mum, discussing cake recipes. Dad was left in charge. He bounced up and down wearing his jolly face, suggesting a game of Musical Bumps.

'Purr-*lease*, Dad, Zeph and Dan have just stuffed themselves silly. They'll be sick if they start jumping up and down,' said Jodie. 'No, we'll play one of my games now. The Deadly Dare Game. OK, Pearl, it's your birthday so you have to go first.

Who's got a dare for Pearl? You have to be willing to do the dare yourself if Pearl can't or won't – and then *she* has to take off an item of clothing.'

'What?' I said.

'This sounds a really intellectually challenging game,' said Harley.

'You shut up. Right, Pearl, I dare you to kiss the boy you like best in this room,' said Jodie.

'*Jodie!* I'm not doing that!' I said.

'No, yuck, don't kiss *me*, I hate kisses,' said Zeph.

'No one in their right mind would kiss you – you've got half your tea all round your face,' said Jodie scathingly. 'Come on, Pearl, get kissing.'

I looked wildly around the room. My eyes swivelled past Harley. I didn't didn't didn't dare kiss him.

'I'll do the forfeit,' I said, and I took off a shoe.

'OK, *I*'ll do it,' said Jodie. She sauntered towards Harley, tapping her high-heeled shoes.

He folded his arms defensively, one eyebrow raised. Jodie stood in front of him, lips in a pout, but then she veered around him and skittered across the floor to Dad. He was squatting down, sorting through his CD collection. She gave him a smacking kiss on the cheek, taking him so by surprise that he keeled over onto his bottom.

'Hey, hey, why the sudden affection?' he said, grinning at Jodie.

'Well, you're a lovely old dad,' said Jodie.

'Your dad isn't a *boy*,' said Dan. 'That's cheating, Jodie!'

'No, it's not. It's my game and I make up the rules and it's only cheating if I say so,' said Jodie. 'OK, Dan, it's your turn next. Dare someone.'

'I dare Pearl to stand on her head,' said Dan.

'That's not fair, choosing me again!' I said.

'It's your birthday, Pearl. Of course we all want to pick you,' said Jodie. 'Come on, stand on your head.'

'No!' I said.

'You can do it,' said Jodie.

'*I* can do it!' said Dan. 'My man can do it too, watch!'

'No, wait, give Pearl a chance,' said Jodie. She gave me a nudge. 'Go *on*. You can stand on your head easy-peasy.'

Of course I could stand on my head – but I was wearing my new short velvet skirt. The ruffles would flap upwards and show everyone my white knickers. I didn't mind about Jodie, of course. I didn't even mind too much about Zeph and Sakura and Dan, though they'd giggle. But I minded terribly about Harley.

'I'm not going to stand on my head,' I said, and I took my other shoe off.

Dad looked up from his CDs. 'This seems a bit of a silly game,' he said.

'No it's not, Dad. It's a great game, if Pearl would just play it properly,' said Jodie. 'Come on then, Dan, stand on your head.'

Dan put his head on the floor and waggled his fat little legs in the air.

'That's rubbish,' said Zeph. 'Look at *me*.'

He did a better headstand and kicked his legs in triumph. Too triumphantly. He fell over with a thump.

'Now look!' said Dad, running to him. 'I *said* this was a silly game.'

'No it's not. I *like* this game,' said Zeph, bouncing

up again. 'I like standing on my head. I'm ace at it. All boys are but silly *girls* can't.'

'I can,' said Sakura. She hitched up her ornate robe and did a perfect handstand, legs together, her toes neatly pointed. She held it steady for several seconds, her face going pink, and then sprang gracefully to her feet. She clapped her hands and bowed.

'That was *quite* good, but mine was better,' said Zeph. 'Now it's *my* turn to think of a dare.' He whirled round and round for inspiration. He looked at the party table. 'I know! Pearl, I dare you to put your head in the bowl of trifle.'

'Don't be ridiculous, Zeph, I'm not doing that,' I said.

'Which is it going to be then, Pearl? Your T-shirt or your skirt?' said Jodie.

'Now, then I don't think we need to go that far,' said Dad. 'Choose another dare, Zeph – that was a daft one.'

'No, it was a brilliant one and *I* dare it,' said Zeph, running to the table.

Dad started running too but he wasn't quite quick enough. Zeph plunged his head ear-deep in the trifle.

'Oh Lordy,' said Dad, seizing hold of him.

Cream and custard and jelly lathered his curls and dripped down his forehead. He wiped his eyes, grinning.

'See! I did the dare!' he spluttered.

Dad picked him up sideways and ran with him kitchenwards. 'Stop the Dare Game this *instant*!' he said.

'I believe it's *my* turn to choose a game,' said Harley.

227

Jodie sighed and rolled her eyes. Harley started explaining how to play Countries. We all had to choose a country and stand on an imaginary world map. Then we had to whirl round while our Earth went spinning. Then Harley shouted, *'Earthquake in Japan'* or *'Monsoon in India'* or whatever, and the afflicted country had to erupt accordingly. Mostly the countries were pitted against each other, but every so often Harley would shout *'Attack by Aliens'*, and then we'd all have to join hands and stand shoulder to shoulder.

I'm sure it could have been a good game, but Jodie kept messing about and Zeph (returned to us totally sluiced down) and Sakura and Dan kept forgetting which country they were, even though Harley made it easy enough for them: Zeph was Africa, Sakura Japan and Dan Britain. The game fell apart without anyone winning.

'My turn to choose the game now,' said Jodie. 'We'll play Murder in the Dark.'

'Definitely not,' said Mum, who had come back into the dining room with Miss Ponsonby to keep an eye on us. Dad was washing up in the kitchen, in disgrace for *not* keeping an eye on Dan. 'We've had enough of your silly games, Jodie.'

'That's not fair, Mum! Murder in the Dark is a proper party game,' Jodie argued.

'I think my children have gone a bit past party games,' said Miss Ponsonby. 'I'd better see them back to their houses now.'

Jodie protested bitterly but I was relieved. Harley sloped off too, carrying little Dan on his shoulders.

'Well, *we'll* still party,' said Jodie, putting the music on loudly.

She seized hold of me and we danced up and down the dining room, round and round until we were dizzy.

'Good party, Pearl?' Jodie yelled.

'This is the best bit,' I panted. 'Just you and me.'

'You funny girl,' said Jodie, but she gave me a hug.

**She disappeared and returned a minute later
with two little badgers.**

16

Jodie and I played together in our bedroom all the next morning.

'You are sooo lucky having me as a sister, Pearl. No one else would play all your pretend games with you. I'm the best at inventing stuff, aren't I?' said Jodie.

We'd resurrected Mansion Towers and were cutting out new cardboard people to live there.

'You're *too* good at inventing. Don't make any of your people murderers or ghosts, will you?' I said.

'No murderers. No ghosts. Nothing scary whatsoever, I promise, Pearly Girly,' she said.

She drew a Victorian man with a smiley mouth. Even his moustache had a cheerful upward twirl.

'He's called Mr Horace Happy and he's just moved into Mansion Towers. He's toddled into the kitchen and seen the cook being horrid to Kezia and

231

Pansy so he's sent her packing. Now Kezia is the cook and she makes Horace ten different cakes every day because he's so greedy. You draw and cut out Kezia and her cakes, Pearl. I'll draw Pansy. Horace has taken *such* a shine to her. He employs little Flossie Floormop and Hettie Hoover to do all the real housework while Pansy just gets to flick her feather duster around the parlour and share Horace's cakes. He buys her a new dress every day so that she looks equally beguiling, and little button boots with very high heels.'

'That's not fair! Why should Pansy get all the new dresses and stuff when she hardly does any work?'

'Because she's extra nice to Horace. I'm sure Kezia could get new dresses too if she'd perch on his knee and feed him his fairy cakes.'

'No, she's not doing any of that!'

'Oh well, Pansy will share her dresses anyway, as they're total best friends. And if you like, Horace can get sooo greedy and eat hundreds of cakes every day until he blows up like a balloon and *bursts*. My, Flossie and Hettie have to labour from dawn till dusk to clear up every little yucky bit of him. But guess what! Old Horace has left all his money *and* Mansion Towers to lucky old Pansy, so she lives there happily ever after with her best friend Kezia, and they *both* have new dresses every day. Get some more paper and get designing the dresses, Pearl – you're better at it than me. But make all Pansy's dresses very low-cut and tight-waisted with very frilly skirts. I'll have a crimson dress and a sky-blue one, and a canary silk and purple velvet for winter.'

Mum looked in on us to see what we were up to.

'I don't know, there's you telling me how grown up you are now you're eleven – yet look at you, cutting out paper dolls! Still, it's good to see the two of you playing so nicely together.'

I'd have been happy to play all day long but Jodie sloped off after lunch. She said she had to take Old Shep for a walk but she was gone a long time.

I played with Mansion Towers by myself for a little while but it wasn't so much fun without Jodie. I started reading *What Katy Did* instead. I raced through the first few chapters. Then I got to the part where Katy is warned not to go on the swing. I started to worry. Katy was such a Jodie-type girl. I knew she'd go on the swing regardless. I knew the ropes would break and she'd fall and hurt herself terribly . . .

I didn't want to read it. I snapped the book shut and slipped out of the back door. I went along the path to the woods and branched off near the badger set. I crept forward, and saw that Harley was already there. He was crouching down with a jar of honey, spreading it all over the leaves and twigs and tree roots. I blinked at him.

'Harley?'

He turned round, smiling. 'Hi, Pearl.'

'Harley, this is such an obvious question, but why are you spreading a pot of honey all over the ground?'

'It's a cunning ploy,' said Harley. 'Badgers *like* honey. If I smear enough around, they'll come out of their set and stay out until they've licked up every morsel.'

'Oh, brilliant!' I said, sitting down cross-legged, looking at the biggest hole expectantly.

'They won't come *now*, Pearl. Not till dusk, probably not till it gets really dark. We have to come back then.'

I fidgeted. 'I'm not sure Mum will let me,' I said, shame-faced. 'She's ever so strict about bed time.'

'Can't you slip out by yourself?' said Harley. He grinned at me. 'I gave you a torch!'

'Yes, I know, but—' I didn't want to tell him I was frightened of going out in the dark by myself.

I wondered about Jodie.

'*Don't* bring Jodie,' said Harley, as if he could read my mind. 'She'll make far too much fuss and noise. *She*'d scare off a herd of wild warthogs, let alone a shy little badger.'

'No she wouldn't,' I said, but I couldn't help giggling. 'I *want* to come on my own, but I don't quite know how I'll manage it. Jodie will want to know where I'm going. I can't just slope off by myself.'

'Why not? *She* does,' said Harley. 'Go on, Pearl, try.'

'All right. I'll try,' I said.

Harley smiled at me. He sat down beside me and offered me the honey jar. We both stuck our fingers in and licked out the remains of the honey companionably.

'Imagine badgers liking honey,' I said. 'I thought they just ate insects and stuff.'

'I think they snaffle up anything tasty. They're keen on peanut butter too.'

'Now you *are* kidding me.'

'No, I read it in a book, honestly. Trust me. I am the Fount of all Knowledge.'

'Is that the badger book or is it *Jude the Obscure*?' I said, pointing to the fat paperback in his jacket pocket.

'No, it's *The Old Curiosity Shop*. I finished *Jude*.'

'You read such hard books, Harley.'

'Dickens is a tonic after Hardy. I'm greatly looking forward to the death of Little Nell.'

'Harley! I *hate* sad books. I can't even read about Katy falling off her swing in *What Katy Did* and yet I know it ends happily. I've had a peep at the end.'

'So you're a fairytale girl. You want happily-ever-after endings?'

'Of course I do!'

'I've never reckoned fairy tales. They always make the ugly guys the *bad* guys. If you're freakily tall, then tough, you're a wicked old giant and any number of young Jacks want to come along and kill you. *You*'re OK though. You're little and pretty and you've got long fairy princess hair, so of course *you*'ll live happily ever after.'

'I'm *not* pretty,' I mumbled, feeling myself going pink.

'You're the prettiest girl in the whole school,' said Harley.

'Well, that's only out of three, and Sakura's only little and you don't like Jodie so you wouldn't pick her even though she's heaps prettier than me.'

'I meant the whole school during term time. And Jodie isn't my idea of pretty – she's too beady-eyed and bouncy. I *do* quite like her actually; she's good fun in small doses, but you're right, I like you much more.'

I wished Harley was a video so I could rewind him saying that again and again.

I chanted, *I like you much more* inside my head all through tea. Afterwards in my bedroom I wrote in my new journal: *Harley is an amazing boy. He is the nicest boy I've ever met. I like him a lot and he likes me too!*

'What's that about Harley?' said Jodie, leaning over and peering.

'Don't peer! This is a *secret* journal,' I said, snapping it shut.

'You don't have any secrets from me,' said Jodie.

'You have lots of secrets so why can't I?' I said.

'Well, I'm older,' said Jodie.

'You had secrets when you were eleven like me,' I said.

'OK, maybe I did, but I'm me and you're you,' said Jodie maddeningly.

I waited until she went to the loo and then I quickly hid my diary at the bottom of my cardboard box of teddies. I whipped my jacket and jeans out of my wardrobe and hid them under my duvet. I got out my new birthday torch and hid that as well, jumping back on top of the duvet as Jodie came back in.

'What?' she said.

'*What* what?'

'You look all funny,' said Jodie.

'I can't help it if I look weird,' I said. I opened Mrs Wilberforce's copy of *What Katy Did*. 'Ssh now, I want to read.'

'Boring!' said Jodie. She lay back and listened to her iPod, dancing her legs in the air. Then she got fed up and went to watch television with Mum and Dad.

I got into my pyjamas and climbed into my over-crowded bed. I read, forcing myself through Katy's long illness and her time spent in her special wheelchair. I wondered if Mrs Wilberforce had read it since her accident. I wondered what she felt about it now. I was almost at the end when Jodie came back, Mum with her.

'Right, girls, get ready for bed,' she said. 'Oh, well done, Pearl, you're all set. Night-night, dear.' She sat down on my bed to give me a kiss and then jumped up again.

'What on earth . . .?' She fished out my torch. My heart started thudding. 'What are you doing with your torch, Pearl?'

'Nothing, Mum.'

'Why is it in your bed?'

My mind went completely blank.

Mum shook her head at me. You were going to read after I put the light out, you naughty girl! You'll strain your eyes.' She took the torch away and put it in my dressing-table drawer. She looked at Jodie. 'You tell me if you catch her reading in the dark, Jodie.'

'Yes, Mum,' said Jodie, saluting. 'The Watch Pearl Patrol is ever alert and ready to report.'

Mum kissed us both and went back to the living room. Jodie shook her head.

'As if,' she said.

'You wouldn't ever tell on me, would you, Jodie?' I said.

'You know I wouldn't!'

'No matter what?' I said.

'Absolutely,' said Jodie, getting undressed. She pretended to be a stripper, humming, 'Da da da

237

daaa, da da da daaa,' as she took off each item of clothing, whirling her bra above her head and rotating her knickers round and round her ankle.

'Idiot,' I said, giggling.

'Why?'

'Because you're acting crazy. Put your pyjamas on.'

'No. Why are you suddenly asking if I'll tell? What are you up to?'

'Nothing,' I said. I yawned elaborately. 'I'm ever so tired. I'm going straight to sleep.'

I lay down and shut my eyes. Jodie went on talking but I kept my eyes closed, not responding. I made myself breathe slowly, in and out, in and out, as if I was already asleep. Jodie gave up after five minutes. I heard her switching off the light and lying down. I waited. She tossed and turned and sighed and pummelled her pillow. But eventually her own breathing slowed. She burrowed deeper under her duvet.

I wasn't absolutely sure she was asleep until I heard her soft snores. I lay still, timing my breath to hers, though my heart was beating hard. I waited another ten or fifteen minutes, and then I sat up and cautiously slid my legs out of bed. I took off my pyjama bottoms and rolled them into a head shape on my pillow. I put on my jeans and pulled my jacket over my pyjama top. I stuck my legs out of bed and stepped into my Wellington boots. It wasn't muddy but I felt they'd give me more protection. I hated the thought of little rodents running round my feet in the dark.

I didn't have time to brush my hair so I tied it

back with a bedraggled ribbon. I was sure Harley wouldn't care what I looked like tonight. It only mattered that I turn up.

I plodded as quietly as I could to my dressing table and pulled the top drawer open. It creaked a little so I had to ease it centimetre by centimetre, but soon it was open enough for me to get my fingers in and find my torch. I gripped it tightly and moved slowly towards the door. Jodie sighed. I stood still, holding my breath, but then she started snoring again.

I got to the door, turned the handle very slowly, and then I was out in the passageway. I saw the light under the living-room door and the murmur of Mum's voice above the television. I made my way swiftly down the passage to the back door. I couldn't really go on tiptoe in my Wellington boots. They made an odd little sucking sound at each step, but the television was on loudly.

I made my way right along the passage to the back door. This was the difficult part. Dad locked and bolted it after we'd settled down for the evening. I prayed he wouldn't go back to check on it when he went to bed. I managed the key in the lock but I was too small to reach the bolt on the door. I wasn't going to give up now. I fetched the stool from the bathroom, clambered onto it and stretched right up. I could just about reach the bolt. I had to push and tug for a minute or more, hurting my fingers, nearly losing my balance and falling off the stool – but at last it gave.

I got down, moved the stool back, and then opened the back door. The fresh night air was a shock on my hot face. It was so dark. The passageway had been dark but I could still see what I was doing. The back yard of Melchester College seemed scarily black in spite of the splash of silver stars in the sky above. I stood with my back against the closed door, longing to rush back inside. But I took a very deep breath, switched on my torch, and went on my way.

The torch was a good one, sending out a strong yellow light so that I could easily see where I was going, but it made the darkness all around seem even denser. It wasn't so bad behind the house, but once I set out along the woodland path I felt terrified. The trees seemed to tower so much taller, a blackly enchanted wood. I heard odd rustlings and tiny cries. They seemed as alarming as jungle roars.

I tried turning the torch in an arc but the swerving light made me dizzy and I kept getting half-glimpses of phantoms: a huge, hideous man who was really the misshapen trunk of a tree; the writhing python that was only a creeper swaying over a branch.

The torch slipped in my hands. I clutched it desperately and forced myself forward, step after step. My Wellington boots were too small for me and were starting to stub my toes. The tops rubbed against my bunched pyjamas. I lost my ribbon in the dark and my hair fell over my face in tangles. I had to press my lips together hard to stop myself bursting into tears. I told myself I was being a ridiculous baby. I wasn't a silly little kid any more. I was eleven years old. I wasn't lost or in dire danger. I was simply out after dark, going to meet my friend.

What if I couldn't find Harley and the badger set? I'd always found him easily enough before, but that was in full daylight. It would be so easy to miss the little windy path that led to the set. There were little paths everywhere. If I took the wrong one, I could get really lost and end up wandering the woods all night long.

I stood at the edge of a path, agonizing over whether it was the right one or not. I thought of calling out to see if Harley was there, but that would frighten any badgers away. I made myself creep forward slowly, looking back over my shoulder every second step so that I could still find my way back – which made me blunder into an overhead branch. It scratched my forehead and pulled my hair horribly as if it had real twiggy fingers. I struggled free, my lips still clamped.

I got to the clearing and shone my torch. There was Harley, crouching beside a tree bole. He waved slightly. I waved back and went to sit close beside him, dousing the light. The sudden dark was immense. He reached out and held my hand. I squeezed his gratefully. We sat there together in the dark. After a minute or so I started to see a little. I focused on the biggest entrance to the set.

We waited. I might have dozed a little every now and then, my head nodding and jerking. Then Harley clenched my hand hard. I saw a snout emerge, then a whole striped head. The badger looked to the left, to the right, seemingly sniffing the air.

He came right out and stood before us, much bigger and stranger and more splendid than I'd realized. He started scratching himself with his long claws. It looked so comical I had to bite my cheeks to stop myself bursting out laughing. Then he stopped, sniffed again, and took several steps forward. He snuffled in the grass, now sticky with honey. Then he started lick-lick-licking.

After a few minutes another snout appeared at the entrance. It was a smaller badger, much more timid. I felt it must be a female. She peered out, retreated, peered again. Then she disappeared and returned a minute later with two little badgers, still cubs. I breathed in joyously, blinking rapidly, as if my eyes were a camera taking photographs. I didn't need real photos. I had the images inside my head for ever.

I'd have sat there all night long, even after all four badgers returned to their set, but around midnight Harley whispered that we should go back.

'You must be tired out, Pearl,' he said.

'I've never felt so wide awake in my life,' I said. 'Let's stay longer, Harley. They might come back.'

'We can come tomorrow, and the next night and the next. You're OK, aren't you, finding your way with your torch? It's not too scary, is it?'

'It's not the slightest bit scary,' I lied.

Perhaps my voice wavered, because Harley insisted on walking me all the way to the back door of Melchester College. The handle turned easily and I slipped inside, waving my fingers at him. It was a struggle relocking the door on the inside but I got the bathroom stool again and managed it. I was on such a high I felt I could rise upwards in the air of my own volition.

242

I tiptoed along the passageway, Wellington boots in my hand in case they left muddy footprints. There was no light under the living-room door now. Mum and Dad were obviously in bed, fast asleep.

Jodie seemed fast asleep too when I crept into our room. She was lying on her side, breathing deeply, not moving. There was just a moment as I got into bed when I thought her eyes were wide open, but it was too dark to be sure. I lay down, hugging myself under the warm duvet, realizing my hands and feet were icy cold. I'd remember socks next time and maybe even gloves . . .

I slept very late the next morning. For the first time ever Jodie was awake before me. She was fully dressed, sorting through the cardboard box of old toys we'd shoved in the wardrobe. The box where I kept my journal.

'What are you looking for?' I said, sitting bolt upright in bed.

'My old rocket,' said Jodie.

She found it wedged at the bottom, under my bears. She waved it around, miming flight.

'I was wondering about giving it to Dan,' she said. 'And you could give these old teddies to Sakura. She'd love them.'

'I suppose,' I said uncertainly. 'But *I* love them.'

'Yes, but you're too old for toys now,' said Jodie. There was a little edge to her voice. She kept her head bent over the box.

'Ooh, what's this doing here?' she said, pulling out my journal.

'Give it here!' I said, leaping up and snatching it from her.

'Don't worry, I don't want to know your silly secrets,' said Jodie.

I wasn't so sure. I wished I could think of a really good hiding place for my journal. I didn't dare write everything in it now. I wrote one small sentence, though I embellished it with stars.

I have such a wonderful secret with Harley!

Jodie was sitting up in bed, arms folded,
waiting for me.

17

I led a weirdly wonderful secret life for the next few weeks. I hung out with Jodie, I played with Sakura, I helped Mum and Dad, I made several shy visits to Mrs Wilberforce – and I saw Harley most afternoons, when we read our books by the badger set.

Harley started keeping a special Badger Watch notebook, writing up each day and night in meticulous detail. He noted every new bedding mound, tuft of hair and pawprint. He even described every trace of badger dung. He drew the badgers in his notebook, carefully shaded accurate portraits. He let me draw them too. I tried to copy his style but I couldn't help giving the badgers humorous expressions. The big male had bushy eyebrows, the female had a smile under her snout, and I drew the two cubs holding paws.

Harley sighed. 'So you'll be calling them Billy Badger and Betty Badger, together with their twin cubs Bobby and Bessie?' he said.

'No! I'll pick much better names,' I said.

Harley smiled at me.

'How do you know they haven't got names for us? They might waffle away in their burrow about Little Soppy Fair Girl,' I said.

'What do they call me then? Great Giant Freak?'

'Of course not. You're Wondrous God Food Provider. They say prayers to you night and morning. Whenever they feel a bit peckish, they grunt, "*God will provide*," and then they go outside their set, and lo, God has indeed been busy with his honey jar.'

The grass around the set was permanently sticky now. I had to watch carefully where I sat down. I stole a jar of honey out of Mum's pantry. Then Harley experimented with a jar of peanut butter he'd bought at the village shop. The badgers licked it up equally enthusiastically.

They didn't come out every night, but somehow those long hours of crouching together watching the entrance of the set were still precious. We even met up once when it was pouring with rain. I got soaked even though I was wearing my jacket. Harley brought an enormous tarpaulin he'd found in one of the Melchester College sheds, and we huddled together under it as if it was our tent.

I hung my jacket outside my wardrobe and pulled my sodden pyjama bottoms off when I got back to the house. I spread them out over the end of the bed, hoping they'd be dry by morning. They were still soaking wet though, and the legs were covered in mud up to the knee.

I got dressed hurriedly, keeping an eye on Jodie, who stayed hunched under her duvet. Mum and

Dad were already up but I dodged them both, my pyjamas a screwed-up parcel in my fist. I got to the bathroom, locked the door, and then ran a bath and leaned over it, trying to pummel my pyjamas clean with soap. I didn't make too bad a job of it, though I had to clean the bath out very thoroughly to get rid of all the muddy scum.

I got back safely intending to drip the pyjamas dry on a hanger inside my wardrobe, but Jodie was sitting up in bed, arms folded, waiting for me. My heart started beating fast. I clutched my pyjamas to my chest as if they were a baby. They started dripping down my jeans.

'Had a little accident?' said Jodie.

I swallowed, going red. 'Yes, actually,' I said. 'Don't tell Mum.'

'Don't tell Mum what, exactly?'

'That I had to wash my pyjamas,' I said, hurriedly hanging them up in the wardrobe and putting a towel under them to catch the drips.

'I see you've wet your jacket too,' said Jodie. 'And my goodness, look at the state of your welly boots. You've had one mighty accident, Pearl.'

I sat down on the edge of the bed, wrapping my arms round myself. My damp jeans dug uncomfortably into my tummy.

'So what have you really been up to?' said Jodie.

'I – I couldn't sleep last night, so I just went for a little walk,' I mumbled.

'As you do, in the pouring rain at midnight in muddy woods,' said Jodie. 'All by yourself?'

'Mmm.'

'Sorry, who are you? You *look* like my sister Pearl but she's scared of the dark.'

'I had my torch.'

'Harley's present. So you could slip out at night and meet up with him?'

'No. Yes! Oh, Jodie, *please* don't tell.'

'I'm not going to tell – but I *should*. What are you playing at, Pearl? I couldn't believe it when you started this lark. I mean, *I* don't think I'd have the bottle. I just can't credit it that you're up for it. You and Harley, of all unlikely people. But what the hell is he playing at? You're only a little girl.'

'No I'm not. What do you mean, anyway?'

'He's got no right to play about with you. Tell him I'll punch his stupid head in if he hurts you in any way.'

'Of course he wouldn't hurt me! He doesn't do anything to me. I never even said I met up with him.'

'Oh yes you do! *Harley and I have such a wonderful secret!*'

'You read my journal!'

'Well, I couldn't help it, you leave it lying around in such stupid places. And I've been worried about you. I didn't know what to say. It's kind of embarrassing. You're too young. You don't do anything really full-on, do you? It is just kissing?'

'What?' I stared at her. 'We don't *kiss*!'

'Well, what do you do then?'

'Promise you won't tell anyone at all. Do you swear?'

'Yes, yes, I swear, I swear,' said Jodie. She said several very rude swear words out loud to be funny but she still looked serious.

I pulled her head close to mine and whispered in her ear. 'We watch badgers.'

'What?' said Jodie, blinking. *'Badgers?'*

'There's a set in the woods. We've seen them lots of times – two adults and two half-grown cubs.'

'Oh, for pity's sake!' said Jodie, starting to laugh. 'You don't have to creep off to the woods to watch badgers. Just sit cross-legged on the lawn, it's heaving with them. Jed's going bananas – they're ruining it all with their earthworks. Oh, Pearl, you are amazing. So that's why Harley gave you that torch! So you could go on your little badger-watching expeditions. Sweet!'

I resented her tone. She was acting like it was a very childish thing to do.

'Lots and lots of people do badger watches and keep notes. Harley started watching in April, that's when all the big watches start. Some are set up so that forty people at a time can watch underground.'

'Oh, wow, fantastic! Forty anoraks huddling together all night watching for dopey Mr Stripy to amble out and have a crap and a scratch for the benefit of his doting public,' said Jodie.

'There's no need to be so snotty about it,' I said. 'I wish I hadn't told you now.'

'Of course you had to tell me. You must always tell me everything,' said Jodie. She nestled up to me. 'So what do you talk about when you and Harley are watching your old badgers?'

'We don't talk. The badgers wouldn't come out then.'

'So you sit there for hours in silence? I'd go crazy!'

'I know. That's why we didn't ask you along too.'

'Oh. So you're saying you would have wanted me along if I'd kept quiet?'

'Yes, of course,' I said, though this wasn't one hundred per cent true.

'So, do you and Harley snuggle up together while you're badger-watching?'

She was teasing again. I glared at her.

'Of course not.'

'Well, Harley's as cuddly as a set of iron railings, I must admit. So you don't even hold hands?'

'No,' I said firmly.

We *had* held hands but I wanted to keep this private.

'Well. I'm glad my little sister's such a good girl,' said Jodie, patting me on the top of my head.

'What about my big sister? Are *you* a good girl?' I said.

Jodie laughed. 'No fear! I'm a very bad girl,' she said.

'Are you a bad girl with Jed?' I dared ask.

'Ah, that would be telling,' said Jodie.

'Well, *tell* then,' I said. 'I know you like him and you do gardening with him, but *you* don't do anything, do you?'

'Like what? We've snogged a bit, that's all.'

'You haven't.'

'Have too,' said Jodie, licking her lips.

'But he's a *man.*'

'Oh, well done, keenly observed, Miss Pearl, Girl Detective. He's not *old* though. He's eighteen. A teenager.'

'He still shouldn't kiss you. That's way way worse than you thinking Harley was kissing me.'

'No it's not,' said Jodie.

'Did he make you?'

'Of course not! No one makes me do anything,

252

you know that. I was mucking around and he was getting irritated and told me to run away and play. I got a bit narked and said I wasn't a kid. He said I was just a silly little schoolgirl. I said, "No, I'm not – come on, give us a snog and you'll see." And he said, "Watch out or I'll do just that," and I said, "Go on then, or are you all talk?" and so he gave me this stonking great kiss. It was just fantastic, you've no idea, but then he pushed me away and said I was a precocious little whatsit and I needed my bum spanked.'

'How horrible! How dare he say that! I hate him.'

'I think I love him,' said Jodie.

'No you don't. You're just playing. You just want him to fancy you. You want *everyone* to fancy you.'

'Maybe,' said Jodie. 'And they do, they do, because I'm so Totally Gorgeous.' She sashayed round the room in her pyjamas, hand on her hip, tossing her head and striking poses. She went to the door on her way to the bathroom. Then she paused.

'I'm going to get every guy in this whole school fancying me. Just you wait till term starts! But don't look so worried, I'll let you keep old Harley.'

I wasn't sure if Jodie was really telling the truth about Jed. I couldn't stand the idea of him kissing her, even though she'd asked him to. I knew I should tell Mum. But then Jodie would get into huge trouble. I couldn't do that to her.

I decided she was probably pretending, the way she often did. Even so, I took to stalking her, wandering round the gardens, peering behind bushes and inside huts, bracing myself in case I discovered Jodie and Jed embracing. But Jed was either working alongside Mr Wilberforce or digging by himself. The one time Jodie was with him he was ordering her about in a lordly fashion, getting irritated with her when she pulled up a flower instead of a weed.

'How do I know whether it's a stupid geranium or whatever? It looks totally weedy to me,' she said, flinging it down on the ground.

'You need glasses, you do. Go on, clear off, you're hopeless,' he said, dismissing her.

We used exactly the same tone when we'd got tired of Zeph and Sakura and Dan tagging along and we wanted to be rid of them. It didn't look as if there was any romance between them whatsoever. But the next day I spotted Jodie squashed up in front of Jed on his garden tractor. They were roaring along at a tremendous pace, zigzagging wildly while Jed let Jodie steer. Jodie was laughing. Now I wasn't so sure.

I asked Harley that evening, on our badger watch. I felt terribly awkward bringing it up.

'Harley, you know Jed,' I whispered.

Harley snorted.

'Do you think there really might be something going on between him and Jodie?'

'I don't know,' said Harley. 'Why don't you ask Jodie?'

'I have. And she says there is. But she would do anyway. I never know whether to believe her or not. I'm worried about it, Harley.'

'I wouldn't worry. Jodie wouldn't fuss so about you.'

'Well, she would, actually,' I said, blushing in the dark.

I'd die if I had to admit that Jodie had given me the third degree over Harley.

'I think Jodie's old enough to watch out for herself,' said Harley.

'Yes, I suppose so. But she can be so mad sometimes.'

'Oh, Pearl. You're driving *me* mad. Do shut up about Jodie. You're making too much noise. The badgers won't come if you keep nattering.'

I shut up altogether, feeling wounded, because I'd been talking in the tiniest whisper. The badgers didn't come out, though we waited till gone midnight. Harley didn't say anything, but I was sure he was blaming me. He didn't understand. He didn't have a sister, a very special sister like Jodie.

I didn't discuss her with Harley any more. I couldn't say anything to Mum or Dad. I found myself blurting things out to Mrs Wilberforce.

I took *What Katy Did* back to her. She gave me a glass of lovely lemonade in a pink frosted glass.

'I made it myself, with fresh lemons and sugar. I used to make gallons of it years ago for Parents' Day, after the staff-versus-pupils cricket match. I served it with cucumber sandwiches.' She sighed. 'But now we don't bother with the cricket match. Half the parents are abroad and the children are collected by chauffeurs, and anyway, I'm not up to catering single-handed. Literally!' she said, holding her one good hand in the air. 'You've no idea how difficult it is to squeeze a handful of lemons when you've only got one hand. I had to hold the lemons steady with my *chin*, as if I was playing a ridiculous party game.'

'Well, it's lovely lemonade anyway. Thank you

very much,' I said awkwardly, my teeth clunking against the glass.

'It's all so much *effort*,' said Mrs Wilberforce. 'Sometimes I wonder if it's worth it. Maybe I'd be better off lying back helplessly, not trying to do a thing. Sorry, I shouldn't moan.' She glanced at *What Katy Did*. 'Cousin Helen would give me a prissy little lecture. What did you think of her? I got so sick of her I wanted to slap her.'

I stared at her in surprise. I'd thought Cousin Helen awesomely saintly.

'She's very . . . good,' I said lamely.

'She's so good she's sickening. All that rubbish about learning to accept pain! Why *should* you? And if you're going crazy with despair and misery because your whole life is ruined, why should you have to try extra hard to be sweet and beautiful and uncomplaining?'

'It does seem very unfair,' I mumbled.

'And then what happens at the end of the book?' Mrs Wilberforce asked me vehemently, as if I'd written it myself.

I shrugged uneasily. 'It all ends kind of happily ever after,' I said.

'And why's *that*?' she demanded.

'Because Katy learns to walk again,' I whispered.

'Exactly! That's what always happens in story-books! Katy learns to walk again. Colin learns to walk again. Ah, have you read *Heidi*?'

I shook my head. 'It's about a girl in the Swiss mountains, isn't it?' I said. 'Does Heidi fall down a mountain and end up in a wheelchair?'

'You read it and see!' said Mrs Wilberforce.

She wheeled herself round the shelves, found the

book and thrust it at me. I jumped nervously and spilled lemonade all down my front.

'Oh dear!' she said.

'I'm sorry,' I said anxiously. 'I'm ever so clumsy.'

'No, no, it was my fault. I can be a terrible bully at times, I know. That's half the reason why I don't teach any more. I did try for a while, when I first used a wheelchair after the accident, but it's left me with such black rages now. I used to rant at the children so. Poor Harold had to wheel me out of the room once or twice. So then I'd rage at him, and yet in many ways he's been a positive saint to me. And I'm raging at you when I've been longing for you to pay me another visit. Now I don't suppose you'll come back any more, and who could blame you?'

I swallowed. 'I'll come back. You can rage at me all you like if it makes you feel better.'

I was trying to be very grown up and serious but she burst out laughing.

'You're a strange little girl, Pearl Wells. In your own way you're just as sparky as your sister. What's she up to now? Is she taking Frenchie's mad mutt for a walk?'

'Well. Maybe.'

'Or is she trailing after Jed?'

I must have looked startled.

'I haven't got much else to do so I crouch behind the curtains and spy on people. It's obvious your sister has got a big crush on our Jed. *Not* a good idea.'

'I know,' I said. 'It's an *awful* idea.'

'That young man's already broken a few hearts in the village. You tell your sister he's bad news.'

'I have,' I said. 'But she won't listen.'

'I hope he doesn't encourage her,' said Mrs Wilberforce. 'Perhaps I'd better have a word with Harold.'

'I think it's mostly Jodie,' I said uneasily.

'Well, she'll soon be able to make friends more her own age when the new term starts,' said Mrs Wilberforce.

I shivered. I didn't want the term to start. I wished it could be the holidays for ever, living this strange dream-like life in the empty Melchester mansion. I was permanently light-headed with lack of sleep, so that I often dozed whenever I sat down. Mum started to worry about the dark circles under my eyes and sent me to bed even earlier. She fussed whenever she caught me yawning.

'Maybe we ought to take Pearl to the doctor,' she said to Dad. 'She seems so dog-tired all the time. I'm really worried about her.'

'I'm *fine*, Mum,' I said quickly.

'Of course she's fine,' said Dad. 'She's bound to feel a bit tired at times with all this lovely country air. It's great to see her going out to play rather than staying cooped up in her room with her nose stuck in a book.' He gave me a quick hug. 'You're growing up, aren't you, Pearly? That's tiring in itself, isn't it, pet?'

'She's still a little wisp of a thing,' said Mum.

'Well, she takes after her mother,' said Dad. He put his big hands round Mum's waist. 'There, I can still circle your waist, easy-peasy.'

'I think *my* waist is the smallest, as a matter of fact,' said Jodie, putting one arm above her head and posing. Her T-shirt slid up, showing her flat tummy. She'd stuck a crystal bead in her navel.

'What in the name of God is that?' said Mum, appalled, thinking she'd somehow sneaked off and got her belly button pierced.

I still didn't always understand Jodie, even though I'd known her all my life. She didn't seem to mind getting into trouble. She acted up deliberately. I wondered how she'd make out in classes in September. Would she be able to do the lessons? Harley had scoffed at Melchester's academic standards, but he was the brainiest person I'd ever met so he wasn't the most reliable judge.

I was sure private school pupils knew masses more than ordinary kids. They did weirdly old-fashioned lessons like Latin and Greek, didn't they? If Jodie didn't understand something, she'd start messing about, and if the teachers cracked down on her, she'd get really cheeky. She'd been excluded twice from Moorcroft Comprehensive for insolent behaviour, though luckily Mum and Dad never found out.

I was anxious about Jodie. I was even more worried about me. Every time I thought about all those posh pupils I felt sick. I wondered how I could ever have fantasized about fitting in with them. They'd look down on me, clonk me with their cellos, hit me with their hockey sticks. I might have been the school swot and teacher's pet at my old school but perhaps I'd come bottom of the class here. I'd never ever be a teacher's pet if the staff were all like Mr Wilberforce and Miss French and Miss Ponsonby, none of whom seemed to like me at all.

Mum and Dad started to get tense as the term approached. Mum pored over her recipe books, multiplying all the ingredients. She costed out each item and had frustrating meetings with Miss French, who seemed to be in charge of kitchen finances.

'Though what the flipping hell does *she* know about kitchen management!' Mum said through gritted teeth. She puffed up her cheeks and put on a posh accent, pretending to be Miss French.

'Oh no, Mrs Wells, silly you, you can't give the children cooked breakfast on a weekday. Much *too expensive! However, we* do *have a tradition of sausages on Sunday at Melchester College. It's considered a special treat for the full-time boarders.'* She swapped to her own voice. 'Two small sausages a *treat*, for pity's sake! And she won't let me cook them proper chicken – oh no, it's that nuggety nonsense where you're paying twice as much per portion for a tenth of the nutrients. Does she want all the kids to get ill?'

Dad had an easier time with Mr Wilberforce, but as the weekend approached when the first boarders were arriving, he got increasingly harassed, running backwards and forwards on last-minute errands, his new shirt damp, his new jeans crumpled. He jangled as he ran, a big bunch of keys swinging from his waist.

'Mind out, girls, Superman has to speed forth,' he said, panting up the stairs. 'I've got to clear a space in the attics for all the blessed trunks now.'

Jodie punched me hard on the shoulder as Dad charged off.

'Ouch! That hurt! What's up with you?' I said irritably.

'Come on, wake up, slowcoach!' said Jodie. 'Didn't you see those keys? Don't you get it? What are those keys *for*?'

'The attic rooms. Half of them were locked,' I said.

'Yeah, yeah, and what *else* was locked?'

'The door to the tower!'

'Yep! At last!' Jodie seized me by the shoulders. 'This is our chance to get up there, Pearl.'

'How? Are we going to ask Dad?'

'No, of course not. He'll say we're not allowed there – he'll make out it's dangerous or something.'

'Well, maybe it is. Mrs Wilberforce fell and broke her neck!'

'We'll be fine. If the stairs have all crumbled away, then we'll just *look*. Oh, Pearl, this is our one chance to get up into the tower. It's been spooking me ever since we got here. We *must* give it a go.'

'*Why*, if it's so scary?'

'I love being scared,' said Jodie, eyes glittering. 'OK, I know *you* don't like scary things. I'll go on my own. Only I don't think I'll be able to reach that bolt, so maybe I'll have to get Harley to come along.'

'Then I'll come too,' I said, as she knew I would.

'Try this one!' I said.

18

I wondered how Jodie was going to get the key from the bunch dangling from Dad's belt. She could be very light-fingered at times but I didn't see how she could possibly wiggle one key off a key ring – and anyway, how would she know which one to take?

'I'll figure something out,' she said.

Dad was busy rehanging a warped door in one of the attic rooms, a difficult heavy job in that close musty air. He came back downstairs covered in dust, hot and sweaty.

'Coo, Dad, you pong a bit,' said Jodie as she gave him a hug. 'You'd better go and have a bath before tea, eh?'

'Mmm, it'll ease my back. It's killing me,' said Dad.

He went off like a little lamb, stripped down to his underpants and ran a hot bath. Mum was safely in the kitchen making cheesy baps.

Jodie grinned at me triumphantly. 'OK, let's go for it!' she said.

She ran into Mum and Dad's bedroom and snatched the whole bundle of keys from Dad's belt. She wrapped them in his T-shirt to muffle them and then we made a run for it. We had to go through the kitchen, but Mum was looking into the oven.

'Don't go off gallivanting. Tea's ready in five minutes,' she said, forcing her lips into a funnel and blowing cool air up her hot face.

'Yeah, yeah, we're just on an errand,' said Jodie.

'Back in a minute, Mum,' I gabbled.

We shot past her, up into the dining room. Miss Ponsonby and the three littlies were already there. Jodie bunched Dad's T-shirt to her chest and we ran past.

'Where are you going? Can me and my Man come too?' asked Dan, unhooking his fat little legs from the bench.

'I'm coming,' said Zeph.

'And me,' said Sakura.

'No no no, this is big girls' stuff,' said Jodie. 'Stay there, little squirts.'

They muttered crossly but stayed where they were. She had far more authority over them than their Undie.

We dashed up the great stairs in the main hall, up and up to the top floor.

'How will we get the cupboard shifted?' I asked.

'We'll do it ourselves,' said Jodie.

I wasn't sure we could possibly manage it no matter how we heaved and pushed, but wondrously Dad had left it half tugged out as he still wasn't finished working in the attics. We went up the stairs and along the long corridor. I was wheezing from the dust. I should have been hot from all the running, but I saw there were goose pimples on my arms.

'We can't,' I whispered as we got near the door at the end.

'Yes we *can*,' said Jodie.

'No, I mean we can't reach the bolt without Harvey. It's too high up.'

'He'll have to open it for us later. We haven't got time to go up the tower now. We're just going to get the door open, stupid, while we've got the keys.' She drew them out of the T-shirt and jangled them in my face. The noise sounded horribly loud. I flinched away from the keys as if they were attacking me.

'Baby!' said Jodie.

I saw *her* hands were shaking as she fumbled with the keys, trying this one and that in the locked door to the tower. The large ones were too big, the little ones too small.

'Oh God, this is ridiculous. We haven't got time to try them all,' said Jodie, sorting through them wildly.

'Try this one!' I said, selecting a stout old-fashioned iron key that didn't match any of the others.

Jodie tried it. It fitted perfectly! It was very stiff though. Her knuckles went white as she tried to twist it.

'Careful! It might snap off altogether,' I said.

'You do it then if you're so clever,' she snapped.

So I tried, pushing the key in harder and giving it a little jiggle so that suddenly it connected and turned with a click.

'You beauty!' said Jodie. 'We'll come back after tea, and bring Harley with us, OK?'

I put my hands flat on the door, as if I was trying to keep it shut for ever. I sensed the darkness on the other side of the thick wood. I could feel how cold it was through the cracks.

'Let's lock it up again,' I whispered.

'Don't be silly.'

'I'm not. I've just got this horrible feeling. *Please* don't let's go up there, ever.'

'You're just playing at being scared, Pearl,' said Jodie, gathering the keys into the T-shirt. 'Come on, we've got to get these back before Dad gets out of his bath.'

'I feel awful *here*,' I said, clutching my tummy.

'You're just hungry, idiot,' said Jodie.

'No, I'm serious. It's a feeling of *dread*,' I said earnestly, nearly in tears. 'I'm sure something terrible's going to happen.'

'Look, I'm the one who makes up the spooky stories,' said Jodie. 'Well, *I'm* definitely coming back after tea. You don't have to come if you don't want to, Pearl.'

We got the keys back to Dad's bedroom with seconds to spare, just as he came padding out of the steamy bathroom with a big towel tied round his waist. He stuck out his tummy.

'Me Big Chief Wobble Belly,' he said, thumping it.

'Dad! You're so gross,' said Jodie.

'Me want cheesy baps for tea,' said Dad.

'Me too, me too,' said Jodie.

'Me too,' I echoed, though I was in such a state I could hardly eat anything, even though Mum's baps were hot from the oven and crisply golden with

266

melted cheese. She'd made egg mayonnaise and tomato salad too. There was a rhubarb fool with sugar shortbread biscuits for pudding, all my favourites, but I could only manage a mouthful.

Jodie sidled up to Harley on the bench, whispering in his ear. His eyes opened wide. He peered along at me. I nodded.

Zeph started messing about with his shortbread, putting two sticks into his mouth to make vampire fangs. He pretended to bite Sakura and Dan. They shrieked half-heartedly, not really scared. I made out I was scared too, to be obliging. I *knew* I was playing at being scared of Zeph. The feeling I had about the tower room was real, no matter what Jodie said.

As soon as Undie herded the three littlies out of the dining room, Jodie, Harley and I cleared the dishes into the kitchen for Mum and then ran off.

'Don't you be long now, Pearl. You're having an early night tonight,' Mum called. 'You're looking really peaky, pet.'

I smiled at her wanly and followed the others. Miss French and Mr Wilberforce were lurking in the big hallway. We couldn't go upstairs in front of them so we had to hang around while they talked endlessly about this and that. Miss French made a big fuss of Jodie, telling her she had a brilliant future career as a dog-trainer because Old Shep was so much more relaxed and obedient now.

Mr Wilberforce must have thought I felt neglected because he told me how much my little visits meant to his wife. It made me feel dreadful because I didn't visit her very often, and when I did, I just seemed to upset her. I wondered what she'd say if she knew we were about to go up to the tower room. I'd promised her we'd never go there. I couldn't help shivering.

'Goodness, Pearl, you can't possibly be *cold*,' Miss French said briskly. 'Maybe you need a good long run as well as Old Shep – get that circulation going.'

I knew why Mum found Miss French so irritating.

'You could do with taking up running too, Harley. You need to put a bit of beef on, broaden out a little,' she said. 'You're *such* a string bean.'

Harley's lips flicked in the briefest smile. I wanted to slap Miss French. We didn't make personal remarks about her grey hair or her wrinkles or her general dumpiness. I couldn't work out why Mr Wilberforce always gazed at her as if she was a film star.

They stumped off together eventually. We all breathed out deeply, sticking out our bottom lips and blowing up our nostrils.

'God, I thought they'd stay rabbiting all evening,' said Harley. He looked at us. 'So, let's go!'

We hurried up the stairs, Jodie and Harley racing ahead of me. I couldn't seem to get my breath. They were ducking behind the cupboard out of sight by the time I'd started down the corridor. I hung back, tempted to sidle back down the stairs to the safety of my bedroom. Then Jodie called me. Well, it had to be Jodie, though her voice sounded ghostly and muffled.

'Is that you, Jodie?' I called anxiously.

'No, my child . . . I am the poor melancholy wraith who haunts the tower . . . the sad white whispering woman—'

'*Stop it!*' I shrieked.

'Well come on, stupid,' said Jodie in her own voice, putting her head round the back of the cupboard.

She reached out her hand. I seized hold of it and she pulled me through, into the stale strange air of the past. We stumbled up the stairs together. Harley was already at the end of the corridor, stretched to his full extent, jabbing at the bolt. He gave a sudden grunt, and then a yelp of triumph.

'Come on, Pearl!' Jodie said. 'He's done it!'

She ran full tilt along the corridor, her footsteps loud and clattering. I imagined all the locked doors opening, and all the Melchester inhabitants frowning out at me, furious because I was disturbing their peace. I saw the four crumbly monkeys crawling out into the corridor, leaving a little trail of withered rubber in their wake.

I rushed after Jodie, terrified of being left on my own.

'OK!' she said.

Harley went to turn the handle but she slapped his hand out of the way.

'No, it's *my* tower!' she said. 'Let me, let me!'

Harley sighed, raised his eyebrows and gave her a little bow. 'After you, madam,' he said sarcastically.

Jodie reached out and turned the handle. She opened the door very, very slowly and then peered inside.

'What can you see?' I whispered.

'Nothing!'

'There must be something!'

'No, really, I can't see anything, it's pitch black. Give us your torch, Pearl.'

I gave it to her. My hand was shaking and I think hers was too, because she nearly dropped it. She fumbled, caught it, and then clicked on the light. She opened the door wider and shone the torch around.

There was still nothing much to see – a little round room with a small spiral staircase leading upwards. There was no furniture, but a pile of rubble littered the floor. Jodie stepped inside.

'Be careful! Watch the floorboards!' I begged her.

'It's fine – solid, look,' said Jodie, stamping her high heel. 'Come in, you guys.'

Harley held out his hand to me. I gripped it tightly and we stepped inside too. It was smaller than I'd thought, as if the brick walls were closing in on us. Jodie swung the torch wildly round and round, making me dizzy.

'Keep it still, Jodie!'

She shone it straight in my eyes. I ducked, turning my head, and saw something glinting at the edge of the floor. I bent down and edged it out of the rubble. It was a silver brocade shoe with a pointed toe. The heel had snapped right off so that the toe curved upwards in my hand.

'What have you found, Pearl? Treasure?' said Jodie, shining the torch at me again.

I blinked, tears brimming and then spilling down my cheeks.

'Are you crying? Don't be silly, Pearl, it's only an old shoe,' said Jodie.

'It's not any old shoe. I think it must have been Mrs Wilberforce's shoe. When she fell down the stairs . . .'

'Oh God,' said Jodie, coming forwards. She peered at the shoe, examining it. 'There's no blood on it.'

'Shut *up*.'

'So she fell down *these* stairs?' said Harley, his hand on the narrow rail.

'Let's go up then!' said Jodie.

'No!' I said.

'Pearl's right. The stairs obviously aren't safe,' said Harley.

'OK, you two stay here. I'm going up. I've got to see the tower room!'

Jodie started clattering up the narrow stairs, shining the torch in front of her.

'*Test* the steps first, idiot,' said Harley. 'Or do you want to end up in a wheelchair too?'

'Shut up, Mr Boring,' said Jodie, but she slowed down a fraction, tapping twice on each step, as if she was performing a little dance routine.

Harley stood at the bottom of the steps, waiting in case his extra weight made the spiral buckle and pull away from the wall. Jodie went up and up and up, her taps getting softer and softer.

'I should have made her let me go first,' said Harley.

'Never!' Jodie called down.

She already sounded a long way away. She had the torch with her so it was pitch dark in our windowless room. It was very cold and damp and smelled sour. Harley reached out and felt for my hand.

'I think I'd better go up after her. You stay here, Pearl,' he said.

I wasn't sure which I dreaded most, climbing all

those rickety dangerous stairs or staying down here by myself in total darkness.

'I'll climb up too,' I said.

'Oh, wow! I'm here! Wait till you see!' Jodie called all the way down.

'Shine your torch down so we can see what we're doing,' Harley called back.

'What? Wait!'

There was a terrible bumping rattling sound.

'Jodie!' I yelled.

It was only the torch, which she'd thrown down the stairs. It landed with a thump, rolling over and over, the light flashing madly.

'My birthday present!' I said, snatching it up. The plastic had cracked but the light bulb still shone brightly.

'Is it OK? Don't worry, I can get you another one,' said Harley. 'Is she *crazy*? You don't fling torches around like that.'

'She doesn't think,' I said. 'Come on then. Do you want to go first, Harley?'

'I'll go behind you, and then if you trip, I'll catch you,' said Harley. 'Let me have the torch. I'll shine it for you. You just keep your eyes on what you're doing and hang onto the rail like grim death.'

He took the torch and aimed it upwards. I held onto the rail and started climbing. The steps were awkward and narrow and quite slippery even though I was wearing my rubber-soled sandals. I had no idea how Jodie had bounded up in her high heels.

I climbed up and up and up. The tower seemed as tall as a church steeple. Jodie kept calling down to me impatiently, telling me to hurry up. Harley encouraged me from behind, insisting I take my time. He kept the torch shining steadily. When I was nearly at the top, I saw great chunks of plaster had been wrenched from the wall. The staircase wobbled precariously, not properly attached.

'Oh God, we're mad,' said Harley. 'I think we'd better go back down – *slowly.*'

'Don't go *down* again! You're nearly there. Come on, come on,' Jodie urged. 'You can't give up now!'

'Let's go right up, Harley,' I said helplessly.

I edged upwards, holding my breath at each step – and then at last I looked up and saw the tower room above me in the flickering light of the torch. Jodie's head appeared at the top of the staircase. She seized my arms by the elbows and pulled. I stepped up, into the tower room.

It was like stepping into a fairy tale! We didn't need the torch up here. We could see dimly in the twilight shining through the lozenge-shaped leaded windows. There was a soft Persian rug on the floor, patterned with birds and roses. Tapestry wall-hangings were pinned all round the room, with woven castles and pale people with tall hats and long pointy feet. There were gold-framed paintings too, of women in dark velvet gowns with long wavy hair falling about their shoulders. Bookshelves ran around the walls, with big red and white gift books with gold lettering on the spines. There was even a rose velvet sofa covered with soft shawls and cushions. It was small, but even so it must have been a terrible struggle to get it up that precarious winding staircase.

I walked on tiptoe as I circled the room. I felt like a terrible intruder. This was Mrs Wilberforce's room – not the sad married lady, bitter and depressed; this was a young girl's secret room, beautiful and romantic.

Jodie snatched up an embroidered shawl and draped it over her shoulders, starting to do a gypsy dance.

'Put it *back!*' I said.

'It doesn't matter. No one comes here any more. It's my room now because I found it, so these are all *my* things, and this is *my* shawl,' she said, stamping her feet with a flourish.

'Carry on like that and we'll all go through the floorboards,' said Harley.

Jodie took no notice, holding the shawl out in either hand and flapping her arms, so it looked as if she had fringed wings.

'If someone crept into your bedroom and declared they'd discovered it and so it now belonged to them, I take it you'd have no objections?' said Harley. 'You'd be quite happy if they wore all your clothes and stomped around in those stupid red shoes?'

Jodie flapped the shawl at him contemptuously, bullfighter fashion.

Harley shone the torch in her face.

'Don't, you're blinding me!' she snapped.

'What's that on your arms?' said Harley.

'Oh, ha ha.'

'No, look – it's all on your shoulders too. I'm not kidding.'

Jodie peered. 'Yuck! What is it?'

It looked as if she was wearing grey lace. It patterned her bare arms and her T-shirt. She rubbed it tentatively and it smeared.

'It's just dust from that stupid old shawl,' she said, shaking it vigorously.

'Just dust?' said Harley. He lowered his voice. 'Maybe it's the Curse of the Tower Room manifesting itself. You're going grey all over, and soon you'll start withering—'

'Don't, Harley!' I said.

'He doesn't frighten *me*,' said Jodie, but she dropped the shawl on the Persian rug. She gave it a little kick and then marched over to the window.

'Look! Just look at the view: you can see for miles,' she said, pressing against the latticed glass. 'I can see all the way over the hills to Galford.'

'No you can't,' said Harley. 'It's in the other direction and it's too dark to see anything properly.'

'I'm like a cat, I can see in the dark,' said Jodie. She bent her head. 'I can see right down down down all the way to the ground – and whoops, I spy with my super-sharp feline eye a little mouse peering up at me, his nose twitching anxiously.'

'Don't lean on the glass like that, Jodie. It's so old it might easily fall out and then *you*'ll go down down down and squash your harvest mouse flat,' said Harley.

'You're such a worry-wuss,' said Jodie. 'Look at the tops of the trees! You could kid yourself you could step from one to the other, all the way to the hills. I've always wanted to be able to fly. Remember my rocket, Pearl? I wanted Dad to make me a rocket to whiz me up to the moon, Harley. Maybe I don't *need* a rocket. Maybe I could just launch myself, one giant leap, and then I'd ride on the wind.'

She raised her arms as if she was going to step

straight out of the window. I snatched a handful of her T-shirt, pulling her back.

'It's OK, Pearl! I'm only kidding!' she said, but I still clung to her.

I didn't let go of her until we were safely back down the spiral stairs and out of the tower altogether.

'How do you know *Harley*?' said the girl
standing next to me.

19

The pupils started arriving on Saturday. Melchester was a small school and only half the pupils were boarders but it still felt as if we were besieged by a vast foreign army. We'd got so used to having the run of the place but now we were horribly restricted. There were lots of new teachers and a proper matron, a large woman who wore such efficient corsets she seemed as firmly plump as a sofa. She was firm in manner too, telling us what to do in a very no-nonsense voice. She didn't cajole the little ones ineffectually, like Undie. She threatened them with a 'good spanking with my hairbrush' and we weren't entirely sure she was joking.

Even the cleaning ladies from the village ordered us around. There were two, a middle-aged woman, Mrs Colgate, and her eighteen-year-old daughter, Tiffany. They were both blonde and plump, but unlike Matron they let it all hang loose. Mrs Colgate wore low-slung jeans, her fat tummy swelling over the waistband. Her protruding navel was clearly visible through her T-shirt. I couldn't look at it because it made me feel queasy. Tiffany wore tiny denim skirts that showed her knickers when she bent over. She had a blue butterfly tattoo on her big white thigh.

When they came to work the day before term started, Mum made them a pot of tea and everyone seemed friendly at first, but when Mum started telling them exactly how she wanted her kitchen cleaned in the future, Mrs Colgate took offence.

'Are you insinuating it was dirty when you came here?' she said.

'I'm not insinuating anything, I'm stating a plain fact. It was downright filthy. I've scrubbed it up to standard now, and I want you to keep it spotless. I prepare my food here. This is a health and safety issue,' said Mum.

Mrs Colgate blew a very rude raspberry. 'The kitchen's your territory, Mrs Wells. *You* blooming well keep it scrubbed. Tiff and I have got the whole school to get round. I've been cleaning here for the last ten years and no one's found fault yet. Just who do you think you are?' she said, folding her arms belligerently.

'I'm the catering manager,' Mum said in her poshest voice. She stuck her chin in the air. 'And that means I'm senior to a cleaner, so stick that in your gob, you dirty mare,' she added, in quite a different tone.

Mum would have been *outraged* if Jodie or I had said that. It was a moment of triumph for Mum, but it meant that Mrs Colgate and Tiffany were our deadly enemies now.

They caught Jodie and me trying to slip up the stairs to the attics.

'Where do you think you girls are going? Those stairs are out of bounds,' said Mrs Colgate.

'They're not out of bounds to us. We live here,' said Jodie.

'This isn't part of your flat, missy. You've no right to be here. Now scoot back to where you belong,' said Mrs Colgate.

'You can't make us,' said Jodie.

'Give me any more of that lip and I'll report you to Mr Wilberforce,' Mrs Colgate threatened.

'See if we care. He's our *friend*,' said Jodie – but she backed down all the same.

We weren't quite so sure he was our friend now. We were used to seeing him in his gardening clothes – his old checked shirts and baggy corduroy trousers and funny floppy sunhat – but now term had started he wore striped shirts and a blazer and grey flannels, striding around in a lordly fashion in highly polished shoes. Some of the teachers didn't even call him Mr Wilberforce. They called him 'Headmaster' in deferential tones, as if it meant *Your Majesty*. Mr Wilberforce still nodded kindly when he saw us and he always gave Jodie a special wink – but we didn't want to try our luck.

Miss French was different too, nowhere near as jolly, dashing around with a clipboard, her reading glasses stuck in her hair like an Alice band. She didn't have so much time for Jodie now. There were a whole *troop* of children eager to take Old Shep for a walk. Miss French chose Jodie if she got there first, but she often wasn't quick enough and some other child had run off with him. Old Shep lapped up the attention, barking joyously at everyone, especially if they fed him treats.

'He's a silly old mutt,' said Jodie. 'I'd got him so well trained. He was even starting to do tricks for me, turning round and lying down, playing Dead Doggie, but now he's got distracted. He'll go off with anyone if they give him crisps or biscuits. It's mad to feed him rubbish like that. He'll blow up like a balloon. I keep *telling* Frenchie, but she won't listen.'

Jodie still spent time with Jed whenever she could, though lots of the older girls vied for his attention too.

'They are so pathetic, that Anna and Sophia and Rebecca,' said Jodie fiercely. 'They just hang around Jed, getting in the way, batting their eyelashes at him, going giggle giggle giggle. *Oh, Jed*, they chorus, over and over. Anna calls him "The Jedi". Honestly. She doesn't seem to get it that he's not the slightest bit interested in her.'

I listened anxiously. Jodie didn't seem to get it that Jed wasn't the slightest bit interested in her either. The only girl I'd seen him staring at was horrible Tiffany Colgate.

Jodie wasn't interested in any of the boys in her new class, as Mrs Wilberforce had hoped.

'They're awful!' she said, after that first day of school. 'Childish, ugly, nerdy, snotty, pathetic and *stupid* too. Thick thick thick.'

'Harley's in your class. He's not any of those things,' I said.

'Childish, ugly, nerdy, snotty, pathetic,' said Jodie, counting on her fingers. 'But he's not thick, I'll grant you that. The other boys really are though, truly. That's why they're still here. They're supposed to be getting special tuition to pass this Common Entrance thingy so they can go to a *really* posh school, but some of them can barely read and write. They've got all these weird fancy names for their so-called conditions, but they're basically thick.'

'What about the girls?'

'They're idiots too,' said Jodie. 'They're hopeless. It's awful that they're all so much younger than me. They think they're dead sophisticated but they're incredibly babyish. And their *voices*! They're just so *fwightfully* silly, squeal squeal squeal squeal. God, it's totally doing my head in and I've only had their company for one *day*. I'm not going to survive a week!'

She threw herself on the bed in mock despair. We were both in school uniform now – grey skirts and white blouses. Jodie had done her best to customize hers, shortening her skirt and rolling up her shirt sleeves, with her grey and red striped tie casually knotted on her chest. She couldn't do anything about her school shoes though, terrible conker-brown flat lace-ups. Jodie waved her thin legs in the air, making her shoes do comical Charlie Chaplin sideways steps.

'This is all such rubbish,' she said, sighing. 'I wish we'd never come here. I'd give anything to be seeing all my mates again. Marie and Siobhan and Shanice.'

She'd conveniently forgotten that they'd all broken friends with her. I flopped down on the bed beside her, peering at her anxiously.

'Don't look so worried, Pearly. We've still got each

other, eh,' said Jodie. 'Who needs any of these posh-nob creeps?'

I kept quiet.

'All right, Harley's not *too* bad. He can be fun at times, when he's not showing off. And the little kids are quite sweet, especially funny old Dan. But all these others are enough to drive you insane.' She gently pulled one of my plaits. 'Was it awful for you too, Pearly?'

'Mmm,' I said into her pillow.

'So your little lot are as bad as mine?'

'Mmm,' I repeated.

I was lying. I didn't dare tell Jodie but I'd had such a wonderful day. I'd been so scared when I had to go to the Year Seven classroom after breakfast. I was sure they'd all hate me. I just didn't have the knack of making friends. I wouldn't be able to think of a thing to say. Maybe it would be better to keep quiet. Everyone always sniggered or groaned when I answered a question in class at my old school. They called me the Snottyswot, the Nerdybrain, the Poncy Teacher's Pet. I was used to being pinched or pushed in class and in the corridors, though when Jodie was still in the Juniors, no one dared touch me in the playground because she'd knock them flying.

I got to the classroom early, hoping to grab a seat right in the front, the safest place. Harley was lounging by the door, looming way above everyone else. I hadn't had a chance to talk to him at break-fast. I'd been in such a state I hadn't been able to stomach the smell of Mum's vast vats of baked beans. I'd nibbled a slice of dry toast alone in our own kitchenette.

'Hi, Pearl,' said Harley, trying to sound nonchalant, though it was difficult with everyone staring at us. 'I just wanted to make sure you were OK. Jodie said you didn't feel well.'

I swallowed. 'I'm fine,' I mumbled.

'Good. Well, see you around after school?'

'Yes!'

'I'll come and find you. Hope it goes well today. See you.' He waved his long fingers at me and sloped off down the corridor towards the senior classrooms.

'How do you know *Harley*?' said the girl standing next to me.

She had very short plaits with lots of wisps, and freckles all over her snub nose. She was only a little bit taller than me and she had a very friendly gap-toothed grin. She really didn't seem at all scary.

'Harley's my friend,' I said proudly.

'But he's in Year Eight,' she said.

'I know.'

'So do you know Harley outside school then?'

'Well. He was here during the summer. And I was too,' I said.

All the other girls were crowding round, listening. There was one girl who was crying, her eyelids very red and puffy. She clutched a sodden hankie and mopped at her runny nose ineffectually.

'What's the matter?' I said.

She just sniffed, knuckling her eyes.

'That's just Freya. She always cries, every single term. She'll get over it,' said a very pretty fair girl with a posh, precise voice. She put her arm round Freya's shaking shoulders. 'Come on, Freya, don't drip all over the new girl. What's your name?' she asked me.

'Pearl.'

'Oh, that's beautiful. I love jewel names. I used to be friends with a girl called Garnet at my old school,' said the wispy girl. 'I'm Harriet. My friends call me Harry.'

'I'm Clarissa,' said the pretty girl. 'We're all boarders; we share a bedroom. How come you were boarding in the holidays, Pearl? Are your parents abroad?'

'No, they're here. They work here.'

'What? You mean they're teachers?'

'No.' I took a deep breath. 'My mum's the catering manager.'

They looked blank.

'She's the cook.'

Clarissa raised her eyebrows.

I stuck my chin out, suddenly brave.

'She's a brilliant cook, just you wait and see what your lunch is like,' I said. 'And her cakes are awesome.'

'Oh, will she make *us* cakes?' said Harriet. 'So what about your dad? What does he do?'

I considered saying he was the site manager. I decided it was pointless.

'He's the caretaker,' I said.

'Oh, so he's that lovely man who took my trunk. He's so funny – he pulled my plaits and called me Polly Pigtails,' said Harriet.

'Oh yes, that's Mr Wells. He gave me his hankie,' Freya sniffed. 'He's ever so kind.'

'Yes, that's my dad,' I said proudly.

'My trunk was *so* heavy no one could budge it but

286

your dad lifted it right up,' said a tall black girl with wonderfully complicated plaits all over her head. 'He called me Polly Pigtails too.'

'You always bring heaps too much stuff, Sheba; you're hopeless,' said Clarissa. She paused, looking at me again. 'So, is Harley your boyfriend?'

'No!' I said.

'Clarissa's got a boyfriend – Jeremy Mendleson. He's in Year Eight too,' said Harriet.

'I think I'm getting a bit fed up with him actually,' said Clarissa, wrinkling her nose.

'Have you got a boyfriend, Harriet?' I asked.

'No, they all tease me and say I'm too little.'

'They all say I'm too *big*,' said Sheba. 'But I don't care. I mostly can't stick boys.'

'I can't stick them either,' said Harriet. 'They're so *silly*.'

'Mmm,' said Freya, blowing her nose.

'Yes, maybe I won't bother getting a new boyfriend,' said Clarissa, glaring down the line at a group of boys at the end. They were making silly belching noises and fighting duals with rulers, proving our point.

'You don't like boys, do you, Pearl?' asked Harriet.

'No. Except for Harley,' I added quickly.

'So you hung out with Harley all the holidays?' said Harriet. 'What did you guys do together?'

I wished I could tell her. I knew she'd have been impressed. But I smiled mysteriously instead, shrugging my shoulders.

I couldn't believe they were all being friendly to me, even Clarissa. I was still worried about school time though. Who would I sit next to? Would the lessons be very different? I'd always been top at my old school, but perhaps I'd be bottom here. Clarissa and Sheba and Harriet and even weepy Freya seemed such bright, intelligent girls. They probably knew heaps more than me.

Our teacher was called Mrs Lewin. She was surprisingly young and pretty with dark hair falling past her shoulders and little rings on every finger. I thought she might even be one of the students at first. She came clacking along the corridor in pointy boots, saying hello to everyone in the queue. She put her arm round Freya and gave her a little hug. She gave *me* a little hug too.

'So you're my new girl, Pearl. I do hope you'll enjoy being at Melchester. Now, who would you like to sit next to?'

I ducked my head shyly.

'Can she sit next to me, Mrs Lewin?' Harriet said.

I felt my face go pink. 'Oh please, yes, can I sit next to Harriet?' I said.

'You can call me Harry because we're friends now,' she said.

I was friends with Harry; I was friends with Sheba and Freya and even Clarissa. By the end of lessons I was friends with all the girls in my class. I knew all the boys' names and quite liked Joseph and Haroon, two quiet boys who enjoyed reading. There were only fifteen of us in the whole class so it was easy to get to know everyone.

I realized I couldn't be top of our class. Haroon was incredibly clever and Sheba was absolutely brilliant at maths – but I seemed to do the best in English and history. We had a wonderful double lesson about the Victorians and then Mrs Lewin

288

told us to write a story set in Victorian times, trying to get all the details correct. Most of the girls wrote about being grand ladies in crinolines, but I wrote about Kezia and Pansy. I got so carried away I wrote pages and pages and pages.

Harry leaned over and peered. 'You're writing like an entire *novel*,' she said.

'I'm sorry,' I said anxiously. I never dared write much at my old school because the others only ever wrote two sides, and that was in very big writing, three or four words per line. You were considered a show-off and a swot if you wrote more.

Harry didn't seem to mind at all.

'Maybe you can write some of mine too!' she said.

We had to read our stories out loud. My heart started thudding when Mrs Lewin picked me. I read in a teeny-tiny voice at first, waiting for the class to start sighing and yawning and poking me in the back. There wasn't a single sigh or yawn or poke! They sat up straight, listening as if they were actually enjoying my story – and when I got to the end, *they clapped*!

I couldn't believe it – all my new friends applauding me as if I was an actress on the stage! I couldn't wait to tell Jodie – but now I *couldn't* tell her. It would be unbearably horrible boasting to Jodie that I had four new friends and a lovely teacher and I'd enjoyed every minute of lesson time.

Jodie wasn't stupid. She saw me wandering along the corridors with my little group of friends; she saw me trading sausages with Harry at lunch time; she saw me sitting on the lawn at break, showing all of them how to make bead bracelets like mine. She saw, but she didn't comment.

I saw Jodie sauntering along by herself, humming a little tune, hitching her skirt up even higher, all alone but acting like she didn't have a care in the world. I saw the other girls in her class, three tall dark-blonde girls, alarmingly alike, so I never quite worked out which was Anna, which Sophia, which Rebecca; they were just AnnaSophiaRebecca. They walked along arm in arm, heads together, all of them giggling. Sometimes it looked as if they were giggling at Jodie.

Jodie had never really got on with other girls, not even back in junior school, but the boys had always been in awe of her. But these Melchester boys weren't the right sort to appreciate her. They were mostly quiet and awkward, backing rapidly out of her way whenever she came near them. There were two loud-mouthed idiots, James and Phil, who chatted her up the first day. Jodie had flirted back automatically. Then they waylaid her after school, wanting her to go off into the woods with them.

'Why? What did they want you to do?'

'What do you *think*?' said Jodie. She sighed at me. 'They certainly didn't have badger-watching on their dirty little minds. Honestly, the cheek of it! As if I'd ever be seriously interested in a pair of spotty goons half my age! I whacked them both hard about the head to teach them a lesson.'

They started calling Jodie names after that. Horrible names that made me burn.

'It makes me want to punch their teeth in,' I said.

'I wouldn't try, little titch.'

'Well, I'll get Harley to punch them. He's tall enough.'

'Harley couldn't punch his way out of a bag of wet

lettuce,' said Jodie. '*I*'m the one who can pack a good punch. Leave me to fight my own battles, Pearly.'

I spoke to Harley in private.

'Why are they all being so hateful to her?'

'They're not *all* hateful. James and Phil are morons but the rest of the boys are OK. The girls are being a bit spiteful though.'

'What are they saying?'

'Oh, just stupid stuff,' said Harley uncomfortably.

'Like what? Tell me!'

'Stuff about her hair and her earrings and the way she talks,' said Harley. 'So of course Jodie plays up to it, acting really tough when she's around them. And she swears a lot. She swore in class today.'

'At the *teacher*?'

'Well, not exactly. Mr Michaels was talking to her about her English literature essay. We had to comment on the balcony scene in *Romeo and Juliet*. Jodie wrote this total rubbish about falling in love and said real teenagers wouldn't say a lot of fancy stuff you could barely understand, they'd just sneak off together and start snogging.'

'Oh no,' I said. 'Was Mr Michaels furious?'

'He was very fair at first. He tried to explain that she'd get no marks at all if she answered that way in an exam. Jodie said she didn't care, she just wanted to say what she thought. Mr Michaels said it was irrelevant what Miss Jodie Wells *thought*, fascinating as that might be, and Anna and the others all sniggered. Jodie got angry and said, "That's just stupid," using the F-word as an adjective, and we all went quiet. Mr Michaels missed a beat and then he said, "Are you calling *me*, etc. etc." and I prayed that Jodie wouldn't get even crazier.

291

Luckily she climbed down a little and said sulkily that she was simply referring to the principle of English essay writing when you weren't supposed to say what you really thought.

Mr Michaels nodded coldly at her and said, "Well, that's just as well, because if I thought you were subjecting *me* to personal abuse, I would have to report you, whereas if you're merely attacking our system of education, I can simply give you extra homework. You're to learn the entire balcony scene off by heart by tomorrow, young lady, and I shall require you to recite it in front of the whole class."

'How mean of him!'

'Well, I thought it was quite good of him, actually. Jodie seems determined to wind him up and yet I can't quite see *why*.'

'She's always been a bit like that. She's OK if she really *likes* a teacher, but she just mucks about if she thinks they're rubbish.'

'But I still don't see why. If she was really thick, I could see why she needed to be the class clown, but she's quite bright. She doesn't *know* that much, but she's ace at arguing her point, and she's very quick to catch on.'

I didn't like Harley talking about Jodie like that. He sounded patronizing.

'Jodie's ever so clever,' I said firmly.

Harley gave me a funny look. 'I bet she's not as clever as you are. Maybe *that*'s why she messes around so – because she knows her little sister will always do better.'

'That's silly,' I said. 'Jodie doesn't think like that at all.'

Harley raised one eyebrow in an extremely irritating way.

'You think you're Mr Know-it-all, Harley, but you know zilch about Jodie and me. I'm not speaking to you any more.'

I marched off with my head in the air. My heart was thumping. I hated quarrelling with anyone. I especially hated quarrelling with Harley. Now I'd walked off, and we hadn't properly fixed up whether we were going badger-watching tonight or not. We couldn't meet up late at night any more. Everything was different now that term had started. The boys' house was locked at ten o'clock now. The male teachers took it in turns to sleep in the master's room, keeping an eye on everyone. We'd tried meeting up in the early evening after tea, but so far hadn't glimpsed so much as a snout.

I stomped back to our flat. Dad was dozing on the sofa, a wood shaving caught in his hair like an alien ringlet. Mum was sitting at the table with her calculator, doing her accounts. Her forehead was puckered as if someone had tried to stitch her eyebrows together. She muttered as her fingers tapped.

'That bloody Frenchie,' she said. 'I'll show her.' She glared and then focused on me. 'All right, poppet? Been playing with Harriet and Freya and Sheba and Camilla?' Mum enunciated each name carefully, so proud of my posh new friends. 'Better get on with your homework now. Jodie's in the bedroom doing hers.'

Jodie was in our bedroom but she certainly wasn't doing homework. She was sitting in front of the mirror in her bra and knickers, her hair piled on top of her head. It was soaking wet and a star-tlingly different shade, a weird purply-black. She saw my face in the reflection.

'Hi! I'm your new Goth sister,' she said. 'Like my new black persona?'

'Oh, gosh. Well. It's different. *Very* . . . Goth.' I touched a wet strand tentatively. 'Is it *meant* to be purple?'

'Yes,' said Jodie determinedly. 'Well, no, it's actu-ally meant to come out black. I don't think it helps that it's already dyed orange. Perhaps it'll get blacker when it dries.'

'Mmm,' I said.

I dabbed at Jodie's hair with the towel to hurry the process. Her scalp was a vulnerable pinky-purple, the colour of a just-born baby. I put my arms round her, resting her damp head against my chest. Little strands of her hair slithered about like lurid earthworms.

'What do you think Mum will say?' I said.

'I don't care what she says,' said Jodie. '*I* think it looks great.'

'So do I,' I said.

Jodie put her head closer to the mirror, peering. 'Maybe I should dye my eyebrows too.'

'No!' I said.

'Well, I need something matching.'

'You could paint your nails?'

'I haven't *got* any nails,' said Jodie, waggling her fingers.

She'd always nibbled her nails, but now they were bitten so badly they were just little slivers, the exposed finger flesh very pink and raw.

'Oh well, paint your nose purple instead,' I said,

trying to make her laugh. She was starting to look anxious.

'Ha ha,' Jodie said, sighing.

She shook the towel off and ran her hands through her hair. 'It really needs a new style to go with the colour. Something wild.'

She started rattling in the drawer. I was scared she was searching for scissors. She had a habit of snipping at her fringe so that her hair already had a ragged uneven look, as if a sheep had been grazing on it overnight.

'Don't cut any more off!'

'No, no, I was looking for . . . yeah, your beads. I could string them on a strand or two, just the purple ones, to make out the colour's deliberate.'

Sheba was next in line for a friendship bracelet. She'd asked for a purple one, her favourite colour. I badly wanted to please Sheba and all my new friends, but I wanted to please Jodie more.

'Purple will look seriously cool,' I said, fishing in my bead jar. 'Though if you stick beads in your hair, it will look as if you're copying Jed.'

'So?' said Jodie. 'Don't you think *he* looks cool?'

'No. I think he looks horrible,' I said.

'So what's your definition of cool? *Harley?*' said Jodie.

'You can be as mean about Harley as you want, seeing as we're currently not speaking,' I said, picking out purple beads.

'Oooh, have you had a lovers' tiff?' said Jodie.

'I wish you'd stop going on about us like that. We're just friends. Well, we *were* before we fell out. Don't you want to make friends with any of the other boys in your class, Jodie?'

'Are you *mad*?'

'Some of them are OK. Not James and Phil, they're horrid, but some of the others?'

'No, I hate them all. And the girls are worse. Do you know their new nickname for me? They think they're oh so witty and hilarious. It's the Ginger Minger. They're so dense they don't even know how to pronounce minger. But anyway, I'm not ginger any more so that'll shut them up. Come on, give us those beads.'

She ran her hands through her hair, suddenly biting her lip, her eyes big. 'Oh God, it looks awful, doesn't it!'

'No, no, it looks great, truly,' I lied. 'Look, I'll go and find Mum's hair-dryer. I'm sure it won't be quite *so* purple when it's dry.'

I blew Jodie's hair bone-dry. The colour looked even more startling now, a freaky purple-plum, deepening to black at the ends. I threaded the beads onto a couple of strands and tied them in place with purple thread.

'There!' I said.

'Well. It's different,' said Jodie. She took a deep breath. 'What rhymes with purple?'

'Nothing,' I said.

'Good. Oh well. I think I'll just go and have a wander,' Jodie said, turning this way and that in the mirror.

'Is Jed working late then?' I asked.

'He's mowing the big field beyond the dormies,' said Jodie.

'So you're going to tag after him?'

'Look, you tag after Harley.'

'No I don't.'

'Come on, you're all set to scurry off for your badger-watching date.'

'No I'm not. I'm staying in tonight,' I said.

'Well, I'm not,' said Jodie. 'I'm going to make myself scarce before Mum clocks my hair.' She took my felt pens, outlined her lips with purple, gave me a wave and then ran out of the room. I heard the back door bang a few seconds later.

I tried not to care. I got out my homework and set about it diligently, though it was hard work concentrating. I didn't know what Harley was expecting me to do. Maybe he was mad at me for shouting at him. Perhaps he'd tell me to clear off if I turned up at the badger set. Maybe we'd never make friends again. I'd had so *few* friends I didn't know how it worked.

I lay on my bed, juggling with Edgar, Allan and Poe. I thought of Mr Rigby Peller lounging on Harley's bed. I knew I'd never find another friend on the same wavelength as Harley. I stuffed my little bears under my pillow and jumped up. I decided to go and find Harley whether he wanted my company or not.

It was much harder sneaking off to the set in the woods now. There were children skipping about everywhere: little girls wandering along arm in arm, murmuring together; little boys charging about playing football; big girls and boys giggling together, six of them sharing a single can of lager, sipping as solemnly as if it was communion wine. They hid it behind their backs when they saw me. I didn't care. They could drink themselves stupid as far as I was concerned.

'Watch out, that's the Ginger Minger's sister,' said one.

'You shut your gob, bumface!' I yelled.

They looked astonished. Then they burst out laughing. I stuck my finger up at them and then scurried further down the path. I heard the distant roar of the garden tractor in the playing fields, then sudden silence. I wondered if Jodie was with Jed. I thought about what they might do together. I couldn't stand the idea that she might let him kiss her again.

I found the little trail that led to the badger set. I looked around carefully, making sure I was out of sight of the lager loonies. Then I dodged into the woods, through the bushes. There was the sandy bank with the entrance to the set and the extensive earthworks and the old badger bedding – and there was Harley, lying on his front, reading a book. He was absent-mindedly running his finger round a half-empty jar of honey. He looked up and smiled at me.

'Hello,' he whispered.

'Hello,' I said, sitting down beside him.

'Was that *you* yelling *bumface* just now?' asked Harley.

'These kids said something horrible first,' I said, blushing.

'About Jodie?'

I nodded.

'Are you going to call *me* Bumface?' Harley asked.

'I might, if you call her names,' I said.

'But you're speaking to me now?' he said.

'Evidently.'

'That's good,' said Harley.

We nodded at each other and then settled down

to badger-watch. We stayed silent while the birds sang in the trees above us and children called to each other far away. Harley offered me the honey jar and I had a little lick too.

'The badgers could have a veritable feast. I've smeared honey all over the shop,' Harley whispered. 'They just need to get up early.'

'Come on, badgers,' I murmured. 'Badger, badger, badger!'

'That's it, badger the badgers to come and have breakfast,' said Harley.

I willed them awake in my head. I made them wriggle and stretch and open their eyes in their musty sleeping quarters. I had the large male scratch himself with his long claws and then scrabble upright. The female nuzzled the two sleepy cubs. They started rolling around their mossy beds, playing hide-and-seek. The male grunted at them irritably. He squared his powerful shoulders and then burrowed his way down the dark earth trench towards the daylight. I willed him onwards, nearer and nearer, his snout starting to quiver as he caught a whiff of honey. Then his head poked out of the set and he paused, peering around.

He was *really* there, big and black, the white streak very marked on his face, his little amber eyes staring straight at me. I sat utterly still, barely breathing. Harley's long body tensed. The three of us freeze-framed for a good minute and then the badger took two steps forward, shoulders right out of the set now. He turned his head to the left, to the right, left, right, as if he was watching a tennis match. Then he padded forward, standing right in front of us. I could have reached out and patted him, but of course I knew better. I stayed still while the badger bent his striped head and idly picked at a grub in the grass. Then he stopped, tasting honey.

He paused a moment, head bowed, maybe saying a badger grace. Then he started rootling round in earnest, sucking at the honey. He made little grunting sounds. After a minute the female emerged, sniffing the air cautiously. She stood by the entrance to the set, waiting, though she could see her mate gorging himself. Then two heads popped out of the set simultaneously, snouts quivering. They barely gave their patient mother a glance. They scrambled over to the thickest grass where the honey glistened and started eating greedily. The mother trotted forwards now, finding her own private pool of honey in the fork of an old branch. She stuck in her snout and feasted.

I took hold of Harley's hand. His long spidery fingers gripped mine. We sat still, watching over our family as the sun slowly sank in the sky. The female stayed by her branch, enjoying honey-sauced beetles and ants. The big male prowled around, sniffing along honey trails, pausing to guzzle. The two half-grown cubs tumbled about, fighting over a honey patch, darting here and there, chasing each other as if they were playing tag. Their mother lifted her head and watched over them, anxious when they roamed too far.

It was getting late now. The children had stopped calling. They were back in their dormitories in the girls' house and the boys' house. The master would be looking for Harley, Mum would be looking for me. We didn't care. We sat there, still as statues.

We heard the garden tractor start up again, far away at first, then slowly getting nearer and nearer. Jed must be driving the tractor along the lane back to the school grounds. It made an ugly rattling roar in the still twilight. The badgers tensed.

'Oh no!' Harley groaned in a whisper.

The male grunted, and then started making for the safety of the set. The female paused, then ran this way and that, trying to organize the cubs. One ran to her, cowering against her, but the other panicked and darted off through the bushes towards the path.

'No, go back to the *set!*' said Harley, stumbling to his feet.

I jumped up too and we started running.

The garden tractor roared – and then there was a high-pitched scream.

It was Jodie screaming.

20

It was Jodie screaming. The garden tractor cut out. There was a sudden ominous silence. I ran right through the bushes, tripping over, staggering up again, desperate to get to the lane.

Jed was at the wheel of his tractor, scowling. Jodie was crouching by the side of the road, making little whimpering noises, her wild purple hair hiding her face.

'Jodie! Are you hurt?' I cried, running to her.

'Look!' she mumbled.

She was cradling something in her arms. Something black and white, only now there was red blood oozing out of the thick fur.

'The badger cub!' I whispered.

'Let me see,' said Harley gently. 'Is he still alive?'

'Yes, but look, he's bleeding so. It's his head – it's all bashed in at the back.'

'If we carry him back to the school, your dad could drive us to a vet,' said Harley.

'You're a right nutter, you are,' said Jed. 'What's the vet going to do, give it a head transplant?'

'The vet could give him an injection to put him out of his pain,' said Harley.

'I'll do that easily enough,' said Jed.

'You've done enough!' said Jodie. She stared up at him, her face contorted. 'You *aimed* at the badger, I know you did. You ran him over deliberately.'

'It's vermin. They all are. They're taking over the whole bloody grounds and you aren't even allowed to gas them any more. They're eating away the Melchester land, making it unstable. Of course I aimed at it.'

'You're horrible!' I said, starting to cry. 'This is one of *our* badgers. He lives in the woods and doesn't do anyone any harm. How *could* you!'

'You don't understand. You're just soft little townie kids,' said Jed. He looked at Jodie. 'Come on, it's practically dead now. Leave it be. Hop back on the tractor. We'll go and have a bit of fun somewhere, take your mind off it.'

Jodie stared at him. 'I'm not going anywhere with you,' she said.

'OK. Suit yourself. Bet you'll be fawning round me like a little puppy dog tomorrow though.'

'I don't think so,' said Jodie.

'Well, your loss, you silly little purple bonce,' said Jed.

He started up the tractor and roared off, dust flying in his wake.

We knelt beside Jodie. She gently rocked the poor badger. He started making awful little whinnying noises. Then his legs started scrabbling horribly.

'I think he's fitting,' said Harley. 'Poor little badger.'

He stroked the quivering paws. The badger gave one last moan, sighed and then went still. We looked at each other.

'Is that it?' I whispered. 'Is he dead now?'

'I think so,' said Harley.

Jodie held the badger close, still rocking him.

'What will we do? We can't just leave him here. It'll be so awful if his mother finds him like this,' I said.

'We'll bury him,' said Harley. 'We'll do it now. You girls stay here. I'll go and get a spade from the garden shed.'

'Don't get into an argument with Jed, will you?' I said anxiously.

Harley shook his head and hurried off. Jodie went on crooning to the badger, swaying from side to side.

'He's *dead*, Jodie,' I said.

She took no notice. She was getting blood all over her. I found an old tissue in my pocket and dabbed at her ineffectually. I kept thinking of the badger's family, frantically searching for their cub.

'Did Jed *really* run him over deliberately?'

'Yes. Well, I think so. He didn't try to swerve, though I *told* him when I saw the badger. I even tried to grab the steering wheel. Then there was this awful crunchy-pulpy sound when we went smack into his little head.' Jodie stroked the badger's head though her hand got sticky with blood.

I stroked the badger too, but I kept to his back and his stumpy little legs.

'I think he was a bit sorry after. He didn't realize it would upset me so. I don't know, maybe he thought I'd *laugh* or something. He thinks I'm crazy. He was going on about me being mad today because of my hair, yet he's the crazy one. How can you want to hurt a little animal even if it's a nuisance? What's he going to do, start aiming at little kids like Zeph? Mow them down because they get on everyone's nerves?'

Jodie sniffed furiously, hugging the badger harder. Mum was going to be mad at the state of her T-shirt but it wasn't the right time to point this out.

'You were right about Jed, he *is* horrible horrible horrible,' said Jodie. 'I knew it all along really. But he just – well, I know it sounds mad but he made me feel kind of special.'

'You *are* special!'

'You think I am, simply because I'm your sister. No one else does.'

'They do, they do, you're the one everyone notices!'

'Yeah, but only because I act crazy and mess around. No one really *likes* me. Mum likes you heaps better than me, you know she does. And Dad does too, though he makes a fuss of me to make me feel better.'

'No, that's rubbish! They love us both equally. they always say so – and they *do*.'

'They might *love* me the same as you, but they don't like me. And the kids in my class positively hate me, you know they do.'

'No they don't. Harley doesn't.'

'Harley likes you best.'

'Well. Maybe. But listen, back at Moorcroft *everyone* liked you best. They all looked up to you.'

'That was only because I hung out with Shanice and the others. And even *she* didn't like me much. She hated it when that boy she fancied snogged me at that club. That's the thing, Pearl, boys like me, older ones. That Bernie liked me, remember. And Jed liked me too. I made him laugh and he called me his little crazy girl.'

'I wouldn't want anyone to call me crazy.'

'No, he was just kind of teasing,' said Jodie, leaning forward. The badger's head suddenly moved.

'He's alive!' I squealed.

'No, no, it's just because I shifted about. Look, his head's all floppy.'

'When . . . when will he go stiff?'

'I don't know. Soon, I suppose.'

'I hope Harley hurries up.' I looked at the badger anxiously. His eyes seemed to be looking straight back at me, but there was no gleam in them. His mouth hung open a little, a drool of blood trickling down one side.

'Do you think we look like this when we die?' I said. 'Eyes all funny and our mouths open?'

'I suppose.'

'I hate the thought of looking like that.'

'Well, I'll probably die first because I'm the oldest, but if you die first, I'll shut your eyes and turn your mouth up in a little smile. Yes, I'll comb your hair and put you in your favourite outfit and I'll tuck a book or two in your coffin with you, just in case you get bored being dead,' said Jodie.

'Do you think that's it, then? We die and we go stiff and then just moulder away?'

'I don't know,' said Jodie.

'There's a lot about God in Mrs Wilberforce's books. Do you think there really is a place like Heaven?'

'Well, I hope there isn't a place like Hell because I shall probably end up there,' said Jodie. 'No, I don't believe in all that stuff.'

'And you don't really believe in ghosts either?' I said.

'Oh, I believe in *them*,' said Jodie. 'Especially here. What about the sad white whispering woman?'

'You made her up, you know you did.'

'I wonder if you get animal ghosts? Maybe this little badger will pad along the path every night on his small ghostly paws, and you'll feel him brushing your ankles but you won't be able to see him—'

'*Stop it!*'

'OK, OK. Poor little badger, we'll put you to rest in the earth. It will be just like being tucked up in your bed, and you can sleep and sleep and stay safely in your bristly badger skin. You won't even be a ghost and haunt anyone, I promise.'

Harley came loping back at last with two big spades.

'What did Jed say?'

'I didn't ask him. I just took them,' said Harley breathlessly. 'Where shall we dig, then?'

'Near the set, so he's near his family,' I said.

I led the way while Jodie held the little badger and Harley clanked the spades. We got to the clearing where all four badgers had been feeding so happily. There was no sign of the male and female and the other cub. I thought of them huddling together underground. I hoped they would stay inside in the dark. It would be awful for them to see their dead cub.

'Let's dig here,' I said, sketching a rough oblong with the toe of my sandal.

I tried to take a spade from Harley.

'Not you, Pearl, you're not strong enough,' said Harley.

'Yes I am,' I said, trying to demonstrate. But the spade was very big and heavy and I could hardly get it to go into the hard earth. I stuck it in as best I could and struggled to lift the clod of earth. It was such an effort I could feel my eyes popping.

'Here,' said Jodie. She laid the dead badger carefully on the ground, dabbed at her bloody T-shirt, then pulled the spade out of my sweaty clasp. She spat on her hands and then started digging. She managed much better than me, even though she wobbled in her high heels.

Harley dug too, and they set up a rhythm, digging alternately, as if they were a mechanical toy. I wandered into the woods, trying to find flowers. I had to make do with blue borage, but they looked pretty even if they were weeds. I picked a lot of big dock leaves too.

When the hole was ready, I lined it with the green dock leaves. They were soothing when you stung yourself so I hoped they felt comforting. Then I approached the badger, a bit scared of picking him up.

'I'll lift him in,' said Jodie.

'No. I want to,' I said. 'Please.'

I took a deep breath and then took hold of him. He still felt warm but he was quite unmistakably dead now, his eyes glazed over, his poor bloody head dangling. I supported him as best I could in both hands and then bent right down and laid him carefully on his green bed. I arranged the borage around him, the flowers very blue against the black of his fur. His little paws looked especially sad. I reached out and held one, fingering the claws. 'Rest in peace, poor little badger,' I whispered.

Jodie knelt down beside me. 'I'm sorry,' she said, a tear trickling down her cheek. 'It's my fault. I kept Jed out late because we were messing about, and he was driving fast to show off to me.'

'It's not your fault, Jodie,' said Harley, kneeling down. 'It's mine. If I hadn't smeared that honey around, they'd never have stayed outside their set that long.'

'Then it's my fault too, because you wanted to show them to me,' I said.

I didn't know if we should say anything formal. I tried to think of a prayer I'd learned at school, but none seemed at all appropriate. I wondered if I could make something up, a poem maybe – but *badger* was an impossible word for rhyming.

I sighed, gave the badger another stroke, and simply said goodbye. Then I sprinkled a handful of earth over him. Jodie and Harley did the same. When he was covered up completely, they used their spades until the grave was filled in.

I patted the earth gently and put one last spray of borage on top. We stood still for a moment and then moved away. It was nearly dark and I didn't have my torch with me. We had to stumble along slowly, Jodie and Harley dragging the heavy spades.

310

'I'll take your spade back, Harley,' I said. 'You're ever so late back to the boys' house already.'

'I don't care,' said Harley, trudging on down the path with us.

He came all the way to the garden sheds. Jed was still there, sitting on an upturned pail, smoking. He drew on his cigarette and then blew out a puff of smoke. I held Jodie's hand. She barely looked at Jed. She just flung her spade in a corner.

'Careful with that!' he said sharply.

She didn't bother to answer back. She took Harley's spade and flung that too. Then she marched out, head held high. Harley walked us round to our door.

'Shall I come in and explain stuff to your mum and dad?' he said.

'No, you go back now, Harley,' said Jodie.

She reached up and gave him a fierce hug. I hugged him too, though I could only reach as far as his waist. He patted us both awkwardly and then hurried off.

'Now for it,' said Jodie, opening the back door.

Mum came rushing down the hallway. 'For pity's sake, where have you two *been*? Your dad's been out searching for you this past hour. How *dare* you stay out so late, worrying us senseless.' She caught hold of me, pulling me into the light. 'Look at the state of you, Pearl, you're all over mud!'

Then she saw Jodie and stared at her open-mouthed. Her T-shirt was streaked with blood – and her hair was purple.

Mum wouldn't listen to proper explanations. She blamed Jodie for everything, though I kept trying to explain. She was appalled that we'd picked up our poor badger and buried him.

'It's a wild animal. It'll be all over *fleas*,' she said. 'Get in the bath, both of you, and get scrubbing quick.'

Mum supervised our bath as if we were little again. Then she took hold of Jodie and washed her hair with her kitchen carbolic soap. She rubbed and rinsed and rubbed and rinsed until Jodie's scalp was scarlet but her hair stayed defiantly purple.

'What am I going to do with you, Jodie? You'll be the death of me,' Mum said, beside herself. 'How can you go into the classroom tomorrow looking like that? And you're in trouble already. Mr Michaels came and had a word with me today. He said he was worried about you because you're just messing around in class, acting the fool. I was so ashamed, Jodie. He was being so nice about it, trying to be understanding, wondering if I could throw any light on the situation. Well, *I* don't know why you act like this. All I know is that you're doing my head in, Jodie. Mr Michaels says he can't understand it because you're a bright girl – and that's what I can't forgive. If you were totally dim but tried really hard, I'd be more than happy, but you're clever. You could do really well. I'm not expecting you to come top like Pearl but it's a disgrace for you to come bottom. I could maybe understand back at Moorcroft – that was a totally rubbish school. That was the main reason we moved away, to give you a proper chance. But now you're throwing it away, mucking around in class, not making friends, turning yourself into a scarecrow and hanging round with that horrible leery gardener with beads in his hair.'

312

'Calm down, Mum. Don't get yourself in such a state. You can cross that last one off the list,' said Jodie, grinning.

Mum slapped her hard across the face.

Jodie blinked. 'Did that make you feel better?' she asked.

'Oh, get to bed before I knock your head right off your shoulders,' Mum said.

Jodie sauntered off, whistling.

'Mum, it's not Jodie's fault,' I said.

'So whose fault is it then?'

'They all pick on her, the other girls in her class. They're horrid to her. They look down on her.'

'Do you think I didn't have to put up with a whole pack of bullies when *I* was at school?' said Mum. 'And I didn't have the luxury of any teachers trying to understand me. I came from a bad family and so they all thought *I* was a bad lot, full stop. I wasn't going to let myself be dragged down. I worked blooming hard and made something of myself. I've made it so much easier for Jodie. It's not that easy for *me*, you know. Do you think I like it when that Frenchie keeps telling me what to do in that ever so patronizing way: "Oh Mrs Wells, *dear!*" They all look down on me, even some of the kids come over all snotty with me, demanding more chips without so much as a please. But I put up with things because this is a good job for me and for your dad, but most important of all, it gives you two girls your big chance. Jodie's got this one year to straighten herself out and buckle down. If she'd only work hard, she could win herself a scholarship. But is she grateful for this wonderful opportunity? Does she take advantage of this fantastic education?

Does she appreciate that the boarders cost their parents damn near six thousand pounds per term? You're both getting your education totally *free*. Oh, Lord, what *I* wouldn't have given to be in your shoes. You're working hard and doing very well, Pearl, and I'm proud of you, but Jodie's just making monkeys out of all of us and I'm sick of it, sick of it, sick of it!' Mum shouted as she tidied up the wet towels. She bundled up the towel smeared with Jodie's black dye, knotted it into a ball and threw it violently into a corner.

I backed away and went to find Jodie. She was lying on her bed reading a magazine, flicking the pages every so often, seemingly absorbed. Her cheek was still bright pink from the slap. It contrasted oddly with her purple hair, making her look like a clown.

'Oh, Jodie, I'm sorry she went for you,' I whispered.

Jodie shrugged. 'So what else is new?'

'It's so unfair. I *said* it was, I tried to explain, but she wouldn't listen,' I said miserably.

'Don't look such a saddo. I was the one who got slapped, not you. And *I* don't care.'

'Mum was going on about lesson time.'

'Yeah, yeah, I heard. She was shrieking her head off.'

'Won't you try a bit harder, just in the lessons you like?'

'Shut up about it, Pearl,' said Jodie.

She said it nicely enough but I knew the subject was closed. I got into bed and started reading *Heidi*. It was a strange story about a little girl living with her scary grandfather up a mountain in

Switzerland. It was good to escape all the worry of Melchester College and run bare-footed through the flowers with Heidi. I wasn't sure why Mrs Wilberforce had chosen it – until Heidi got carted back down the mountain to be a little companion for Clara, an invalid in a wheelchair.

I flicked through to the end of the book and found a picture of Clara standing upright, miraculously recovered after breathing in the fresh air of the mountainside. I could see why Mrs Wilberforce got so irritated by all the old storybooks.

Jodie was asleep now, her magazine tossed to one side. I put the light off and read several chapters by torchlight but I got worried when I reached the haunted house part. Jodie had made the ghost in the tower too real.

I put the book on the floor and went to sleep. I woke up in the middle of the night and heard little whimpering sounds. I bit my lip, listening intently. I leaned up on my elbow, peering over at Jodie. She had the duvet over her head.

I slipped out of bed and pattered across to her. 'Jodie?' I whispered.

She didn't answer.

I wriggled under her duvet and cuddled up to her. She was very hot and her face was wet with tears.

'Oh, Jodie,' I said, cuddling her close.

She didn't say anything, just wept on my shoulder. I held her and stroked her while she sobbed a little more. Then she sniffed fiercely, wiping her face with the sheet.

'I've got a tissue somewhere,' I said, mopping her.

'Thanks, Pearl,' she whispered, her voice still all jerky with crying.

'Are you crying because of Mum or the badger or Jed?'

'I don't know,' said Jodie. 'I just felt like crying, OK?'

'But you hardly ever cry.'

'Yeah, well, I see why. It just gives you a splitting headache. Let's curl up and go to sleep, Pearl. Sorry, I've got the pillow all wet. Do you want to go back to your bed?'

'No, let me stay with you a bit.'

I stayed holding her in my arms until she went to sleep. I lay listening to the sound of her breathing. She was still a little wheezy from sobbing. I needed to go to the loo so I eased myself carefully out of her bed and crept to the bathroom.

As I tiptoed out of it again, my bare foot touched a little scratchy edge of paper caught between the bath and the mat. It was just a tiny scrap, part of an instruction sheet that had obviously been torn into shreds. But it still had two words clearly showing.

Pregnancy test.

'My goodness, you've still got this old thing!'

21

I asked Jodie outright the next morning.

'Do you think you might be going to have a baby?'

'What?' She stared at me as if I'd gone mad. 'Of course not, idiot!'

'I found this little bit of paper in the bathroom. I think it's from a pregnancy testing kit.'

'Well it's nothing to do with me,' Jodie snapped.

I peered at her. I was never sure when Jodie was lying, she was so good at it.

'I just thought maybe you and Jed . . .?'

'You *have* to be joking!'

'Well, you kissed him, you said you did.'

'Oh, Pearl!' She took hold of me by the shoulders and gave me a little shake. 'You are such a banana! You don't get a baby from *kissing*.'

'I know that,' I persisted. 'I was just scared you and Jed might have done more than kissing.'

'Will you shut up about me and Jed! You're

319

getting boring. I don't want to talk about him any more. You're giving me a headache going on about him.'

'You've got a headache because of all that crying in the night,' I said.

Jodie stuck her chin out at me. 'What crying?' she said.

I gave up. There was no point persisting. I kept an eye on her for a while, peeping at her stomach, but it stayed as flat as always. I listened hard when she was in the bathroom. She was never sick. I realized it was a ridiculous idea. Of course she wasn't pregnant. No wonder she'd been cross with me. *Someone* had used a pregnancy test kit, but maybe it was a while ago, before we came to Melchester College. Or maybe it was Tiffany, slipping into our bathroom for privacy. *She* had a big stomach all right – and great big boobs and bum too.

We saw her sitting on the back wall with Jed. He was cupping her hand, lighting a cigarette for her. She was looking up into his eyes, laughing. Then they both saw us. We were in our school uniform. Mum had forced Jodie to scrape her hair back into plaits, as if an old-fashioned style could somehow counteract the purple.

'Oh my Lord, what a sight!' said Tiffany, rolling her eyes.

She whispered something to Jed. He roared with laughter and then deliberately put his arm round her plump shoulders. Her black bra strap was showing beneath her tight sleeveless T-shirt. Jed fingered the strap. Jodie marched past, pretending not to notice.

'I'm sorry, Jodie,' I said, when we were in the bedroom together.

'What do you mean?' said Jodie angrily.

'Well, Jed was being horrible, playing up to Tiffany. He doesn't really fancy her – any fool can see that. He was just doing it to annoy you,' I said.

'As if I care,' said Jodie.

She stalked off. I tried to follow her but she yelled at me to leave her alone.

So I wandered off by myself and met up with Harley. We went for a little walk in the woods, though neither of us had the heart to try badger-watching. I told Harley I was worried about Jodie.

'How's she doing in class now?' I asked.

Harley sighed. 'She's weird. Sometimes she joins in and suggests stuff and she's fine, but other times she still messes around and takes the mickey out of everyone, especially Mr Michaels.'

'And she hasn't made any friends?'

'Well. She's got me, sort of. I sit next to her now, and I always get her to be my partner if we have to work in pairs, but she's not exactly thrilled about the situation. Whenever I say stuff, she starts yawning like I'm sending her to sleep. I sometimes see why all the others can't stick her.'

'They're so mean to her.'

'Yes, but she asks for it, she really does.' Harley took a deep breath. 'Still, I'm not going to go on about it. I don't want to fall out with you again, Pearl. *We*'re still friends, aren't we?'

'Of course we are.'

'Even though I didn't punch that prick Jed for killing our badger cub?'

'What?'

'I keep replaying it in my head. When Jed throws back his head and grins, I stride over and go *wham-biff-bash* like a comic book. Jed's front teeth fall out and he grovels away from me, saying, "Don't hit me any more, Harley, I swear I'll never hurt another living creature ever" – yeah, as if!'

'I think *you*'d probably lose your front teeth if you tried to punch Jed,' I said gently.

'I think you're probably right there. And I don't actually see the *point* of being violent, even to idiots like that. But there's still a bit of me that hankers after being Superhero Harley, this tall geeky kid who can suddenly swoop upwards and fell a hundred Jeds with one blow.'

'Maybe your feet could grow big and you could just go splat and trample all the Jeds into the ground.'

'Or my head could blow up like a giant balloon and I'd pucker my lips and spit on all the Jeds and drown them in the torrent.'

'What about me? Can I be a comic-book hero too? I'll be Pearly Girly and I'll do the opposite. I'll shrink down down down until I'm like a tiny insect but I've got this big big *sting*. I fly through the air and sting Jed on the end of his nose so that he gets this big pus-filled spot, and every time any of that AnnaSophiaRebecca crowd say the slightest thing mean about Jodie I'll sting them too, right on the mouth so their lips swell up and they can't speak.'

'Is this you then?' said Harley, fumbling for the notebook and pen in his pocket and drawing a weeny mosquito creature with little fangs and a ferocious expression.

'Yes, yes, exactly! Now draw you.'

He drew a huge foot with a totally flattened Jed underneath. We sat at the side of the lane inventing a story as we went along, dividing the notebook into squares like a proper comic. It was great fun, and very distracting – but I still couldn't help worrying about Jodie. I didn't have any idea where she'd gone. I was sure she hadn't gone chasing after Jed. And yet I worried about her even more if she was moping in a corner somewhere, all by herself.

It was a huge relief to find her back in our bedroom looking much cheerier.

'I took Old Shep for the longest walk. Frenchie was *so* pleased to see me. She said Shep's been really pining for me, not at all his usual self. As soon as he saw me, his ears went up and he absolutely *leaped* at me and licked me all over. So I took him for his run, and then when we got back, Frenchie made us baked beans on toast. She had a glass of red wine with hers and she gave *me* half a glass too.'

'What was that?' said Mum, putting her head round our door.

It was obvious she was still furious with Jodie.

'That Frenchie gave you *wine*? Is she mad?'

'She says the French give their children small glasses of wine on a regular basis. She says it's a very civilized habit.'

'Oh, she does, does she? You didn't act very civilized that time you went out with that awful Shanice and came home drunk. You were sick all down yourself. And it doesn't sound very civilized to me, drinking wine with *baked beans*. Why is she taking it on herself to feed you tinned muck

323

anyway? Doesn't she think I make a proper tea for you?'

'If you could just hear yourself sometimes, Mum,' said Jodie. 'Nag nag nag. I'm amazed Dad can stand it.'

'You leave your father out of it. *He*'s got no complaints!'

'Well, I wish *you*'d stop complaining.'

'I'm not the only one. That Frenchie might make a fuss of you, but she's not a proper teacher. I asked Mr Michaels if you're making more of an effort and he said . . .' Mum quivered, hardly able to get the words out. 'He said that when he was trying to teach you algebra, you screwed up your paper and said you couldn't be bothered and that you thought it was a load of old rubbish. Did you *really* say that?'

'Not in those *exact* words,' said Jodie. 'I might have used one or two expletives too.'

'How could you! I suppose you think you're clever! I'd have given anything to learn algebra and geometry and trigonometry and all that stuff. I was always good at sums and yet I was only ever taught the basics. When I was your age, my mum kept me home half the time to mind my little brothers. You've no idea how lucky you are!'

'I think your record's got stuck, Mum,' said Jodie.

'If I'd spoken to *my* mum like that, she'd have knocked me into the middle of next week,' said Mum.

'Well you're a bit slap-happy yourself,' said Jodie. She held her head out at an angle. 'Go on, have another slap now if it'll make you feel better.'

Mum raised her hand. I gasped. Mum looked at

me, looked back at Jodie, and then burst into tears. She ran out of the room sobbing. We heard her calling Dad.

'Oh God,' said Jodie. 'Now she's telling tales on me. Why can't she just leave me alone? You wait, Dad will lumber in here in a minute, all solemn, and he'll start, "Now, Jodie, I'm not having you upsetting your mother like this."'

There was a knock on our door. Dad came in, sighing, running his hands through his hair.

'Now, Jodie. I'm not having you upsetting your mother like this,' he said.

Jodie rolled her eyes at me. I couldn't help giggling.

'It's not funny, girls!' Dad said sorrowfully. 'Don't be like that, Pearl. And Jodie, oh dear, Jodie, what are we going to do with you, eh?' He sat down on her bed and she cuddled up to him.

'Mum keeps nagging at me, Dad.'

'Well, you're such a bad girl, and you keep doing such crazy things. You shouldn't cheek your mum the way you do. It really upsets her, and she's having a tough time as it is. This has been a big strain for her and she's having to cope with all sorts.'

'That's not *my* fault. I never wanted to come to this stupid school in the first place.'

'Now, now, it's not stupid, it's a lovely school. You just need to settle down and try a bit harder with your lessons. You're a bright girl. You both are. Not like your old dad! I'm as thick as two short planks. I always came bottom at school, apart from wood-work. But you could really do well, Jodie, if you'd only try.'

His foot nudged one of the boxes Jodie had shoved under her bed. She'd still not bothered to unpack properly. He pulled it out, sighed at all the junk, and then picked out her old wooden rocket.

'My goodness, you've still got this old thing!' he said, smiling. 'You were always such an odd little kid. A rocket, eh! Not that it looks much like one, I must admit.' He gave her a gentle poke with the nose of the rocket. 'So how about being my little rocket girl? Don't you want to work hard and fly all the way to the moon?'

Jodie seized the rocket and went whirring round the room with it, making childish *pow!* noises. Dad shook his head at her.

'I give up,' he said. He looked at me and raised his eyebrows. 'Oh well, just so long as you're happy, Jodie. I suppose that's all that matters.'

Dad didn't seem to get that Jodie *wasn't* happy. She laughed loudly and clowned around but her face didn't light up and her eyes were dead. She steered clear of Jed, never even nodding in his direction, but I knew she was missing him terribly.

I took *Heidi* back to Mrs Wilberforce and told her that Jodie was no longer keeping company with Jed.

'That's good,' said Mrs Wilberforce.

'Yes, I suppose so. But Jodie doesn't see it like that. She's not very happy.'

'She's not making poor Mr Michaels very happy either. He came to tea the other day and seemed at his wits' end. I felt sorry for the poor man. He's teaching Harley, who's much cleverer than all of us put together, and Jodie, who's going out of her way

326

to be disruptive. So Pearl, she's being really really bad – what is Jodie *good* at?'

I thought hard.

'She's good at heaps and heaps of things. She's funny and she makes up wonderful stories and she's always looked after me and made sure I'm safe. That's what she's totally best at, being my big sister.'

Mrs Wilberforce nodded. 'Mmm. That's a splendid testimony. Well, I shall ponder that. Now, perhaps you might fancy borrowing a book about sisters? Let me see – you must have read *Little Women*?'

'Well, I've heard of it, but I've never really got round to reading it,' I said.

'It's a *lovely* book. You'll especially like the relationship between Jo and Beth. Oh, you lucky girl, to be reading *Little Women* for the first time. Which book are you reading in class at the moment?'

'Oh, it's not like your lovely books, it's about nowadays. It's a story about twins. I've read it before, but it's so sad – they break friends, and then one of them goes off to boarding school and the other doesn't and it *ends* there. I wanted it to end with them living together again and never ever being separated.'

'Maybe you could write your own new ending for the story?' said Mrs Wilberforce. 'Are you still writing your journal?'

'Oh yes,' I lied. I hadn't been able to bear writing about the badger cub dying and all the sad things since.

Mrs Wilberforce was watching my face. 'What about you, Pearl? I know you're doing brilliantly in class. Mrs Lewin waxes lyrical about you.'

'Really?' I said, blushing.

'And she says you've made lots of friends too.'

'Yes, well, sort of,' I said. 'I especially like Harriet.'

'So why don't you run off to the girls' house now and play with Harriet for a bit?'

I hadn't ever gone calling for Harry before. We sat next to each other in class and we chatted together at play time, but I always went back to our flat after tea. I felt stupidly shy of going to find her. What if she didn't really want to see me?

'Off you go!' said Mrs Wilberforce.

'Am I allowed?' I asked pathetically. 'I mean, the matron won't mind?'

'You're not frightened of Matron, are you, Pearl?' said Mrs Wilberforce, laughing at me.

'I'm frightened of everyone,' I said.

'Are you frightened of *me*?'

I hesitated. She burst out laughing, but then she covered her mouth with her good hand, looking concerned.

'The little children are frightened of me, I know. Because of the wheelchair and the way I look now.'

'No, no,' I argued awkwardly.

'Yes, yes. And it's so sad, because I used to teach the little ones and they were always so sweet. Some of the boarders used to call me Mummy. I'd go and tuck them up at night and read them a story. Matron's very good with them but she doesn't have the time, she's got so much else on her plate.'

'Perhaps you could still go along, in your wheel-chair?'

'No, it's too awkward, and the littlest ones are up on the first floor. I'm not up for that sort of stuff any more anyway. I just can't make the effort. But maybe . . .' She smiled at me. 'I've had a little idea. I'll mull it over. Now off you go. Bravely beard Matron in her den and ask if you can play with Harriet.'

Beard was the appropriate word for poor Matron. She didn't have a *real* beard, but she had whiskers on her chin and heavy down on her upper lip. She was fat, but she squashed her very large chest and stomach and bottom into some kind of corset so that she didn't wobble when she walked. She had surprisingly slim legs with elegant ankles and little pointy shoes. She looked like a well-upholstered sofa on tiny wheels.

I'd always scuttled out of her way, imagining she'd be ultra-scary. The door to the girls' house was open so I wandered in uncertainly. I knew Sakura's bedroom was upstairs but I didn't have a clue where to look for Harriet.

I could hear laughter and a television somewhere but I didn't like to barge in uninvited. I stood shifting from one foot to the other until Matron suddenly shot out of a room at the end of the corridor, balancing an enormous pile of pillowcases and sheets and duvet covers. She peered at me from over the top.

'Ah! You're Mr and Mrs Well's little girl . . . Jodie?'

'No, I'm Pearl.'

'Yes, that's right, Jodie's the one with startling hair. Lucky she's not boarding with me. I'd have held her under a hot tap until I'd scrubbed all that purple out.'

'Mum tried that,' I said.

'Oh dear. Perhaps it's indelible, like those pencils. They're purple, aren't they? Anyway, my darling, how can I help?'

I wondered if I could play with Harriet?' I asked timidly.

'Of course you can, you silly sausage! Her dorm's on the second floor. You'll find it easily because it's the noisiest, what with Harriet gassing and poor little Freya grizzling and Sheba singing and Clarissa showing off.' She laughed fondly. 'You can carry these sheets up for me and pop them in the airing cupboard, there's a darling.'

I staggered up the stairs, found the airing cupboard, stuffed the sheets in as best I could – and then listened. Matron was right. I could hear all the girls laughing and playing very loud music. I went over to their door, wondering whether to knock or just stick my head in. I licked my lips, rehearsing in my head what I was going to say.

Can I play with you? sounded so young, like I was six and wanting to play with Barbies. In the end I tapped once on the door. The music stopped. I heard squeals and giggles and a lot of scuffling. I waited, heart beating. Then Harriet opened the door a few centimetres.

'Oh, Pearl, it's only *you*! Come in, come in,' she said, grabbing hold of me and pulling me into the dorm. 'We thought you might be Matron!'

Harry had a dressing gown on and the other three were in bed, their duvets up to their chins.

'Oh, sorry! I didn't realize you went to bed this early,' I stammered.

'We're not in bed. We're hiding,' said Clarissa, jumping up from under her duvet. She wore her knickers and a silk scarf tied round her chest and fishnet stockings on her skinny legs. I stared at her open-mouthed.

'We're playing at being lap dancers,' she said.

'Well, I'm a *fan* dancer,' said Sheba, kicking off her duvet. She was wearing her swimming costume and had a big feathery fan in her hand.

'I'm a dancer too,' said Freya. She wore a proper bikini and she'd crayoned roses and hearts around her belly button.

'Tra-la!' said Harry, flinging off her dressing gown. She was wearing her school knickers and a little lacy bolero over her flat chest. She twirled around, bumping and grinding her hips. 'You do it like this, don't you, Pearl? Funny old Freya thought lap dancing was actually dancing in someone's *lap*, but they'd get all squashed, wouldn't they?'

'You don't think we're terribly *rude*, do you, Pearl?' Freya asked anxiously.

'Don't tell Matron!' said Sheba.

'Of course I won't. Look, my sister Jodie and I often mess around like this. Hey, it was soooo embarrassing when we first moved here. We were painting our room and getting all messy so we stripped off down to our knickers, and guess what, *Harley* walked right in and saw us!'

'Harley saw you in your knickers!'

They all exploded with laughter.

'Did he see your sister too?' asked Clarissa.

'Yes, but she didn't mind. She doesn't get fussed about stuff,' I said.

'I'll say,' said Clarissa.

I swallowed. 'What do you mean by that?'

'She didn't mean *anything*, Pearl,' said Harriet.

'I just meant that your sister truly doesn't seem to care about anything. My cousin Anna's in Year Eight and she says she's . . . incredible.'

'Yeah, well, that's Jodie,' I said.

I stared hard at Clarissa, silently daring her to say any more.

'You're so different from your sister,' said Freya.

'I know,' I said. 'I wish I was more like her.'

'I'm glad you're like you,' said Harry. 'OK, are you going to lap dance too, Pearl?'

I felt a total fool, but I dared to whip off my skirt and shoes, and then I pranced about a bit, winking and wriggling, copying the way Jodie danced. The others all laughed and clapped and joined in.

When we got tired of lap dancing, I suggested we pretend we were a new girl band and we made up our own dance routine. Matron really did come knocking on the door because of all the thumping, but she didn't come in, she just called out for us to quieten down because she was starting to put the little ones to bed.

I decided I'd better get back myself. Harry begged me to come and play with them the next day.

'It's such fun when you're here, Pearl,' said Harry, giving me a hug. 'I wish you were a proper boarder and could sleep in our dormie.'

I almost wished it too. I skipped back along the path, waving at the bungalow in case Mrs Wilberforce could see me. I slowed down when I got near the little trail to the badger set. There was a brown smudge on the lane which might have been blood from the poor badger cub. I went to see if Harley was crouching by the set, but there was no one there. I went and knelt by the main entrance.

'I'm so sorry,' I whispered into the darkness. 'You must be missing your cub so much. I hope you have lots and lots more children and they all live long happy lives.'

Then I went back to our flat. Mum had a bad migraine headache and had gone to bed early. Dad was watching sport on the television, his shoes kicked off, his belt unbuckled. He was sipping beer straight from the can and eating a packet of salted peanuts.

'Don't tell Mum!' he mouthed.

Jodie wasn't in our bedroom. I didn't know where she could be. I wondered if she might be taking Old Shep for another walk. I waited and waited. It was past our bedtime now. Mum was asleep, thank goodness. I crept into the living room and saw that Dad had nodded off too, his hand lolling over the arm of his chair so that the dregs of his beer can dripped onto the carpet.

I wanted to climb up onto Dad's lap, but if I woke him, he'd fuss about Jodie, maybe even wake Mum. I tiptoed back to our bedroom, worrying about the back door. When Dad woke up, he'd bolt it and then Jodie would be locked out all night. It was raining outside. I could hear raindrops pattering steadily against the window. I thought of Jodie trudging through the dark, getting drenched.

She slipped into our bedroom at long last. I threw my arms around her in relief. She was warm and bone dry.

'Where have you *been*?'

'Just around and about,' she said vaguely.

'But where? I was so worried. I wish you wouldn't go off without me.'

'*You* do!' said Jodie. 'I went to meet you at the Wilberforce house but you weren't anywhere. What were you up to? Badger-watching with Harley?'

'No.' I hesitated. I felt so guilty having friends when Jodie didn't. 'I was just playing with Harriet.'

'What, she came calling for you?'

'No, I went to the girls' house.'

Jodie raised her eyebrows but didn't say anything.

I swallowed. 'You don't mind, do you, Jodie?'

'Of course not,' she said. 'So, did you have fun?'

'Well, sort of. We played this lap-dancing game and then we made out we were a girl band. That was my idea, actually.'

'Good for you,' said Jodie.

'Well, it was all a bit silly really. *We* have much more fun,' I said.

Jodie shrugged.

'You know we do,' I said. I pulled her nearer to me. 'Jodie, where were you? Don't have secrets from me. I hate it so.'

Jodie tapped me lightly on the end of my nose. 'Nosy!' she said.

'Were you seeing Jed?'

'*No!* Look, I wasn't seeing anyone, I just went for a walk.'

'No you didn't. It's pouring with rain outside.'

'I didn't say I was outside. I went for a walk *inside*.' Jodie made her two fingers walk upwards.

'You were upstairs? You didn't go up to the attics all alone?'

'I went all the way up to the tower room.'

'You didn't! How did you get the door open by yourself?'

'I moved a trunk out of one of the rooms and stood on it to reach the bolt. We didn't relock it after we went up there, you and me and Harley. So I could get in easy-peasy.'

'In the *dark*?'

'Yeah, I should have taken your torch. But I was OK once I got up the stairs. It was so weird up in the tower room by myself.'

'Weren't you scared, Jodie? What about the ghost?'

'I wasn't scared,' she said. Then she grinned at me, tucking her mad hair behind her little pierced ears. 'Well, of course I was scared at first. So scared I was practically wetting myself. All the way up those dark stairs I kept thinking that the ghost would be up there, waiting for me, reaching out with her pale hands—'

'Stop it! Oh, you're so mad, how could you still go up!'

'I wanted to see if I had the bottle. It was like a test. Could I risk the Curse of the Tower Room! The more frightened I got, the more I simply had to make myself. When I got up to the tower room at last and stepped out onto the carpet, I felt something trailing over my face and I just about died. I screamed like a total nutcase and swatted the air, shrieking, "*Get away from me!*" Then I realized it was just a stupid cobweb and I started laughing at myself and then I wasn't scared at all. I felt fantastic, up there all on my own, with the rain beating against the windows. I walked round and round in a circle. I even started running round until I felt completely dizzy.'

'You shouldn't run! Those floorboards are so old

and creaky. You could have fallen right through. Oh, Jodie, please, please don't go up there ever again, promise me.' I clung to her, nearly in tears.

'OK, OK, don't get in such a state! I promise.'

But we both knew Jodie didn't always keep her promises.

...had really have fallen right through
...to her ...
...to her heart an tears
...In a state I wouldn't
...didn't always recognise her

Mum sat me down carving pumpkins.

22

I decided I wouldn't go and play with Harriet and the others after school no matter how much I wanted to. I wouldn't even go off with Harley. I'd find Jodie and stick with her, no matter what.

I saw Mr Wilberforce go over to the Year Eight table at tea time the next day. Jodie was lolling on the end of the bench, staring into space, taking no notice of the girls giggling opposite her. Harley was sitting beside her but she was ignoring him too. She was staring up at the ceiling. I wondered if she was imagining herself up in the tower room. She jumped when Mr Wilberforce came up behind her and put a hand on her shoulder. He murmured something in her ear and then walked off. Jodie slid off her bench and followed him, everyone staring at her.

I scuttled over to Harley.

'What's happening?'

'Mr Wilberforce just said he wanted to see her in his study,' said Harley.

'Your sister is *so* much trouble,' said Jessica, her eyes shining maliciously. 'You should have *heard* what she said to Mr Michaels today! I shouldn't wonder if she gets *expelled*. I mean, the way she acts, the way she looks!'

I took no notice of their silly tittle-tattle. I turned and went to follow Jodie. Harley came with me. We sat on the stairs, waiting for her to come out of Mr Wilberforce's study. I kept picturing him, stern but still kindly, cataloguing all Jodie's crimes, minor and major. I saw her cheeking him, trying to make him laugh. He'd get fiercer then, cutting her down to size. I turned his big pink hands into scissors going *snip snip snip* at my sister, so she got smaller and smaller until she was just little shreds of skin and purple fluff.

I craned my head, listening anxiously. Harley dared to creep right over to the door and put his ear against it. He tried listening for a while and then tiptoed back.

'I can't really hear anything,' he whispered. 'There's just the buzz of Mr Wilberforce's voice but I can't make out what he's saying.'

'And Jodie?'

'She doesn't seem to be saying anything at all.'

This seemed a very bad sign. I started biting my nails.

'Don't,' said Harley, pulling my hand away from my mouth and keeping hold of it.

'He wouldn't really expel her, would he?' I whispered.

'I don't know. *I've* been expelled, because I never fit in anywhere.'

'Jodie doesn't want to fit in here,' I said.

'But you do. You've made friends with that funny girl with the plaits.'

'Harriet.'

'And all her cronies.'

'Yes, Freya and Sheba are OK. I suppose Clarissa is sometimes.'

'And you've made friends with me too. I'm OK-ish, aren't I?'

'You can leave out the *ish*,' I said. 'You know I like you best, Harley. I like it here, ever so. But if Jodie gets expelled, we'll have to leave and Mum will be so cross with Jodie, and Dad will be so hurt and it will be just awful for her.'

I pictured Jodie, pale and defiant, trying hard not to cry. I felt my own eyes getting watery. Then the study door opened and Jodie bounced out, positively beaming. She saw us, shut the door behind her, and then strutted over to us, grinning all over her face.

'Hey there,' she said, giving us a little wave. 'What are you doing here?'

'Waiting for you!' I said.

'Oh, sweet,' said Jodie. 'Well, I've got to run.'

She started striding off down the hall to the main door.

'Where are you going?' I said, running after her. 'Oh, Jodie, are you really all right? What did Mr Wilberforce say to you? Did he get really cross with you?'

'No! We're like *friends*, you know we are. Oh, he said a bit of boring stuff about working harder and not cheeking that sad sap Michaels – but mostly he's ultra pleased with me.'

'Who are you trying to kid, Jodie?' said Harley.

'It's true! He said he's noticed how good I am with the little kids, Zeph and Sakura and Dan, and how they're all a bit unsettled now that term's started, so he wants me to spend more time with them, especially after tea. Not just our three: *all* the littlies under seven. He wants me to read them bedtime stories and make a fuss of them.'

I wondered if Mrs Wilberforce had had a word with her husband.

'That's a brilliant idea,' I said.

Harley pulled a face. 'More like crazy,' he said. 'Jodie's not exactly Mary Poppins.'

'Jodie's *better* than Mary Poppins,' I said firmly.

Harley's eyebrows hitched an inch up his face.

'No, truthfully,' I said. 'Jodie was always wonderful to me when I was little.'

'You're still little now and Jodie's frequently horrible to you,' said Harley. 'She bosses you about so.'

'No she doesn't, she just looks after me. She was like a second mum to me, always playing with me and teaching me stuff. She was magic,' I said.

She proved herself magical to all the little ones. She went along to tuck them up that evening. She told them she was a purple princess and she gave every small child a tiny purple tattoo to show they were her special princelings.

Zeph wanted an elephant tattoo. Jodie did her best. It didn't show up very well on his dark brown skin so she outlined it with silver. Sakura wanted a purple lotus flower, which was easy enough. Dan wanted a daisy, even easier. The other children were also easily pleased, the boys mostly wanting flash cars and jet planes and guns, the girls wanting cuddly teddies or birds or butterflies.

Jodie told the boys a bedtime story about a superman schoolboy who drove his own limo, and then she went to the girls' house and told them a story about a baby teddy called Little Paws. The boys loved her, the girls loved her. They all begged her to kiss them goodnight.

She went to visit them for an hour or so every evening. I sometimes went too, lurking in a corner, listening to her. I didn't mind a bit when she talked to the boys, in fact I sometimes cuddled up with Dan and his man while Jodie told everyone stories. Dan was always a little stand-offish in his odd little outfits, but when he was dressed in his soft striped pyjamas, he seemed to lose several years and become this cuddly little baby. Even his man stopped being so freaky because Dan wrapped a big hankie round him for a nightshirt, covering up his disconcerting innards.

It was a much weirder experience going to the girls' house because Jodie treated them exactly the way she used to treat me. In fact 'Little Paws' was *my* story, made up to celebrate the birth of my first teddy bear. I felt so proud of Jodie when all the little girls ooohed and aaahed at every aspect of the story – and yet I also wanted to clap my hands over their ears because 'Little Paws' belonged to me.

I caught Jodie fishing Edgar, Allan and Poe out from underneath my duvet.

'They're *my* bears, Jodie,' I said.

'Of course they are, baby. I just want to show them to all the littlies. I've made up the coolest bear story for them called "Purplelocks". They'll simply love it, especially if I act it out.'

'You're not acting it out with *my* bears,' I said childishly.

Jodie stared at me and then laughed. 'Who's gone all green-eyed then?' she said.

'Don't be ridiculous,' I snapped.

She was right, I *was* jealous, especially when Sakura hung on Jodie's every word and begged to hold her hand. I'd always felt that Sakura was my special little girl but I hardly got a look-in now.

Jodie was still ostracized by most of the others in her class but she truly didn't seem to mind now. Both Matron and Undie complimented her on her relationship with the little ones, though Undie seemed understandably peeved. Miss French congratulated her. Mr Wilberforce took Mum and Dad to one side and told them that Jodie was doing a sterling job with the small children and seemed to be settling down at last.

'You're turning into a little treasure, Jodie,' said Dad, picking her up and whirling her round, the way he did when we were little. 'We're so proud of you, aren't we, Shaz?'

Mum nodded and mumbled something vague but she didn't really praise Jodie properly. She seemed distracted, not properly focused any more. She concentrated hard when she was cooking but the rest of the time she seemed in a daze. She watched a lot of television, but she didn't laugh at any of the sit-com jokes or shout out the answers to the quiz shows. She didn't nag us or question us or correct our grammar. It was much more peaceful but a little weird.

Mum still got irritated when Miss French told her what to do.

'Pumpkins!' Mum exploded. 'That stupid woman's ordered thirty blooming pumpkins so that the little kids can carve silly faces for Halloween – and then she wants me to make pumpkin soup and pumpkin pie and pumpkin tart and pumpkin risotto and pumpkin kiss-my-bum. What a ridiculous waste of money – pumpkins are the most tasteless, useless veg. Then she wants umpteen kilos of apples, and these aren't even for eating – they're for *bobbing for apples*! What a waste of bloody food, pardon my French, getting kids sticking their heads underwater to bite lumps out of apples. I ask you!'

'You have to enter into the spirit of Halloween, Mum,' said Jodie.

'It's all silly American nonsense,' said Mum. 'It's all rubbish, this trick-or-treating lark, little kids dressing up as ghosts and ghoulies and skeletons and pestering for money.'

'Yay!' said Jodie.

She started preparing all her little children for Halloween. She sweet-talked Matron into letting her have a stack of old worn sheets so that most of the little kids could have ghost costumes. She invented specific and wonderfully scary costumes for Zeph, Sakura and Dan. She stole an old-fashioned scythe from Jed's garden shed and made Zeph a Grim Reaper. She dressed Sakura in her black gym leotard and black tights and then painted white bones all over her, turning her into a skeleton.

'*I* want to be a skellington and look like my Man,' said Dan.

'You're too chubby to be a skeleton, Dan. No, I've

got a better idea for you. You're going to be a scary monkey,' said Jodie.

She made him a papier-mâché monkey mask and purloined Dad's old brown wool balaclava to be the fur on his head. She dressed him in a big woolly jumper and then gave him two rotting rubber hands from the toy monkeys in the attics.

'You hang onto them inside your sleeves and offer to shake hands with people and then let go, so that they're left holding a severed hand,' said Jodie, demonstrating. 'See, Dan? You'll give people such a fright.'

Dan whooped triumphantly, turning round and round, juggling with his horrible monkey hands.

'You're getting them all over-excited,' I said sourly. 'And you're totally mad letting Zeph near a scythe. 'He'll kill everyone.'

'It's all blunt and rusty and I've wrapped sellotape round it to make it safe,' said Jodie. 'Now, what are *you* going to wear for Halloween, Pearl?'

'I'm not wearing any stupid costume,' I said. 'I'm not one of the babies.'

'You're *acting* like a baby,' said Jodie. 'Look at that lickle sulky face, diddums!'

She ran her finger over my lips, making a silly noise. I bared my teeth suddenly and bit her.

'Ow! That *hurt!*'

She shook her hand, rubbing the finger, showing me real tiny toothmarks. I started to feel terrible. Jodie traded on this, holding her hand in her armpit and looking anguished.

'It was only a little bite,' I said.

'You broke the skin. Don't you know what damage a bite can do, even a little one? Remember

346

when that dog bit me? I had to go to the doctor's and get an injection. You could have given me any old infection. Tetanus. Maybe even rabies.'

'I haven't *got* tetanus or rabies so how could I possibly give them to you?'

'You could easily be a carrier. It might not affect you but you could pass it on to me and I could get desperately ill, even *die*.'

'You're just being silly,' I said, but my stomach clenched and goose pimples crawled up and down my arms.

'Oh, well, if I die, I'll turn into a ghost and then I won't need a Halloween costume, I'll *be* one!'

'I'm sick to death of Halloween and I'm sick to death of you!' I shouted.

I didn't speak to Jodie any more that evening, not even when we went to bed – but in the middle of the night I climbed under her duvet and hugged her tightly, crying.

'You're making my pyjamas all wet,' she complained sleepily.

'I'm sorry. I'm so sorry I bit your finger. It *is* all right, isn't it?'

'Well, I *think* so,' said Jodie. 'It's just – oh God!'

'*What?*'

'Feel!'

I scrabbled for her hand in the dark. I felt her thumb – and one, two, three fingers.

'It must have fallen off in the night!' said Jodie.

'It can't have!' I gasped, feeling again frantically. She was hiding one finger in her palm. I shook her furiously while she howled with laughter.

'You are so *bad*,' I said.

'And you are so stupid,' Jodie chortled.

I found Harley at breakfast on Halloween morning and asked if he was going to wear any special costume.

'I look enough of a freak in my natural state,' he said. 'Miss French said I had to email my ma for yet more trousers. I've grown another two centimetres since the start of the summer. It's so unfair. You'd think I'd start contracting after all that time spent crouching, badger-watching.'

'We could maybe watch again tonight?' I said. 'While the party's going on? You know I hate parties.'

'You liked your birthday party, didn't you?' said Harley.

'Well, yes, but that was different. I still hate parties where you have to dress up and do silly things.'

'I'm afraid it's a Melchester College speciality. There'll be a Bonfire Night party soon and a Christmas party at the end of term. Attendance is absolutely compulsory. Mr Wilberforce and Frenchie examine our faces every five minutes, and woe betide us if we're not grinning widely enough.'

Harriet and Freya and Sheba and Clarissa weren't looking forward to Halloween either.

'It's, like, so childish,' said Clarissa, pretend-yawning.

'You don't even get any proper prizes for winning the games,' said Sheba.

'And there are still forty-five whole days until the end of term,' said Freya. She had a special chart on the two middle pages of her school jotter and crossed each day off with her best pink gel pen.

'I quite like the apple-bobbing,' said Harry. 'You

get to eat any apple you catch with your mouth.'

'My mum's going to make toffee apples,' I said.

Mum hated the whole Halloween hullabaloo, but she was determined to show off to Miss French. She snapped out of her strange new apathy and scurried around the kitchen all day making ghost gingerbread biscuits with spooky white-icing faces, five huge square sponge cakes, each decorated with orange marzipan pumpkins, and tray after tray of red toffee apples oozing stickily onto greaseproof paper.

Dad tried hard too, scrubbing out a big trough for apple bobbing and fashioning makeshift wooden stocks, boring holes for arms and legs.

'Are you going to shut a child up in that?' I asked anxiously.

'No, no, you mustn't tell, it's a secret, but Mr Wilberforce and Miss French are going to dress up as witches and take turns in the stocks and all you kids can throw wet sponges at them,' said Dad.

'I'll be first in line when it's Miss French's turn,' said Mum.

My whole family were absorbed in preparations for Halloween. I felt unsettled, left out. Mum sat me down carving pumpkins. It was fun fashioning the eyes and mouths but it was awkward and uncomfortable scooping out all the flesh and it made my hand ache. I did five pumpkins and then tried lighting candles inside them. I hated the way they sprang to life, five leery grinning heads. I blew out the candles quickly and went to my room.

Jodie was there, painting her face white. It contrasted eerily with her purple hair. She was dressed in a black T-shirt and leggings with a black net skirt. She had skull stickers up and down her arms and legs, and chains clanking round her neck.

'Where did you get the chains from?' I asked.

'Well, let's hope no one needs to go to the loo for a bit,' said Jodie.

'You're mad,' I said.

She grinned at me. She'd blackened her teeth revoltingly.

'You'll scare all the littlies to death,' I said.

'That's the point of Halloween,' she said. 'They *like* being scared, it's fun. Come on, let me make you up too, Pearl. Then you can put on your black skirt and I'll give you a chain or two and you can be my little Goth ghost sister.'

'No, I don't want to. I hate Halloween,' I said.

'Don't be such a spoilsport. Please. Join in with me,' said Jodie.

I gave in and let her paint and decorate me ghoulishly because I didn't want her to be the only older girl dressed up. I let her whiten my face and blacken my teeth.

'You could dye your hair too to match mine,' said Jodie.

I wasn't going to go that far, but I let her braid it into lots of plaits and tie them with black ribbons.

'There! You look so cool, Pearl!' Jodie said at last, spinning me round so I could stare in the mirror.

When I was little, I'd have been thrilled at the sight of myself, but now I was acutely aware that I looked ridiculous. I wanted to scrub myself back to my old self but I couldn't hurt Jodie's feelings.

'Yeah, ultra cool,' I said lamely.

'You've really entered into the spirit of things,
my dear,' said Mr Wilberforce.

23

I didn't feel cool. I felt burning with embarrassment
when the party started in the dining hall at half
past six. The little ones were all capering about in
their costumes but very few Juniors were dressed
up, and none of the Seniors. They all smirked at
Jodie and me. They smirked at the teachers too.

Mr Wilberforce came as a witch, though he wore
rolled-up trousers under his skirts to show he
wasn't seriously trying to be a drag queen. He had
a silly floormop wig but he didn't wear make-up.
Miss French had gone to town on hers, adding
warts and wrinkles and an entire false nose that
looked alarmingly authentic. (Mum chortled at the
sight of her.) Matron looked the closest to a real
witch naturally, so perhaps that was why she didn't
dress up at all.

Undie tried too hard, hidden under a ghost sheet
while she clutched a severed papier-mâché head in
her hand. She'd modelled a startling likeness but it

353

didn't upset any of the littlies. Halfway through the evening, bored of endless apple-bobbing, Zeph bounced the head out of her arms and used it as a football all around the room.

Lovely Mrs Lewin had turned herself into Good Witch Glinda, wearing a pretty pink dress with sequins and carrying a wand. Mild Mr Michaels came as the devil in a black jumper and trousers with a long black forked tail sticking out the back and two little twists of horn stuck to his forehead.

They were all varying figures of fun, but this was intentional, a deliberate reversal of power to give the Halloween party some point. Jodie and I just looked like losers, babyish for wanting to dress up and tackily tasteless in our mad make-up and net and lavatory chains.

Mum looked shocked when she saw us, and Dad raised an eyebrow, but they couldn't really tell us off, not when all the teachers had dressed up too. Miss French clapped us both on the back, cackling in character, and Mr Wilberforce nodded and winked at Jodie.

'You've really entered into the spirit of things, my dear,' he said. 'And you've been utterly inspirational to all the younger ones. I've never seen such a splendid turn-out of wee ghoulies and ghosties. Well done!'

Jodie grinned at him and started organizing all her little gang into a game of Tag the Ghost.

'I'm not sure that's such a good idea. They're all a bit excited already,' said Miss Ponsonby.

'Nonsense! It will do them good to let off steam and run about a bit,' said Mr Wilberforce. 'You show them, Jodie.'

Jodie showed them with a vengeance, charging around on her high heels, her purple hair flying, getting so hot that her eye make-up started running. Her net skirts kept flying up, showing the skulls on her thighs and her skimpy knickers, red to match her shoes. All the girls in Year Eight rolled their eyes at her and some of the boys started muttering horrible things.

Mum would have said something now, regardless, but she was in the kitchen making mulled wine for the adults. Dad tried hissing at her, 'Watch your skirts, our Jodie,' but she took no notice.

Harley came over to me. 'Can't you stop her making such a fool of herself, Pearl?' he whispered.

I glared at him. 'I don't know what you mean,' I lied. 'She's just helping the little ones have fun. They're loving it.'

This bit was true. All the children scampered after Jodie, calling to her, desperate for her approval. I knew how they felt. I'd been led by Jodie all my life.

I walked away from Harley, even though I knew he was only trying to help. I went to watch Harry apple-bobbing. She made me have a go but I was hopeless at it. I kept getting mouthfuls of water instead of apple and smeared my purple lipstick all over my chin. Harry pursued her apples relentlessly, like a seal snapping up fish. Her dress got soaked but she didn't seem to care.

Mr Wilberforce and Miss French were soaked through too as they took turns in the stocks. Harry queued to throw squeezy sponges at them, so I did too. I threw my first sponge aimlessly and it landed thump on the floor a metre away from the stocks.

Then I overheard Clarissa whispering that Jodie looked a total tart. I flexed my arm and aimed my sponge at her, catching her fair and square in the face. She shrieked at me furiously.

'Sorry, Clarissa, I've got lousy aim,' I said, shrugging.

'Good for you, Pearl,' Harry whispered, and we squeezed hands.

We all ate Mum's special Halloween cake. Mum wrapped a special slice in tinfoil for Mrs Wilberforce.

'Doesn't the poor soul want to come to the party too?' she said pointedly. 'My husband would be happy to wheel her over from the bungalow.'

'That's very kind of you, my dear, but she doesn't really care for this sort of fun and games nowadays,' said Mr Wilberforce.

Mum tutted. She cast a glance at Miss French, who was shrieking in the stocks. 'Miss French certainly seems to be enjoying herself,' she said.

'Oh, dear old Frenchie's a jolly good sport,' said Mr Wilberforce.

Mum raised her eyebrows and handed round toffee apples, sniffing. Dan tried to share his with his man, holding the apple precariously with his false monkey hand. Zeph barged into him and Dan dropped his toffee apple. It rolled stickily across the floor. Dan went to pick it up.

'No, don't, Dan, it's all gritty and fluffy now. Here, have mine,' said Harley.

Dan took his toffee apple, barely pausing to say thank you. Then he chased after Jodie, leaving poor Harley standing there.

I went up to him. 'Look, you have *my* toffee apple.

I don't really like them that much,' I said.

'No, you eat it, Pearl. I'm fine,' said Harley.

'You don't sound fine,' I said.

'Well, I've never been top of the pops when it comes to popularity, but I did feel I was going OK if I could count on you and little Dan. Now Dan can't be bothered with me and you stalk off like I'm a bad smell. Aren't we friends any more?'

'Oh, Harley, don't. Of *course* we're friends. You know I just can't stand it when you criticize Jodie.'

'But I was only—'

'I know. I'm just a bit twitchy about her, that's all.'

'So's everyone,' said Harley. 'Jodie has to be the centre of attention. It's as if she's got a neon sign flashing on and off, saying, *Look at me! Look at me!*'

'You're criticizing her again.'

'No, I'm not, I'm making a purely objective statement.'

'And I think you're a weeny bit jealous that Jodie's so good with the little ones. That's not criticizing, it's a – what was it? – a purely objective statement.'

'I'm not the slightest bit jealous. *I* don't want them all trailing after me all the time, it's incredibly tedious. I'm sure there's going to be trouble getting them all to sleep tonight because they're all so wired up and over-excited but that's not *my* problem. Jodie's the girl who reads them their bedtime stories now. Let *her* try to settle them all down.'

Jodie seemed willing enough. Dan started crying because his second toffee apple fell on the floor and Sakura started rubbing her eyes and Zeph kept bumping into everyone deliberately. Undie clapped her hands and announced it was Time for Bed. No one took any notice until Jodie put her finger to her purple lips and made all the little ones stand as still as statues.

Jodie nodded at Undie as if to say, *See!*

'Now listen, you lot, let's hurry back to your houses, and if you're *very* good, I'll tell you all a special Halloween story when you're in bed,' she announced.

'*What* Halloween story?' I asked anxiously.

'Oh, we'll make one up,' she said. 'You come too, Pearl. You're my little sister witch.'

'Don't make it *too* scary for them, Jodie,' I said. 'You always used to frighten me. Well, you still do.'

'Yeah, but you're a little wuss, dead sensitive. The littlies will just think it a laugh if I tell them a ghost story. Look at the way Zeph was kicking Undie's head around. Come on, let's gather them up.'

I'd sooner have stayed with Harley or Harriet but I helped round up all the younger children and walked them in a crocodile up the dark pathway. Mr Wilberforce led the way, swinging an old-fashioned lantern, and Undie sloped along behind, her sheet wrapped round her neck. I tried to make conversation with her but she answered in monosyllables. She sniffed when she looked in Jodie's direction.

Mr Wilberforce was obviously still thrilled with Jodie, clapping her on the back and kidding her he ought to put her on the staff payroll. She skipped along beside him, her weird teeth flashing in the lantern light. Mr Wilberforce went past his bungalow so that he could light the little troupe of children safely to the girls' and boys' houses.

Undie cleared off to her own room the moment he'd gone, deciding to let Jodie and me get on with it. All the children were desperately tired now, whining and yawning and rubbing their eyes.

'Tell you what, Pearl, you get the girls into their pyjamas and tell them a Halloween story, OK?'

'No, I can't!'

'Oh come on, you can make up just as good stories as me. *Better!*'

'Yes, but that's just for *us*,' I said.

'Go on. Be a sweet sister witch,' said Jodie, starting to herd the boys into their house. 'Make up any old thing. Just get them settled.'

Sakura slipped her hand into mine. 'Are *you* going to tell us a story, Pearl?' she said. 'Goody goody!'

So I went into the girls' house and supervised all ten little girls as they got into their pyjamas and cleaned their teeth and had a last wee. Then they all climbed into their little red beds and looked at me expectantly.

I sat down on Sakura's bed and started telling a story about a little girl called Cherry Blossom who grew pumpkins in her garden for Halloween.

'Is it going to get very scary?' Sakura whispered.

'No, don't worry, my stories aren't scary at all,' I said.

Sakura relaxed, stretching out her legs as I told her how Cherry Blossom watered and fed her ten pumpkins every day. Her feet wriggled against me like little puppies under the blanket.

'Then at Halloween Cherry Blossom went down

her garden to her pumpkin patch, ready to pick her ten fine pumpkins. They had grown absolutely huge, practically bursting out of their bright orange skin. Cherry Blossom thought it a pity to pick them but she reached out her hands nevertheless. And *then* the first pumpkin opened up with a loud pop' – I made an explosive popping noise and each little girl tried hard to copy me – 'and out flew . . .' I paused.

'It's not a ghost, is it?' said Sakura. 'Please don't let it be a ghost.'

'No, no ghosts, I promise. This is something small, with wings.'

'It's a bat!'

'No, a bee!'

'A butterfly?'

'It was a *fairy*,' I said. 'A little plump pumpkin fairy with a bright orange fairy frock and little green satin ballet slippers and sparkly green wings. She spread her lovely little wings and flew round Cherry Blossom's head. "I am your very own pumpkin fairy and I will grant you a special Halloween wish," she whispered.'

If Jodie had been listening, she'd have made vomit noises at this stage but all my little girls went, 'Aaah!'

'So what do you think Cherry Blossom wished for, Sakura?' I asked.

'I think . . . I think she wished to see her daddy,' she said, wriggling.

'OK, so the pumpkin fairy puffed up her cheeks and blew out a stream of magic fairy dust, like this . . .' I blew, and all the little girls blew too.

'And Cherry Blossom's daddy came running

down the garden and he picked her up in his arms and gave her a big cuddle.'

'And he promised to stay with her for ever and every,' said Sakura.

I made nine more fairies pop out of a pumpkin so that every little girl could have their own wish. I was sick to death of the pumpkin-patch fairies by this time.

As soon as the tenth wish was chosen, I said firmly, 'Now *I* wish that you all go to sleep straight away like good little girls.'

Astonishingly, they all slid down under their duvets, closing their eyes. Sakura asked me to kiss her goodnight, and then I had to go from bed to bed, tucking each little girl up properly. I suddenly felt as fond of them as if they were all my little sisters. They liked *me*. Maybe they liked me almost as much as Jodie!

I thought she'd be waiting for me impatiently as the Cherry Blossom story had been incredibly long-winded, but when I went to find her in the boys' house, she was only just finishing her own story. It was dark in the dormitory. She was telling the story by flickering candlelight (a nightlight stolen from a Halloween pumpkin). The boys were lying on their backs in bed, unusually still, eyes big, all of them staring transfixed at Jodie.

'So the sad white whispering woman still weeps up in her tower,' Jodie said very softly.

I clutched her arm in protest but she shook me off.

'And every now and then she steps silently down and down the winding stairs, slides straight through the door and wanders along the corridors, whispering . . . If you listen carefully, you might hear her yourself one day, but beware. She's so lonely. She'd love a little boy to keep her company during the long dark nights. Watch out she doesn't whisper in *your* ear . . .' Jodie's voice faded. The little boys didn't move. They scarcely breathed.

'Right, come on, sleepy byes,' said Jodie in her normal voice. 'Night-night, everyone.'

They mumbled under their duvets.

'You've scared them silly,' I said.

'It was just a story. They *asked* for a ghost story. They *liked* it. Didn't you like the story, boys?'

They mumbled again.

'You're not scared now, are you?' said Jodie.

'I'm not a bit scared,' said Zeph, and the others echoed him.

'*I*'m not scared,' Dan whispered. 'But I think my Man's a bit scared because he's so little.'

'Well, you give him a big cuddle and tell him to go to sleep,' said Jodie. 'Night then.'

She took my arm and clacked out of the room in her high heels. I pulled away from her when we were outside the house.

'Jodie, you *shouldn't* tell them stories like that. I don't care what they say. They're only little. They'll have nightmares. You used to give *me* terrible nightmares but at least I had you there to comfort me.'

'Yeah, I can still give you nightmares, easy-peasy. I'm truly great at ghost stories. Maybe I'll make horror movies when I'm older.' Jodie started humming creepy music, dancing her fingers over my face in the dark.

'Stop it! I'm serious. I don't think you should tell

362

that story anyway, to anyone at all. It's horrible and it's totally tactless because of Mrs Wilberforce.' I lowered my voice because we were going past her house. I wondered if Mr Wilberforce was making her a drink, then sitting by her wheelchair, ridiculous in his witch outfit, telling her about his silly party. She must long to struggle out of her wheelchair, take command of her withered legs and run and run and run right away for ever.

'My story hasn't got anything to do with Mrs Wilberforce,' said Jodie. 'I made most of it up before I'd ever even *met* her.'

'Yes, but it's still horribly similar in parts.'

'She's not *dead*. Though she's as good as.'

'Jodie! Shut *up*! How could you say such a terrible thing? She might hear you.'

'Don't be stupid, she couldn't possibly hear. I'm not being terrible, I'm simply stating a fact. I'd sooner be dead than shut up here, barely able to get out, while old Wilberforce carries on with Frenchie.'

'*What?*'

'Well, it's obvious, isn't it?'

'He couldn't be! Do you think Mrs Wilberforce *knows*?'

'Why do you think she's so depressed all the time? She can't exactly flounce off, can she?'

'I think you're just making it all up, distorting everything. And if it *is* true, then it's even meaner to go on about your sad white whispering woman creeping along corridors.'

'Creeping, right, on her own two legs. It would be truly tasteless if I had her bowling along in some ghostly wheeled chariot,' said Jodie. She made weird creaking rattling noises.

I ignored her, stomping along in the dark, wishing I had my torch with me.

'You're just jealous because the littlies like my stories,' said Jodie. 'Don't worry, Pearly, you're still my favourite girly.'

I said nothing, humming a little tune so as not to listen to her any more. She ran after me, then stumbled and turned her ankle.

'Ouch! Flipping heck, that hurt! I hope the heel hasn't come off my shoe. Pearl? Pearl, wait for me. I'm totally crippled, I need your arm.'

I walked on. I knew she hadn't really hurt herself. She was just playacting. I didn't *always* have to do what she said. I hummed louder, hurrying.

'Pearl!' she called. 'Don't leave me. Please?' She sounded suddenly forlorn. My heart turned over. I gave in and ran back to her.

**She stood in front of the whole school
at half past nine.**

24

Jodie was sent for the next morning.

'*Now* what have you done?' said Mum. 'Mr Wilberforce had a word when I was serving him his breakfast. He wants to see you at ten to nine and he doesn't look happy.'

'I haven't done *anything*! Don't look so worried, Mum,' said Jodie chirpily.

'I've got a whole load of worries, young lady,' said Mum, sighing. 'And half a dozen of them feature you. I couldn't believe my eyes when I saw you prancing around at the party in that silly get-up, showing off like anything.'

'Thanks, Mum,' said Jodie. 'You're going overboard with the flattery, as always.'

'I'm just trying to stop you showing us all up,' said Mum. 'I'm sure it was your idea for Pearl to wear all that witchy nonsense too.'

'Hey, what about Mr Wilberforce and Frenchie? Weren't *they* wearing witchy nonsense?'

'Well, they certainly both looked a right pair of idiots, I must admit. I could barely look him in the face. What kind of a message was he giving to the kids? He hadn't even bothered to shave his legs. And as for that Frenchie, well, she looks a bit of a witch to start with, so I suppose she was off to a flying start, but *really*! Anyway, you run off to Mr Wilberforce – and for pity's sake watch that cheeky mouth of yours. Just hang your head and say you'll try and do better, whatever it is.'

'It's *nothing*, Mum. Mr Wilberforce was singing my praises last night. He thinks I'm Little Miss Wonderful.'

Jodie flounced off, fluffing her purple hair and doing a little tap dance in her high heels.

'That . . . girl,' said Mum. Heaven knows what adjectives she was adding inside her head.

'*Our* girl,' said Dad. 'Why do you always have to be so hard on her, Shaz? I can't see that she's in any kind of trouble. She's right, old Wilberforce thinks the world of her.'

But Jodie had blown it this time. I lurked near Mr Wilberforce's study, waiting for her. Mrs Lewin took the register at nine but I hung on, though I didn't want to get into trouble. Jodie didn't come out of Mr Wilberforce's study until twenty past. Her head was bent, her hair in her eyes. I knew something was horribly wrong even before I saw her face properly. She'd been crying, her eyes still brimming, her eyelashes spiked with tears.

'Oh, Jodie,' I whispered. I went to give her a hug but she pulled away from me, pushing me hard in the chest.

'What? What's the matter? What have *I* done?' I gabbled.

'You haven't done anything, as always, Precious Pearl,' said Jodie. 'You're the good girl, the clever girl, everybody's favourite storyteller. All the little girls loved your story last night and curled up sound asleep, bless their little cotton socks. But two of my boys wet their beds, Zeph was sick and Dan had nightmares and screamed the place down, yelling that the whispering ghost was coming to get him. I wish!'

'Oh dear,' I said, not knowing whether the laugh or cry.

'And now Dan's running a temperature and Undie's had to keep him in bed, the silly little diddums.'

'Oh, Jodie, it's not his fault. You know what he's like.'

'Yeah, a wimpy little tell-tale, out to get me into trouble.'

'He's *not*. He adores you, you know he does. All the littlies love you to bits. You're brilliant with them.'

'No I'm not. Mr Wilberforce says I've let them all down, deliberately frightening them. He acted all sad and wounded and said I'd let him down too. I don't know why the old fart's making such a song and dance about a silly little story. It was all *his* idea to have a Halloween party.'

'I know, I know, but—'

'How do they know it was *my* story that upset them anyway? It could have been the sight of a daft old man in drag – or how about Undie with her ridiculous *head*. So OK, what was she dressed up as?'

'A ghost?'

'Yeah, absolutely. And what does old Wilberforce want me to do? Stand up in front of the whole school and tell them all there's no such thing as ghosts. Is he making Undie do that? Is he hell.'

'It's unfair, I know. Have you *really* got to get up in front of everyone? I'd absolutely *hate* that. Still, you won't mind too much, will you, Jodie? Then everything can get back to normal and all the littlies can have their proper story time again.'

Jodie looked at me strangely, wiping her nose with the back of her hand. 'They'll have their story time all right, but not with me. With *you.*'

'What?'

'Apparently you and your soppy fairies were a huge big hit with all the little girls. They've all been burbling about you non-stop. You're going to be the chief storyteller now.'

'No I'm not,' I said. 'I'm not taking your place!'

'Yes you are, because Mr Wilberforce *says* so and you're the little goody-goody two shoes who always does exactly as you're told,' said Jodie vehemently.

She pushed right past me and stalked off to our bedroom. I didn't dare follow her. She stood in front of the whole school at half past nine, her crazy hair brushed back, her head held high. Her skirt was hiked up high above her knees and she was wearing her red high heels. There was a little gasp as she clacked across the stage. Mr Wilberforce glared at her footwear, but decided not to be distracted.

'Now, Jodie, you have something to tell the younger children, haven't you?' he said.

'If you say so,' said Jodie.

'I do indeed say so,' said Mr Wilberforce sternly.

'Right. Well, pin your ears back, you little ones,' said Jodie. 'Apparently *some* of you got worried by my Halloween story last night, which was very silly, because it was only a *story*. I made it all up. Mr Wilberforce wants me to tell you that there's absolutely no such thing as ghosts. People might dress up as ghosts for silly parties, but there aren't any *real* ghosts, OK?'

The little ones stared at her, stunned. The Juniors shifted around uncomfortably. The Seniors smirked.

'Whoooo!' someone whispered, and there was a ripple of laughter.

Jodie's pale face went pink. 'No ghosts,' she repeated. 'No sad white whispering women. Mr Wilberforce says she's a figment of my imagination, so remember that, right?'

She tip-tapped off the stage. Mr Wilberforce let her go, though he shook his head at her. At the end of assembly he beckoned me. I knew what he was going to say. I so want to write that I utterly refused to take over the bedtime storytelling from Jodie. I *did* mumble to Mr Wilberforce that Jodie told wonderful stories and that I was sure she'd never tell the little ones a ghost story again.

'Are you *really* sure, Pearl?' said Mr Wilberforce.

'Oh, absolutely,' I lied.

'Mmm. The trouble is, *I'*m not so sure. Your sister Jodie is a law unto herself, a lovely girl in many ways, but a problem child. I've got to think of the other children. I can't risk having them frightened into fits every night. No, dear, I'd like you to take over bedtime duties for the moment. Miss Ponsonby says the little girls were enchanted by your story. I think you ought to write it down and show it to Mrs Lewin.'

I couldn't help being thrilled, even though I felt so bad about Jodie. So I said yes, I'd be happy to tell the girls a story every night. I had to tuck the little boys up too. I knew enough not to tell them a pumpkin fairy story. (I was planning new stories about the gooseberry-bush baby fairies, the giant sunflower fairies, the ever-so-good-for-you broccoli fairies – an entire *allotment* of fairy stories.) I told the boys badger stories instead – Mr Badger, Mrs Badger and their two children, Bobby and Bessie.

Harley sloped into the little boys' dormie when I was in mid flow. My throat dried and my voice trailed away.

'Go on, Pearl,' said Zeph.

'Tell us more!' said Dan.

I tried hard to ignore Harley and carried on telling the story. It was very babyish and twee. Mr Badger smoked a pipe of dandelion tobacco and wore long green dockleaf slippers, Mrs Badger chalked her white headstreak every day and painted her long claws, and Bobby and Bessie wore cute denim dungarees and attended Badger Infant School. Jodie would have groaned and fidgeted, but Harley lolled on the end of Dan's bed, seemingly absorbed.

When I'd finished and tucked them all up under their duvets, Harley walked with me to the door.

'They're loving your story,' he said. 'I hope you're not going to traumatize them by having little Bobby ambling off and getting run over.'

372

'Of course not. My stories never have any sad or worrying bits.'

'Unlike Jodie's stories.'

'Oh, don't. I feel so bad taking over from her. She says she couldn't care less now but I know she *does*. And people keep making silly ghost noises around her. They're all so horrible.'

Jodie was hunched up on the sofa with Dad, watching television, when I got back. Mum was dozing in her chair, a cake recipe book open on her lap. I went to sit on the sofa too. Dad's arm wound round me automatically and I cuddled up close. But then Jodie stretched and stood up.

'Where are you off to, Jodie?' Dad said.

'Oh, things to do,' she said.

I swallowed. 'Can I come too?' I asked.

'No, I've got things to do. Without you,' said Jodie. She walked off, whistling.

'Uh-oh,' said Dad. 'Have my two favourite girls been having a tiff?'

'Not really,' I sniffed. 'Jodie just doesn't seem to like me much any more.'

'Nonsense. Jodie thinks the world of you, you know she does. She's just having a bit of a hard time at the moment. You know that.'

Dad held me close, his head on top of mine. I felt his chin move as he glanced at Mum, checking she was still asleep. 'I can't help thinking it was maybe a big mistake to come here. Your mum thought it such a fantastic opportunity – well, I did too, the chance for my girls to have a top-notch education, all for free. We'd have been mad not to go for it. Especially for you, Pearl. You're our little brainy-box and it's worked for you, hasn't it? You like your lessons and you've made some nice little friends. You've even got yourself a *boy*friend, you cheeky baggage.'

'Dad! Harley isn't a boyfriend, you know that.'

'Yes, well, he's a kind lad, and means well, though he can't help sounding a bit of a twit at times. But some of the snotty brats in his class make me boiling mad. I've seen the way they call after our Jodie. I've felt like giving them a piece of my mind but I know Jodie wouldn't thank me for it. It's not working out for her, is it, Pearl? Your mum so hoped she'd settle down here. She's always been a bit wild and maybe she was hanging out with a bad bunch back at Moorcroft, but she was happier there, I'm sure of it. I can't stand to see her all pale and droopy, it just about breaks my heart.' Dad heaved a great sigh. 'Maybe we should move right away, start over somewhere else? What do you think, Pearl?'

'I don't know, Dad,' I said helplessly.

Dad gave me a hug. 'Of course you don't know, poppet. Take no notice, I'm just being silly. We'll sort something out somehow and see our Jodie get her bounce back.'

He settled back into watching his programme on television, a compilation of greatest rock hits. He started humming along, his socked foot tapping, his fingers drumming my arm.

He told me all about the different rock bands and I pretended to be listening, but I didn't take in a word. I was thinking about Jodie, wondering if she was creeping up the stairs, along the corridor, squeezing behind the big cupboard, going through the door, up the spiral staircase to the tower room.

I wondered about following her up there, but it would be so scary going by myself. What if I got all the way to the top and found Jodie wasn't there after all? I thought about being there all by myself in that round room, knowing I had to feel my way down that shaky staircase.

I couldn't do it.

I stayed snuggled with Dad for over an hour. Mum woke up and made a pot of tea. She didn't even comment on Jodie's absence. She said she had a headache and took her cup of tea into the bedroom with her.

'You see the girls to bed, Joe,' she muttered, as if Jodie and I were still small.

Dad looked worried, wondering what he was going to do if Jodie stayed out really late. But she was back by half past nine, acting as if she'd just popped along the corridor to the bathroom.

'Right, girlies, beddy-byes,' said Dad, as if we really were tiny tots.

Jodie and I played along with this without conferring. It made everything so much easier for all of us.

'Hop, skip and into bed,' said Dad briskly.

We hopped and we skipped and then we jumped into bed. Dad came and gave us big hugs.

'Another one!' Jodie demanded, so I did too.

'You pair of soppies,' said Dad.

'Tell us a story,' said Jodie.

'Once upon a time there was a little girl called Jodie and she had brown – no, purple – hair and a little girl called Pearl and she had fair hair. Jodie put her purple head on her pillow and Pearl put her fair head on her pillow. They fell *fast asleep*,' said Dad.

This was the only story he'd ever told us, and we could chant it all backwards. Then Dad backed out of the room, blowing kisses, and we were left alone together.

'Can I come in your bed, Jodie?' I asked, keeping my voice little-girly.

There was a silence.

Then, 'No,' said Jodie.

My heart started thudding.

'No, because my sheets are all tangled up. I'm getting into *your* bed,' she said, and she bounced in beside me.

I cuddled her close. 'Let's play Big Sister, Little Sister,' I said.

It was a silly game we played years ago. I was the Big Sister and I had to look after my very naughty Little Sister Jodie.

'OK, OK, Big Sister,' said Jodie in a funny little lisping voice.

We played until we fell asleep. When we woke up in the morning, Jodie was still in my bed. She was curled up facing me, her fist under her nose so it looked as if she was sucking her thumb. Her face was soft, her cheeks flushed from sleep. She looked so young, as if she'd really become my little sister overnight.

We all gazed up at the golden stars expoding
way above the tower.

25

It was the fifth of November on Monday, Bonfire Night.

'Another blooming party,' said Mum. 'That Frenchie! "Don't you worry, Mrs Wells, we don't need you to prepare a *banquet*. Just bangers and baked potatoes, traditional firework grub. You could get your husband to set up a barbecue outside." Silly cow, how can you cook for all the school on a blooming barbecue?'

Mum huffed and puffed, but she made huge trays of special iced cake sprinkled with hundreds and thousands to look like fireworks, and she sent Dad into the village to buy bags of marshmallows to have with hot chocolate.

Jed built a huge bonfire on the front lawn at lunch time, with half the school helping him pile on the branches. Even the senior girls joined in, Anna and Sophia and Rebecca throwing a few twigs haphazardly and squealing with laughter at everything Jed said.

'Idiots,' said Jodie contemptuously, stalking past.

Anna and Sophia and Rebecca giggled, then pursed their lips and went, 'Whoooo!'

'Hiya, Purple Bonce,' Jed called, grinning at her. 'I hear you've been scaring all the little kids with your stories.'

'Yeah, she is, like, *so* weird,' said Anna.

'Tales of ghoulies and ghosties, eh? So you believe in that crap, do you?' said Jed.

Jodie stopped. Her fists were clenched. I put my hand on her wrist. I could feel her shaking.

'I believe *you*'re crap,' she said, and walked on.

'Good for you, Jodie,' I said. 'I thought you were going to punch him.'

'I nearly did,' said Jodie. 'But I'll show him. I'll show all of them.'

'What are you going to do?' I asked anxiously.

'You wait,' she said.

Harley was crouching in the bushes at the side of the lawn, waddling around like a giant duck, sticking rockets into bottles.

'Oh cool! I love rockets,' said Jodie. 'We'll help you, Harley.'

'No, wait, Mr Wilberforce has drawn up this terribly complicated grid. They've all got to be placed in a specific pattern and then we've got this ridiculous team plan - Mr Wilberforce, your dad, Mr Michaels, Jed and me. It's like a battle. We've even got to dress up in ridiculous gear – balaclavas, special gloves, rubber boots – like we're a creepy SAS squad.'

'What time do the fireworks start, Harley?'

'Half seven, on the dot.'

'Great,' said Jodie. She peered along his line of

bottles. 'It's not going to be a very *big* display.'

'I know, yet old Wilberforce is bigging it up so half the kids are expecting the entire sky to light up like the Aurora Borealis.'

'Like the *what*?' said Jodie.

'Northern Lights,' I said without thinking.

'You two whizzy-brains,' said Jodie. 'Well, I think the kids will have lots to look at tonight, one way or another. Happy rocketing, Harley!'

She walked off. I linked arms, walking with her.

'I hope there won't be bangers. I hate them,' I said. 'I'm not even sure I like rockets very much. I like it when they explode into stars but I hate that whooshy noise they make. I always get scared one will fall down on me. I liked it best when I was little and we just had sparklers in the back yard, you and me.'

We'd hold the sparklers in our mittened hands, letting them sizzle and flash. Jodie showed me how to write in the air with them. I couldn't write proper words the first time and only managed a wobbly P for Pearl so Jodie wrote both our names in the air. When the sparklers went out, there was still a golden trail of writing hanging there in front of our eyes, *Jodie and Pearl*, linked together.

'I hope Mr Wilberforce has got some sparklers,' I said.

Jodie mimed holding a sparkler, whirling it round.

'Yes, you used to write our names,' I said. 'You've always been such a great sister to me.'

'That's what sisters are for,' said Jodie.

Then the bell for afternoon school rang and we went off to our classrooms.

'*There* you are, Pearl!' said Harriet. 'We were looking for you everywhere. We were trying to make a guy for the bonfire but he kept falling to bits. We needed you to sort him out – you're *much* better at art and craft.'

So straight after lessons I went over to Harriet's room and inspected their limp little guy. I decided he needed a major operation. I snipped and sorted and stuffed, and then I sewed him two buttons for eyes and a red felt smiley mouth. He looked cute and friendly now he had a face and we all fussed over him.

When I went back to our flat at last, Dad was dressing up in his firework-lighting gear. He pulled on big gum boots borrowed from Mr Wilberforce and then did a funny jackboot strut around the room. He tried marching into the kitchen to make Mum laugh but she swotted him away irritably, jabbing at row after row of pale pink chipolatas.

'Where's Jodie?' said Dad, knowing she'd probably chuckle at him.

I didn't know where Jodie was. I wanted to watch the fireworks with her, arm in arm. I wondered if she'd gone to buy a packet of sparklers for us down at the village shop. It was just the sort of thing she'd do.

I put on my jacket and wound a scarf round my neck and stuck my feet into my own wellie boots. This was my badger-watching outfit. The cuffs of my jacket were still slightly sticky with honey. I thought of the lonely cub curled up by itself in the dark set, with no one to romp and chase and play with. I shut my eyes tight to stop myself crying. I needed Jodie to scoff at me and call me a baby.

I thought my torch would be useful outside in the dark. I couldn't find it anywhere. I had to go into the pitch dark by the side of the building towards the bonfire. All the pupils were huddled together, unrecognizable in the dark. The fire was already lit, flames flickering upwards. Small hooded figures danced round and round the bonfire. I knew it was just the little ones in their winter uniform duffel coats but they looked like strange goblins.

I hung back, feeling stupidly shy, wondering if Jodie was already there.

'Pearl! Pearl! Over here!'

It was Harriet, jumping up and down, making our guy jump too.

'Pearl! My Pearl! Come and stand with *me*!' Dan shouted.

'See the bonfire!' said Sakura. 'We're dancing round the bonfire, making wishes!'

'We're going to get sausages!' Zeph yelled, careering towards me.

I was suddenly surrounded by capering children, crazy with excitement, all of them wanting to see *me*. I gave the little ones a hug and then went to stand with Harry and Freya and Sheba and Clarissa.

'At last!' said Harry. 'We have to burn the guy now.'

'Do we really *have* to?' said Freya.

'It won't be a proper bonfire without a guy!' said Sheba.

'Of course we have to burn him, that's the whole point,' said Clarissa. 'Give him here, *I*'ll do it.'

'No, let Pearl, she made him,' said Harry, thrusting the guy at me.

His head tilted, his button eyes glinting in the firelight. His body shifted, almost as if he was struggling. I wanted to keep him tight in my arms but I took a deep breath and hurled him.

He whirled through the air and landed right on the top of the bonfire. He straddled it, arms up, head wagging. Then a flame leaped up over his leg, then another attacked his thigh, and in split seconds he was alight all over, his arms still up, as if signalling for help. I wanted to snatch him back from the flames. Freya started crying. Harriet gripped my arm agitatedly.

'Oh dear, now I wish we hadn't,' she said.

'It's my fault, I made him look so nice,' I said. 'Jodie made a guy last year but he was really scary with a devil's mask and long toothpick teeth. We were glad to get rid of him.'

'Where's Jodie now?' Harry asked.

'I don't *know.*'

I was starting to get really worried. I was sure Jodie was plotting something but I wasn't sure *what*. Maybe she'd invented some kind of Bonfire Night game?

Mum was trundling a food-laden trolley over the grass. She caught hold of me.

'Help me hand all this stuff round, Pearl, there's a dear. Get Jodie to help too.'

'I'll help,' said Harriet. 'Oh, yum – your mum's such a good cook, Pearl.'

I darted around, thrusting paper plates of sausages and baked beans and potatoes at everyone. Then I poured jug after jug of hot chocolate. Half the little ones spilled their chocolate all down their duffel coats but at least it didn't show in the dark.

'My Man wants his *own* cup,' said Dan. 'And he ate my marshmallow, so can I have another one?'

I knew this was a deliberate scam but I still gave it to him.

'I do like you, Pearl,' Dan said happily. He paused, sucking his marshmallow. 'I like Jodie too though, lots and lots. I didn't mean to get her into trouble.'

'I know you didn't, Dan.'

'I can't find her.'

'She's around somewhere, Dan,' I said, trying to sound reassuring.

'She's missing the food!' said Zeph.

'She won't miss the fireworks, will she?' said Sakura.

I remembered Jodie asking what time they started. It must have been for a reason.

'I'm sure she won't miss the fireworks,' I said.

The first rocket soared high in the sky at exactly half past seven. We all gazed up at the golden stars exploding way above the tower. And then there was a gasp. There was an eerie light inside the tower room, spotlighting a figure standing inside, right up on the window ledge, a strange ghostly figure in a long white dress, a shawl draped over her head.

'It's the sad white whispering woman!' Dan shrieked. 'It's a ghost, it's a ghost, it's a *ghost!*'

Everyone was peering up and pointing, and the little children were all crying, and even some of the Seniors were screaming. Harriet nearly snapped my arm in two.

'It really is a ghost!' she whispered.

Another rocket went up, but no one looked as the new stars exploded. Everyone stared transfixed at the tower-room window. I stared too, seeing my sister Jodie making them all believe in ghosts.

Dan was screaming hysterically.

'It's OK, Dan, truly. It's not *really* a ghost,' I whispered, but he pulled away from me, scared senseless.

'It's the ghost woman and she's coming to get me!' he yelled, throwing himself on the ground.

I saw Jodie banging on the window, shouting something, but of course we couldn't hear. She struggled with the catch, hitting it with her hand until it opened. Another rocket soared, illuminating Jodie with its green ghostly light.

'It's only *me*, Dan!' she yelled. 'Look, it's just silly old Jodie.'

I'm sure that's what she said.

She hung right out of the window and tugged at her shawl to show her purple hair. She tugged too violently, she jerked forward, she wobbled in her crazy red shoes – and then she fell.

She fell all the way to the ground, the shawl billowing out behind her, the white lace dress floating, one shoe falling off. Her mouth was open and I heard her scream high above all the others. She fell onto the lawn with a terrible thud, head flung back, arms and legs spread open, while another rocket showered the sky with lurid sparks.

Melchester seems like a dark dream.

26

They wouldn't let me hold her. I wanted to rock her the way she'd rocked the badger cub. They said she mustn't be touched in case her neck was broken. I screamed at them then because of course her neck was broken. She was broken all over, my sister Jodie, and I needed to hold her to keep her together. But they took her away in the ambulance and I didn't get to see her again.

I begged and begged and begged to go to the funeral parlour. I needed to see Jodie when she was put in her coffin. I knew exactly what I had to do. I had to shut her eyes and turn her mouth up in a little smile. I had to comb her dear purple hair and dress her in her shortest shirt and slip her crazy shoes back on her upturned feet. I wasn't sure if she'd want books tucked into her coffin too. I planned to give her all my stories instead and I wanted to put her old wooden rocket in her hand.

Mum wouldn't listen. She just cried and cried.

Dad tried to understand, but he kept shaking his head.

'I can't let you do that, darling. It's too morbid. I don't think it's allowed anyway. It would likely give you terrible nightmares seeing our poor Jodie now.'

Dad started crying then and I couldn't argue any more with him.

There was so many tears, so many arguments. We couldn't have the funeral straight away. There were mad questions and enquiries. Some people thought Jodie had killed herself deliberately. This was so crazy I started screaming again. Of course my sister hadn't committed suicide. She'd been trying to reassure Dan and the other littlies. She'd leaned out of the window to show them she wasn't really the sad white whispering woman, she was just our mad Jodie with her purple hair and her red shoes. She's slipped in those shoes, she'd lost her balance, she'd fallen. It was an accident.

I said it was an accident, Mum and Dad said it was an accident, Mr Wilberforce said it was an accident, but the newspapers wrote all kinds of sleazy lies about my sister. They suggested she was a total misfit at her exclusive boarding school, treated harshly by the teachers, bullied by the other pupils, made so miserable that she took her own life.

They couldn't prove it though. I'm the only one who knows everything about Jodie, because she was my sister and she loved me more than anyone else in the whole world. As if she'd ever kill herself and leave me behind!

When we could have her funeral at last, Mum and Dad wouldn't let her be buried at Melchester church. They couldn't bear the thought of leaving her, lonely and moulding in the grounds. We were moving far away immediately afterwards. We needed to set Jodie free.

They held the funeral in the nearest crematorium, twenty miles away in Galford. They wanted the ceremony to be private, but the whole school attended.

'I don't want them there! They just want to show the school in the best light possible after all that bullying scandal in the papers,' Mum said bitterly.

'Maybe. But maybe they want to mourn our Jodie too,' Dad said.

Everyone was in their neatest uniform. Every little girl had snowy socks, every little boy had his hair grimly parted. Every Junior had their tie neatly knotted and their shirt tucked in. Every single Senior carried a lily to put on top of Jodie's coffin.

Mr Wilberforce wore a dark suit and a black tie. He pushed Mrs Wilberforce in her wheelchair. She wore a black net veil over her long white hair and a black velvet cloak that covered her legs. Miss French stood humbly behind them in a shiny navy suit that was too tight for her. The teachers stood in a sober line, gripping their hymn books.

Jed was there too, in an old donkey jacket because it was clearly the only dark garment he possessed. His head was bowed. He looked white and watery-eyed. He could have been grief-stricken, but then again he might simply be suffering from a hangover.

Mum and Dad and I were right at the front. Jodie was wheeled in alongside us, flowers heaped on her mahogany coffin. I pictured her lying on her back, pulling faces at all the false sentiment, yawning when the vicar went on at length about 'this beautiful vibrant young girl', making vomit noises when Anna of all people stood up to sing part of Fauré's Requiem.

I whispered to Jodie throughout the service and she talked back to me, telling me she was OK, indeed this was her finest moment, everyone united in celebrating her life. The little ones were sobbing, Dan and Sakura totally sodden, and even Zeph was snivelling.

'Tell them to watch out,' Jodie joked. 'If they wail *too* much, I might creep back and haunt them. I'm the sad white whispering woman now, and I'll go *Whoooo* in their little earholes.'

She chuckled and I laughed too. Dad put his arm round me, holding me tight. His face was already salmon-pink, suppressing his tears. Mum was huddled beside him, head bowed, hands over her face. Her shoulders shuddered up and down as she sobbed.

'Get Mum!' said Jodie. 'It's killing her that I've got purple hair for my own funeral.'

'It's killing her that you're dead, Jodie. She loves you so. We all do,' I whispered. 'Look at poor Dad.'

'I know. You look after him for me, Pearl. Give him lots of big hugs. I do love him so much. But I love you more, babe. You're my best ever little sister and I love you the most, remember?'

'I'll always remember. I love you the most for ever and ever and ever,' I said as the organ music blared for the last hymn.

There were other sounds too, weird clankings. Then Jodie's coffin jerked, and just for a split second I thought she was going to jump straight up out of her coffin, scattering all the flowers, and go, '*Joke!* I'm not really dead, you suckers.'

But the lid stayed on, the wreaths in place, Mum and Dad's huge roses and my heart of freesias, but the coffin shunted slowly forwards, towards the curtains at the end.

'No!' I shouted. 'No, don't go, Jodie! Don't leave me!'

I struggled with Dad, desperate to get to the coffin before it disappeared for ever. He hung onto me, pinning me into my seat. Jodie chugged off through the curtains without even saying goodbye.

There was a reception back at the school. Mum insisted on doing the catering herself, with Dad helping her. I helped too, handing out cups of tea and sandwiches and fruit cake. It seemed bizarre for anyone to want to eat at a time like this. I'd been allowed to invite Harley and Harriet as they were special friends.

Harry was howling, her eyes red, her nose running. I gave her a hug.

'Oh, Pearl, I'm supposed to be comforting *you!*' she wailed. 'I'm so sorry. It's so awful for you. And I'm going to miss you so when you go away. Please please please let's stay friends and write to each other heaps.'

'Of course, Harry. You've been a lovely friend. I promise I'll write lots,' I said.

Harley didn't cry, but his voice was oddly thick, as if he had a bad cold.

'You're being so brave, Pearl,' he said. 'I wish there was some way I could make it easier for you. I've never really had a friend like you before. It's been so great hanging out with you, watching the badgers, making up daft games, all of it. I'm going to miss you terribly.'

'I'll miss you terribly too, Harley.'

'You know something? I'm going to miss Jodie so much too,' said Harley.

I could talk to my friends but I didn't want to talk to the teachers, not even lovely Mrs Lewin. I kept right away from Mr Wilberforce – but I wanted to talk to his wife.

She saw me hovering. 'Could you wheel me out of the room for a moment, Pearl?' she said.

I pushed her into one of the empty classrooms. She reached out with her one good hand.

'How are you coping, Pearl?'

'I'm OK,' I said.

'No, you're not,' she said. 'Come here.'

I went nearer, reluctantly. She managed to pull me close.

'What are you thinking right this second?' she whispered.

'That I want Jodie,' I said.

'Of course.'

'And that nothing will ever be the same again.'

'It won't be, I know.'

'And – and – it's all my fault she's dead!' I said, and then I started weeping.

She sat there, her good arm round me, while I cried on her chest, leaving snail trails of tears and snot all over her black velvet.

'Tell me why you think it's your fault, Pearl,' she said, stroking my hair.

'I should have stopped her going up to the tower room. I should have stood up to her more. I should never have said I wanted to come to Melchester College. She only said she'd come for my sake.'

'Yes, I see why you could argue it's all your fault, Pearl,' said Mrs Wilberforce. 'But so could all of us. I'm sure your mother and father are blaming themselves for coming here. I know my husband is hating himself for giving Jodie such a hard time over the Halloween story. Maybe poor little Dan is sobbing that it's all his fault for being scared. I'm sure half the school are feeling bad because they made the poor girl's life a misery. I'm sure Jed *should* feel bad, but I don't have a clue what he's thinking.

'I know what *I'm* thinking though. I feel terrible because I should have guessed you girls were going up to the tower room, and I above all know how dangerous it is. But listen, Pearl, listen hard. Terrible things happen by *chance*. We don't make them happen. The worst thing in the world has happened to you and you'll never properly get over it and never stop missing Jodie – but don't let it wreck your life the way mine is wrecked. You owe it to Jodie to live a life for her as well as for yourself. She'll still be there with you, in your head. You know that, don't you?'

'I know she will.'

'You'll remember everything about her always.'

'Yes, always.'

'I know you must hate Melchester now – but perhaps you could write to me once or twice, just to let me know how you're getting on?'

'Yes, I will. I want to do that. I'm going to write and write, I promise.'

*

I've kept my promise. I write to Mrs Wilberforce every month and tell her what I'm doing. I write to Harley and Harriet too. I even write big illustrated story letters to Dan and Sakura and Zeph. I need to write to them so they all remember Jodie.

Most importantly, I write to you, my special baby sister. I've written our whole story in this beautiful manuscript book from Mrs Wilberforce. I tore out the first few pages of my journal and started telling our story properly. It's your story too, little May.

It was such a shock when I found out about you.

I was crying the night of the funeral, lying there in bed, desperate for Jodie herself to come sliding into my bed to comfort me. Mum and Dad came into my room after a while. They were in their night-clothes but hadn't gone to bed themselves. None of us had slept much since Jodie's fall.

Mum sat on one side of my bed, Dad the other. They found my clenched fists in the dark and each held a hand. For a little while we all cried, and then Dad gently mopped my face with his big hankie.

'There now, our Pearl,' he murmured huskily.

'Oh Dad, I can't bear it,' I sobbed. 'I want Jodie so.'

'I know, pet, I know.'

'If only I hadn't nagged her so,' Mum whispered. 'I just wanted her to do well, that's all. I loved her dearly, even though I didn't show it. Do you think she knew that, Pearl?'

'Yes, Mum.' I tried to think of something else to say to comfort her but I couldn't find the right words. I was hurting too much.

I buried my head in my pillow. 'I want Jodie *back*,' I said. 'I want my *sister*.'

'She can't come back to us, Pearl,' said Dad, 'but – but maybe this is the best time to tell you. You're going to have another sister.'

'What?'

'Or a brother. Whatever. I'm going to have a baby,' Mum said, sniffing.

'*You're* going to have a baby?'

I could barely take it in. So it was *Mum*'s pregnancy test! Jodie and I had never suspected a thing.

'I – I didn't know you wanted another baby,' I mumbled.

'Well, it came as a surprise. It wasn't planned at all. I thought I might lose the baby, what with the shock of our poor Jodie, but everything still seems OK,' said Mum.

I could feel the soft weight of her as she sat beside me. I could make out the shape of her rounded tummy in the gloom. You were inside there, curled up, tiny as a tadpole, swimming in the dark.

'What do you think, Pearl?' said Dad. 'Are you pleased?'

I didn't know what I thought. I didn't want a new baby sister then – I wanted my own big sister Jodie. She was all I could think of. Sometimes she's all I can think of now, a year later.

Melchester seems like a dark dream. I still have nightmares about it. I'm running down endless corridors after Jodie, in and out of attic rooms, up and up and up those spiral stairs, and there she is, at the window of the tower room. I run to her, screaming her name, but she's falling before I can grab her, down and down and down. I fall after her but I always wake up before I hit the ground too.

We'll never go back, Mum and Dad and me. We couldn't bear to see that tower ever again. We live in London now, in a large block of flats. We live rent-free because Dad is the caretaker and odd-job man for the whole estate. Mum doesn't work yet. She's still too tired and anxious and haunted by the past, plus she's kept busy looking after you. We have the garden flat, so we can wheel you out onto the small strip of grass. You've had such a happy first summer, lying on your mat, kicking your little wrinkled heels in the sunshine.

You were born in May so that's what we've called you. Our little May. I sometimes call you Queen of the May and dress you up in your long white christening frock and string garlands of daisies round your neck.

I wasn't sure I'd like you at first, let alone love you. I thought I'd used up all my love on Jodie. I so wanted you to look like Jodie, be like Jodie. But you're not a bit like her, you're not like me either, you're utterly yourself. You're pink and plump and so serene, smiling and holding out your starfish hands whenever you see me. I can make you screw up your lovely blue eyes and give small giggly gurgles whenever I kiss your fat tummy. That's the only thing that reminds me of Jodie, that little laugh. You laugh a lot, May, because you're so happy, and you don't yet understand why Mum and Dad and I are still so sad.

I'm trying to get on with my life even so. I read, I write, I do my homework. I go to Greenhill, the big secondary school down the road. It was pretty scary the first few weeks, but I'm OK now, really. I've got friends – though there's no one like Harley. I like most of the teachers, especially Mrs Goodhew, who takes us for English. She's encouraging me to write stories. She has no idea I've written the most important true-life story in the world in this book.

It's all for you, May. You're my baby sister and I love you with all my heart and I'll always look after you. If anyone teases you or hurts you or scares you when you go to school, I'll make mincemeat of them, I promise you. But I'll never ever be such a great big sister as Jodie. She's your sister too, May, and she always will be. You'll understand why when you're old enough to read this story. We're never going to forget our sister Jodie.